W9-BND-886

SHAVETAIL

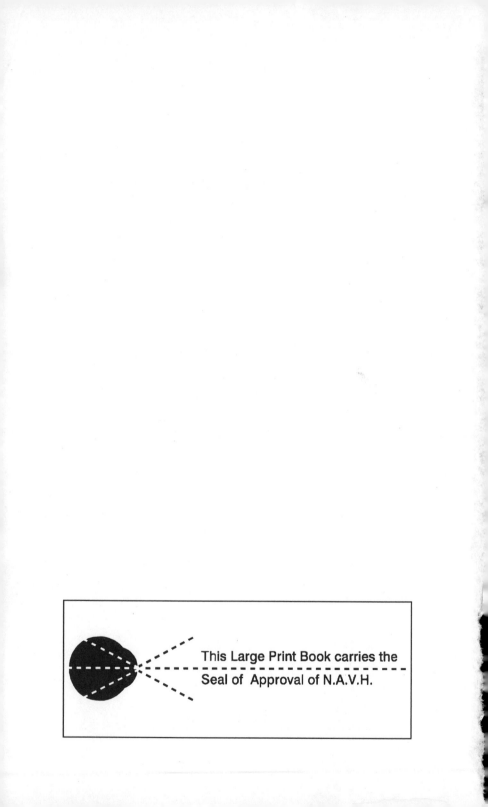

This Large Print Book carries the
Seal of Approval of N.A.V.H.

SHAVETAIL

THOMAS COBB

THORNDIKE PRESS
A part of Gale, Cengage Learning

GALE
CENGAGE Learning™

Detroit • New York • San Francisco • New Haven, Conn • Waterville, Maine • London

GALE
CENGAGE Learning™

Copyright © 2008 by Thomas Cobb.
Thorndike Press, a part of Gale, Cengage Learning.

Thorndike Press® Large Print Historical Fiction.
The text of this Large Print edition is unabridged.
Other aspects of the book may vary from the original edition.
Set in 16 pt. Plantin.
Printed on permanent paper.

LIBRARY OF CONGRESS CATALOGING-IN-PUBLICATION DATA

Cobb, Thomas, 1947–
   Shavetail / by Thomas Cobb.
    p. cm. — (Thorndike Press large print historical fiction)
   Summary: Fleeing a shameful past, seventeen-year-old Ned Thorne joins the U.S. Army and, in 1871, is sent to the dangerous Arizona territories, where he joins his captain and a ragtag troop in the search for a missing woman supposedly kidnapped by the Apache.
   ISBN-13: 978-1-4104-0924-9 (alk. paper)
   ISBN-10: 1-4104-0924-4 (alk. paper)
   1. Young men — Fiction. 2. Soldiers — Fiction. 3. Frontier and pioneer life — Arizona — Fiction. 4. United States. Army — Military life — 19th century — Fiction. 5. Arizona — History — To 1912 — Fiction. 6. Large type books. I. Title.
PS3603.O226S53 2008b
813'.6—dc22   2008018144

Published in 2008 by arrangement with Scribner, an imprint of Simon & Schuster, Inc.

To Randy

In Memory

*Donald Barthelme, Frederick Busch,
Gary Caret, and George Cobb*

May 1871:
Private Ned
Thorne

Under the feathery branches of a mesquite tree twenty feet in diameter, among the litter of the tree — small oval leaves, rotting beans, bits of cholla dragged by pack rats trying to build refuge — lay a diamondback rattlesnake, thick as a grown man's forearm, coiled in folds, suspended in a state neither asleep nor awake.

Some thirty yards away, the boy, having conceded the only shelter for hundreds of yards to the snake, tried to cram his body into the makeshift shade of a crate stenciled with "Property of the United States Army. Fragile." The crate was delicately balanced on a trunk, similarly stenciled. The first had been placed so that half its length extended into the air, creating a scant few feet of shade on the ground underneath.

The boy got up and shifted the crate. The day was moving into afternoon, and the angle of the sun was giving him the chance of wider patches of shade. It was not yet fully hot, perhaps ninety degrees, not much more, but the sun was unrelenting, and he felt his skin burn. He had spent the last four hours alone here, with no water and only the boxes for shade. He was considering going back to drive the snake from under the tree, but he was afraid.

Around him he saw nothing but brush, grass, and tall stalks of yucca. In any direction he looked, there were distant peaks of mountains, but for miles around him, there was nothing more than the repetition of what was right here.

He was seventeen, had been seventeen for two months. Handsome and thin, though not frail, he looked older, in part due to a full but sparse beard that he had grown for the express purpose of looking so. Without it his delicate features and perpetual scowl gave him away for the boy he really was. He was lately of Jefferson Barracks, Missouri, where he had done his training, learning the craft of weather observation, becoming proficient in horsemanship, and, much to his own surprise, proving himself a superior marksman. Before that he had been in Baltimore, where he'd enlisted after fleeing his home in Hartford, Connecticut, in the dark of night.

Just two days earlier he had arrived in Tucson, the Arizona Territory, by stage from San Francisco. Tucson was the ugliest town he had ever seen in his life. It looked as if it had been constructed by an enormous, addled child who'd simply thrown mud on the ground. He had nearly missed boarding the stage and had to ride the entire trip backward, coming into his future just as his father had always told him he would, back-side first.

The stage had dropped him here, which, he now understood, was nowhere. A set of wagon ruts moved roughly south by south-west. On these, the driver had promised, an escort from Camp Bowie would be by to pick him up. That had been long ago. Hours. He was vaguely curious about the hour, though knowing the time would have made the wait and boredom intolerable. He curled up into a tighter ball under the shade of the trunk and slept.

He was awakened by the snort and stamp of mules. Later, he realized he had been dreaming the sound of tack and the creak-ing of a wagon for some time.

"You Thorne? New meat for D Com-pany?"

He scrambled out of his barely con-structed shelter. "Water. I'm dying."

9

A canteen came flying over the heads of the mules. Ned misjudged it, let it fall, and had to scramble on hands and knees in the burning dirt.

"No. Probably you ain't. When you still know how awful you feel, you ain't even close to dead yet. You go slow on that water. I don't need to be driving you back and you got the squirts all the time. My life ain't that much joy as it is."

Ned forced himself to pull the canteen from his lips. He hoisted it and poured some of the rest over the top of his head. "Private Ned Thorne," he said, saluting in a perfunctory manner. "D Company, Camp Bowie."

"Brickner. D Company, all right. But not Bowie. We're at Ramsey now. And don't salute. I ain't no officer. I'm a corporal and a human being same as you." Brickner was a big man, round in the face. His hat was a battered straw that seemed to come nearly to his eyes, which were only slits against the sun. His mouth was set in an ironic half-smile in the middle of a black beard going heavily to gray.

"What? Where? Where's Ramsey?"

"Nowhere. Or next door to it. Where's the nails?"

"Nails?"

"They supposed to be sending nails with

you. You were going to pick them up in Camp Lowell. Didn't you do that?"

"I didn't go to Camp Lowell."

"You come through Tucson, didn't you?"

"I did. But I didn't go to Camp Lowell. I stayed in a hotel."

"Hotel? You stayed in a damned hotel? Hotels is for rich bastards, fine ladies, whores, and thieves. Which of those is you?"

"I wanted a bed."

"And we're wanting nails, which you didn't get. What the hell good are you? And what's all that over there?" He nodded toward the crates.

"Weather instruments."

"Whether what?"

"Weather. Rain. Snow. Wind. Weather."

Brickner looked around at the depth of blue in the sky. "Weather. Goddamn. Ain't none here."

Ned stood in the middle of the desert, his head and shoulders wet, his belly already starting to bloat from the near canteen full he had drunk. He had no idea what use he might be. "I haven't slept in a real bed in almost two months."

"I ain't slept in a bed in years. What other complaints you got about your miserable life?"

Stung, the boy stood and glared, saying

11

nothing.

"That's what I thought. Get in the wagon here, Marybelle. And don't talk to me. It makes me sick to look at you."

They rode in silence. The small breeze stirred by their motion carried the dust and the smell of the mules back to them. Ned held another canteen in his lap, taking small swallows from time to time. His thirst was mostly memory by now, but a memory of which he could not completely rid himself. He kept his eyes straight ahead, looking only occasionally over to Brickner. The heavyset man's face was shining in the afternoon light from the sweat that came down in enough quantity to combine with the dust to form a light sheen of mud, which streaked into his beard. The rest of his skin was dotted with rough patches, burned and peeling.

"You know what time it is?" Brickner asked.

"I don't have a watch."

"I won't take it from you."

"Can't. Someone else did."

"Damn." Brickner looked off toward the horizon where the Dragoon Mountains gave way to the Little Dragoons farther to the west. "Three, maybe four, o'clock," he said.

"Who got your watch, then?"

"A sergeant. Back at Jefferson."

"How'd he get it? He just take it off you?"

"Him, three jacks, and a pair of fours."

"And what was you holding?"

"Not enough."

"I reckoned that. What, exactly?"

"Three sevens, if it makes any difference to you."

Brickner snorted and snapped the traces against the haunch of the nearest mule. The team picked up and then settled back to their same pace, man and mule seeming in agreement that this was all to alleviate the boredom of the road. "Take these. Go on, take them. I ain't going to hurt you." Brickner handed Ned the reins while he loaded and fired a long-stemmed clay pipe.

"It does make a difference. A man could go ahead and lose his watch on three sevens. That's bad luck. Bad luck is better than stupid."

"It seems to all come out about the same."

Brickner drew on his pipe as if thinking this over. "Not so. Luck changes. As I see it, stupid is as constant as sunshine."

"Sunshine isn't all that constant."

"It is out here. Sun and stupid don't give up out here. Both of them will kill you as soon as you forget to worry about them.

13

That kepi you got there for instance." He nodded at the short-billed blue cap Ned wore. "Sun going to bake your brains into a johnnycake you wear that Army issue out here. When we get to Bowie, you buy yourself a broad-brimmed hat and save your head."

"I don't have any money left."

"Well, you're dead, then. Hope you liked them whores."

They made their way up a gradual but noticeable ascent, the mules digging them through the path — hardly a path but a pair of wheel ruts — past mesquite, yucca, and creosote. Black-banded grama grass grew knee high over everything Ned could see.

They rode mostly in silence. Ned held the canteen between his knees, keeping it capped against the violent lurching of the wagon as it passed over rock and rut, counterpointed by the obscenities of Brickner, who held a bottle of whisky between his knees. He did not offer to share it.

Dear Thad,

It is stranger country than any you could make up or even hope to hear of. There are no real trees, though there are plants that might stand for them. Mostly

14

it is grass and large bushes, perhaps the size of a grand pussy willow, though they lack any of that charm.

Yesterday, I saw plants as tall as any oak or pine at home, but bearing no leaves at all. They were large bare trunks rising straight up with just the occasional branch almost as thick as the trunk about halfway up. Their skin is a thick green hide, near to leather, with ridges of thorn long enough to pierce a finger or hand.

They would seem the very sentries of hell, for it is hot enough here to qualify. From a distance, you would think that the sun had scorched the earth until there was nothing of the surface left. Up close, though, I am surprised to see that everything is full of life, though a hard and scraggly one.

I have seen a rattlesnake, though I was not bitten by it.

I trust you will keep a watchful eye on our mother, whose great sorrow is a burden for her small shoulders. Take care, too, of our father, whose sorrow and anger continues to grow, in great part the result of mine own actions . . .

The letter broke off in his head, as it

always did when he got to the part where he had to ask for the forgiveness he needed. He felt as though his shame were too great a burden to be carried by words. The weight bore on him tremendously.

"This is a bad place," Brickner said. He indicated the road before them, rising between two ridges, all scrub brush and rock. For the last several minutes they had been traveling along what appeared to be part of an actual road, one, Brickner explained, that had been the old Butterfield stage route. "If you could pick the best place in the world to stage an ambush and kill someone, it would be here or somewhere just like it. You ever hear of Cochise?"

"No."

"Cochise is an Apache Indian. Chief of the Chiricahua tribe. Smart old rascal. Lives right over yonder." He waved off to the west, where yet another range of mountains formed the horizon. "Those is the Chiricahua mountains, meaning they belong to Cochise, not us. And he's heard of you. He knew you was here before you knew you was here. You ain't real sure where you are right now, but, by Jeesums, he knows right where you are.

"And twice he's done ambushes right here at this spot. Killed him a lot of people. This

16

is called Apache Pass, and it's a lot of bad history. Last time he tried something it was against the Army, only we had us a couple of howitzers. You try to imagine what it's like when you are a ignorant old Indian and the Army starts shooting howitzers at you. It must feel like the world is breaking apart. Here, you take this."

Brickner handed Ned the trapdoor Springfield he had taken from under the seat. "We're coming right up into the pass. You keep that at the ready, now. You can shoot, can't you?"

"I can shoot."

Brickner looked at him, a long sideways glance. "And I can dance the cancan so's it would break your heart. At least make noise."

Ned held the carbine across his chest, his thumb next to the hammer, his finger lightly against the trigger. He turned his head from side to side, keeping his arms loose, ready to swing the rifle to either side.

"You can't see it," Brickner said, "but Cochise laid a lot of that rock across the top of the ridge. He and his Apaches made a real breastwork of stone and made it so good that when the patrol came through here, they never even knew it was there. All the sudden, there was the Devil's own abundance of Apaches shooting rifles and arrows at them."

Ned looked up. To either side, ridges sloped up twenty or thirty feet above their heads. There were big rocks and bushes everywhere. He strained, looking for signs of Indians. He brought the Springfield to the ready, levering back the hammer with his thumb. He wanted an Indian to show himself so that he might shoot it and finally silence the fat man.

"Mostly, it's about this," Brickner said, halting the mules on the trail. He nodded to a small green spot next to the trail. From eight feet away, Ned could hear the small trickle of water, and even before he heard it, he smelled it.

Grotto, he thought. Not more than three yards off the trail, four or five feet lower than the trail itself, a small area opened about eight feet across. A mesquite formed a canopy above it, and the ground was thick with mud. Even from outside, he could tell the temperature was a good twenty degrees cooler than the temperature on the trail.

"Hold on there, Marybelle." Brickner dug a shovel from the bed of the wagon. "If it's cool, it's got snakes. Remember that. And the best snake killer ever made is a long-handled shovel."

He followed Brickner. Over the years, the trickle of water had cleared out a hollow as big around as a small stock tank. There was enough room for the two of them to stand side by side. A series of barrels, linked by pipe, caught the thin twist of water that slid down the mossy surface of rock and onto a metal trough that emptied into the first barrel. As the water reached the top of the first barrel, it leaked into the pipe inserted through the staves and fed the second barrel, which eventually filled the third, and so on. They had, momentarily, stepped out of hell and back into the world.

They drank, then filled the canteens and the canvas bags for the mules. Ned sat in cool, wet shade while Brickner watered the mules. He felt his body gather strength in the moist air. Over his head, he heard the buzz of dragonflies that moved up and down around the water in short, nervous bursts. Lizards moved through the branches of the mesquite trees and, above them, birds in the topmost branches, as if all the life of the desert had concentrated itself in this one small spot.

"Let's go," Brickner said.

"What's the hurry? Let's stay here for a while."

"The hurry is that I say 'hurry.' We got business yonder. Get to moving."

Out of the spring, he was momentarily blinded by the sun and staggered by the heat. He was conscious of the effort he put into pulling the hot air into his lungs and pushing it back out again.

They had gone less than half a mile when the trail opened up into a valley, stretched out in front of them. "Bowie," Brickner said.

Camp Bowie was a collection of mud and stone buildings, squat and low, grouped casually around a wide flat area, all dirt and sand, save a flagpole in the middle. Ned guessed that was the parade ground, though he could not imagine troops drilling in such an area without raising clouds of dust that would obscure everything.

"This is an Army camp?" The question was clearly rhetorical. Everywhere they looked, soldiers were moving on horseback or foot, singly or in formation. "There isn't much to it."

"Enjoy it. This is the best you're going to see for a long time. You can get a real meal in a real mess here. You can sleep on a real cot tonight, you being so particular and all. You can go to the sutler's store if you've got money, which it seems you ain't. Or you can go to Sudsville for laundry and whores. If it ain't what you're used to, you're going to be wishing you was used to it soon."

"There's whores?"

"Marybelle, there's always whores if you know where to look."

"Where do you look?"

"Damn near everywhere I go."

Brickner left him at the barracks, one of the low, long mud buildings with a roof of sticks laid across thick round beams and a floor of dirt. Inside, it was dark and cool against the late afternoon heat. A corporal led him down the row of cots without a word. Soldiers coming back from duty wandered in and out of the barracks, regarding Ned with little curiosity. The corporal pointed to a cot that held only a ticked straw mattress, no blanket or pillow.

"Mine?" he asked.

"Boyer's. He's dead."

The corporal turned and left, and Ned stripped off his fatigue coat. He looked for a pillow, found none, and rolled his coat into a tight ball and put it at the head of the bed. He sat down and pulled off his boots and swung his legs onto the mattress.

"I wouldn't do that."

Ned looked up. A tall, thin soldier, going bald, shook his head. "Get up."

21

The soldier walked toward him, and Ned swung his legs down and stood, getting ready for the fight. "I was just going to lay down. The corporal told me I could use this bunk. I've had a hard coming of it."

"Don't ever just lay down out here," the soldier said. He stopped, grabbed the mattress by the corner, and wrenched it from the cot, flipping it over. As he did, a scorpion nearly the size of his hand spun in the air, landed on its back, righted itself, and scurried toward Ned's stocking feet at surprising speed.

Ned jumped, flat-footed, over the scorpion toward the aisle, catching one foot on the bottom of the bunk and falling heavily to the floor. The tall soldier stepped over him and ran after the scorpion, stamping his foot as he went.

"Got away," the soldier said. "Damn. Those things sting like the Devil hisself." He stepped back over Ned. "You hurt yourself?"

"No. I'm all right." He got up and brushed himself off. He reached down for the mattress and touched the corner of it gingerly.

"That'll be all right, then," the tall soldier said. "It's gone into the wall somewheres. Have a good sleep."

Ned gingerly touched his arm, which

tingled with small sharp pains where he had landed. He raised his arm a little and shook it gently, then turned it in slow circles.

"You're going to always want to shake your bedding, your uniform, your boots. Always look before you put anything on or set yourself down. There's a million creatures that is meaner than dirt out here. You best be on your guard. I can't say, though, that most of them are worth busting an arm for. You sure you're all right, then?"

He nodded, picked up the mattress, and slid it onto the cot, forcing himself to use the injured arm. "I almost stumbled onto a rattlesnake today."

"Well, that ain't hard to do. You'll learn to see them pretty soon. Remember that most every cow patty you see is just that, but every once in a while, it's a snake. And they love shade more than we do. Usually, they'll give you a warning, but not always. Just don't go putting yourself where something else already is, and you'll be fine."

Ned lay flat, using the coat for a pillow. The rough fabric chafed his red, burned skin. His body tensed against the thought of snakes, scorpions, and spiders. He would nearly drift to sleep but then wake with a start, sure that a scorpion was making its way across him. In the empty barracks, unable to sleep, he thought about the two days he had spent in the Territory.

On the street in Tucson where he was nearly positive he had found a pleasant-enough cantina the night before, three men were arguing in the middle of the street.

Two of them were white men, involved in a heated exchange. The older white man wore a full, uneven beard, stained yellow with tobacco at the edges of his mouth. He was dressed in a patched wool suit, stained at the lapels and shoulders. His shirt, yellow or ecru, perhaps once white, was buttoned at the collar, which he wore without a cravat.

A younger man, dressed in a faded calico shirt and voluminous canvas pants, leaned into the older man, waving his arms like a man trying to keep balance on a log. On one foot he wore a black boot that Ned recognized as infantry issue; on the other, a busted brown brogan. Slightly apart from the two, but held at the elbow by the older man, was a man yet older, with long gray hair held off his face by a red rag that circled his head just above his dark, darting eyes.

This was an Indian, but different from the half-naked, mud-caked Indians that had served him at the stage stop only a day before. Ned looked at him closely, thinking that this might be, finally, an Apache. A battered pair of yellow moccasins reached just above his ankles. His shirt was a pink gingham print with a frilled round collar and a flare at the waist. As Ned got closer, he saw that it was a woman's dress, cut down.

"I'm telling you," the younger man said. "It's my watch, and he done stole it."

"He says he found it," the older man said.

"Found it in my pocket. That's where he damned found it."

The old Indian looked straight ahead, saying nothing.

"Well then, here it is back. You got your watch. What more do you need?" He held up a cheap, plated watch showing a lot of brass at the back and edges. It dangled and spun on a thin lanyard of braided horsehair.

In exasperation, the younger man yanked off his wide sombrero, whose brim had come detached from the crown on one side. It made a flapping sound as he waved it up and down. "Justice is what I want. That was my daddy's watch. He done give it to me. Why the hell would I go and lose something like that? He damned stole it off me."

"You say stole, he says found. Just take the damned watch and go about your business and save us all a lot of trouble."

The younger man reached out for the watch, then drew back his hand as if the watch were something he would not even touch, much less possess. "It's the word of a damned thieving Indian against the word of a white man. That's what it is. Why is that giving you bother? Why is it you can't get this straight?"

The older man reached up and ran his hand through his thick, graying hair, pulling at a handful that stood straight up from the rest, which was oiled down. "Take the damned watch."

The old Indian did not move or look at either of the men. He looked straight ahead toward Ned, though Ned doubted that he even saw him. The only sound was that of a passing wagon, pulled heavily by black mules.

"The hell of it," the older man said. He reached into the pocket of his coat, dropped the watch, and extracted a small, plated pistol. He put the pistol to the Indian's head and pulled the trigger.

The Indian's knees collapsed and he went down, held for a second at the elbow by the older man's hand before slipping on through, landing on his backside, then falling flat onto his back in the dirt, his blood making a dark thick puddle of mud under his head.

"There," said the older man. "Does that satisfy you now?" He replaced the pistol in his pocket and pulled out the watch.

The young man grabbed at the watch and stuffed it into the pocket of his shirt, turned on his heel, and stomped off. He stopped and turned back. "Well, I guess it does."

And then Ned's body released, and he slept.

CAPTAIN ROBERT FRANKLIN

They were nearly down from the mountain and onto the broad plain that stretched east and south. To look over the plain was to see immediately that this was rich land that would one day be studded with farms. Though it was still early enough to provide ample daylight, he had asked Little Sam, his favorite among the Apache scouts, to find a campsite for the evening bivouac. Defensively, it was better to stay in the foothills than down on the plain, where their fires would be a beacon to anyone within twenty or more miles.

The Chiricahua Apaches were at peace and had been for some time. But to play the fool was to be the fool, and, in the Army, fools brought death and grievous hurt. He had seen his share — been responsible for his share — of harm, and he wished no more of it. His reputation as a soldier had suffered over the years, he knew, but he had vowed that those who served under his command would never be put into the path of harm through any foolishness of his. His men did not regard him with great affection, he knew, but they stayed alive to give him what regard they wished.

He was a large man, thick in the shoulders and back. He wore fatigues and a broad-brimmed campaign hat against the ferocious sun of the Southwest, which had toughened and furrowed his face. Though this was a routine patrol, designed to aid in the mapping of the southernmost parts of the Territory, he rode like a man on parade, his head back, his arm held precisely against his body, the reins light against his fingertips. He was a man so long in the Army that he had become the Army.

It was heading toward late afternoon, almost time to halt the line of march, when he saw Little Sam riding up fast. They were traversing a long, alluvial plain of grama grass that reached nearly to their stirrups. The expanse of grass that stretched nearly horizon to horizon was studded with clumps of yucca and the occasional dome of a honey mesquite. But mostly it was grass, moving like the fur of a large dog caressed by an unseen hand. And through the very middle of it, a parting, caused by the approach of the scout.

He received the news with the same equanimity with which Sam reported it. Two or three miles up ahead, beyond the ridge and into the lower reaches of the valley, was a ranch, which had been attacked. There were dead, and the dead were white.

He brought Sergeant Triggs forward, informed him of the situation, then sent him to ride at mid-column and gave the orders. Following the lead of Little Sam, the column set out at full canter.

He kept the column together at the top of the ridge, where the scouts waited. The ranch was modest — a small hacienda, surrounded by an adobe wall, which anchored and protected it. Beyond the wall was a crude corral, constructed with lashings of mesquite and yucca. Beyond the corral was another, smaller building, and behind the house an adobe hut, fenced with yucca, that might serve for a chicken coop. There was a small garden and a circle of stone that, no doubt, marked a dug well.

He considered the situation. The Apaches had found no evidence of anyone alive at the ranch, but he did not like the looks of it. The hacienda had been built with fortification in mind, and the possibility that someone still lurked in the house or behind the walls, waiting for them, could not be discounted.

He sent the scouts ahead, on foot, trusting in the Apaches' ability to move unseen through the terrain. When the scouts had moved two hundred yards ahead, he split the column so as to come down flanking the hacienda from the north and south, spreading the troops at twenty-yard intervals to present a wide and difficult target for any who might be behind the walls.

Triggs led the south flank and he led the north, bringing his men in a wide arc, hoping to draw fire at a distance that would make accurate shooting unlikely. They moved slowly, steadily, carbines loaded, drawn, and at rest across the pommels of their saddles.

He had never fought the Apaches, but he knew their reputation as fighters and tacticians. And he knew from his experiences on the Pit River the advantage that knowledge of the territory gave the aboriginals. He rode his column in steadily and slowly, keeping his eye alternately on the hacienda and on Sergeant Triggs's column coming in across the valley. The Apache scouts were nowhere to be seen.

He felt the anxiety of anticipation descend into the tranquility of purpose. Everything

31

he had done and learned fighting the Pi-Ute and studying at the Point, and even the games he had played as a boy, distilled into this moment. Each step of his mount was precise, considered, alive with the possibilities of the moment. He himself was more alive in this moment than he had been for longer than he cared to remember.

They moved the last fifty yards on foot, keeping their mounts between themselves and the hacienda. He kept them moving in a descending arc until, arriving at the outer wall, they met up with the other column, effectively surrounding the ranch.

Signs of struggle were everywhere. The thin mud coating of the wall was pocked from the impact of bullets. Bits of glass, which had been embedded atop the wall to discourage intruders from scaling it, littered the ground. At the front entrance of the wall, near the remains of what had been a gate, now a mere scrabbling of sticks, were traces of flour and beans. A couple of rags of cloth were snagged on the low-growing brush outside the wall.

The door of the hacienda gaped wide as though thrown open in welcome. And through it the contents of the house spilled out — furniture, cloth, maize, flour, and broken crockery. Beyond the door was only wreckage. The lives of those who lived here had been picked up and whirled and tossed about by someone. It seemed like the work of a tempest or a cataclysm.

"Someone's made a mess of this, for sure." Triggs stood in the doorway next to him, hat off, like a man paying his respects to an agency above and beyond his own powers. "The Apaches, then?"

"Most likely. Fan the patrol out to search the premises. There may be survivors, or at least remains. And, Sergeant, there will be no looting. It will not be tolerated."

"Understood, sir."

The troop moved through the hacienda four abreast, through the ruins of someone's life. They looked for nothing in particular and for everything. They searched for some sign of those who lived here, or had lived here, and they searched for signs of those who had come in and destroyed it. They kept their eyes down because there was nothing to see above the level of their knees.

The house was a large, single room with an area for sitting and sleeping on the west side and another area for eating and cooking on the east, centered around a large, rounded fireplace of adobe slathered over with mud, in the style of the Mexican.

There had been good furniture set up. A

bed, now on its side. A chest of drawers, fallen facedown onto the dirt floor. Thin chairs were scattered about. A table of rough wood stood miraculously upright, but bare except for a scattering of flour, sugar, and corn. A small writing desk lay on its back, its contents of paper scattered about it, much of the paper in a dark area that had been, for a short while, a pool of spilled ink.

He stooped among the wreckage. In the storm of paper, flour, and beans on the packed earthen floor lay tangles of clothing. Denim and canvas trousers, shoes, stockings, shirts of calico and muslin. What caught his eye was a long swirl of pink fabric. He tugged at a corner of it, pulling it from the mess of the rest of the clothing. It was a woman's dress. As he pulled it free, a small scorpion, not much larger than his thumbnail, leaped from the bodice and into the pile that remained on the floor — a tangle of shirts and undergarments, stockings and shoes. The dress was hardly new. The hems were fraying and showed the signs of repeated washings. He held the dress at arm's length. It belonged to a small woman, perhaps no more than a girl.

Outside, the sunlight blinded him. He walked beyond the walls and sighted the area until, in the distance, he located Little Sam. He waved him in.

"What have you found?"

Sam raised two fingers, then pointed off in the direction from which he had come.

"Men?"

"Yes."

"A woman?" He held up the pink dress.

Little Sam regarded the dress impassively. He shook his head. "Two men. White. Mexican. No woman."

"Damn it all." He stared off to the horizon, focusing less on what he saw than on this new complication of an already troubling problem. "Keep looking," he told Little Sam. "They may have taken her out a bit further and . . ." He paused. "Killed her."

Sam shook his head. "No. They kill, she here. No. Take."

"Perhaps she escaped, then. Maybe she is out there somewhere, hiding. I'll send some troopers to sweep the area. She may be hiding from you and the other scouts. Maybe she wasn't even here. We don't know for sure that there even was a woman."

Sam was looking at him, expressionless. He nodded, and Sam turned and went back the way he had come, yelling to the other scouts in Apache.

He threw the dress over his neck and

gripped it with both hands, pulling down. He pushed his neck back against it, glad to have a pressure he could resist. He called out Pack and Birdwood and sent them to sweep the area in widening circles around the hacienda, calling out "Miss" at every turn. He called out Richmond and Kent and ordered them to the outbuildings to find shovels.

The men had been dead for two, maybe three, days by his reckoning. God knew he had seen enough of the dead to make a pretty good estimate of it. They were about fifty yards apart, the white man on his back, the Mexican facedown.

The vultures and coyotes had been at the bodies for a while. As the troopers lifted the two men and brought them together where they were to be buried, the ants and flies paused only a bit, then resumed their labors.

It was clear how they had died. Though the scavengers had taken enough flesh to release some arrows, there were still some lodged in bone. The white man had been hit head-on. The Mexican had tried to run and been hit in the back.

"Damn you. You could have died on someone else's watch. Why is it always me who draws the most foul assignments?" Royal Kent cursed quietly and unrelentingly as he jabbed at the soil with his shovel. Richmond worked quietly but slowly. He had already vomited once, and his face shone white under the glistening sweat.

"Private Kent. Hold your tongue," Franklin said.

"Sorry, sir."

"The poor brutes can't hear your complaints and neither God nor I want to."

In the distance he could hear Pack and Birdwood still calling out "Miss" as they rode, their voices getting less distinct as their circles widened. He would let them ride awhile longer, though he already knew their efforts would be futile.

Private Ned Thorne

When he woke, it was nearly dark. At the far end of the barracks there was faint light from an oil lamp on a small table near the door. He blinked to focus. A pair of eyes stared at him from the cot on his right.

"What time is it?" he asked.

"Half-past May."

"When's mess call?"

"Been. It was pretty good, too. You slept in Boyer's bed. He's dead. I thought you might be him. He knew his Bible, Boyer did."

Ned assumed that he was still nearly asleep. He ran his hands over his face, then down his belly. He was hungry. He swung his legs off the bed and sat up, facing away from the person who was talking. "I need to get something to eat."

"Canned peaches. Sweeter than candy. You know Boyer?"

"No. I don't know Boyer. I'm not him.

I'm from Connecticut. Where's the mess?"

"Where's Connecticut?"

"A long way. It's all the way back in the United States."

"Is it nice there? I was in Tennessee once. It was nice there. Pretty. And the air smelled sweet as all get-out."

"Yes. Connecticut is nice. Used to be. I'm not well thought of there anymore."

"I don't believe I'm thought of at all. Can't think of who might want to think on me."

"Perhaps that's for the best. I need to eat something. Where's the mess?"

"Yonder. I had extra on the peaches. I really thought you was Boyer come back. He was a regular whiz at that Bible reading."

"No." He started to pull on his boots, then remembered and shook them out. It was too dark to tell if anything came out, but he supposed not. He shook them again and put them on. "Boyer's dead, and I might be, too, if I don't get something to eat."

" 'He will come as a thief in the night.' That's wrote in the Bible. Boyer read me that. I can't forget that. I ain't going to, neither. Not ever."

"I guess not. Mess 'yonder' this way or that?"

"Yonder. Them peaches is sweeter than candy. 'Like a thief in the night.' Boyer, he's coming back."

He sat by himself in the mess. Most of the troops had already eaten and left. He had stopped groups of them walking and talking easily in the dark, saluting them all in case there was an officer he couldn't see in the dark, and asked them for directions.

He had taken all he could on his plate and was thinking of going back for more. It was good American food, mostly from cans. There was beef in thick gravy and salted small potatoes and stewed tomatoes and slices of thick bread with lard. It was the first food he had eaten in days that was not slathered with thick, hot chili to hide its origin. He had a tin cup of milk that was fresh and cold because there was ice at Bowie. He ate leaning forward, his left arm curled around his plate in a protective pose.

He woke to a hand over his mouth and nose. Still in sleep, he struggled to rise. Another hand and arm held him at his shoulder and chest.

"Marybelle. Hush. Get up." The voice was a rasping whisper, the breath fetid with whisky and sex. Coming up from sleep, Ned struggled, then relaxed. "It's time."

It was dark. The barracks was filled with the snoring and thrashing of sleeping troopers, counterpointed with groaning and a few mumbled words from a sleep talker. He could just make out Brickner's face.

"Quiet," Brickner said. "It's time to go. We're getting on. Get yourself up. Come. Quiet, now." Ned opened his mouth to ask the time, only to have Brickner's hand clamp over it again. "Hush."

He swung his legs off the cot and groped for his hat and boots. He fought against the sleep that had him suspended in a haze. He reached for the boots, remembered, and shook them. Brickner pulled him up and away from the cot.

Outside, they made their way by moonlight, Ned still carrying his boots in one hand, coat in the other, hobbling and pussyfooting along the rocky path that led past the butcher's shop and stables to where the wagon stood, hitched and ready.

He shook out his boots once more in the wagon as Brickner snapped the traces and headed the mules forward. They lurched forward, then back, as the wagon went up the road in the dark.

"What's the hurry?"

"It's a long way to go. When the sun gets to blazing, I got to go easy on the mules.

This is the time."

"Can't we stop for food? That was awful good food I had at the mess."

"It's no time for that. Don't need it anyhow."

"What time is it?"

"It'll be dark for a while yet. You worry an awful lot about time for a man who let some candy-belly sergeant tote his watch for him."

Ned looked around at the strangeness of the desert at night, the stunted, twisted shapes of the desert life glowing white in moonlight. "Is this safe?"

"The mules know the way."

"No. I mean Indians."

"Apaches? They don't fight in the dark. Bad medicine. It makes the owl spirit stronger. They don't want none of that. We're safe as babies."

When light began to slowly define the landscape, they were several miles from Bowie. They had traveled down steep and rocky trails that slowed but didn't stop the mules. Ned fought to stay awake against the sleep he had missed. In the rocking, creaking wagon, he would slip back into sleep, only to be jolted out of it as the mules adjusted their gait to the trail. The journey had the feel of a dream whose beginning had already faded from memory.

They moved nearly due south, out of the mountains that held Camp Bowie and down into a broad prairie of grama grass nearly as high as the seat of the wagon. The tallest mountains were the ones they had just left, but in every direction, other mountains defined a ragged and chewed horizon.

The sun had been up for nearly an hour, the heat already building steadily enough that Ned could feel his uniform weighing down with sweat. Brickner pulled the wagon off the trail onto a broad, level expanse near a clump of mesquite trees. "Chow," he said. "I'm near starved. Food takes up belly room a man needs for whisky. Go over yonder and get us some firewood."

Near the trees, he found only small dry twigs of the mesquite that had lain on the dry ground so long they were beginning to fossilize. He made wider and wider circles around the tree, gathering up a small armful of the sticks.

With handfuls of grass and dried mesquite beans, they built a small and smoky fire. Brickner handed him a tin coffeepot, crusted a couple of inches deep in the bottom with old, hardened coffee, and a canvas water bag. "This is dirty," Ned said.

"Ain't dirt. Coffee."

"How old is this coffee?"

"Coffee's like a good whore, new ever time."

While Ned tended the fire and the coffee, Brickner dug through the back of the wagon, rearranging tarps. When the coffee had come to a good boil, Brickner hauled out a skillet, then an ammunition crate. From the crate he took packages, which he untied and unwrapped — a good-sized, thick slab of bacon and biscuits. He held them out at arm's length for Ned's approval. "And you never knew, did you, what a fortunate thing it is to ride with Obediah Brickner?"

Ned took a biscuit, held it to his nose, and inhaled deeply. "Wonderful."

"Wait. Wait." Brickner waved his hands in front of him. "Wonders from a world few men know." He dug in the crate and brought out another package, soaked and dripping. He tore the paper and revealed a fist-sized chunk of butter, nesting on melting ice. He took a piece of the ice and put it in his mouth, offering another to Ned. It was slick, cold, and sweet.

Then from the bottom of the crate came handfuls of straw, tossed in the air to spin crazily to the ground. From under the straw, six brown, speckled eggs.

They ate chunks of salty bacon, whose

grease mixed with egg yolk in a delicious paste they licked from their chins and lips. They ran whole biscuits across the lump of butter and crammed them into their mouths.

"Eat it. Eat it all. Save us from fighting the others for it."

"If there is something better than this in the world, I couldn't think what it would be."

Brickner took a long slug of coffee and wiped the drips from his mouth, smearing butter and bacon fat across his round face and through his beard, making it shinier than it had been before. "I know what's even better." He grinned broadly.

"What? What could be better?"

"There's officers in Bowie who ain't getting no seconds on breakfast this morning."

Ned clapped his hands and rolled onto his back, laughing. "You are a man of miracles."

Brickner sat cross-legged on the ground, smiling, a fat, smiling Buddha, like the Chinese people worshipped, but in a filthy Army uniform. "Ain't nothing more to life than what you can make of it."

While Brickner saw to the mules, Ned scoured the skillet and tin plates with sand and loaded them in the wagon. He took the shovel and buried the fire. When he replaced the shovel, he stepped back in puzzlement and tried to comprehend what he was seeing and what he wasn't seeing. "It's gone."

"What's that?"

"My trunk. My instruments. My instruments are gone."

"Damn," Brickner said, pulling off his hat and running his hand through his thinning hair. "Damned if you ain't right."

"Where is it?"

"Damned if I know. Bastards at Bowie, I suppose. Bunch of lying, thieving bastards."

"We got to go back. I got to have those instruments."

"Don't reckon we can do that. We got hours to travel yet. We'd be a day late if we was to turn back now. It's a damned shame, though, those weasels stealing your gear like that."

"We got to get it back."

"Wish I could help you on that, Marybelle. But what's stole is stole. It don't come back. We got enough grief without going back and looking for some more."

"But they're my instruments. They're valuable."

"Now, it was my thought that those was the Army's instruments."

"They are, but they're my responsibility."

"Well, that's a way to look at it. Here's another: they's the Army's responsibility. Now it's true that you've bungled it a bit, but so did the Army in giving them to you. It's the Army's fault as much as it is yours. More. It's their belongings."

"But I'm the one who's going to be in trouble."

"What's the Army going to do to you? Bust you to private? Send you to the very ends of the earth? You're already there. Boy, you are so low, the Army can't get in a good swipe at you. You get a couple weeks in the guardhouse is all. Hell, Ramsey ain't got a guardhouse. They can't touch you."

"It was my responsibility. I lost hundreds of dollars' worth of instruments."

"No. No. You ain't thinking right. You got your petticoats all knotted up over nothing. They ain't lost. Lookit here. Those is Army things, right? Am I right?"

Ned nodded, feeling empty and defeated.

"Where are they? In Camp Bowie. And where's Camp Bowie? The Army. They's where they's supposed to be, just not in the exact location the Army thought they were putting them. That what belongs to the Army is still in the Army, and that ain't lost. It just can't be. You're getting yourself all stove in over nothing. And nobody in Ramsey is going to care much. You know what they want in Ramsey? Nails. Nails is what they want, and nails is what we got." Brickner pulled back the tarp to reveal three kegs of nails.

"Nails don't have anything to do with me. The instruments do."

"Believe me, when they see these nails, no one is going to give the first thought to your lackings. Now, come on aboard. I'm moving out. You don't want to be walking to camp, days late and charged with desertion."

"Where did the nails come from?" They had been riding south for nearly an hour when the thought finally clawed its way into his consciousness.

"Where nails come from."

"You didn't have any nails when you picked me up. You wanted some nails. Now you've got them. How did you get nails?"

"What are you saying?"

"I'm asking how you got nails."

"I got them. Ask what you want to ask."

"Where did the nails come from?"

"It don't make no difference, and you don't care. Ask what you want to ask. I'll tell you true, but you got to ask."

"Where are my instruments?"

"Back at Bowie. That ain't the question.

You know that."

"Where at Bowie?"

"How the hell am I supposed to know that? I ain't no seer. Those instruments is there, and I am here. Now ask the question."

"You steal my stuff?"

"Yep."

"And traded it for the nails?"

"Yep."

"Why?"

" 'Cause I needed the nails more than you needed that gear. I might be wrong, but I don't much care. That's how I see it."

Ned said nothing. He stared straight ahead and tried to adjust his life to fit this new injustice. His hands hung limp at his knees and there was a slight burn behind his eyes.

"So. You wanted the truth. It seemed real important to you to know the truth, and now you do. And it makes you feel worse than you did. And now you got to make some decisions. And they're hard ones. But they're yours to make. Let me know. I'm waiting on you, now."

He wanted to turn and face Brickner, but he couldn't force himself to do it. He tried to cipher out his options. He could wait until Ramsey and report Brickner. He should do that, but it seemed no way for a man to live his life, always running to a momma, or a teacher, or an officer for help. He could fight it out with Brickner. Even without looking, he knew he would lose. Brickner was a grown man and much bigger than he. He was supposed to be a man now. He tried to know what a man should do. He couldn't do anything. He simply stared ahead.

He looked over at Brickner, and simultaneously, almost before he was conscious it was what he was going to do, he landed a fist below Brickner's right eye with a loud crack, causing Brickner to buckle at the waist, ducking his head out of range.

He saw Brickner's hand coming toward him, and he saw Brickner rein back the mules, and he heard the long, low, guttural moan Brickner used to slow them. He was amazed how it all unfolded, as if time itself had bogged and slowed. He could not understand why he couldn't get his own hands, which had become mired in time, up to protect his face.

And then time pulled free, and the back of Brickner's hand, which had swung from completely across his body, passed just over the tips of Ned's ascending fingers and exploded into his face with the sound of an oak stave smacking a melon. His sight went red, then black. Everything jumbled, then righted itself, and he knew he was on his back in the bed of the wagon. And he knew he had to get himself up, but his arms and legs just weren't working right.

Brickner came over the seat of the wagon quickly, his right boot landing squarely on Ned's wrist, pinning his arm. Brickner dropped, his knee coming down on Ned's shoulder. His fist, with all his weight behind it, came down on Ned's face. His shoulder pinned, Ned could only turn his head a few inches from side to side. He raised his legs and bucked his hips to no avail. For a while, he watched Brickner's fists coming at him, first feeling the impact, then hearing the even worse sound. He shut his eyes.

It was a bad dream, impossible to comprehend in reality. He couldn't be being beaten this badly. He had been in fights before, plenty of them. And he had lost some of them, too, but that experience was nothing like the way Brickner was efficiently, unemotionally hammering him, a journeyman methodically carrying the task to proper completion.

"You've had enough." It wasn't a question. "You know that, don't you?" Brickner stood over him, looking at him with calm

51

concern.

Ned turned his head away.

With his toe, Brickner gently pushed Ned's head back. "You understand? Don't be proud, now. This ain't that time. You're beat. You're not going to try anything stupid, are you? I don't need to give you any more."

Ned shut his eyes and shook his head.

"All right, then. You just ride back here. Take it easy on yourself. I'm heading us on."

"You all right?"

Ned had moved from the bed of the wagon back to the seat. Riding in the back was too painful, too full of defeat. He nodded. "I'm all right."

"I didn't want to do that. Do you know that?"

Ned nodded. His left eye was swollen, his jaw hurt badly, and his left shoulder had stiffened until he could barely move his arm.

"I done what I had to. I done what you made me. No more."

Ned nodded.

"You was robbed." Brickner looked over at the small, pained smile on Ned's face. "I mean back at Tucson. I been thinking on it. They stole your stuff. You was robbed in Tucson."

They rode farther. The light brought everything into sharp focus. More grass, scattered trees. They were heading for a band of mountains pretty much due south. "How come I didn't report it?"

" 'Cause it's all thieves in Tucson anyway. They'll try and steal your pecker while you're taking a whiz."

Ned said nothing.

"They beat you and threw you unconscious on the stage. You didn't wake up 'til later."

"That's stupid."

"That don't matter. They ain't going to believe you anyway. Officers only believe other officers. It only matters if they can prove you're lying. You wanted to report it to your commanding officer. That's what you're doing."

"It's weak."

"It's what you got. You should have been more careful, anyway. Here." He handed Ned the reins. "Just don't drop those." Brickner climbed over the seat and began untying tarps. "Take this." He handed Ned a revolver, butt first. "That's for you. It's the latest thing. Cartridge loading, forty-five caliber, courtesy of Mr. Colt. The Army is just trying them out. You can't get one anywhere. I'm going to give it to you because I feel bad that I had to hurt you like that. I'm a good man, once you learn to stay on my right side."

Ned looked at the gun, smaller and lighter than the Army Remington. The cylinder was open at both ends to receive metal cartridges, rather than the standard-issue paper ones. "You got bullets?"

Brickner smiled at him. "Do I look like a man would give a fellow he just beat a gun with bullets? You just put that away for a while. I'll find us some bullets later on."

"Why are you giving this thing to me?"

"Because I beat you pretty good. And I didn't want to have to do that. I'm not a bad man. I'm a hard man, and I protect myself and that what's mine, but I don't take joy in giving beatings. I'm hard on my enemies, but I'm good to my friends. I would be obliged if I could call you my friend. It would go good for you, too."

Ned looked at the Colt and spun the cylinder. It was the prettiest gun he had ever seen. He raised and sighted it to the horizon. "All right, then."

"Then good. All right." Brickner swung his right arm again and backhanded Ned in the chest, knocking him across the seat and into the wagon. "There. That's a reminder of what can happen if you do me wrong.

I'm all kinds of badness if you do me wrong, but I'm a good man to know and be friends with. You tell the story the way I tell you to, and we're going to be just fine here. You're going to be glad you made my acquaintance.

"Let me tell you what I think. You're a baby. You don't know that, but everyone else does, and everyone's going to want you, 'cause babies is what you make of them. You're in for some hard times. What I'm offering you is a chance for better. Better than any what the others is likely to give you. You see that mule there, the one with the short tail? That's a shavetail, a young, green mule that hasn't learned his tasks yet. He can't go by himself. He's always got to be paired with an older, smarter mule. He's you, and I'm the older, smarter one. I'll teach you what you got to know. You throw in with me, you're going to do all right. You don't, you going to wish you had. And that's no threat. That's just how it is, how I know it's going to be. I'm a patient soul. I'll wait on your answer."

"You had no call to do that. I wasn't going to do anything to you. I wouldn't tell what happened. We agreed."

"Yes, we did. But one man can never know what another is thinking. That there was just to keep you thinking along the right track. Here. This will ease the sting." He handed Ned a bottle of whisky, which Ned uncorked, drank, and handed back. Brickner took a drink. "Nothing ever as bad as you think it's going to be. And nothing's as good, neither."

LIEUTENANT
ANTHONY AUSTIN

The insect made its way in a ragged scurry, moving through chutes of sand, coming up on rocks smaller than a bird's egg, and then turning to move back and go around. It explored bits of leaf and pine needle crushed by the boots of soldiers. It came up the side of a tall, flat rock, traversed that on the vertical, then lost its purchase and fell down, coming to rest on its back, waving its legs frantically until it righted itself and went on, going at an angle oblique to the one it had previously tried.

The insect was little more than half an inch in length, its anterior sections black, the posterior a bright and pure red, the whole body covered with a fine, smooth hair. Between thorax and abdomen, a slight waist was barely visible under the fine, plush hair.

"Antlike." The man leaned forward, taking the spectacles from his face and holding them at various distances and angles between himself and the curious insect. He replaced his spectacles and leaned back, resting his weight on the heels of his boots. With a bit of pencil taken from behind his ear, be wrote the word in a small package of papers stitched roughly together at the top. "Antlike?" He crossed out the word and rewrote it, displacing the question mark into a set of brackets. "Antlike [?]."

The creature scuttled toward a haven of piled leaf and needle. The man reached out with a long straight pin and knocked it back, flipping it onto its back one more time, forcing it to struggle to the upright and begin the difficult journey up the small draws of sand and stone yet again.

The man leaned forward again, holding the pad of paper on the tips of his fingers, bringing it up parallel to the insect so that the creature's body matched up against lines carefully inked into the heavy top page. He pulled the packet back, flipped back to the page he had been on, and wrote "5/8 inch."

The hairy little insect made progress up the draw, only to encounter the pin again, which knocked it back. It stopped as if confused or frustrated, then began again. Unrelenting. The man relaxed his legs and stretched himself across the draw, resting on left hip and elbow, and with tight, small strokes of the pencil, sketched the insect, pausing every so often to reach out with the pencil to knock it back, then resume his drawing. Drawing done, he wrote.

"Order, Hymenoptera. It would seem to be a member of the family Formidae, having only a narrow waist between thorax and abdomen. Its head, though covered with the fur that coats the rest of the body, resembles — in general — the other members of that family. Its mandibles, however, do not seem disproportionately large as would be expected, and it exhibits no aggressiveness to the pencil. The hair that covers its body, especially the bright, posterior scarlet hair, is smooth and velvety, as fine and soft as the fur of a young pup, as bright and beautiful as anything worn by the finest of ladies." He reached forward toward the insect, aligned his hand above it to push the pin through its hairy thorax, and lifted as its legs waved for the last time.

He closed the packet of papers, pinned the insect to it, and put it and the pencil into a fringed buckskin pouch, then drew his legs up to him and sat. It was early afternoon. Above him were the small but profound sounds of the riparian forest — the wind through the leaves of cottonwood and sycamore, the birds calling from branch to branch. Somewhere in the distance, he heard the tiny bark of a gray squirrel scolding some coyote or bobcat that had come too close to the tree it had staked out as its own. From far below, the sounds of the camp became more insistent on his attention — the omnipresent hammering and sawing, the clank of the chain and crack of the whip as mules leaned into the labor of moving logs as the camp continued to spread outward, displacing tree after tree. And as a background to all of this, the murmur of men's voices, rising and falling in pitch, with the irregular counterpoint of laughter and cursing. From this distance, the noise was indistinct and as calming as the sound of water moving steadily on. Closer, it was mundane, quarrelsome, and more often than not, profane.

He reached behind him, picked up his broad-brimmed straw hat, gathered his long hair back with his left hand, and placed the hat onto his head so his hair was simultaneously pushed back and trapped by the hat's crown. He took the strap of the buckskin bag in his hand and stood, bringing it over head and hat and letting it rest on his shoulder, the bag against his hip. He tested the firmness of the rock and sand with the side of his boot and started back down the draw toward camp.

The camp rode a flat plane nearly a mile wide between two forks of the White River at the very base of the Chiricahua foothills, the transition from desert to mountain. It had, twice he suspected, been a floodplain when enough water had run down the forks to turn them into a single, broad, flat table of water. The result of that was a crown of rich topsoil and river silt well above the banks of the river, rich with grass, shrub, and tree. From where he stood, the camp was barely visible, small wedges of grass and canvas seen through narrow frames between trees.

He crossed the north fork of the river on a series of flat rocks placed as a breakwater, forcing the river farther north and away from the camp. At his tent, he entered and stowed his gear, pushing the pin with the impaled insect into a piece of cork resting on a makeshift desk. He sat, unstoppered the ink well, dipped his pen, and wrote "May 15, 1871, Camp Ramsey" on a slip of paper, which he placed below the insect and pinned to the cork.

He took his blue tunic from the peg on the tent pole and put it on. He reached for his tasseled helmet, thought better of it, and

61

kept on the straw. Then he removed his spectacles, folded them carefully, and put them away in his desk.

"As you were." He returned Sergeant Stonehouse's salute and stood side by side with him, observing the troopers who were scaling the rough log walls of the building under construction. "It goes well?"

The sergeant laughed. "As well as it can. It's the last of the nails. We'll run out before we run out of light."

"Brickner will be back tomorrow. He'll have nails. You can take some of these men and move them to felling or splitting." He turned around and motioned with his chin to where soldiers were driving wedges into long lengths of ponderosa pine.

"If he does come back," the sergeant said.

"Pardon?"

"Brickner. He'll bring nails if he does come back."

"You believe he will not be back?"

"What more can be done to him?" The sergeant asked. "All that's left is to shoot him, and he knows that won't happen."

The lieutenant smiled. "That's why he always comes back. Anybody else would shoot him. The dog returns to where he gets his food without a kicking to accompany it.

Brickner will be here and he will have nails with him."

"Yes, sir."

"You have my word on it, Sergeant."

"Sorry, sir. I don't mean to question your treatment of Mr. Brickner."

"Yes, you do, Sergeant. You mean very much to question it. That's as it will be. And Corporal Brickner is as he will be. And he will be here tomorrow. And if he is not, it was not you who sent him. It was me. I will be the one responsible, as I always am."

"Yes, sir."

"Carry on, then, Sergeant."

From the distance came the bright ring of metal on metal. Three soldiers, stripped to the waist, took turns hammering metal wedges into a pine log some twenty feet long. The hammers came down alternately, one striking and recoiling as another was at the top of its arc and the third was being brought back to begin its upward arc.

The distance kept sound and sight unsynchronized. The ring of the hammer would be followed by the sight of the hammer coming down again, as if the ring were merely an anticipation of the strike. All of this was followed by the creak and sharp crack of the wood fibers letting go as the log split into two pieces, ready to be split again.

The screaming came from beyond the hammering and to the north of it. He called for Stonehouse and nodded in the direction of the commotion. "See to that," he said, and went back to his tent to record and preserve his little insect.

He had them arranged on a piece of cork some nine inches by twelve. There were thirteen of them all together, Hymenoptera, or what he thought were Hymenoptera, and Hemipesis. They were arranged with military precision, or were after he had arranged and rearranged them several times.

"Sir. Your skills are required here," Stonehouse said.

"What is it?"

"Borchert. He is badly hurt. A tree fell on him. His leg took the worst of it."

He came outside where a group of soldiers was gathered, four at the ends of a stretcher, where Trooper Borchert, no doubt the one who had been screaming earlier, lay.

Borchert, who kept up a quick monologue of the mundane and irrelevant, like a man too embarrassed to keep his peace, smiled. "I'm not sure," he said, "that I can walk on this leg." He nodded toward the pant leg, soaked in blood, that seemed strangely empty from just below the hip, past where the knee had been. His foot was canted ninety degrees from forward. He seemed the gracious center of attention, smiling and nodding to his comrades who had seen him transformed from friend, companion, and soldier to simply "the man the tree fell on." Seemingly enjoying his new role, Borchert did his best to put the rest of them at ease.

The lieutenant watched as the smiling Borchert, saying a quiet and heartfelt thanks to the rest of the troop, began to lose color, his face progressing from florid to fish-belly white in only seconds. He looked at the lieutenant as if he had been struck by a new and strange thought he could not be sure of. His eyes rolled up, then shut as a shudder passed through his body.

It was after the noon hour when the captain and his patrol came back into camp. The lieutenant had stayed up with Borchert most of the night. He had undressed and cleaned him. Borchert came briefly into consciousness several times. He said nothing, but took the occasional sip of the whisky the lieutenant offered him. He would then slip back into unconsciousness. When the captain was apprised of the situation, he asked neither for the details of the accident nor for an accounting of responsibility. He asked only of remedy.

He must be sent to Camp Bowie, the lieutenant explained, some forty miles away. He was in desperate need of a surgeon. Bowie had one, Ramsey had barely a first-aid box. The question was how to get him there.

"We will have to build a travois," Captain Franklin said.

"May as well line up the men and give them turns whacking on that leg with their rifle butts. The trip will kill him."

"Then what will we do, Tony? Brickner won't be back with the wagon until late tonight. Probably tomorrow. And when he comes back, he'll be drunk as a dog with a team of tired mules. It will be useless to turn him around and send him back. Borchert will lose the leg for sure."

"The leg is lost. It was lost immediately. There's no bone left in there, only a bunch of chip and powder where it was. I'm not concerned with the leg. That's out of it. Completely. My concern is Borchert. Keeping him alive if we can, keeping him comfortable if we can't."

"It's his leg. He's lost his leg is all."

"Bobby, we've seen this before. His leg is crushed. He's in the rapture of dying. Like a rabbit in a snare. He's given himself over. He's bleeding to death on the inside. Moving him by travois would just kill him faster. I see no use in it."

"What, then?"

"Wrap him in blankets. Tie the legs together to keep the bad one from flapping around like a bit of cloth, and if he wakes, all the whisky he can handle. If he lives through the day, we can put horses to the wagon when Brickner returns and send him up then."

"He's wanting real attention now."

"We have no real attention to give him. What he wants is to have that leg cut off, but we can't do that without killing him in the act. No, Bobby, he's wanting the last bits of comfort he's likely to get from this life."

Borchert came to consciousness in the afternoon, looking around like a man visiting a strange town. He accepted the whisky gratefully, drinking it steadily but calmly, pushing himself further and further toward unconsciousness. By mid-afternoon, with Lieutenant Austin at his side taking discreet sips of the whisky Borchert was no longer using, Borchert died.

"There is no culpability."

Lieutenant Austin raised his head from the bracket of his hands. Beside him were the inkwell and his pen, the point still dry. Captain Franklin nodded to the paper in front of Austin. "There is no culpability. It was an act of God. There is no way to know with certainty how a tree may fall. A man can't know what's inside." Franklin sat heavily on the stool next to Austin's make-shift desk, a couple of ammunition crates nailed to vegetable boxes.

"It's not a report," Austin said. "I'll be at that later. It's a letter to his people, to let them know."

"I have questioned Fenner and the others on the felling detail. I am satisfied that there was no culpability. You would have thought that tree had purpose, they told me," Franklin said. He appeared older than Austin, though they were, in fact, within months of each other. He was taller, broader, his skin weathered about the eyes. His mustaches, meticulously waxed, showed gray woven through the black. A first lieutenant brevetted to captain, he outranked Austin, but their relationship was one of old, close friends deeply familiar with each other, rather than one based on rank. "The men said that it was like the tree was after him,

Tony, just coming at him, always coming at him."

Austin removed his spectacles and rubbed his eyes, a man profoundly weary. He had tended Borchert through the night, giving him what aid he could. He had not gone to help when he heard Borchert screaming. He could not have helped. Still, he should have gone. It was his place to go.

"He started up the hill, his only chance," Franklin said. The tree was falling straight down the draw, like it had eyes. If he'd kept to the draw it would have gotten him straightaway. They all saw him slip trying the hill. He slipped, went down, and gave up. He knew then he had no chance. He watched the tree come down on him. They said it looked like he might get up to try again, but he didn't. It was no use."

Austin looked at the paper in front of him. "That's no comfort to the people who cared for him. I can't think what in the world might be comfort for them. Perhaps I should write that he died in a heroic effort to establish a bakery in the last outpost of the United States of America."

"The broader purpose is achieved through the trivial incident. You know that as well as I. It is no matter to his people whether he died fighting the aboriginals or cutting down a tree. He is dead, and he died in the line of duty. We shall leave the matter there. There are other, more urgent things we must attend to."

The lieutenant raised his head and looked at his old friend, seeing now that in his own concern for Borchert, he had ignored what was written on the captain's brow. "What, Bobby? What has happened?"

"They're Apaches. That's all we know. They're not Chiricahua Apaches, at least Sam says not, but some other tribe. They attacked a small ranch maybe twenty-five miles from here. Killed two. And worse."

"Worse?"

"There's a woman. Missing. Gone with them, I've no doubt. Probably to Mexico. They will likely try to sell her there. White women are a commodity of value in Mexico."

"If they are not Chiricahua, who are they?"

"We can't tell. They are Apaches, for sure. Arivaipa, I think. It's my bet that they are the remnants of the unpleasantness up at Camp Grant last month. Some leading citizens of Tucson recruited some of the Papagos who live just west of there to help them pull a surprise raid on the Arivaipa Apaches who had surrendered to the Army

70

at Camp Grant. Together they killed over one hundred of them. Most of the Indians killed by the good citizens and their Papago friends were women, children, and old men. They did the usual — scalped, raped the women, disemboweled the children. Just a massacre. The Papagos and Apaches are ancient enemies. *Apache* is actually the Papago word for 'enemy.' Most of the able-bodied at Grant appeared to have been away, most likely hunting. I think that they came back, saw what had transpired, and ran for Mexico."

"Camp Grant is a long way west of here."

"Indeed. But there is a fairly solid line of rugged mountains coming in this direction. They are mountain people, the Apaches, and if they are running for their lives, they would stick to the mountains, where all advantages are theirs. I think it might be possible, even likely given the state of calm among the Chiricahua Apaches, that this band has come near us and onto the ranch. There is no conclusiveness, but it seems likely enough — the taking of the woman, the ransacking of the ranch for supplies. It was a messy job. This was done in a great hurry, and those Apaches are in a great hurry."

"We should notify Bowie."

71

"I shall. And I will request orders from George Crook himself that I go in pursuit of the Apaches."

"George won't hear of it."

"He will. I will pursue them, and I will retrieve the woman."

PRIVATE NED THORNE

He lay face down on the parade grounds, his mouth and nose pressed to the dirt and pine needles. While his mind told him he must rise and go on, another part of him urged him to stay down as long as he was able. The exercise was called "toting the stick," the stick being a pine log some eight inches in diameter and five feet in length. So that the stick would not come free from its perch on his shoulders and possibly injure him, they had kindly lashed his wrists to it. The stick that now pressed his face into the earth.

This was the third time he had fallen in what seemed an eternity of marching in a wide circle around the rough and barely cleared parade ground, where he had to dodge rocks and tree stumps every few feet. Worse were the soft pits where tree stumps had been pulled and the ground newly filled. Twice before, he had stepped in one of those pits and sent himself sprawling, the log smacking his face hard to the ground. The wound high on his cheek reopened and bled freely.

The toe of the sentry caught him just under his right arm, with not so much a kick as a push, though neither gentle nor benign. The kick was a reminder that he had to right himself and go on marching his stick around the perimeter of the parade ground. He waited just a second to let Brickner, who, much practiced in this exercise, was dully plodding the circle, pass him by. Then he drew his knees up to his body and made the effort to rise. Again the stick pushed him back down. He tried again, with no better result, and then, as if by magic, he was hauled upward by sentries lifting either end of his stick. "Now, march," one said. And he did.

After he had fallen for the fifth time, unable to rise and given over to tears, the sentries who had overseen his punishment appealed to the captain, lifted him, and freed him from the pine log.

He now sat before the captain in the captain's tent, his tears stopped but his legs wobbly, his left eye nearly closed, and his face caked in blood, which had formed a thick, ropy scab down his cheek to his jaw. His uniform was torn and filthy.

"Quite remarkable," the captain said. "You have made it to the stick within half an hour of arriving in camp. Few men have ever had the temerity to arrive in camp drunk. You must be a young man of most exceptional qualities, though those are not noted in your transfer papers. But then, Jefferson Barracks does love to post surprises. And the implements for the measurement of weather changes that were entrusted to you? Those you exchanged for drink?"

"No, sir. They were stolen from me at Camp Bowie."

"Oh? By whom?"

"I don't know, sir."

"Well, I'll tell you, then. His name is Brickner, and you would be advised to keep your distance from him. I would imagine that's a sample of his artistry on your face, is it not?"

When he said nothing, the captain gave him a tight-lipped smile and nodded as though he had now decided something, and what he had decided would not be good for Ned. "There is also a notation here that you proved yourself a quite superior marksman at Jefferson Barracks. You're a hunter?"

"No, sir. I never much used a gun. I just

took to it in training."

"I see. A gift, then."

"I suppose."

"Yes. Of course. You suppose. You have some education behind you, isn't that true?"

"I have been to school, through grade twelve," he lied, being a year shy of that. "But I did not go to college."

"But you can read and write and do numbers."

"Yes."

"Here." The Captain pulled out a chair at his desk. A sheet of paper, a pen, and a bottle of ink sat on a blotter. "You are familiar with these implements?"

"Pen and paper."

"Let's see how you use them. I want you to take a letter. You will write it exactly as I say. You will not drop any words, change any words, add any words, or invent new spellings for any words. You will, above all, not attempt to correct anything I say. Is that understood?"

"Yes, sir."

"Very well. Then write this:

"My Dear General Crook,

"I have the honor to report that a recent scouting expedition south and east of our current position has revealed a most unfortunate turn of events. A small ranch had been at-

tacked and depredated. Are you getting this?"

"Yes, sir, I am."

"We discovered the bodies of two men, one white, one Mexican, both killed by Apaches. It is my belief that these Apaches are Arivaipa Apaches, the survivors of the misfortunes at Camp Grant some weeks earlier, now fleeing for their lives to Mexico, taking what they can on the run. The depredation of the small ranch is, of itself, a grave misfortune, but I have further evidence which leads me to believe that there was a woman at said ranch and that the Indians are now in possession of her with the intent to take her to Mexico, where, as you are aware, white women are a commodity of great value.

"Though I remain cognizant of our mission to merely scout and map this new territory, I believe it imperative that I send a patrol against the marauding Indians, with the intent to recapture the woman and return her safely to what relatives remain or, at least, to the civilization to which she belongs. The fate that awaits her at the hands of the Apaches and Mexicans is grim indeed.

"I request at this point that you might countermand your order not to engage the Indians unless attacked in order to facilitate the pursuit of the renegade, fleeing Apaches with

the sole intent of procuring the safe return of the unfortunate woman.

"Awaiting your orders,
"Robert Franklin, captain
"D Company, Eleventh Cavalry
"United States Army, in command of post
"Camp Ramsey, Territory of Arizona.

"Do you have that? All of it?"

The boy handed him the letter, written in a studied but clear hand. The words were spelled correctly and there was no excess of blots or stains on the paper.

"Very good, then. I am going to make you an offer that holds considerable fortune for you. I and the lieutenant are in need of a competent aide-de-camp. Private Birdwood, who now holds that position, is somewhat less than competent at most things and possesses no abilities to either read or write. You will report directly to me, and to the lieutenant when I am not available. You will accompany me on patrol, and you will serve me at my pleasure. You will serve me coffee that is both hot and potable, and you will keep my uniform, including the leather and brass, in tip-top shape. You will act as my secretary as well. And you will perform these same functions for the lieutenant. As you perform these duties well, we will reduce your indebtedness to the Army accordingly. My calculations are that you are indebted in the sum of four hundred dollars, plus, a figure that would take you an astonishingly long time to pay off on a private's salary of thirteen dollars a month.

"For the time being, you will bunk with Birdwood. You will accompany him and watch what he does. What he is not competent to perform will become your duty. You will not find a shortage of that. Is that understood?"

"Yes, sir."

"Good, then. Make sure you understand. To not understand is to fail."

Lieutenant
Anthony Austin

He held the boy's face in his fingertips, cradling the chin as though it were a rare and wondrous egg. There was a thin and soft beard there, but it seemed clear that under it the chin had not grown used to being shaved and was still smooth and delicate. The boy's was an altogether pretty face, delicate and even of feature, and it pained him to see how Brickner had misused it. The boy was polite and submissive, though sullen and silent unless spoken to, and though he said little, he seemed to carry with him an air of intelligence and good breeding.

"Mr. Brickner is a rough craftsman: far too rough for such a face. And so, too, am I, I fear. You will have a scar."

"Yes, sir."

"That doesn't worry you, does it?"

"No, sir."

"Such is the carelessness of the young.

80

Having had only such a fine face, you think nothing of it. Once gone, it will not return. You're thinking that a good scar will give you character, aren't you? That you shall be judged more a man for it."

"Sir?"

"Never mind. Give it no thought. It will all come clear to you. Someday, much later. I'm afraid that this will hurt, a good deal, most likely. There is whisky. You may help yourself. It eases pain." He saw the boy's expression change as his body convulsed at the thought of yet more whisky. "Or not. It is your choice." He took the bottle himself, took a long pull, then wet a cloth with carbolic acid and pressed it to the boy's face, causing him to flinch and cry out just a bit. "You will excuse me. Comfort yourself in that it doesn't hurt nearly so much as what's to come."

He wished he were better with the needle and had finer thread. The boy was trembling now, but would not allow himself to cry out as the needle pierced his skin. He then drew the heavy thread taut, and the boy's face went white. He kept an eye on him against the eventuality that the boy should faint, causing the stitches to pull out, or worse, get his eye impaled with the needle. But the boy kept consciousness with a grim determination to withstand the ordeal. A small but steady stream of tears moved along the side of his nose.

When he was done, the boy's cheek was a ragged line of thick blue stitches up to the eye, badly trimmed. The boy would look better when the swelling went down, and perhaps the scar would give him some character. He felt, though, that he had desecrated something precious, just as the rest of the world would continue to desecrate this boy.

Private Ned Thorne

And so he had become a charwoman. In part he had joined the Army to prove his worth by performing deeds of heroic daring. Instead he found himself a washer of dishes and linens, a blacker of boots, a polisher of brass, a brewer and server of coffee, and a brusher of uniforms. He worked alongside Jarbal Birdwood, who was also his tentmate, an affable and diligent idiot who labored at the same small tasks with disastrous results. Jarbal Birdwood was short and blond with a hank of hair down his forehead, cut on the diagonal. Under blue eyes that stared intently as if demanding something not quite spoken, his nose skewed off to the right, giving him the look of someone always pointed in not quite the right direction. Though he was Ned's bunkie, Birdwood had so far chosen not to say any more words than absolutely necessary, forsaking even greetings beyond a nod and a stiff raising of the hand like the beginning of a salute. Now, as Ned filled the pot with water for the morning coffee, Birdwood was arranging the crockery on two serving trays, carefully and methodically placing plates, saucers, cups, napkins, and silver on the trays.

Ned set the pot on the fire to boil and sat back on his heels. He reached over to the trays and transposed the spoons and forks. Birdwood turned his head, studying Ned with first one eye, then the other, which Ned understood to serve as the question he would not ask. "Yes," Ned said. "That way. This is correct."

"Hell and villainy," Birdwood said. "How is a man supposed to remember such things? Isn't it enough that there's fork and spoon? There's need for both? They have to be in some special way? Where's the use?" Birdwood was greatly fond of licorice and his curses were scented with it. He kept a supply wrapped in clothing, stuffed in a sack that lay pushed far back under his cot. Ned felt sure he was not supposed to know it was there, though Birdwood crept under his cot on hands and knees with a frequency that could not help but draw attention.

Ned shrugged. "It's the custom. Haven't you ever set a table before?"

"I set at many a table. There wasn't such rules. You learn that going to school?"

Ned started to say, No, at home, but thought better of it. He waved his hand as if to dismiss the question, pulled the coffeepot from the fire, poured a little into a cup to test the color, poured out the sample, and replaced the pot. "Another minute or two, I think."

"It's coffee, ain't it?"

"Almost."

"Hell and villainy. I believe you have more learning than any man I ever met, except the lieutenant and the captain and some others, but you don't beat a man over the head with it."

"Does the captain beat you?"

"Not yet, but he's waiting on his chance just like everyone else. Every minute of your life is another chance for a beating, and what you got to do is figure how to dodge it."

"The captain's a hard man, that's for sure. The lieutenant's all right, though."

"The lieutenant won't beat you, but he'll tell the captain to do it."

"I don't believe lieutenants tell captains to do anything."

"This one does. They're the same person. Different suits is all. You spit on the lieutenant and the captain busts your jaw."

"You spit on the lieutenant?"

"Not me. Others do. They don't think he's much of a man. Can't figure out why he's in the Army. Should have ought to been a preacher or a schoolmaster or such. The captain, he may not be the greatest soldier in the Army, but he's a soldier. The lieutenant is always off looking at birds and clouds and such. But the two of them, they've been together for years and years. They fought the Pi-Ute at the Pit. They got lots of men killed up there, and that's why they're here."

"Is that true?"

"It's what's said. Might be true. I don't know. This doesn't seem like the kind of place to send the pick of the litter. I don't think we're the best the Army has got." Birdwood smiled, his teeth black and probably rotten from the licorice.

"Well, why do they keep them together? Why are they still in the Army?"

"The captain, his father is some pumpkins back in the East. He's a congressman or secretary or something. Maybe he's the president, I don't know. But he's some pumpkins, I know that. Ain't no one can touch the captain. So they put him out here, where he's out of the way, and they put the lieutenant with him, and no one has to deal with either one of them but us."

He had never been in a place so strange as the lieutenant's tent. It seemed something out of a circus or a carnival. It amazed him that so much could be packed into such a small area. Everywhere were boxes and, on top of the boxes, jars filled with a nearly clear liquid in which odd creatures floated. There were small animals, gutted and hung to dry. Boards with bright dots of color rested against the jars. Badly stuffed birds perched next to the boards.

He leaned over to examine one of the boards splotched with white and discovered that the splotches were butterflies or moths, pinned onto the surface. He found nowhere to set the tray of coffee and biscuits he had brought.

Dear Thad,

One could not imagine a place on earth more strange or bizarre than the United States Army. I have been on active duty at my new posting for two days. In those days I have been robbed, beaten, tortured, and transformed from a weather observer/recorder to a chambermaid. I am, further, the only one in this world who finds any of these occurrences in the least odd. In the infinite possibility of worlds, there certainly must be one such as this, but I wish that I hadn't been the discoverer of this one.

Take loving care of our parents and all others.

CAPTAIN ROBERT FRANKLIN

He heard them making their way to the officers' quarters before he saw them. It was just getting ready to grow light. Reveille would sound in less than half an hour, and the approach of the troopers bearing his and Tony's breakfast kept his exasperation from boiling over and tainting the day. He did not ask much of his troop; he understood that he had been allotted the dregs and that D Company, "Dog Company," was apt, for they were the tick-infested, the flea-ridden, and the mangy, the yappers, the cowerers, the leg humpers, the heel nippers, ball lickers, and tail tuckers of the Army. Yet it should be within the power of even such as this to get his breakfast and his coffee prepared and served a good thirty minutes before reveille.

The presence of the boy, and he was no more than that, gave him some hope that at the least, his morning routine might change for the better. A good cup of coffee, one that had not been boiled to the thickness of strap molasses, would brighten his day considerably. And the boy — who he suspected was a ponderer, a sneak, a grumbler, and probably a coward — understood the rudiments of dining and might make a cup of coffee that did not offend the palate. And soon he would be able to send the sincere but dim Birdwood back to more suitable activities like shoveling out the corrals for Brickner. There he would present no danger to anyone, since Brickner despised Birdwood as too deficient in imagination to participate in any sort of mischief.

"Sir." The boy carried the tray, cups melodically ringing against saucers, while Birdwood scrambled to set up the folding legs that would hold it. The fare was simple, beans and salted meat with hardtack left over from the great war. He did not eat better than his men, despite the difference in service. He would eat the beans, and he would eat hardtack until the bakery was completed and bread was available, but he would not eat any of it from a tin plate.

"Good morning," he replied.

The boy merely repeated "Sir" and sat the tray on the makeshift desk.

"Shall I wake the lieutenant?" Birdwood

asked, nodding in the direction of the lieutenant's tent.

"No. I think not. He had a rough night of it. Best let him sleep while he can." The regrettable incident with the falling tree had sent Tony back into a deep melancholy, as he'd assumed it would. He had taken whisky liberally the night before, as that was the only palliative that had any effectiveness. But for that relief, he paid a high price, too, for in the daytime he would be weary and open to the very effects of the melancholia from which the whisky had rescued him. When these bouts came, they stayed for a long time, and Franklin was prepared, yet again, to go through the despair with his friend.

"Will that be all, sir?"

"For now. Inform Sergeant Triggs that I wish to see him before reveille." He gave the boy a long and unpleasant look, just to keep him on his toes. Though his service had, all in all, pleased him considerably, he found the boy's downcast countenance an irritant.

"You will apportion the day," he told Triggs, "to include rifle practice as well as an exercise in horsemanship. I will also require a rider to be sent to Bowie with a message to be forwarded on to General Crook. Have someone ready for riding immediately after mess. Whoever you send should be prepared to insure that the message gets relayed to the telegraph at Camp Lowell and should wait at Bowie for a reply."

"Yes, sir." Triggs nodded in affirmation and raised, just the tiniest bit, his right eyebrow. He liked Triggs, a trooper cut in an earlier fashion. The sergeant was a difficult man, who was severe with those who strayed or attempted shortcuts. For the man prepared to go about his duties in a serious, straightforward manner, he was rigorous but fair. Franklin thought it a shame that such men were falling out of fashion in the postwar Army.

"We will be seeing action soon," the captain told Triggs. "The matter of the ranch has fallen to us, and we will carry out our duties — the first of which is to find the woman and rescue her, and then to deal with the aboriginals who took her. We cannot allow such depredations to occur and go unpunished within our very shadows. When the word comes from General Crook, as it will, we must be ready for a mission of some duration and danger."

"Shall we forgo our other projects then — the bakery?"

"Allot what time and manpower you can spare, but for now our priority must be to prepare for what is to come."

Private Ned
Thorne

Dear Thad,

The Army is nothing like I thought it would be. The picture painted so prettily does not reflect the reality, and I suppose that is true of much in this world. I hope, though, that it is not true of everything.

He had joined the Army to become a hero and a success. Granted, his primary aim had been to put as much distance between himself and those in Hartford, Connecticut, as was possible. In that, he had succeeded. But he had become a washer of dishes and waiter at table. He had learned the intricacies of the thermometer, barometer, and hygrometer, studied the messages written in clouds, but he spent his days cleaning and arranging. He had hoped to see action against the fierce Apaches, but instead, he laundered officers' linen. He had joined the service, but instead had gone into service, and soon even the small help that Birdwood offered would be gone, as Birdwood was being reassigned.

"You can write?" This came accompanied by a powerful gust of licorice.

He looked up from the crockery he was washing in a small pool of the river — the porcelain coffeepot, cups, and saucers he had used to serve the officers' breakfast — to find Birdwood standing behind him, standing hipshot, bent slightly at the waist. His question confused Ned, who had been writing in his head, while in front of him was only river water and porcelain. He looked up at Birdwood, who seemed to be accusing him. He tensed, ready for the fight. "I beg your pardon?"

"You can write?"

"Yes. I can."

"Letters and such? Things that people can read? Other people?"

"Yes."

"Even to people you ain't never met?"

"Yes. I can write letters."

Birdwood adjusted his stance, turning his head slightly to look at Ned from different angle, perhaps to see if this changed things. His tongue darted out and worked his teeth as his lips curled back. "I never took to it. They tried to learn me, but I couldn't see the sense of it."

"You need me to write something for you?"

Birdwood nodded, saying nothing.

"All right, then. I can do that. I have to finish this first." He continued to rinse the crockery, half expecting Birdwood to just turn and go away. But he continued to stand as he was. Ned set the breakfast service on the rocks to dry. "Let me go to the tent for paper and pencil."

When he came back, Birdwood was still standing just as he had been. "All right, then. What do you want me to write?"

"A letter. Can you do that?"

Ned nodded. "Who do you want me to write it to?"

"My pap," Birdwood said. "My pap in Ohio."

"All right. What's his name?"

"Birdwood."

Ned nodded, again. "Mr. Birdwood, then. In Ohio. What part of Ohio?"

"Lynchburg. Near to there."

"Is there a street number? A road or anything?"

Birdwood considered this. "Nearby."

"What's the name of the road? So I can

get this to him."

Birdwood shrugged. "The road to Lynchburg."

"Doesn't it have a name? We need to get this as close as we can."

Birdwood was still baring his teeth and had now begun to open his mouth wide and turn his head rapidly from side to side. He stopped suddenly and glared at Ned. "Forget it, then."

"No," Ned said. "No. This will be all right. The postal authorities will find him. They are very good at that. I'll just write to Mr. Birdwood, outside of Lynchburg, Ohio. Someone will know how to get it to him. Now. What do you want to write?"

"A letter."

"Yes. Yes. Certainly. What kind of letter?"

"One he can read."

"Yes, of course. What should the letter say?"

"That I ain't dead."

"All right, then. You just say it to me, exactly as you want to say it to him, and I'll write it down just the way you say it."

"Just the way I say it?"

"Exactly. It will be just as though you were talking to him."

Birdwood considered this. He kept working his lips and mouth and had now begun to pull at the strands of straw-colored hair that fell across his forehead at a perfectly mitered forty-five-degree angle. "You'll write it just as I say it?"

"Word for word. Try not to go too fast, though."

"Pap," Birdwood nearly yelled. "I ain't dead. Hope you ain't, either. Jarbal."

"That's it?"

Birdwood nodded. He turned to his right as if to move away, then turned back. "Ain't it enough?"

"I don't know. Does it say what you want it to say?"

Birdwood considered this. "It does."

"I guess that would be enough, then."

Birdwood nodded and turned to go, then turned back again. "And you wrote this so that others can read it?"

Ned nodded. "Does your father know how to read?"

"No. Does that count?"

"No. No, it doesn't. He can find someone who will read it for him, I'm sure."

"And can you read what others wrote?"

Ned nodded again. "Do you have a letter you need read?"

Birdwood shook his head and took a quick step back.

"If you get one, I would be happy to read

it to you."

"Who's going to send me a letter?" His expression registered real alarm, as though this were the first time he had ever considered such a possibility.

"I don't know. Maybe no one. Probably no one."

"I got to let you read it?"

"No. But I would if you wanted me to, but . . ." He caught himself. "I don't think anyone is going to send you a letter. I'm pretty sure you won't get one."

"I don't want one."

"Then you won't get one."

"You ain't going to send me one?"

"No. No, I won't. If I need to tell you something, I'll just tell you."

Birdwood nodded once more, hard. "Obliged," he said. "Obliged." He didn't move away, but kept shifting his weight from one foot to the other.

"Even if it's someone you ain't met?"

"What?"

"Who wrote something. You can read what was wrote, even though you ain't never met the one who wrote it?"

"Yes. Of course. In school I read books by Mr. Shakespeare and Mr. Bunyan and Mr. Milton. And lots of others. And they're all dead. I read what they wrote, though."

"You can read what the dead wrote?" Birdwood was very agitated now, shifting his weight and twisting and contorting his mouth.

"Certainly."

Birdwood considered this for a moment, looking at Ned as though he were some sort of spirit from another world. He reached inside his blouse and retrieved a small book and handed it to Ned.

It was bound in blue leather with marbled endpapers. A good-quality book, the pages filled in a fine, neat hand.

"I stole that."

Ned thumbed through the pages. It was a diary. A woman's diary. "You stole it from whom?"

"Back there. Where we was. Where the dead ones was. The ranch. I found it out there. I took it. It's a good book, ain't it?"

Ned ran his fingers over the smooth blue leather. It was not new. Some of the luster was off it, and his fingers detected a fine web of cracking from the drying of the leather. The stitching was tight, despite the fact that it had been opened and handled innumerable times over the years. "Yes," he said. "It's a good book."

Birdwood looked off into the distance toward the peaks of hills to the southwest.

"What's it say?"

"It's someone's diary. A record of what they did. A woman, I would guess. You found this at the ranch?"

Birdwood nodded.

"We should turn this over to the captain. He would want to know about it. He should know that there was a woman there."

"Can't," Birdwood said. "I stole it. I saw it and I took it. Can't turn it in. I stole it after the captain give orders not to steal nothing. But I done took it anyway. If the captain finds out, I'm in big trouble. You can't unsteal what's been stole. He could hang me for it, and I believe he'd like to do that. No. If you give it to the captain, you got to say you stole it. See if he'll hang you."

"I wasn't there."

"You can't give it. You can't. He'll know it was me, and he'll hang me. I ain't no loss to him."

Ned turned the pages slowly, carefully. The entries were written in a beautiful hand, with great care. The ink switched from black to blue and then back to black a couple of times. He thought about the person who had written this, and then he thought about Birdwood, who had done a stupid thing and stolen the book. It was a stupid thing, but then stupid people did

101

stupid things. He couldn't peach on him, not after Birdwood had trusted him, and he couldn't take the load on his own shoulders. "Still," he said. "It's not ours."

"That's 'cause it was stole. Can't steal what's yours. I give it to you for writing me that letter. You going to turn me in? You going to get me hanged after I give it to you?"

"I won't turn you in."

"All right, then. I'm obliged on the letter. And that book is now yours. Whatever comes of it, it's yours. A woman, you say? I'd be obliged as well if you was to tell me what she said."

Ned tucked the little book into his blouse "Someday. When I've read it, I'll tell you what it says. It's just about her life, though. I don't think it will be very interesting."

"I stole her life? That's pretty interesting, right there. Obliged again."

"Each of you has a dozen cartridges," Triggs said. "Four of those will be used for sight alignment and practice. After those four cartridges are spent, step back and take your ease. We will then replace the targets." He motioned to his right, where sheets of writing paper had been attached to straw bales. "You shall then, from fifty yards away, fire four times at the target — once from the standing position, once kneeling, another prone, and for the final shot you shall stand with your back to the target, turn, sight, and fire within a count of three. Once that round has completed, the entire squad should retreat another fifty yards and repeat the sequence from the distance of one hundred yards. The soldier who hits the target the most times at the end of eight shots will receive the afternoon relieved of all duties."

"That will be me or Brickner," Birdwood said to Ned. "We're the two best in the company."

"Who's the better?"

"Me. Except he always wins these things. You got a knife on you?"

He took a penknife from his pocket and offered it to Birdwood.

"No. You keep it. These cartridges jam something fierce. You want to be in the competition, you got to get after it with your knife, scrape it out and keep shooting. And don't waste a lot of time on the turn and fire. No one hits much on that one anyway. If you got a jammed cartridge, do the others. Just pretend on that one."

"Thanks."

Birdwood stared at Ned as though he had said something in French or Persian.

"Obliged," Ned said.

Birdwood nodded. "I'm going to win this one. A day off is a day nobody yells at you."

When the order came to fire, Ned paused just a second, the way he had learned in training, and let the first volley of shots pass. Even though you know it's coming, that first concussion of shots makes you jump just a little. He counted, one, then fired and went down to one knee, listened for the big volley, then fired again.

It was a simple process, really, and it was one he liked. You simply put the notch of the rear sight into the target, then waited for the ball of the front sight to nestle into it. You squeezed the trigger, taking out the slack, and when the ball was heading into the notch, just before it actually reached it, you tripped it, and then went through the process again. Lying on his belly, elbows braced by the soft, sweet-smelling ground, he let the ball roll into the notch and fired for the third time. It was mechanical, logical, and easy, and though he had little experience with guns before he reached Jefferson Barracks, he liked the drill more than anything else in Army life.

As the exercise went on, the reports from the other rifles became more rhythmic. It was always this way, the soldiers unconsciously coming into a rhythm with each other, loading, sighting, and firing, even breathing in an unconscious unison. He wondered sometimes if it were also so in battle. Did a troop of soldiers with Springfield rifles become a being unto itself, breathing, seeing, moving, and firing like some mythological beast?

Though he seemed, to himself, to be moving at a snail's pace, far slower than a human being could move, there were still troopers firing at their targets when he had finished the drill at fifty yards. He came to another consciousness, as though waking from a dream, and was aware now of the raggedness of the gunshots around him, the sharp smell of the powder, and the thin layer of smoke that floated above them.

On the sergeant's order, they turned their backs to the target and marched forward another fifty yards to where a rope laid across the ground marked the second line of fire. He reached into the cartridge box on his belt and palmed another four cartridges. Holding three cartridges in his hand, caught between the ring finger and heel of his palm, made the first shot somewhat more awkward than it would be if he left the cartridges in his box, but the first shot was the easiest, and then there were only two to hold and he did not have to rush his aim. By the time they reached the final shot, his hand was empty and resting comfortably on the small of the buttstock. In this way, he was not hurried and overly hasty in taking his aim.

It was not precisely like loss of consciousness, or dreaming, either. But on the firing range, he found himself somewhere else, as if he'd somehow absented himself from his own body. Detached and free, he watched himself firing steadily and deliberately at the target.

They stood down. The air was quiet around them, the birds and small animals that normally kept up a small cacophony now terrified into silence by the noise of twenty rifles being fired at more or less the same time. Sergeants Triggs and Stonehouse gathered the targets from the straw bales and put them off to the side of the makeshift firing range, where they compared them.

"Here, Marybelle." Brickner's hand came across his shoulder, bearing a black and fetid-looking cheroot. "This will take some sting from the defeat."

He turned, took the cigar, and waited while Brickner fired it for him. "Thank you." He was just learning to smoke, and he had worked hard to calm the coughing reflex that came with the activity and was only now beginning to see it as a source of small but still-bitter pleasure. He might have turned it down, but he was afraid of Brickner and his scorn. Though he did not like Brickner, he desperately wanted to be seen as a man, a creature of at least the same order as Brickner.

"We have two targets with seven hits apiece," Triggs announced. "Both Corporal Brickner and Private Thorne have outshot the rest of you considerably. However, Private Thorne has grouped his shots into an area I can cover with my hand. He is the winner and receives the remainder of the day free of other duties."

He came to mess late, as he always did, having seen to the presentation of supper for the officers. Since the mess hall was nothing more than some logs driven into the ground, they ate outside, sitting on the ground or whatever they might find to keep them off the ground — rocks, tree stumps, of which there was an abundance, or logs. He took a seat on the ground, next to Birdwood. There were plenty of stumps available, but to get one, he would have to go over to where Brickner and the rest of the toughs sat, and he wanted no part of that.

Birdwood did not acknowledge his presence, or Ned believed he did not. In his eating habits, Birdwood was remarkably feral. Mess was meager — beans and hardtack in as great quantities as one wanted — but Birdwood protected his as though it were something precious, hunching his back to get his face low to the tin pan he used for a plate. His head was in constant motion, dipping and rising to and from the pan and turning side to side to catch a glimpse of any intruder who might want to take the slop from him. This seemed to Ned a ridiculous notion, since there was plenty and no one in his right mind would want more than his share anyway.

Birdwood seemed on the verge of saying something to Ned, then went back to pushing beans into his mouth with a square of hardtack, but perhaps what Ned saw was merely the curl of Birdwood's lip as warning in case Ned should get his hand too near him and have it bitten.

"That was some fine shooting, Marybelle," Brickner said from across the small clearing that separated them.

"I should say so," opined another. "That boy's a likely one with the rifle at a hundred yards. He bears watching."

"Shut pan, Shattuck. He outdone you and me and all the rest of us."

"It should have been mine or Brickner's day off, not his. He's just brand new and nothing but a lick finger, going to spend his time off polishing the lieutenant's piss pot."

"Leave him be," Brickner said. "It was a square deal."

"Oh, he's good at a hundred yards, all right. It's an easy thing to give some whacks to a piece of paper at a hundred yards. But shooting a man, that's something else. What are you going to do when that day comes, boy? You going to be steady on the trigger when you're sighting in your first man? You think it's going to be easy to kill someone? Killing your first man, that's a task for you."

"I already have."

"You already have what, Marybelle?"

"Killed a man. I've already done it."

Someone snorted as if to dismiss the remark, but other than that, there was no response except silence. Finally, Birdwood raised his head from his mess. "You ain't never."

"Yes," said Ned. "Yes, I have. I have killed."

LIEUTENANT
ANTHONY AUSTIN

He had spent the morning by himself, in the woods. There was a bird there that interested him. From a distance it seemed very much like a cardinal, though shiny black like ebony. He would need to capture the bird for study, but he wondered whether it was a cardinal, indeed, or a close relative. Did cardinals, like men, have brothers that were a different hue, or was this another species altogether? Of course, the same question was still being debated about men, he supposed, though that question did not compel him overly.

When the firing had begun, all life in the trees and surrounding area vacated the neighborhood and left him with nothing to contemplate but his own thoughts. And his own thoughts he did not wish to contemplate. Of what species and what use in the world he might be was not a line of questioning that profited him in the least. He had risen from his spot under a pine tree before he became rooted to that spot, before he became so mired in inertia that he might never move again.

In his tent, he poured a small glass of whisky, not more than two fingers, and sipped it carefully, aware how easily sipping became gulping and how quickly the easing of the darkness gave way to the darkness of unconsciousness. A small pain gnawed at the front of his brain, just behind his eyes. A result of too much whisky the night before, the headache reminded him that the cure, though better than the disease, was not free of ill effects.

"Well, Tony, we're on our own tonight." Bobby had opened the flap of his tent and walked in as he was used to doing, removing his hat and throwing it on the bed while running his hand through his hair, causing it to stick straight up. "Triggs has given our aide the afternoon free. It seems that the shuffling, sullen boy is something of a remarkable marksman, just as advertised. Is it so bad, then, that you need to be at the whisky this early?"

He waved his hand dismissively. "It's just a dram so as not to shock the body. I'm all right. You needn't worry."

"Needn't worry and not worry are different things altogether. I'm worried now that word from General Crook may come too late to be of help to the woman. It's not far to the border with Mexico. Those Apaches can get down there and have her sold before we're ever able to put our backsides in the saddles. Once the Mexicans have her, there's precious little we can do."

"Don't get ahead of yourself, Bobby. Cranston has barely had time to arrive at Bowie if he's riding full-out, which he's hardly likely to be doing, being finally relieved of tree-sawing duties."

"That's what worries me. How much longer can we wait? And then the general is likely to take his sweet time in ordering us to action, the telegraph being useless unless it's actually used."

"Or won't at all. That's what worries you, Bobby, not that he will delay in the consideration but that he won't order you after them at all and will likely send a detachment from Bowie."

"No. George knows us better than that. He knows we're good soldiers and trustworthy. Things like what happened at the Pit simply happen in battles. We've been reassigned out of politics, nothing more. Certainly not out of a lack of confidence on George Crook's part."

He had heard this before and was weary of it. Bobby's insistence that their exile was political was as familiar to him as an old song one has long tired of hearing. They were here because the Army wanted shunt of them but had to keep them because Bobby was the son of a senator. But he had learned that, often enough, his melancholia spoke for him, interpreting everything in its darkest possible light. Optimism was a rare state, like solipsism that overtook him for a few brief seconds, then vanished with the mere shake of his head. "Of course," he said. "Of course. George loves us better than he ought."

"Don't mock me."

He shook his head. His cynicism was able to transform itself to a thousand shapes, all of them unpleasant. "No. No. I don't mean to. You're right, of course. I'll fetch our supper tonight. Let the boy enjoy his freedom for the rest of the day. He's paid dearly enough for it."

"Triggs showed me his target. The shooting is commendable, and he takes orders well. I think I judged him too harshly. He is just a boy, but a good one, with some promise, I think."

"There's the glimmer of intelligence in his eye. God knows we don't see much of that with the pack we have." Of course Bobby liked the boy. He was young and clever and good-looking. What was there not to like?

"I'm thinking I might organize a scouting expedition in the next day or two. Not to engage the Indians, but just to keep their track fresh so that we can go in pursuit once the word comes from Bowie. I'll take the boy, so you might want to get Birdwood back for a day or two."

"I don't think it's wise. An expedition, I mean. Word will come. You should be here when it does. And if you do go, which I suppose you're bound to do, I won't need Birdwood. I can attend to my own needs well enough."

"But you're having a spell of it again. You'll be in charge here. Let someone aid you." Bobby's eyes softened, somehow accentuating the lines around them, a feature that Tony dearly loved. But now, Bobby's show of concern angered rather than soothed him.

"And when I'm in charge, I do what needs to be done, don't I? Yes, I do. Of course. Just like a real officer in the United States Army."

"I didn't mean that, and you know it. You're not well at the moment. That's all there was to it." Bobby was hurt and averted his eyes, trying not to show it.

Austin sighed heavily and nodded his head. He was, he supposed, not well. Well. Was he ever "well"? Could he even remember what "well" felt like? He had known the darkness of melancholia his whole life, but since the incidents on the Pit River, it had become his constant companion and torment. He could feel it come at him — and it came at him often — as a faint blackness at the edge of his sight that grew ever larger and blacker until it had taken him completely.

Private Ned
Thorne

The problem with liberty here was that there was nothing to do with it. He thought to go exploring the area around the camp, but he was afraid he would get lost in such unfamiliar territory. He could spend the afternoon hunting, he supposed, but the killing of other creatures held no allure for him. So he found a quiet spot where the thin river ran well, somewhat distant from the camp but still close enough that he had only to listen to know exactly where it was.

The river hardly deserved the name — it was a thin channel of water, not more than six feet across and less than one foot deep, that rode a bed nearly fifty feet wide and so deep that the walls were above his head. It had been diverted somewhere, he imagined. For there were trees growing in the bed now, as well as small, bristly bushes scattered along the walls of the bank. It was no longer a river, only a creek, though he could not remember by what standard one flow of water was designated a river and others brooks, streams, and creeks. In Connecticut this would be no river, but then, in Missouri, the rivers in Connecticut weren't likely to be considered that, either.

There wasn't much water in this haggard and emaciated stream, but it made a pleasant sound as it fell over the rocks below his perch at the base of a wide, feathery tree. Someone had piled rocks to form a pool with an entrance and an exit where the water spilled over, creating the sound. He watched the water rolling over the stones of the entrance and wondered how much water came in and out of the pool. How much water, indeed? There was a way to calculate that, he knew, but he couldn't think what it was. They had covered that back in Jefferson. It should be part of his job to be able to report on exactly such matters.

He found everything he needed in the rubbish heap behind the stables. He took a six-foot length of thin board, and, measuring it against his thumb, he marked approximate one-inch intervals with tar on the stick. When he had finished that, he took the stick, a length of rope he had found, and one of Brickner's empty whisky bottles and headed back to the river. There he drove the stake into the riverbed, banging on it with a rock. At the midpoint, he tied the rope, which was now tied to the corked bottle, and let the bottle go.

The bottle moved slowly, following the flow of the river until the rope stopped and held it. Ten feet in four seconds by his count. The rate of flow, he then calculated, was 2.5 feet per second. The river covered three marks on the stick, approximately three inches. The small run where he had set up his contraption was twenty feet long by six feet wide. He multiplied that to get 120 feet of surface. An approximation, but he thought that even if it were significantly off, the guess might provide information about the amount of change in the river's flow. On impulse, he climbed from the streambed, put on his boots, and ran and got the lieutenant.

LIEUTENANT
ANTHONY AUSTIN

"Clever. Quite clever." It really was. He could not help but smile as the boy, trousers rolled past his knees, white feet picking carefully among the rocks of the creekbed, took the bottle back to the stick and let it go one more time. The bottle floated bottom first to the end of the rope and, tethered there, rode the current as if there were a tiny ship inside it.

"I don't think it very accurate," the boy said. "I wouldn't record it and say that is the actual flow of the stream, but it might be good for comparison. I don't know. Perhaps it has no value at all. Do you think it does?"

"Inestimable. I think its value inestimable. As you correctly say, its accuracy is in doubt. But that is as it is. Comparison is a valuable tool. We learn much through comparison. This is like that, unlike another. By seeing the likeness and difference in things, we come to understand their relationships.

"But that is only a small part of it, I think. There is great value in that it has provided you with a way to spend your free time that shows you as a young man of resource and curiosity. Curiosity, perhaps, killed the cat. But it proves the human alive. It is the great urge of the human — to know about the world around him and to interact with it. Galileo, Copernicus, Harvey, Newton, and Darwin. All men with a great curiosity about what they saw around them. And because of them, we know about the world and about ourselves. This doesn't, I think, rank among those discoveries, but it is cut of the very same cloth, as, I think, you are."

"Darwin insults God and man."

"Nonsense. That is the drivel of the frightened and incurious. Afraid of what they might find in front of them, worried that they might be called upon to improve their lot by doing more than falling on their knees and wishing for improvement, frightened that they might actually have a responsibility for the betterment of themselves and others, they find those who don't share their fears 'godless.' And it's a pathetic God they serve, a big, ignorant Papa, who punishes what he doesn't understand and who understands quite little. Who told you Darwin insults God and man?"

"Well, everyone. I mean, Reverend S[...] of course, but others, too."

"And you believe all that Reverend Spiller tells you, of course?"

"Well, yes. He's a reverend."

"And why do reverends always revere the wrong things? I wouldn't have you turn your back on your reverend or completely disregard his teachings. Such men, I think, have great value and a genuine desire to be helpful. But the world is changing now, perhaps more than it has changed in several hundred years, certainly more than it has in the hundred years or so since Mr. Newton got curious about things. What your reverend learned when he was a boy may no longer be so true as he thinks. You may have the advantage of him in some matters, the workings of the world being one of them."

"I wouldn't think so."

"No. Of course you wouldn't. But please, go on with your explorations of the world around you. You have a valuable mind, the mind of a scholar, perhaps. And don't worry too much about God. He can't be so jealous of all His secrets that He would deny a young man the chance to witness a few small ones and marvel at them. He must rather like that, I'm sure."

and put his hand on Thorne's
m fairly sure I'm right on this
vays, but on this one. This is
you have done here with your
ttle. Enjoy it. It is a fine thing.
And on your calculations, remember that
we are dealing not with square feet of water,
but with cubic feet." He moved his hands
to indicate the idea of depth.

"Yes, sir. I had forgotten that. I'm sorry."

"Wrong does not require sorrow, only correction."

Private Ned Thorne

He picked up the bottle and let it go. It moved slowly to the end of the rope and stayed there. He tried to imagine it moving swiftly in a real river, reaching the end of the rope in a mere second or less. How, then, would he be able to count the time without a watch, and a much better watch than the one he had lost at Jefferson? He pulled the bottle back and let it go again. It moved slowly, and he soon tired of watching it drift to the end of the tether. But he was happy. He had done something of value here, at last. And he was sure others would be pleased. He climbed out of the river, rolled his pants back down, but left off his boots, and sat under the scrub oak and took out the diary that Birdwood had given him.

April 8. There is nothing to be done. Both Father and Michael are persuaded that our future lies in California. There is no further use for tears or protest. They are adamant, certain in that way that only men are certain, and all that had held our lives secure in Massachusetts is sold or for sale. What a tragedy it is to see your life carted off by strangers. It is slow torture to watch yourself stripped bare of all that has been dear to you, piece by piece, gone into the lives of people you meet only briefly, placed in wagons, and disappeared down the street.

California remains a dream I pray I shall wake from months from now. All I am allowed is my writing desk and dresser, my clothes and a few books that are precious to me. All else is lost forever. The china and silver are packed in crates, Grandmother Hodgins's set in my hope chest, to begin our life in California. Much of the fall I spent gathering seed of lupine, Queen Anne's lace, yarrow, and black-eyed Susan, that I may plant them when we reach California and thus have a bit of New England left to me. Bulbs of daffodil, tulip, and iris sleep deep in the bottom of my trunk.

In only eight days we are off. I inhabit the back of the house, which is now sold, for not wanting to look out the windows and see more of the wagon in which we shall live for the next month than is necessary.

I do not mope or complain, though that would seem a luxury to me now. I am and shall be strong and pay no heed to the thoughts that come in the quietest hours of the night.

April 10. Michael is my comfort and solace. It is not the present or the past that matters, only the future. In California we will prosper in ways we could not in Massachusetts. We shall raise strong and beautiful children, and they shall be provided for through abundance. When doubts have taken their strongest hold on me, it is Michael who, with a word or touch, banishes them to the forever darkness, and he stays alert, my protector should they attempt to regain entry in my thoughts.

April 13. As the days burn out and departure looms, a dread grows deep inside of me. To leave our home, climb aboard the wagon, and trek across the great prairies to begin a life no one knows anything of seems, to me, near to death. I wake in the middle of the night in fear and trembling, and while awake I find myself catching my breath as hard and fast as though I had just stepped into freezing water.

What keeps me from falling into complete despair is Michael. He and my father have become like boys running out to play in the storm, while Mother and I watch from a distance, trying to control our fears. They, both of them, but mostly Michael, are full of the spirit of adventure. And their excitement becomes mine when I remind myself that it is my role to assume the new life and that I would be doing thus even were Michael and I to be married at home. Home. I must learn that that word is for what we go to, not what we leave.

He is a strong man. Though he is young, he has a wisdom and courage that I wish were mine, but I know his is to become mine by and by. That he loves me sincerely, I could never doubt, and though I am full of vague fears and concerns, there is no place I should not go so long as Michael went there with me. I know that Michael is decent and honest and hardworking, and I put myself into the strength of his hands and arms and heart at the same time I work to pack away the small, trembling doubts that nip at me.

April 15. Michael's and Father's enthusiasms grow as our day of departure nears. Their enthusiasm is much like having a living thing that has continued to grow beyond proportion of what began it. It begins now to envelop me, and I cannot discern which is greater, my eagerness to get to California or my sorrow to be leaving behind nearly all that is dear to me.

In the hurried and hushed conversations between Michael and Father, I catch the word "virgin" pass between them, and I try to decipher whether the conversation is about the new land to which we go or about myself and our coming marriage. And then I remember that they are one and the same, finally, a journey into a new life and a new being.

April 17. The day so long anticipated and dreaded has come and gone. After such a long time of waiting, we have left our home and embarked on the journey. That such a day was so full of import seems now incredible since it has come and gone like all days do. We are not yet out of the state of Massachusetts. The swaying of the wagon is most disagreeable, and we are still on good, well-journeyed roads. I fear what will happen when we reach the much more primitive roads, trails perhaps, that reach into the frontier. When I mention my fears to my mother, she only smiles and pats my hand as though I were a child.

April 19. I have learned to write with the swaying of the wagon, the clink and plod of the oxen having become so familiar to me that when we stop for the night, I feel myself unsteady on my feet as though we were still moving forward. Some hours, it is a grand symphony — the creak of the wagon and the tack, the musical rattle of the metal livery, all playing the steady rhythm of the feet of the oxen, with their deep bass thuds, striking the ground as steady and dependable as a big drum. And at other moments it is all din and cacophony that threatens to drive one to madness before too long.

The land passes slowly before us. Since the hard climb over the Berkshire mountains, our pace has quickened over long rolling hills and broad stretches of plain. I realize that before us still lies the great prairie and beyond that the desert. I sometimes fear monotony more than any of the dangers forecast.

Last night we found a slow, clear river, where going a ways upstream, we women were able to bathe and later wash the clothing and linens. What a treasure is privacy, and what a relief to be clean and dressed again in clean clothes. Last night, lying in the river, watching the last of the sun drop toward the horizon, feeling my skin come back alive in the cold, running water, I felt new strength. When we reach California, and Michael and I are married, I feel I will be able to build with Michael a new life, and a finer one than I have ever known. All thoughts now begin with "When."

April 20. At times I catch sight of Michael performing some chore, putting his back into the task of lifting a barrel or bringing one of the oxen to the traces, and a thrill goes through me to think that one day he shall be mine. And I want to touch the smooth skin that covers his sinewy arms. And then I stop myself and know that I cannot think more on this or the wait until we reach California will become unbearable.

April 25. What a sight is the Hudson River. It moves from the mountains that build to the north, heading down to the sea some hundred miles below us. It moves at a stately pace, wide and bold. It is a fine procession of water, moving endlessly onward. It took us all of a day to cross it by ferry. The ferry was grand and wide, but it held only one wagon at a time. So the early hours were spent on the eastern shore waiting our turn to cross. The later hours we spent on the western shore, waiting for those behind us to cross. Having crossed this great river, we have accomplished something grand, and it begins to dawn, what a wonderful thing this is, moving from Massachusetts to California.

Above his head a small wind rattled the needles of the pine. He flipped the pages of the diary, running his finger over the neat, tight lines of script. He held his page with his finger, brought the book to his nose and inhaled, hoping for a smell of New England and home from the dry pages.

What he smelled, of course, was dust, gently overlaying the scent of pine around him. He had thought little of New England in the past weeks, in fact he had worked with diligence not to think of it, except as a place and time he had to free himself from. Now it came to him at once and overwhelmingly, like the snow of a nor'easter, covering him with a sadness that caught in his throat and threatened to choke him.

He felt an oppressive sadness now, a darkness gathered around him, just barely out of his sight. He felt homesickness for Connecticut, for his family and for Edith, who he thought perhaps he loved and to whom he had explained nothing, but just ran. He could not help but think of her. When he read the words written in the diary, they came forward in Edith's voice. Except for Thad, he felt no other loss as deeply as he felt the loss of Edith, who could talk to him and comfort him and who held him in a regard no one else did. He had kissed her, not just because she allowed him to but because he held her so dear. And he felt the absence of his brother Thad as he would feel the absence of a limb violently torn from him. At the core of him was a terrible aloneness that he willed himself not to feel during most times of the day. Now, as it

131

sometimes happened, aloneness grew and welled within him until it reached a point where it could not be contained by the force of his own will. It washed over him and carried him along in its wake.

And here he was now, as far from home as it was possible to be, and he was already a failure, having lost the weather instruments just barely after he had received them. He had traveled all this way, done all he had done, just to find himself the failure he had hoped he wasn't. Under the tree, at his ease for the first time in days, he began to cry — not just weeping but great, racking sobs that forced him to struggle for clear breath.

Though he was alone, he fought to compose himself and did so with great difficulty. He coughed, blew his nose, and daubed at his eyes to dry them. Then he looked around to see if anyone had witnessed his fit. But as soon as he had himself composed, a huge and abiding sense of shame overtook the sadness. He had first sensed it in reading the diary. The woman's admiration for Michael seemed to him evidence of his own shortcomings. Whatever he was, and Ned did not know what he was, he was no match for a man such as Michael, a man in whom all, but especially a girl, could put her confidence, sure that he would rise to be worthy of it. He hoped that Edith had once held him in the same esteem, though surely that was long gone and changed. In his own life, he had betrayed the confidence of Edith and everyone foolish enough to entrust him with it.

In a troop of soldiers that even he understood were misfits and the detritus of the lowest classes, he was himself the least worthy. He had been tested for moral character and he had failed, and when given another opportunity, he had failed again, and yet again. He had always supposed himself a man of character. Now he had grave doubts that he was possessed of any character at all, or that he could trust himself if things came to that.

Though he had shown himself good with the gun and had made a tiny attempt at recording the weather, he was, all in all, a coward and a thief. He wondered how it was that he had become the things he most detested in the world. And he wondered if the lowest of the low, the other cowards, thieves, murderers, liars, drunks, shams, and weaklings, had similarly loathed those occupations. Perhaps one was just born to them, and the cruelty was that you were chosen to hate that which you truly were.

And he began, again, to cry.

"Aye. There's the brave little soldier."

He opened his eyes and scrambled to his feet, scraping against the rough bark of the pine tree to see Brickner standing off just to his left, shirtless and grinning.

"You're not having a good time of it, then, Marybelle?"

"What are you doing here?"

Brickner held up a bottle. "Making sure the best of the day isn't wasted." He took a long drink, wiped his mouth and mustaches, and then held the bottle out to Ned. "You might could use some of this."

He shook his head. "I came here to be alone."

"And a world of good it has done you, too. Here. Drink. I'm offering a kindness."

"I don't want kindness, or need it."

"And there you're wrong. It's kindness we all want and need, and it's a precious commodity we seldom find enough of. Instead, we go looking for aloneness, which we don't need. We're alone, boy. We carry aloneness with us everywhere we go. You don't search for aloneness, you search to find a way to get shuck of it. No, it's kindness we want, and you've come to a place where there's damned little of that." Brickner smiled a full smile, his whole round face a part of it.

"Leave me be. I came here to be with my thoughts."

"You're a smart fellow, and a tough one, too, maybe." He looked over at Ned with a small remnant of the smile. "Though not as tough as I am. But you are smart, and smart's in short supply around here. I could use a smart fellow. There are real gains to be made here. All of this out here, this nothing we're riding herd on, this is opportunity. You and me could be rich if you'll just do what I tell you to do."

He wanted just to send Brickner away, but he did not know how to do that. He wanted to be left alone with his own misery. But to have any chance at repairing the wrongs he had done, he had to have, at least, money. And, finally, he supposed, the notion he held of moral superiority to Brickner was mere vanity. "Leave me," he said. "Would you please just leave me alone?"

"All right," Brickner said. "But think on this." He unbuttoned his fly and withdrew his thick penis. He tilted back his head and drank long from the bottle while sending a stream of urine foaming into the carpet of pine needle and earth a few feet from where Ned stood. "We're all leaky vessels, boy. You're full of notions of yourself and the world that people told you were proper. And you don't know enough yet to tell whether they're right or wrong. I'm here to tell you they're wrong. What's proper is not what's schooled into you. What's proper is that you void what's of no use to you and keep yourself filled with what's likely to give you some ease."

Dear Thad,

Is it true, as the Reverend Spiller has said? That God is not angry with us when we sin or fail, but is, rather, disappointed in us? I think it must be more than that. I cannot imagine that God, who is huge, would not be angry and even hate us when we do things that we should not. Father is angry. Isn't God angry as well? Is disappointment enough? No. God is angry with me. He must be so. It is why He is God.

CAPTAIN ROBERT FRANKLIN

He took the patrol out before dawn, moving in quick march, walking their mounts for no more than half an hour at a pull, then remounting and continuing the march. They came out of the mountains at midday and then picked up the pace of the march as they came across the broad plains of grama grass, heading east by southeast toward yet another chain of mountains that had been in sight all day without seeming to come any closer.

They rode under orders of silence. He liked moving this way, quietly, efficiently, the creak of tack, the dull concussion of hooves, and the snorting of the horses being the sounds of the march. Thorne rode at the lead, bearing the guidon without complaint, though the captain could tell from the way Thorne kept changing hands that the chore was wearing hard on him. Far ahead, out of sight now, were the Apache scouts. Occasionally, one of them who spoke English, either Little Sam or Buttons, would report back, often appearing as if by magic or sleight of hand at the head of the patrol, then disappearing as quickly. The ability of the Apache to move swiftly and without notice was as wondrous as anything he had witnessed in his life.

In the hours of their march, they had come through enough landscapes to make up an education. Out of the low pine and juniper of the encampment, into the tall pine and oak of the mountains, back down into scrub oak, then to plains of grass, and on into the occasional stands of yucca and mesquite. They had surprised herds of both deer and antelope. Birds of every description broke cover at their approach, especially the coveys of quail that waited until the horses were right on them, then broke with a whirring of wings that sounded like a flock of children's whirligigs taking the wind in an instant. Hawks and vultures circled above in the endless blue of the sky. At each congregation of vultures, he and Triggs would exchange looks, asking silently if this might be the location of the woman they sought, but they never changed course or stopped to find what it was that the vultures circled. The Apache scouts, he knew, had already done the checking. This was the way it was. You moved forward, toward the unknowable, as prepared as you could be based on the knowledge you had. This was the way it was to go to battle.

Private Ned
Thorne

Dear Thad,

We have ridden some thirty miles today, riding under the guidon of D Company, which I carried. Though the pole is anchored in a socket attached to the saddle, it still requires holding with the hand, and mine, both of them, are weak from the pain and cramping. Still, as we rode, myself next to the captain, I could not help imagining what it looked like, a line of United States soldiers on march under the company flag. I wish I could both do it and see it. It must be a wonderful sight. It cannot but stir you.

They took their mess under the shade of trees that seemed to have been planted long ago, as if where they were had once been somewhere but had come to be nowhere. They encamped early to save the horses and to have fires to cook their meals. To have fires going past sundown would be to advertise their presence for tens of miles around. Even in the shade, it was treacherously hot.

"Hot? Why hell, this is not hot, is it, Mayapple?"

"No, I should say not. You ought to go to Yuma or some such place if you want to learn hot."

"It was in Yuma that Hastings died, wasn't it?"

"Indeed it was. Have you all ever heard the story of Hastings?"

There was general groaning. "Thorne. Thorne there. He hasn't heard."

"We had been posted at Yuma for five or six months," Mayapple said. "It was the hottest damned place ever was. One day the temperature dropped below one hundred, and Hastings caught himself a chill and died."

"But that wasn't the half of it."

"I should say it wasn't. One night we was all in our bunks, and we heard a sound. We lit the lamps and what do you suppose we saw?"

"Hastings?" Someone asked.

"His very self. Back from the dead. The stink of the grave still on him something awful."

141

"Tell the boy what Hastings said."

"I was just about to. Hastings, he says, 'Go back to sleep, boys. It's only me. I was posted here so long that I got used to it. And now hell feels a tad chilly.' You see, he had just come back for his blanket."

Ned laughed, then realized that he was the only one laughing. It was, he saw, an old story that the others had heard before, and his laughter only served to prove him the new one, the boy. He colored, then rose and went to the captain, who was regarding him with the slightest of smiles.

"Will you be requiring anything more, sir?"

The captain shook his head. "Take your ease. Today's was a long march. Tomorrow's will be, too."

When people had turned to their own concerns and that of their comrades, he headed off for the brush, walking as if just seeking a place in which to relieve himself. On a rock under the shade of a mesquite, he took the diary from his blouse and went on with his reading.

April 30. If all goes well, if there are no further accidents of wagon or animal or sickness, we will, within several days, be in sight of the Mississippi River, and

142

then across it by ferry and out into the great prairie beyond. It is, by accounts, a wondrous sight, wider by far than any two other rivers placed side by side, though this I can barely imagine, still refreshed in the sight of the mighty Hudson. Last evening, Mr. Brangwen brought out his fiddle after supper. We all gathered, listened, and soon began to dance. Arm in arm with Michael, I sensed in him a vitality I had not known he possessed. He is, I know, a good man who will take to responsibility well. His prospects limited in New England, he becomes more excited, more alive, as we push into the west. Each day he and Father become more sure we shall prosper in California. I slowly grow into their enthusiasm, though I cannot keep entirely from my mind thoughts of home and, therefore, sadness.

May 2. It has been a day of tragedy for our party. Mr. Farmer's wagon lost a wheel and had to be repaired. While a party of the men held the wagon up with a long oaken pole, Mr. Farmer put on the new wheel. Before he could accomplish this, however, the axle of the wagon slipped from the pole and came down on him. It tore a terrible gash down Mr. Farmer's chest, clear past the hip. It's said that one can see his ribs and the inside, the gash is so wide. Poor Mr. Farmer. All day his screams have been interrupted only when he slips from consciousness due to the pain. Father says we have no proper doctor to see to him and are several days' journey to anywhere where such a doctor might be found, and since such a journey is near impossible, we will press on, hoping that Mr. Farmer survives. The screaming has stopped some time ago to be replaced by a desolate moaning. I think that this does not bode well for Mr. Farmer, though, regrettably, it is much easier on the rest of us.

May 11. Today Mr. Farmer is buried. What a lonesome thing is a grave at the side of a trail as the train of former comrades moves ahead.

May 18. Today, the Mississippi River. It staggers the mind and blocks the tongue. Never has there been a river so huge. The Hudson seems a brook in comparison. We again wait our turn to be ferried across. This is momentous. To cross such a river is to forever put our old lives behind us. We cross this expanse of water into the future, our future. And we must only take heart to succeed in coming near to our dreams.

June 8. Across the expanse of the Mississippi, we move steadily west, having left the comforts of the country behind us. We are now past the regions of doctors and traders where we might stop to resupply. There is coughing and fever among the travelers, and it is as if on cue, there now being no medical help for hundreds of miles on the journey. I do not write as often as I should, the incessant rocking of the wagon and the slow unrolling of the scenery fostering an indolence that shames me.

No matter how hard one tries not to count the crosses that line our route, it is unavoidable. Yesterday, in making only fifteen miles, I counted the graves of five unfortunate souls. I do my best to comfort myself that the graves are not fresh, and that with each train that passes, the journey is better known, along with its dangers, and is, therefore, less treacherous than the previous.

June 10. The Neideckers, two wagons ahead, seem to have the fever worse than all the rest, though Mr. Neidecker has improved slightly in the last days, while Mrs. N seems only the worse. The Johnson boy has taken over the duties of driving their wagon while the unfortunates rally against the sickness that has so cruelly caught them. Michael has begun, in the last two days, to cough as well, though he says he feels well enough, all in all. I worry about him continually. Father and Mother assure me that he is a strong, young man, and no harm will come to him.

June 13. Before setting off this morning, we buried Mrs. Neidecker at the site of last night's camp. The irony is nearly too much too bear. This morning the sun broke brightly, and surely the fine weather is here. The rains that have followed us have stopped, and we will be able to move at a much quicker pace as the trail dries out. Had Mrs. Neidecker been just a bit stronger, I'm sure the turn of the weather would have aided her recovery.

The good news is that Michael, after four days of coughing and two days of weakness, showed good color and spirits this morning, despite the grim news brought by the dawn. Though he did not, at the insistence of Father and several of the others, take part in the burial of that fine woman, it was clear to me that the strength and health that has always been his is rushing back into him with the advent of the good weather.

Michael's brother James has taken over most of the chores of driving and tending the team, though that is only temporary. It has fallen on James's wife to tend to Michael, and I know that is wearisome for her and should, by rights, be my duty more than hers. I asked Father this morning if I might ride the day in their wagon to keep Nancy company and aid her in the tending of Michael, for it is burdensome for her, I know. Father declined, fearing for my health. It is difficult not to express the displeasure I feel toward Father in his recalcitrance. It is difficult to watch the afflicted struggle for their recovery. I want desperately to join them in the effort.

June 20. We buried Michael this noon. I may as well write in cipher, for though I can say and write the words, I have no

147

understanding of them. Though I stood in the high grass of the prairie, watched the men break through and overturn it with shovels and other instruments, revealing underneath the cool brown earth that flew up from the shovels and mounded near the grave, spilling and tumbling down the side of the mound like small creatures glad at last to be freed from the deepness of the earth, I cannot say I could comprehend what had happened and was about to happen. I looked on the innocent clots of dirt and rock as dreadful foes who were taking Michael from me to enjoy the embrace of him that was by all rights mine.

He stopped. Michael dead? How could this be? Michael had been improving, his coughing considerably lessened. He must have skipped pages. He leafed back through and found nothing to say that Michael's condition had worsened. He bent back the pages of diary from the binding to see if any pages had been removed. They had not.

How the world has suddenly changed. Its length and breadth have stretched beyond the comprehension of someone such as I. At the same time, time itself has shrunk into something so small there is no room to breathe in it. It is a piece of fruit that has begun to rot and shrivel into itself. The future no longer exists. The past has gone hollow and might as well not exist, either. There is only the present, alternately hot and cold, bright and dark, and moving by with the dry, hollow sound of the wind in the grass.

I catch myself at the worst moments thinking to myself, "Oh, I must tell Michael of this," only to be brought up short by the knowledge that there is no Michael. This is a terrible knowledge. A demon or imp that I keep catching, only to lose again in just another instant. Yet it scurries after me always, mocking me, and I am condemned to catch and lose it and must again repeat the same. I feel myself a small and pitiable Sisyphus. I would know what outrage I had perpetrated against God, except that is sacrilege.

He felt a sudden and profound loss, as if Michael or this woman, whose name he did not know but whom he thought of as Mary, were his relation. He understood the absence of death, the way the dead left their place behind, a gap in the world that they had once filled. He knew how vivid and clear that space appeared in the hours and days shortly after the death, then gradually began to close as the world healed itself, and how then the space was merely glimpsed at the odd time and you understood it had been there always, you had simply forgotten to see it, and in that, you once again betrayed the beloved dead.

He read on, at once reluctant and compelled.

June 22. We made good progress today. A small wind accompanied us, blowing across our way from the north. It brought with it the smell of flowers growing across the prairie. Suddenly my heart would lift, as if my soul were a small bird, catching the wind and soaring like the mighty. Then would come another of the awful crosses or cairns of rock that mark the resting place of another traveler lost to the world, or in the midst of joy, Michael would fail to lay his hand on mine or to smile, and the joy that had, of the sudden, begun to build within me would crumble like a painted eggshell that had been holding me up, and I would feel myself go heavy and fall in around the ruins.

June 23. What is the way to love? Once in, how out, though the loved one be dead? I try to remember how it came about that I first loved Michael. At what point did his life become more important to me than my own? Did it ever? Did I fail to value it sufficiently and, thus, let it slip? When did the touch of him, the smell of him become more dear to me than anything else in the world? I cannot remember. I know it was not always this way, but I cannot remember how it came to be. Trying to remember the way into love is like trying to remember one's own birth. Surely it happened, here is the very evidence of it, but in memory, the actual happening has been blasted away. Why cannot it be that we remember the beginning and not the end? Why is it loss we experience again and again and have only the feeblest sense of the wonders of the finding?

June 25. Death continues its cruel mockery, its grotesque capering across a sterile and dry landscape. Mr. Estes, who has recently lost his wife, came to see Father last night. He would propose that he and I should marry, he being newly widowed and I losing Michael so suddenly. He finds that the two of us, our futures tumbled over in the odd turnings of disease and death, have a bond that might lead to partnership. I am, of course, sickened by the notion of it, and Father sent Mr. Estes away, harshly, protecting both my feelings and my virtue. I cannot imagine how one could even conceive of such an enterprise.

No. He stopped. No. Do not listen to Mr. Estes. He does not love you like Michael, or . . . He stopped himself. Or, what? What were these people to him, these people who did not even know him? Still, he felt a part of them. The soft voice of Mary, that so closely echoed the voice of his own Edith, though it had taken on a timbre of its own now, soothed him. He was pulled into the reading to hear again that voice.

June 26. Could there be a more loathsome creature on the earth than myself? Those stirrings I had begun to entertain so frequently in anticipation of my new life with Michael run on, unabated, despite the absence of Michael. It is as if some part of me has broken off and marches on toward some foolish vision constructed only of the flimsiest of dreams. Yet the dreams are what remain, and to let go of them would be to let go of my very existence right now. What small and pitiful things are our lives. I begin to question whether or not I have a life and whether I ever did or merely dreamed it.

June 29. We move steadily on across unending plains. We are pulled forward by the steady, dumb, unrelenting pace of the oxen. The oxen move forward, unencumbered by notions of what was or what might be. They simply move their great dumb hooves again and again, ever forward and toward the west. I would envy them but that in my best moments I feel that I am one of them, moving steadily forward, plodding, step by step, toward what I neither know nor desire. For knowledge and desire are the cruelest things that are on the earth. How fervently I wish that I could, by reaching in and dragging out, rid myself of both.

At mid-morning of the second day, they had reached the foothills of the mountains to begin an immediate climb that tired the horses and forced them to dismount and lead the horses up steep and gravelly trails, little more than deer paths. The air was cooler already, and his legs had regained feeling. He now regretted the dismount, which less than an hour ago had been such a relief. The pain that had inhabited his legs now turned its attention to his feet, which, hot and sweaty, moved around inside his boots, raising blisters. As they climbed, the horses dislodged pebbles and debris, which caused the horses behind them to slip and dislodge more debris. There was soft cursing all down the line. Relieved of carrying the guidon, he was back in the line, the dirt and pebbles clouding his eyes and stinging his skin. He climbed with his feet angled out for purchase and his arm bent in front of his face to shield him from the debris being sprayed back at him, the other arm yanking at his own mount's reins, which he had doubled around his fist so that they were now biting through his gauntlet into the flesh of his hand.

After a harsh climb, they reached a level *cienega,* a meadow of grass, bordered by a ring of scruffy oaks. Here they were ordered to dismount and rest. He was called out along with Brickner, Wortham, Park, Mayapple, and Sergeant Triggs. The captain had taken his ease under one of the oaks, his blouse unbuttoned and his sweat-soaked hat perched on his knee. He had soaked his kerchief in water and draped it across his head. He remained in that position until Little Sam came scurrying out of the brush to the west.

They rose as the captain approached, but he put them at ease. "They are directly above us, two miles, maybe less. Sam thinks they are a small band, two dozen, maybe fewer. They seem to have been camped for a while and have established a small *rancheria.* We have no confirmation on the woman. We will proceed, just the seven of us, up this draw on foot until we meet up with Sam and Lucky below the *rancheria.* Our purpose is to reconnoiter only. We will march under orders of complete silence. You will bring with you only your carbines, ammunition boxes, and canteens. You will make every effort to march in complete silence. Upon contact with the aboriginals, your job is to observe only, unless I order you otherwise. We will commence the patrol in ten minutes. Prepare yourselves."

The draw was more treacherous than the deer trail to the *cienega* had been. No matter how he watched Brickner in front of him set his hands and feet, he seemed unable to find any spot for his own that would not send rocks spilling down behind him onto Wortham, who under the orders of march said nothing but whose silent curses Ned felt well enough. Though Brickner's climb sent rocks and gravel spilling down to him, Ned knew the amount he was sending to Wortham was greater and worse.

The air continued to cool as their way up the draw took them higher, but the sunlight became more intense, glaring off the rhyolite of the mountainside and burning the skin at his neck and wrists. His eyes watered, but that did not wash away the sweat that poured down his forehead and into his eyes, burning them, drawing more tears, and, finally, nearly blinding him. His heart pounded and his breathing became more ragged and forced. He was sure that the stock of his carbine, scraping and banging against the rock, set up a noise like thunder.

After a few hundred feet of scrabbling through the draw, squeezing between the boulders that lined it, and clutching at the sorriest of ragged plants for sufficient leverage to pull themselves along, the small patrol reached a low ridge. The captain, crouched at the opening of the draw, directed them with hand signals to positions along the ridge. Brickner was sent to the left and Ned to the right, where he had to scramble over Wortham to find position between two boulders.

He threw himself down, belly to the ground, and pressed his face to the cool rock, hugging his carbine, expecting at any second to hear bullets whining and whizzing and ricocheting around him. After what seemed to be a safe amount of time, he raised his head a little and took a look over the outcropping of rock.

Below was a small valley, nearly a bowl in the mountainside, studded with fine trees and bordered on the east by a small pool of water fed by a thin stream that came out of the side of the mountain and exited to the southwest. Here and there along the shaded ground were piles of branch and brush and just an occasional patch of dark ground. He had no experience with either the Apaches or with trailing and tracking, and though he saw immediately what a likely spot for an encampment this was, nothing here suggested the presence of Indians.

They waited and watched. As they did, the sounds of the place grew. From the trees in front of him, birds called back and forth to one another. The high notes of the birds were woven over a steady, quiet bass formed by a small wind that moved continually through the feathery branches of pine trees. Somewhere to his front right, a squirrel angrily scolded them from deep inside the branches. The winds were swirling gently so that from time to time, a quick breeze of fresh air would cool his face as it spun past him. His breathing, quick and ragged from the climb, slowed and steadied. He wiped the palms of his hands on his trouser legs, but as quickly as he did, they sweated up again. He could not slow his heart. Though nothing had happened yet, he was in a fight. Somewhere, out there, in the bowl or beyond, someone was waiting to kill him.

He was aware of the sergeant's presence before he saw him, crouched there, holding his hand palm out to Ned in a silent order to neither speak nor move while he whispered orders to the prone Wortham some four feet to Ned's left. When the sergeant had gone, scuttling back, crablike, to his original position, Wortham backed out, still nearly prone, and in a crouching run made his way behind Ned and beyond the boulders.

Ned continued to watch the empty bowl before him. If there had been Indians here, as he guessed there had been, perhaps they were long gone. The place was, save for birds and squirrels, as quiet and empty as a midweek chapel. But the birds and squirrels kept a commotion, and he thought maybe they knew that nothing of significance could happen here. A motion to his right drew his eye, and he caught his breath and swung his carbine toward it.

It was Wortham, coming down the rocks below, as agile and quick as a monkey. He moved in sure motions, stopping momentarily after each step to scout his next move, then came again, stopping and moving until he made his way down the wall of the little canyon. It was a fine and skilled performance, and Ned watched, fascinated, as Wortham, who was at least ten years older than he, moved though the rock and scree better than Ned ever could.

He could not help thinking of the rope dancers he had seen a year or two before. Had it been only one or two years? It seemed like ages since he had sat in the tent, his mother on one side of him, Thad on the other, watching a man in red tights and soft, white shoes maneuver the ropes and swings set up before him. The rope dancer pointed his toes carefully but surely, the rope taking his weight with a slight sag, then a bounce, for which he compensated with the movements of his outstretched arms. He moved from step to step, each step a separate act, but each flowing to the next so that the journey across the rope, no more than fifty feet, was as skilled and pretty a construct as any building was a construct of brick and stone. His throat caught at the danger, and his eyes welled with admiration for the feat. He looked over to Thad, who was sitting wide-eyed, mouth open, as the man reached the end of the rope only to grab onto a swing that dangled above his head. The sight of Thad's open mouth reminded him that his own mouth was open in just the same way, so that to anyone watching, though there was no one not watching the rope dancer, Ned would have seemed an entranced child, just like his brother, though he was fifteen years old, nearly a man. He clamped his mouth shut and put on the look of one who has seen such things so often that they held little charm.

The odd motion of Wortham, who had reached the canyon floor, caught his attention before he heard the crack of the shot that picked Wortham up off the ground, twisted his body, and threw him backward, very much like a rag doll. There was a pause while Ned and everyone else tried to register and make sense of the absurdity of Wortham's fall. Even before the echo of the shot had completely faded, Wortham lay awkwardly prone among the rocks, in no position anyone but a dead man could maintain.

If there was an order to open fire, he did not hear it. Nonetheless, he did open fire, along with everyone else stationed along the ridge. At what he was shooting he did not know, maybe just the place, an odd, pretty place where a terrible thing had happened. He fired straight ahead, ejecting spent cartridges, loading another, and firing, unable to see anything except the smoke of gunpowder that hung across their position. The air was thick with it, the smell acrid and choking.

He did hear the order to cease fire. The shooting came to a ragged end, the final shot coming from his far left. Then Sergeant Triggs was lying nearly on top of him, breathing hard in his ear, his breath sharp and sour. Triggs's left hand held his shoulder just below the juncture of his neck.

"Do you see him, son?"

He saw very little. Smoke hung in wide strands across his plane of vision, but the strands were beginning to thin and pull apart. There was no sound to be heard except that of breathing, which might have been Triggs's or his own. They had become the same.

"There's two of them I can see," Triggs said. "Brickner's taking one, and you're to take the other. Take your time. Don't waste a lot of ammunition. Find him, sight him, and kill him. He's right across there, just between those two rocks there."

He followed the line of Triggs's hand and finger to an outcropping of rock nearly directly across and just above him. He wasn't sure he saw anything at all. Perhaps a small flash of light. But he heard the sound that occurred as the bullet whirred like an angry bee just above his head.

"You best hurry up and see him, boy, because he, by God, sees us. Do you have him?" Triggs settled his weight into Ned as if trying to become as small as Ned or to become part of him.

He nodded, though he was not sure he did. He could not help thinking of the angry bee that had just flown over him, a bee that wished to sting him to his death. He squinted at the distance, which seemed all rock and brush. If there was a man over there, he could not make him out. And then, in a small flash of light, he saw the rifle, perhaps some small part of the man behind it. A shot just above the rifle would surely do the job.

"He's yours. Take him." Then Triggs was gone.

It was impossible that the shot missed. He clearly saw the quick burst where his bullet hit rock to the right of the rifle. He pulled back out of the opening, spun onto his back, sheltered by the rock, and flipped open the trapdoor of the Springfield. The cartridge did not eject. Speed was essential now. The target knew he'd been spotted and would likely try to move or get away altogether. He remembered Birdwood's warning about the soft copper cartridges and dug in his pocket for his penknife. He pried out the bent casing and ran home a new cartridge. When he rolled back into the opening, he heard the buzz yet again. Without thinking, he spun away from the opening and onto his back again. His breath was coming in great, heaving gulps now. He turned over and scooted on his belly up to the rock. He could see the barrel of the rifle, there against the rock, under the brush of some tree. Another bee buzzed by his head. He stayed in this time but held his fire. He waited for the rifle across the canyon to move, but it didn't.

He rested his sights just on top of the rifle and then moved it slightly to the left to adjust for the windage that must have caused the last miss. He struggled to get his breath under control but could not, so he just held it. He would have to stay put, to not move even if another of the bees came buzzing at him. He felt his mind go free as he watched the little ball of the front sight come into the notch of the rear sight. It balanced for the slightest of moments, then tumbled into the notch. Just as he squeezed the trigger, he felt the concussion and recoil that slammed his face into the rock below.

He was alive. He knew that because he could still hear shots to both sides of him. He was alive, but he was not right. Though he wanted to stand up, to find out what was wrong with him, to see where he was hurt and how badly, he lay still, hugging his carbine to him, afraid of the bullets like deadly bees all around. He lay there and felt the cool rock at the side of his face. He was alive because he could see. He could see the speckled stone in front of him, mottled with blood. His blood. He knew it was his blood, pouring out of him, with no stopping until he was dead. There seemed to be a flood of it, and it was coming out of his own head, it was in his ear and in his eye. And with the blood came the pain.

Above him, the sky snapped open like an

umbrella. Faces looked down on him as though he were a curiosity. "He's alive. He's been shot, but he lives." A voice echoed this back across the canyon. He blinked and made out Mayapple and Triggs looking at him in a way he did not like. He tried to pull himself up onto an elbow and failed, falling heavily back.

"Sweet Lord, Jesus," someone said. "He's had his brains shot out."

"Easy there. Don't be moving." Sergeant Triggs reached out a hand and held him at the shoulder, then pushed him down and rolled him back over. He felt the sergeant's fingers in the hair at the back of his head. The pain made him jerk his entire body. "At ease, soldier. At ease. You've a scratch. That's all. Just a scratch, but you'll be fine. Just fine. Stay at ease."

He turned and looked up to the sergeant's face, trying to read his own story there. The mixture of fear and concern at once frightened him and comforted him. The sergeant's expression was not unlike his mother's when he was ill, and in that moment, he loved the sergeant dearly. But the sergeant's hands were covered in blood. And he knew it was his blood, still pouring out of him until he would be dead.

The sergeant smiled down at him. "You

got him. There were two of them. Just two. You got yours and Brickner got his. You did your job, just like you were supposed to. You made a fine shot. It's over now. You're all right. You took a little nick, but you're not hurt. You're all right. We'll be headed back to the camp soon. You're going home. Just take your rest. You've done a fine job."

He prayed the prayer for grace before eating, knew that was wrong, and then he prayed the prayer for going to sleep, knew that was right, and he went to sleep.

The smell of ammonia yanked him back into consciousness, then the captain pulled him upward until the world spun itself back in front of his eyes.

"Can you sit up, Private?"

He considered the question. He thought he probably could not. "I've been shot," he explained.

"I know that. But you're going to have to sit yourself up like a big boy, now, or I won't be able to tend to you. I've got scissors in my hand. I think you'll be wanting me to use both hands for this. You still need to be a soldier for this, now sit up straight."

And he did. He had trouble getting his eyes to focus on what was in front of him, but he was able to sit, and the world did not darken and spin like it had before. Below him, troopers were in the bottom of the canyon. Sometime while he was sleeping, the rest of the patrol had joined them.

"I have to cut off some of your hair, here. Otherwise I can't see what I'm doing. You'll look like a damned fool for a while, but that can't be helped."

"Am I going to die?"

The captain snorted. "You're going to have a painful head for a bit. I think that's about the length of it. You took a nick from a bullet, but just a nick. You two must have shot about the same time. You did the better job. He's dead." The captain continued to tug on his hair, sawing away with the scissors, cutting bloody chunks from an area that hurt like fire. He gritted his teeth and tried not to flinch.

"That doesn't hurt," the captain said. "But this. This will hurt." The captain pushed a wet bit of cloth into the back of his head. The liquid was cool, then cold, then hot as fire. He did not flinch. He screamed.

"That's enough of that then. Shut your mouth and be a man. It's carbolic acid. It burns a bit, but it cleans the wound right out. And as long as I'm giving you pain, I should probably tell you, I don't think you were shot. The wound looks too uneven and dirty. You took a bit of the rock from up there, I would say."

"A rock?"

"That would be it. You've been whacked in the head with a rock. His shot went above your head, hit the rock, and knocked off a chunk that smacked your head. Now hold still. I'm going to take a sleeve off your union suit here and bandage your head. It's kind of an odd spot. It's going to be difficult to make it hold without covering your eyes and nose. I'm going to bring it up under your chin and tie it off at the top of your head. You have permission to forgo the kepi for comfort.

"Brickner. Cease and desist. This instant." They were standing on the ridge. Below, Brickner had one of the dead Apaches prone on the ground, knife in one hand, hank of the Indian's hair in the other.

"I done killed him. His scalp is mine."

"Corporal Brickner, you will unhand that man or I will see you hang. If anyone under my command will desecrate the body of an enemy, he will be bound over and hanged. Is that understood?"

Brickner dropped the Indian's head so that it landed with a thud, like something slightly rotten. He threw his knife down, violently, so that it stuck in the ground, handle up. He began to stalk away, then stopped, turned back to the captain, came to attention, and saluted. "At your orders, sir."

"Brickner, I have kept you from the gallows before. Don't count on the continuance of my goodwill. Sergeant Triggs, form a burial detail for the Indians and prepare Wortham for transport back to camp. Mr. Brickner, pick up your damned knife and put it away. I do not wish to see it again." He flicked a half-salute at Triggs that also relieved Brickner of his still-held salute.

Dear Thad,

Today saw a fierce battle with a band of hostile Apaches. You will know I am wounded but alive. I write now from that far country that is known as manhood. An Indian's bullet has driven all things of boyhood from my life.

Do keep the news of my injury from our parents. I would not cause them any more grief than I already have, and I know now this is the price of honor and courage, which is always sold dearly. I would hope that my absence would find them great peace.

"It's a terrible thing, isn't it?" the captain asked. "Looking into the face of a man you have killed. Even one such as this."

Ned looked at the bodies of the two dead Indians lying on the ground while two troopers dug their graves. "They're old."

"Maybe not so old as you think. They lead a hard life, harder than ours. But, yes, they're old. The main band of the Apaches left them behind to hold us off because they were expendable. They did and they were. You were expecting killing to have something more of the romantic to it, weren't you?"

"No, sir. I know."

"Yes, of course. You know. Everyone young 'knows.' "

He could not keep his eyes from the head of the Indian he had killed. His bullet had entered just to the side of the Apache's nose. There wasn't much more than a jagged hole there. But it had come out behind the man's other ear, and in so doing, it had taken most of the left side of his face. The eyeball hung precariously without a full socket of bone to secure it. It was open, lidless. The top part of the mouth was gone, and he was aware that the big red thing he was looking at was the man's tongue. Here and there were loose, scattered teeth. Blood was everywhere. He turned his head away, but not before he had seen enough that he would never forget the sight.

He wanted to tell the captain that he knew more than he was credited for, but he clamped his jaw shut and did not speak.

They returned to camp at a slower pace than their leaving. He rode in the back of the column this time, relieved of guidon duty, next to Brickner and behind the horse that carried Wortham. He tried his best not to look at the bundle — Wortham, sewn into his blanket, which was stiff with blood, crossed, and tied with ropes over the saddle of his mount, which was tied to the saddle of the horse in front of it. Like the rest of them, he had stood at Wortham's body and remarked at the damage a small bullet can do. Wortham had lain with a surprised look on his face as if he had just turned the corner to find himself dead. The front of his blouse was soaked in blood, and in the upper left corner of the stain was a small round hole, about where Ned thought Wortham's heart lay. He had not wanted to look at Wortham's astonished face, but he had not been able to look away from it. Now, as they rode, remembering what he had seen, he tried not to look at the remains in the blanket. But there was too much time and not enough landscape to keep his eyes off the bundle that bounced and groaned against the saddle as the horse plodded steadily forward.

Neither did he want to look at his own shadow, which began at his left, shortened as they rode, and vanished just for a while, only to return at his right, lengthening out as the march continued into the late afternoon. He might have been able to imagine himself an Indian of the plains from his shadow. Above his head, two points stuck up from the back like feathers of an Indian brave. He knew, though, that not seen in shadow but in flesh, he did not look like an Indian brave, but rather, with bandage cut from his union suit, wrapped around the back of his head, and tied at the top, like a man suffering from toothache.

There was little talk on the way back, though they no longer moved under orders of silent march. The grim remains of Wortham following their line sobered them considerably.

He tried, as well, to avoid conversation with Brickner, who was no doubt still smarting from the captain's rebuke and, Ned feared, contemptuous of Ned's wound, caused not by a bullet, but by a piece of dislodged rock.

"It wasn't smart soldiering, that's for damned sure," Brickner said.

Ned watched the shadowed ends of his bandage bounce along the ground like the floppy ears of a storybook bunny.

"He got Wortham killed. Near got you killed, too. It smelled of ambush from the get-go. I knew it right aways, and so he should have knowed it. You take a look at them Indians we shot?"

Ned went on watching his shadow. He had tried being proud of shooting an Indian, and he had also tried feeling ashamed. Neither seemed to fit him right. He was now working on trying not to think about it at all.

"I asked, did you see them?"

He shook his head. The ends of the bandage bobbed violently.

"Old men. Old granddaddies. They was the two oldest Indians I ever saw. Hell, they might be the two oldest Indians ever. They might have been the first two Indians ever made, shooting at us with the first two rifles ever made. But they stopped the United States Army in its tracks. Two old men with a couple of old repeating carbines. They got one of us, wounded another, and turned us back so the rest of them could get away.

And I'll tell you what. They are having one grand old time with that white woman tonight. The damned circus is in town and he led us right into it."

His head snapped up. "The woman?"

"Hell, given a little time, you could have figured out to go around that little bit of canyon. So, you tired of the Army yet?"

"No. But I'm damned sure tired of you."

Brickner laughed. "That's good. That's some real fine talk from a man with his underwear around his head. You think on how long the Army's going to have you if you don't get some money pretty soon. You're damned useful with that rifle there. You and me, we may be the best this company's got. I can help you out, Marybelle, and I believe you can help me out."

LIEUTENANT
ANTHONY AUSTIN

He awoke to cold coffee. After staring at the cup and marveling at the incompetence of Birdwood, he remembered. He had been awakened at first light, addressed the cretinous soldier, and then had sat down on his cot to ponder the day. At some point, he reasoned, he had lain back down and slept.

He was not used to the rigors of command. When Bobby went off on one or another of his expeditions, it became his duty to survive the day as best he could. Largely, that meant submitting a formulation of the day's events to Stonehouse and letting him implement the formula, apportioning chores as he saw fit. But even that seemed to him a bother. He had once relished the scraps of command that came his way, but as he grew older and found that command was not his particular strength, he became less desirous of it, and he had been truly happy that Bobby had been brevetted to captain and, thus, the sole commander.

He was good at what the Army was deficient in, observing the world that the Army seemed intent on stomping, flattening, subduing, and destroying. As their postings had gone farther and farther into the west, they had come into more territory containing wonders heretofore unseen by white men. As the Army tramped across the earth with its big boots and lines of hooves, what had been unseen became trampled. More and more, he saw his job as the recorder of what was once wild and was soon to be tamed, then extinguished.

But the world was not that bleak. He needed to remind himself of that, to drill it into his consciousness. That was the melancholia, he knew. But knowing and escaping were not, unfortunately, linked. When the darkness came upon him, as it had after Borchert had been killed by the tree, it became a slowly advancing cloud of pessimism that engulfed him and everything around him. The earth was a place that transformed itself as did all living things, and the Army and the advance of the civilization it preceded were simply an agent of that change. There was no more sense in grieving the advance of the Army than in grieving the continued arrival of one's birthday.

He had wondered if perhaps Cranston had returned from Bowie. As much as Bobby awaited word from George Crook, he awaited word from his friend Orville Stanhope at the museum in Philadelphia. Over a month ago, he had sent a description and drawings of a Calypte he had found not a mile from the campsite. He had quite simply stumbled upon it. Taking his ease from a long morning's walk, he had seen what he thought was a large moth working the chaparral. Quietly, slowly, he had removed his hat and then caught the tiny creature with a great swipe through the leaves and flowers. It was no moth at all but a hummingbird, so delicate that the force of his hat had stunned it. He reached in and took the bird in his hand, still alive, the tiny heart whirring like a child's whirligig. With the slightest pressure of his index finger, he snapped its neck and stilled the whirring. He had spent hours studying the creature. It was a hummingbird quite unlike any he had seen before, and he was nearly positive that no other white man had seen one, either. He proposed the name *Calypte austinus*. His hummingbird, his tiny creature, carrying his name into eternity.

The bird rested in Philadelphia now, in a box that once held plug tobacco, stuffed with cotton batting. Before he had sent it along, rarely a day had passed that he had not opened the box, very carefully lifting and pulling the batting and staring at the tiny creature, remembering the rapid trill of its heartbeat, suddenly stopped by the smallest of pressures from his finger. This was the way of his work. To find and identify, to immortalize a creature, to add the creature to the list of the known and understood, required first that you kill it. And he never looked at the tiny bird without remembering how it sped from flower to flower in quick jerks, stopped, then sped again. The bird was his because he had seen, captured, and killed it. And one day it would carry his name down the centuries he would not occupy except in the name of the bird no bigger than a large moth.

But Cranston had not returned from Bowie, and so there was no news of any kind. And as put out as he was not to know the fate of his little bird, Bobby would be more put out that he had no answer from the general. As much as he needed to identify and name something no one else had, Bobby needed even more to go off into the wilderness and be heroic. To rescue the woman, if indeed there was a woman, was exactly what Bobby needed most from the world. To wrest a woman, a white woman, from the hands of Apaches before they could take her to Mexico and sell or trade her would make up for so much that had gone wrong in Bobby's life. Bobby seemed to the rest of the world a bit of the old Army, a soldier who soldiered as it had been done before him for centuries, who was able to transcend himself until he was nothing but soldier, carrying forward the mission of his country and his president. But in the late hours, the dark hours, he was a man who, like other men, felt deeply his own shortcomings and grieved them and the misfortunes they had cost.

If he could perform a daring rescue, perhaps in the eyes of the world, and more important, in his own eyes, he would be the soldier who found and saved the woman, rather than the soldier who made the mistake on the Pit River. How well Marc Antony, also an Anthony, had understood the way one's failings could overtake and obliterate one's successes in the blink of an eye.

But Cranston had not returned, and he held out little hope that he would soon. Perhaps this was the dark whispering of the melancholia and would be washed away with just a little more whisky. But he felt and worried that it was not. General Crook was an honorable man, but he was a general. And generals found themselves promoted nearly out of the Army and into the life of the politicians. If George had faith in Bobby, and perhaps he did, he still answered less to his own conscience and understanding than to the politicians who were generally unburdened by conscience and understanding. He did not want to think about the toll George Crook's rejection would take on Bobby and then, necessarily, on himself.

But such thoughts were their own punishments, and he tried to put them out of his head. Nothing had yet happened, because it was not yet time for anything to happen. Events would continue on their course, and there was no utility in judging that course before its time.

He thought that he might make a productive day of crossing the river, which one could do safely without fear of wetting one's boots, and walk to the south a bit where there were stands of mallow that should attract a population of both birds and insects. He preferred the birds, simply on grounds of the aesthetics, but the world of insects was, by comparison, vast, and there seemed an infinite number in this area that had yet to be described, named, and cataloged.

All in all he would prefer to just put on his boots and go on his own, unnoticed, unaddressed, to make his studies. It was nearing mid-morning now, and Stonehouse had taken command of the troops and set them to work, no doubt. And when he came to address him, Stonehouse would give him the supercilious look of a noncom who has taken, in his mind, the rightful advantage of a superior officer.

He respected more than liked Stonehouse, although he thought him a soldier of better-than-average merit. He was younger than Triggs, cut out of rough and uneven material. Having lately risen out of the dirt, Stonehouse thought himself a soldier of considerable worth, and so he would have been had he not been so cocksure of it, arrogant and unbending. The respect that Triggs had won with hard service over the years, Stonehouse simply considered his due. He would deal with Stonehouse as he could, having the advantage of rank, if not skill.

"There are crews at work on felling and splitting, but I have taken the largest number to finish the bakery," Stonehouse said.

He did not question whether that was the proper thing to have done. It was. "The oven is finished, as are the chimney and walls. The rafters have been raised and the roof shall be completed before darkness today. By tomorrow, I should think, we shall be having fresh bread."

"Good. Tomorrow, make sure there is a surfeit of it, so that every man who put his labor into that building will have as much of it as he likes. I don't know about you, Sergeant, but I've had a sufficiency of hard-tack."

"You'll get no argument from me," Stonehouse said.

"Tomorrow, we'll post a guard, do some general policing of the area, I think. Then let the men have some time off. A baseball game, perhaps. Or a musical. Next week we can start on the mess."

"Yes, sir. Is there anything else, sir?"

"No. No, there won't be anything else, Sergeant. I leave the post in your hands. Carry on."

"As you wish, sir."

To all intents and purposes, it was a courteous and formal exchange. Stonehouse had received his orders and had sworn to carry them out. But underneath that, he understood and Stonehouse understood that he had ordered Stonehouse to do what he was already doing and to keep on doing it. He had turned over control of the camp to Stonehouse long after Stonehouse had taken control on his own.

But now he was free to spend the day as he pleased. And that pleased him tremendously. He went to get his notebook and glass and his pouch of supplies. He had ordered himself a day off.

It was a small lizard, maybe six inches overall. He could not measure without startling the little beast and he preferred, where possible, to observe rather than to kill and collect. Its tail was longer than its body and bright blue. It perched on a stone the size of his head, doing the little push-ups that lizards were wont to do.

He consulted his notes and thought it must be some branch of the whiptail family, as the tail was quite long and thin, but he found no reference to any such lizard with a bright blue tail. It might be a juvenile of an already identified species, or it might be a branch of the family not yet noted. There was no way to discern. He opened his book and sketched the small creature as best he could. It was patterned with stripes of light skin, speckled with spots and lines, the markings radiating the length of the small body. The throat was a clear and clean white. Though he could not see the belly without drastically altering his position and, no doubt, scaring the creature into flight, he suspected that it was a continuation of the same white that marked the neck.

He did not wish to be an overidentifier, one of those who continues to flood the museums and universities with descriptions of species already identified, mistaking the normal differentiation of individuals within the species as marks of yet another species. But here, where so little had been identified, he felt compelled to note and describe anything he could not already identify. He would, he knew, identify a number of new species, and in doing so, would necessarily misidentify a number of individual variants. There seemed no remedy to the situation, so he wrote and he drew. He loved drawing, for drawing existed in the present moment only, and only the present moment was certain and safe.

CAPTAIN ROBERT FRANKLIN

He brought the patrol back on an arcing course farther north than they needed to go, but this route took them well beyond the ruined ranch that was their source of their latest difficulties. He rode with a kind of grim determination, Triggs next to him, neither of them speaking or acknowledging each other's presence. The pressure he felt was palpable, a weight that rested on his shoulders and pushed both down and forward. He rode with his head upright and straight. He had changed the straw sombrero he had worn on the way out for his helmet. He could feel the horsehair plume brushing back and forth across the helmet in a nearly mesmeric rhythm.

But it was important that the men see him this way, proud and sure. It had not been a defeat at the small *cienega*, though he had lost one man and nearly lost another. And though he had found the trail of the

Apaches, he knew little more than he had known before he set out with the patrol. He had found no sign of the woman, nor did he have a good idea of the size of the Apache band. He did not know if they were, indeed, survivors of the ugliness at Camp Grant fleeing for their lives into Mexico or whether they were a group of the locals, come off their word to leave the white settlers be as long as their home base deep in the mountains was left unmolested.

What he knew is that he had another dead soldier, the second in little more than a month. He would go back to camp, regroup, rest the men and horses, and by the time they were ready to go out again, he would have word from Crook, ordering him to go after the Apaches and retrieve the white woman. And the first death, though it was part of his command, did not pertain to him. That one was Tony's, though there was nothing Tony might have done to prevent it. Still, that one was Tony's, not his. But this one — this one was his and his alone.

It was grand country they were riding through. They were just at the foothills of the Dragoon mountains, where Cochise had his stronghold. The land sloped down into a long and fertile plain. One could look over the sweep of grama grass, dotted with the sprawling, messy mesquite trees and the tall spiky stems of yucca, and understand that someday this would not be grama grass, but wheat and barley, and the few clots of mesquite would have given way to apple, peach, and pear trees. It was like looking at Eden, before the hand of the Creator had so lovingly sculpted it and long before the folly of the woman had brought an end to it.

And then Little Sam appeared next to him, having come up from behind the column unseen and unheard until he was right there. As much as he admired the Apache's ability to keep out of sight until he needed to show himself, it unnerved him, too, and he wished that Sam would instead come into the column head-on so they would know he was coming instead of coming up from the rear, letting the hoofbeats of his horse join the others.

He had sent Sam forward in the early morning to scout the best path through the mountains and back to camp. He tried his best to remain respectful of Cochise, and he would have preferred not to even cross the mountains. But on this northern swing, missing the mountains entirely would entail an extra day's ride, something he was not prepared to undertake, traveling with a wounded man and a corpse that was wanting burial soon.

They could take a course to the northwest, Little Sam informed him, that would take them through a draw in the mountains, which was far enough from the stronghold that the Chiricahua should take no offense. They would be watched as they rode up and over a trail that was only moderately difficult for the horses, but they were always watched anytime they were within a few hours' ride of the stronghold. Cochise was a man who did not like surprises, and he had seldom found himself surprised since the Army had opened up with the howitzers on his fortifications in what was now called Apache Pass.

But what was even more promising was a small herd of pronghorn antelope that the scouts had found. Buttons and the other scouts were watching them while Sam, who had the best English and the best understanding of what the captain wanted, would bring the patrol up. It was a good opportunity to get fresh meat without going out of their way back to the camp. What would be a required bivouac anyway could now be an opportunity to refresh their provisions.

He did not particularly like the idea of

stopping to hunt while he was transporting casualties, but Little Sam assured him that they could take the meat at their leisure. And it would be good for morale. Wortham, bouncing along the trail sewn into his blanket, was a great and dreadful weight on the spirits of the men. A little productive sport would ease the grimness of the day, and the taste of antelope could surely sweeten the taste of defeat.

It was a small box canyon, the final cut of a meager stream in the mountainside before it spilled out to the desert floor and dried to a sandy wash. They came, under Little Sam's direction and crawling on their bellies, to the rim of the canyon. Even the wounded boy, Thorne, eased his way, gingerly, to the edge. At the bottom of the canyon, a small herd of pronghorn antelope, seven or eight, already starting to skitter, were gathered around a pool hardly more than a large puddle.

He raised his hand, open palm back, the signal to hold fire. The antelope moved in small steps in tight circles, heads up, trying for a scent. The lead animal, a big buck, moved around the herd, quick, agitated, ready to bolt. He spun and kicked as the first arrow hit him just behind the right shoulder.

The herd moved with him, alarmed now, as one bolted for the outlet of the canyon, from where more arrows came, striking the buck at the base of the neck, another embedding in the back of the antelope directly behind him. The Apache scouts rose now from the scrub oak and juniper where moments before there had been no one. The twang of bowstrings released joined the sound of the antelope screaming as they bounded over and into each other and spun back into the canyon where the soldiers waited.

The captain rose to his knee, tried to draw a bead on one of the spinning animals, and fired, hitting nothing. Around him, the rest of the patrol rose and began to fire. It became a battle immediately, the Apaches continuing to loose their arrows first, then to fire their carbines; the soldiers, standing now at the rim of the canyon, firing into the swirl of antelope that were jumping and spinning, crashing into one another and into the ground. The air grew indistinct with smoke and bitter with the smell of gunpowder.

The reports of the .50 Springfields were constant, nearly a single, long sound, as the troopers ejected spent shells, ran home fresh ones, fired into the swarming animals, and then began the process again. Above even that racket, the hoarse screaming of the antelope and the cracking and rustle of the brush as the antelope struggled in their terror played counterpoint to the spouts of blood and explosions of tissue as U.S. Army rounds slammed into the crazed animals who had innocently stumbled into hell.

Soon he could smell the blood under the heavier, sharper odor of gunpowder. It was chaos below. Bullets whirred in and ricocheted off rock. The animals spun and stumbled over each other, throwing up arcs of blood and tissue. He watched as one doe was struck so often that her haunch snapped and her leg flapped uselessly as she went down in the fusillade. He yelled the order to cease fire, but the firing went on, and he had to yell it again, then scream it, and only then did it gradually die.

After his order to cease firing, a couple of the troopers continued, ejecting shells, running new ones home, and firing without bothering to aim. He had to move around the lip of the canyon, ordering them to stop, placing his hands on their shoulders to draw them out of near trances.

There were seven antelope in all. All were dead or dying. He had thought when this began that they might take two, but instead they had annihilated the herd. The patrol climbed down into the canyon to haul them out. He moved from animal to animal, looking into the calm, glassy eyes of those still alive but moving, like so much freight, into death. Two continued to struggle, including the big buck. He was penetrated by half a dozen arrows, and .50-caliber slugs had torn great chunks from his flesh and had left his front leg hanging by the strings of his tendons. Another, a doe, its spine shattered, twisted on the ground, lashing at the air with her delicate forehooves. These he dispatched with his side arm.

The air was full of the smell of blood, and the rocks were slippery with it. It was disagreeable business, slaughter. No one could dispute the improvement in weaponry over the years. Still, the loading of primed cartridges directly into the breach of the rifle allowed for a rate of fire that itself allowed for the worst in a man — fear and rage — to come to the fore and suppressed the best of him — the ability to reason and to consider his actions. It occurred to him that the fall of the muzzle loader was also the fall of a wiser, more considered soldier.

There were moments in command, and they were mercifully few, when the command to open fire took on a life of its own, like a horse beyond the reach of control. Men who had been trained to operate as a unit did so, but they became a unit under the command not of him, but some power no one knew but all recognized. The storm had to be ridden out until it passed and command could be reestablished.

He took command now, over troopers who had returned to the order and patterns to which they had been trained. While three of the troopers went back to fetch the horses, the others began setting up camp, gathering wood and rocks for fire, filling canteens in the stream above the small pool gone murky with blood.

The Apaches set to work cleaning the kill, opening up the antelope and drawing their entrails into steaming piles. When the animals were cleaned, they stacked them like so much cordwood and covered them with leaves and branches to keep off the animals and insects that were already gathering. One small doe they kept out and skinned, waiting for the fires. Two others they lashed upside down in trees just inside the mouth of the canyon for the Chiricahua, whose range this was and who, from somewhere, had watched as they slaughtered the herd. The Chiricahua had, no doubt, counted on the herd to supply them with occasional meat for a long time yet. He had no doubt that they held considerable anger now, and that the two carcasses would be small consolation for the loss they had endured.

He ordered them to make camp. He had set off with the full intent of riding into the dark in order to return to camp that evening. And though he himself did not relish another night in the field, sleeping on dirt and rock, the men needed some time to recover themselves. In the morning they would resume the march, calmer, rested, and back to operating as a unit.

The patrol gathered around the fire where chunks of antelope sputtered, crackled, and sent up sweet smoke. They sat to clean their weapons and refill cartridge boxes, carefully wiping down the copper casings that wanted to turn green and corrode, further softening the metal and increasing the possibilities of jamming the receivers of the carbines and rendering them useless.

Foster and Exeter were assigned the first watch, which called for special attention to the horses, which were no more accustomed to the sudden eruption of gunfire than were the soldiers. They pastured in the canyon wild-eyed and skittish from the fusillade and the smell of blood still in the air.

PRIVATE NED THORNE

Dear Thad,

As we ride back to the camp I cannot help looking at my hands, the very hands that held yours when we were boys, the hands that caressed our mother as she put us to bed at night, and think how awfully they have changed. Though no one else would see the difference, except for an occasional scratch and callus, to me they are the hands of someone I never met and never wished to. When, I wonder, did these hands draw the duty of opening the doors of death? These hands that measured beans and flour and cloth in our father's store, that took money and gave back the change, now move the living into death as if that had been their purpose all along.

I would extend my hand to you and ask you to take it, if that were possible, in the hope that the touch of your hand again would return mine to me. I would not be a killer. No one knows the pain of that until he himself becomes one. At what point, I wonder, did my hands draw that onerous duty, and when shall I be relieved of it?

He did his best to ignore the throbbing of his head. He did his best to not look at his shadow on the ground, the ends of his shirt bobbing ridiculously over his head as they rode. He did his best to ignore the constant grumbling of Brickner. He did his best, but accomplished none of it.

"It's going to be near an extra day of riding," said Brickner. "That little adventure in the canyon is just an extra day of riding, for a mess of meat that is going to be gone bad before we can even get it salted and smoked. And the Chiricahua are going to be plenty displeased at that little show of firepower we put on back there. And our good friend Wortham here is smelling none the sweeter for the extra time."

"Hush," he said, sounding far too much like his own mother.

"What? Hush? Hush, Marybelle? Boy, don't you ever tell me to hush. There are things that must be said, and I, by God, will say them. The Army has taken most of what was ever mine. What I have left is what I see and say, and neither the Army nor you is going to stop me. You best not try."

"I am tired and my head hurts. Leave me in peace."

"Peace? You want peace? You chose a hell of a place to try to find it. Peace is not what the Army manufactures, though they're loud in the boast that they do. Marybelle, how many mistakes do you plan to make? Are you bucking for officer? You're so far advanced in foolishness that you've got captain in clear sight. I would be damned worried that I wasn't just about to catch up to him if I were you."

"Leave me be."

"Fear that, Marybelle. Fear that I will leave you alone. That I'll leave you to the United States Army to do whatever they will with you. Fear whatever the Army will do on its own. Fear that, Marybelle, and especially fear what this Army under this command will do. Tell them to leave you be and see if maybe they will."

They came out of the mountains late, under the light of a full moon that had risen in front of them like a beacon. They came the last miles down the banks and into the bed of the river, the shod hooves of their mounts clanging on the stones and splashing up the thin pools of water that comprised most of the river. They were nearly in sight of the camp when they came across the vedette, who had most likely been off drinking or sleeping or both.

They rode into a dream. They came into a camp that was blazing with light and music. After they were challenged by the lone vedette, they rode into the camp and across the parade ground with no contact with another soldier. The captain led them to the stables and then gave the order to dismount and to unsaddle and bed the animals. A hundred yards from the stables, the bakery was awash with light that poured from the holes in the mud walls that stood for windows and from the roof that now covered half of the building.

Dismounted, they stood at their horses and stared. Perhaps it was a dream, a common dream of light and music, and everywhere, the smell of bread.

Captain Robert Franklin

He stepped into a whirlpool of light and music. Troopers laughed and danced in front of him, swinging in wide, drunken circles as the throbbing scratch of accordion, fiddle, and flute formed a kind of dyspeptic music.

It seemed as if every lamp in the camp had been pressed into the service of the bakery. Along the floor and on the crude tables, candles flared and wilted. The blaze of lamps along every wall sent long, black shadows bending and scraping the wall and floor. Thin towers of black oil smoke rose toward the rafters.

At the far end of the bakery, Putnam worked his squeeze box, bending from the waist as he pumped the bellows, an overgrown marionette bouncing and stretching in time to "The Blue Tail Fly," which seemed to grow in volume and intensity as the sweat gathered and splashed from his head and body to the wall behind him. Pack and Hermann, fiddle and flute, struggled to keep up with him, and the song became a strange distortion of itself as the troops were pushed and pulled spasmodically by the sounds of instruments that seemed to be struggling against one another.

Half of the troopers wore their scarves knotted at their biceps, a traditional sign that designated them "ladies" for the night, or for that particular song. Some few had gone beyond the traditional and danced with scarves, or worse, mops, on their heads. Bottles were being passed liberally as they danced, clapped, and sang.

Everywhere, there was bread. On crude tables, planks fitted to sawhorses pushed against the wall, there were round loaves, both whole and torn, and sometimes just the grainy reminder of what had been a loaf. Troopers tossed loaves of the stuff over the heads of the dancers, and great white chunks of it were being waved about and stuffed into mouths. Its sweet perfume was everywhere in the room.

He was aware that more of the patrol, having unsaddled their mounts and left them to cool in the corrals, had come up behind him. He put out his arms to hold them back like a parent shielding his children from the sight of tragedy or scandal. They strained against him, caught by the music and the smell of fresh, warm bread that overpowered even the smell of sweat that rose from the middle of the room.

"Ladies!" someone shouted. "We have new ladies." The music kept on as the musicians continued dismembering the song, but much of the dancing stopped as troopers cheered and encouraged the new arrivals.

"Bobby." Tony appeared from the center of the swirling mass. He was relieved to see that Tony wore neither mop nor scarf. But his hair was pulled back and caught with yarn like a girl's. His spectacles sat far down on his nose. "Bobby. Come, Bobby. We have bread."

"What?" was the only question he was able to frame.

"I called the recreation for the evening. They need it. They are weary and bored with the constant construction. And we have bread, not old, weeviled hardtack, but bread, good, fresh, wonderful *bread*. It's a time for celebration." He was aware that Tony spoke too quickly, flush with excitement and, he smelled now, drink. Tony held up a large chuck of bread, the crust light and tan, the inside a swelling, pillowy white.

"The bakery is ready, Bobby. We have bread!"

He could not and did not judge why this drove him to near fury. It was no more than any other exercise in recreation he had called and participated in hundreds of times himself. Perhaps, had he been the one left at camp, he would have done the same to celebrate the completion of the bakery. But he continued to stare at Tony, hoping his glare would cause Tony to ignite, burn, and consume himself on the very spot he stood. "Bread? We have bread? We have one dead and one near to it." He caught the gross exaggeration of the boy's condition, but he could not help himself from uttering it. "That's what we have. But fresh bread takes all sting from death. That we all know."

"Dead? Who is dead?"

"We were attacked. There is no choice now but to go after them."

"No. Bobby, no. Not yet."

"Voice your concerns to Private Wortham, not to me. You'll find him sewn into his blanket."

"This is dreadful," Tony said, his voice low with disbelief.

"Indeed." He spun on his heel and turned, not bothering to issue further orders to the troops who stood behind him. When a couple of them followed, he stopped and turned again. "At your ease. You are dismissed. Entertain yourselves as you see fit, but, for God's sake, get Wortham from his horse and under shelter. If you do not honor the mission or yourselves, honor the dead."

PRIVATE NED THORNE

He watched the scene in disbelief. He had
seen the captain utter cross words before.
He was, after all, a prickly man, easily
angered. But the fury he saw in the captain's
eyes frightened him. The captain was an
impressive man, his jaw square under stiff,
waxed mustaches. And his eyes, squinting
now, were pale blue and cold with fury. He
had seen such only a few times before —
once in the eyes of his father at the beginning of the troubles — and he saw, as he
had seen before, that the tissue that separated civilization from barbarity was thin
and easily torn. He had thought to follow
the captain to see to what needs he might
have, but thought better of it, and, dismissed, stayed were he was, glad to see the
distance between himself and the captain
grow.

They stood then, in the still-unfinished
bakery. The music had stopped, and the

men who had given themselves over to it stood idly now, as if suddenly aware of the strangeness of their own situation. It was as though they had stumbled into an occurrence of great indelicacy and were doubly embarrassed to find themselves a part of it.

The lieutenant picked out a couple of troopers and ordered them to see to the remains of Wortham. "This is an entertainment. Those of you who find it inappropriate in the light of our recent loss should excuse yourselves. For the rest of you, there is, I think, no harm in continuing what had been a well-deserved celebration of your labors. The captain has ordered you to entertain yourselves as you see fit. What you choose is a matter between yourself and your own conscience and beliefs." He turned and nodded to Putnam, who bowed at the waist and began to squeeze out something that, with some imagination, could be taken for "Old Dan Tucker." Pack and then Hermann joined in and limped along behind Putnam.

The soldiers stood for a bit, then with a shout, a group in the middle of the building began to wave their hats and stamp to the music in a rough approximation of a dance. Soon, all around him, bodies began to reel and twirl to the tune. The lieutenant watched for a moment, then turned to go. Ned followed.

"No," the lieutenant said. "You stay here. The evening is yours. It looks like you have earned it. Your services will not be required until the morning. There are somewhere here a few bottles of a quite passable whisky, probably better than what you are used to. But be moderate, for your services will be required in the morning. In the meantime, enjoy yourself as best you can. Let me see your wound before I retire." He took the bandage from Ned's head and ran his fingers over the swollen and jagged injury. "Ah," he said. "The captain has the delicate hands and skills of a smithy, as, I fear, do I." He ran his finger down the clumsy stitching he had done on the boy's face. "But this scar will be well covered by hair soon enough. Let me tend to it in the morning so that infection does not set in. In the meantime, I think you can forgo your headgear. It does not favor you." He handed him the blood-crusted bandage of torn undershirt, then turned and left.

He made his way through the throng of dancing, clapping soldiers to the makeshift table set up against the wall, where there were still small, whole loaves of bread. He took a loaf in his hand and felt the heft of it, the rough dry finish of the crust. It smelled wonderful, and he was reminded of Christmas many years before. Thad, who he missed more than all of the others — his mother, his father, his sweetheart Edith — had come to his bed in the morning, when it was just beginning to turn light. Thad had been on a mission of stealth and had come back to where Ned slept, holding a round package of thick red paper. "Ned, Ned, wake up. See what we have got."

He sat up in his bed, more asleep than awake, and took the package from Thad. It fit in his hand with a good heft, like a fine ball. He brought his nose down to it, and inhaled the wonderful scent, sweet and pungent, that lurked behind the drier, slightly dusty odor of the paper. He knew what it was, and his hand trembled slightly as he held it.

"Oranges, Ned. Four of them. Two for us each."

"Come. Be my lady."

"I beg your pardon?"

"Take up the scarf. Be my lady. Let me dance with the finest partner to be had in this camp. It's a poor excuse for music we have in Putnam, but there is no sense in compounding the misery by not dancing.

Come. Dance. Let's enjoy the opportunities we are given." It was Bliss, a corporal with some time served. Ned knew him by sight, but could not recollect ever exchanging a word with him. Bliss was a tall, gangly soldier, clean shaven, with thinning hair. He smiled brightly at Ned.

"No. No. I don't think so."

"Come. Take up the scarf and bottle. You will feel the joy soon enough. The Army life provides precious little respite. Never overlook an opportunity." Bliss quickly knotted a scarf around Ned's biceps, grabbed him by the hand, and pulled him toward the center of the building.

"I don't dance. I'm not a lady."

"For tonight. Tonight only. You will be the lady, or I shall be. It is of no concern. We shall enjoy ourselves while we can. Tomorrow we're back to duty, back to sweat and leather. Everyone can dance if only he will." Bliss stepped hard to the sound of the music and pulled Ned with him. And Ned did something that might have been mistaken for dancing, but was more a stumble to music as he was dragged by the strong arms of Bliss.

Around them soldiers were spinning and whirling, alone and partnered. Several had begun to caper in the very center of the building, stamping their feet and clapping as others of the men cheered them on. Bliss and Ned stopped their rhythmic lurching to clap as Hermann cut caper, dancing on one leg, while he swung the other in ways that suggested his bones were jointed differently from those of the others. He put on an extravaganza of stepping and jumping, twisting and contorting as all others gave over to cheering.

When the song came to an end, the ragtag band mounted an assault on "Buffalo Gals," and Ned was back dancing with Bliss. A jug of raw whisky made its way to him, and he drank long and hard and passed it to Bliss, who passed it back after he had drunk. "Damn the Army life," someone yelled out, and Bliss yelled back, "But bless those who live it." Soon they were shouting the phrases back and forth, more or less in time with the wheezing of Putnam's squeeze box.

He was, he was surprised to find, having a good time. To be a lady for the moments of dancing he found did not discomfit him in the least. And though he thought of dancing as an activity of care and social skill, here it was as though they were Hottentots, throwing their bodies into the fire of the music until they were consumed with it.

He had, just the day before, killed a man.

He had come more than a thousand miles just to see one of the noble Indians of the fearsome Apache people, and on finding one, had promptly killed him. But that and his other misdeeds, which on some days he thought might devour him, seemed far past, part not of his, but someone else's, life. He was getting gloriously and freely drunk and understood that life was to be lived as best one could and the errors and misjudgments of any man should best be forgotten as though they had never existed.

When a bottle of whisky made its way to him, he took it eagerly. He had been given new life by the whisky and the music, and he wanted to give himself over entirely to it, to live only in this new life and to never again think on or be bothered by that other life that had turned out so horribly different than he had ever imagined it could.

"Are you having a good time, then?" Bliss asked.

"To be sure," he said, speaking each word deliberately.

"That's the boy, then," Bliss said. "If you're going to live the Army life, you're going to need to learn to take your pleasures where you find them, to drink deep of them. The moment is for you to use, for you might not like what the next one brings." Bliss's strong hand gripped Ned's shoulder, pulling him toward him, then, with a laugh, pushed him away. Ned took another big drink and laughed along with Bliss.

"I think I could learn to like the Army life, after all, given the time," Ned said.

"Then you, sir, are a great fool, not unlike the rest of the fools you see before you." Both Ned and Bliss exploded in laughter, in recognition of the fact that they were both great fools. "Here," Bliss said. "Eat some bread. You've been having a good tussle with that bottle. In the end, the bottle always wins."

He took a great chunk of bread that Bliss offered and stuffed it in his mouth. The taste was familiar and wonderful, but his mouth was dry, and he found chewing difficult and swallowing nearly impossible. He took more whisky, but it did not improve the condition.

Bliss was holding him up now, an arm around his back, his hand under Ned's arm. He leaned back into Bliss, still bravely chewing on the dry bread. "Thank you," he said. "You're a good friend."

"You bet," Bliss said. "That's what I am. A good friend. And I think perhaps your time for dancing is through. What do you say you take to quarters for the evening, leave the dancing for the more able-bodied?"

"No. Dance."

"I'm not sure you're up for it, my boy." Bliss let him go and Ned took a step, stumbled, and fell heavily into a couple of privates who were dancing. They laughed as he slid to the floor, and Ned laughed, too.

"Come then," Bliss said. "It's time for bed."

Ned was still laughing when Bliss hauled him upright, took Ned's arm over his shoulder, and began the laborious walk-drag of the sober and drunk out of the bakery and into the cold air of the evening.

"Thank you."

"There's no thanks necessary," Bliss said, throwing his arm over Ned's shoulder. "You've had a rough go at it this trip."

"I killed an Indian."

"I heard that. You're quite the marksman."

"I killed him. He's dead."

"That often happens when you shoot them."

"How do I end up killing everyone?"

"Not everyone. An Indian. An Apache. Trying to kill you and the others."

"No. Everyone. Everyone I get close to. You better get away. I could kill you, too."

"Not likely. I guess you think you make a

fist of killing people, but I don't think you're all that swell. You're a boy. Nice looking, too. You have to free your thoughts from that killing business. You're a nice boy."

"You think I'm a nice boy?"

"I think you're nice. I think you're a good boy who finds himself in rough circumstances." Bliss brought his hand up from Ned's shoulder to his head and brushed Ned's hair gently with his fingers.

"I'm a killer."

"It's the Army. It's the occupation."

"No. I'm a killer. I kill people. I'm death's best friend."

"No. No, you're not. You're a boy, like we all was. You're just a good boy. Killing's a hard thing, but it will come easier with time. You're a soldier now, and killing is what soldiers do." He pulled Ned more tightly to him. "Before this, what did you kill? A rabbit? A mouse? Or, no, a louse. I bet that was it. You killed an evil little bloodsucking louse. That's nothing to be ashamed of."

Suddenly angry, Ned pushed at him hard. Bliss went back a step or two, then came forward, trying to get his arms around Ned. Ned brought his elbow back across his body and into Bliss's nose, which crunched like a stepped-on snail shell. The sound of the bone breaking and the sound of Bliss's cry hit him like a wave, taking him off his feet and throwing him forward onto Bliss.

Bliss hit him once, a glancing blow against the side of Ned's head, just forward of his wound. He gave himself over to fury and had Bliss down on the ground, pummeling him with his fists. He could hear the sound of screaming, and he had to stop it. He grabbed Bliss by the neck, pulled his head forward, then slammed it into the ground. He heard the hard expulsion of Bliss's breath, but the screaming did not stop. He kept hammering Bliss's head to the ground, but he could not make the screaming stop.

He went to the ground heavily, pinned by the weight of someone's body, which he desperately tried to buck off. Hands were at him from everywhere, trying to grab his arms, then his legs. The screaming continued. He fought to get away from the hands that grabbed at him, and he fought to get back to Bliss, to smash him until the goddamn bastard son-of-a-bitch quit screaming, but more bodies piled on him. His arms were held and pulled back, and his legs were bound, then his wrists. A piece of cloth or rope or something came across his face, then into his mouth, where it was pulled tight. The screaming stopped.

■ ■ ■ ■

He awoke, prodded by another boot pushing at his ribs. His head hurt him fiercely. His mouth was dry. He thought he might be sick, and then he was. He lay on his belly, feeling sicker from the smell of his vomit.

"Get up."

He made an attempt, but his arms did not work, and his legs were not much better. He came slowly to the realization that his arms and legs were bound, his arms behind him, and that lengths of rope were wrapped tightly across his chest.

"I said, get up. Sit upright. You can manage that." It was Sergeant Stonehouse. "The captain is on his way. I want you sitting upright when he gets here. I believe he has a few things to say to you." Stonehouse gave him another small push with his boot. "You've done it this time, boy. You've really done it. Sit up. Don't make yourself worse off than you are."

He struggled his way upright, pulling his bound legs up toward his waist until he could get them under the weight of his upper body. He threw his shoulders back to bring himself upright, and each time he did, the pain and the sickness got worse, but he struggled until he was seated, kneeling.

An end of the rope that went around his chest was secured to the trunk of a pine some five feet away. He had scrambled memories of hitting and choking someone last night and understood why he had been bound.

He sensed the approach of the captain before he saw him. He tried to turn his body by scooting on his knees in the direction from which the captain came, but that only caused him to fall over, back on his side. As the steps approached, he felt someone pull up on the rope that encircled his chest and tug him to an upright position, unsteady on his feet. He came upright face to face with the captain.

"In just one week, I have seen you twice for drinking and fighting. I don't believe that's the record, but it suggests great promise for the future. If you have a future, which is doubtful."

"I am sorry, sir."

"It is well and good to apologize to me. Certainly it is my due, but Corporal Bliss may be more deserving. You've left him in a bad way. Would you like to tell me what that was all about?"

"No, sir."

"Because you won't, or you can't?"

217

"Some of both, sir."

"You will notice that, having no guard-house, we have to improvise for your punishment. Had I known the quality of the man they were sending me, I should have put building the guardhouse ahead of building the bakery. How do you go from being meritorious one day to the brink of court-martial the next? Is this a special talent of yours?"

"I don't know, sir."

"Your bonds there suggest some of the quandary in which I now find myself. You have toted the stick with no apparent effect. Our next recourse would seem to be the guardhouse, yet we have none. Further, you have caused me to press Private Birdwood back into service as the aide-de-camp, a role for which he is spectacularly unsuited. You are fully capable of fulfilling those duties when you are sober, but those times now appear to be rare. I find it difficult to put you back into a preferred role in this camp when your conduct is so unbecoming. Would you like a discharge from the Army? Is this life too strenuous for you?"

"No, sir. No. It is not. Do not dismiss me, sir."

"Are you so enamored of drink that you cannot give it up?"

"No, sir. I can give it up. I will. I have. I promise you."

The captain spit on the ground, then covered it up with the toe of his boot. "That," he said, "is the value of your word as far as I am concerned. One cannot expect honor from a boy, more than one can expect elocution from a dog. Tell me what the fight was about."

"No, sir. I cannot."

"For that you have honor? A man does something to you so exorable that you beat him to unconsciousness, do great damage to his face, perhaps blind him, and you will not say what it was that drove you to that state?"

"No, sir."

"If you will tell me, I will return you to your former duties after you have served a sufficient time enjoying the shade of this tree."

"I cannot, sir."

"Do you understand that serving as my aide-de-camp will allow you to advance to a position of honor in the service, perhaps to command, even?"

"I cannot, sir."

"Your service in the action against the Apaches proved to me that you are a young man of some potential. You have a gift. That we knew. Your skill with a weapon is considerable. But you also kept your wits about you in the mountains. To draw a bead and fire, accurately, when bullets are whizzing about you speaks to a different but related talent. Most men stumble into the job of soldier, stumble through, and then back out of it. A rare few are born to the profession. I believe you might be one of those, if only we can dispose of these bad habits you seem intent on cultivating. They are neither merits nor assets and will earn you only condemnation from the fraternity of the military. Will you put those aside with your boyish notions of honor and tell me the cause of the unpleasantness?"

"I still cannot, sir."

"My God, boy. Have you no ambition greater than the manufacture of turds for the rest of your life?"

"I could not say, sir."

Lieutenant Anthony Austin

"He is, after all, a boy. We have known that. To make a soldier of him requires considerable effort."

"It is, perhaps, an effort to which I am unwilling to commit." Bobby did not look up from his writing.

"Did he tell you what happened between himself and Bliss?"

"No. He has a boy's notion of honor that prevents him from peaching on a fellow soldier."

"That's not necessarily a bad thing. That he has some notion of honor."

"It is schoolboy honor, nothing more."

"Honor is learned, and it must begin somewhere. You might see this as the foundation on which something more grand might be built."

"I see it as a pain in my backside, and I have ample sufficiency of that without playing nurse to a boy."

"A boy, as once you were, as once I was. You cannot create a man without beginning with a boy. Someone once took the trouble with you and with me, and with every other boy who grew to be a man of some strength and honor. This is a boy with much to recommend him."

"Indeed." The captain gave Tony a hard look.

"I meant he is bright, and we have seen he has breeding and some sense of himself, and he has talents that have great value to us. If we don't take the trouble with him, who is going to?"

"The Army sends me men, and with those men I accomplish the missions that the Army requires. They do not send me boys and require me to build them into men."

"Except that this time they have, whether in error or not. It does no one any good to send him packing into who knows what kind of future."

"I don't intend to send him packing, not this time at least."

"Then what is your thinking?"

"Brickner. I'm going to give him to Brickner. Let him deal with the wrong ends of the mules for a while. Let him see what life holds in store if he does not bother himself to make a better go of it."

"Brickner? Brickner, Bobby? You're going to give him to Brickner? You would do better by him, us, and the rest of the world to assemble a firing squad and be done with it. Brickner has no business with control over a boy who is bright and has a curiosity about the world that could lead him to fine things. He could be the sort that reveals and defines this part of the world."

"If he has any of the intelligence and backbone you suggest he does, he will soon come to see the error of his ways and to where it will lead him. I refuse to reward bad behavior. Duty with Brickner is the most odious on the post. It is fitting that a boy who cannot follow the rules and routines of our life should pay the penalty for such failure. He will redeem himself for his failures, or he will be sent packing. And redemption cannot be purchased on the cheap."

"The penalty will be greater for us, Bobby. Brickner will mold him into a model of himself. Do not confuse retribution for reformation. He will not leave service with Brickner a better man. You know that, and I know that you do. The price will be ultimately paid by us. It is better that we just forgive the debts and go from there."

"And so we hold what he did to Bliss at

no account?"

"Bliss is a horse's ass when he drinks. And it was only time that kept him from a beating by someone. It was little more than an accident that the boy was the one to administer it. What he did, he did because he was provoked. I am not sure how, but I am sure that he was, and I think you are, too. Bliss was taken by that sweet face, and it led him where he should not have gone. The boy needs to learn to control himself, to understand that his actions necessarily have consequence, something it takes a boy some trying times to learn. But you're going to correct his actions by sending him to one who is far worse? Good Lord, Bobby, think what you're about."

"This boy has been given great opportunities here, but he shows no regard for that at all. He seems to think that the duties of aide-de-camp are odious, because he does not know what odious duty is. A few weeks with Mr. Brickner should dispel any of those misapprehensions he has. It is precisely because I think this boy has value that I'm doing this. Do you think I relish the thought of any more time with Private Birdwood than has already passed? Do you think I'm a fool, Tony?"

"Of course not, and there is no justice in

that question."

"Do not suggest . . ."

"I do not suggest at all. I caution. In your anger at the boy, whatever its source and inspiration, do not send this boy down the wrong path. Steer him away from drink, it does not become him; make him love and fear your authority, strip the roughness from his spirit, mold him into a soldier, but do not cast him so far from us that we may not retrieve him. If you won't bother with him, put him under my command."

"He will be where I can keep my hands on him if need be," the captain said. "My hands, Tony; mine, not yours. I think I'm not the one trying to mold this boy into an image of myself, here. I am not the only one who has noticed that the boy is, indeed, pretty. He will remain under my command, as will you. And he shall redeem himself, but only if we give him the opportunity."

Private Ned
Thorne

Dear Thad,

There is no improvement, and I fear there will never be. I beat a man severely last night. Again I was given over to the darkness, and I seemed to leave myself and watch someone who looked very much like me go on a rampage as if no better than a wild Hottentot, or even, I am sorry to say, the Devil himself. I fear something deep inside of me is defective and beyond mending. What I might do to repair this defect, I do not know. I am haunted by the fear that I may never.

Pray for me and intercede if you might that I be worthy to be thought of as . . .

Your brother

If he was careful of his direction and his turns about the tree, he had an eight-foot tether. The ropes that had bound him last night had been exchanged for shackles that kept his arms in front of his body and allowed enough freedom in his arms to feed, drink, and to relieve himself. His feet were bound with hobbles meant for a horse, and though uncomfortably tight, they gave him latitude in the movement of his feet, though let loose he would have been capable of not much more than a quick, shuffling walk. The hobbles were attached to a chain that was looped around the base of the pine tree. The chain was secured by bolts, which, with some effort, he might have loosened in an attempt to escape. But there was nowhere to escape to. Except for the sake of inconvenience and embarrassment, there was no reason to keep him attached to the tree. He had seen enough of the country that surrounded him to know that he did not wish to take his chances with it on his own.

So he sat. The length of his chain allowed him to reach the deeper shade of some brush behind the tree. He had already unluckily chosen that spot for his latrine since it afforded him the most privacy, but it was also the coolest, most comfortable area within his confinement. He wished now that he had taken that spot for his water bucket and principal place of rest, relieving himself in the path of those who came to tend to him. But neither his manners nor modesty afforded him that. When he tired of sitting, he rose and walked around the tree until he had wrapped his chain completely around it, then he walked the other way until he was tired of that, and then he sat again.

He was forbidden visits from any other of the troop, which he did not consider a hardship. He had not learned to relish the company of soldiers, though he found himself missing the company of Jarbal, his bunkie. He missed his daily duties, and that was a surprise. And as much as he dreaded the anger of the captain, he was anxious to be at something again, anxious to walk more than the eight paces he was allowed by his chain. He had sat quite enough, and he assumed he had several more days to endure.

He thought of the captain and his words. Did he, indeed, have a gift? Was killing a gift? Killing could be only a curse, not a gift. Still, that the captain thought he showed some promise, whatever promise it was, was surprising and not unpleasant. He preferred the lieutenant and his science. He had liked learning about weather and how to measure it. Had he not failed in that pursuit, he thought he might be happy now, if happiness were ever possible. That he was able to do so much, so wrongly, in such a short time, amazed him. If he had a talent, it was surely the talent to make muck of everything he tried.

In the late afternoon, Birdwood brought his evening mess. They were forbidden any communication, but with a series of glances, nods, and smiles, he felt he had at least some contact with what passed as his closest friend. Birdwood sat down a plate of beans with a large chunk of bread and a cup of thick, black coffee. As he sat down the cup and plate, Birdwood maneuvered himself so his back was to the rest of the camp and reached into his shirt and produced the little blue journal.

"I can't talk to you," he said.

"But you are."

"No, I ain't. Don't you talk to me. I ain't talking. I'm just letting you know that."

Ned nodded his head.

"Do you understand that? That I ain't talking to you, because the captain, he might hang me or put me on a firing squad if I make an attempt. Do you understand?"

Ned nodded his head one more time.

"Do you understand?"

"Yes."

"Hush," Birdwood said. "I can't talk to you. Do you want to see me hanged?" Birdwood leaned toward him, his urgent words rushing out on a wave of licorice.

Ned shook his head from side to side.

"Do you? I'm asking you. It's important."

He nodded.

"Well, just damn you, then. Here, take this. I brung it from the tent. I took it from the cot where you hide it. Don't let anyone see it, or it will be the end of Jarbal Birdwood. Do you understand?"

Another nod.

"Well, hell. There just ain't no reasoning with you. Read your damn book. I'll be damned if I'm going to get myself hanged for the likes of you." He held the book in front of Ned's face, dropped it on the ground, rose, and left.

The problem, Ned saw immediately, was light. In the early afternoon, there would be an hour or less when it was sufficiently dark to provide him cover to read, but sufficiently light that he could see to do so. When there was ample light, he would be in full sight of the camp and the officers.

The journal promised respite from the tedium of sitting, rising, walking in circles, and then sitting again. But there was no privacy in which to read the journal. To be caught with it would be deep trouble indeed, and a great deal of that trouble would land on Birdwood's shoulders. He wished now that he had turned it in to the captain, claiming to have found it on the grounds somewhere that anyone might have dropped it, but he had promised Birdwood, and he could not break that promise.

The answer was his latrine. Again, he wished he had thought his earlier decision through. If he could sit in the bushes, hidden from view, he could read the little diary at his leisure. But if not, he had to sit out in plain view waiting for the light to fail sufficiently to provide cover. At best it would give him brief spans of time twice a day. To have reading material and not to be able to read was a kind of slow torture. The enforced hours of boredom became even less bearable.

He did his best to make the area inside the bushes habitable. He dug holes with his boot heels and kicked the matter he could into the holes. It clung to his boots, of course, and he carried the smell with him. The smell of his urine also bothered him, and barring a good rain, there was nothing he could do about that except accustom himself to it.

So, several times a day, for short periods of time, he would be able to retreat into the bushes, stoop, sit on his heels, and read the journal he had hidden in a bush. The position would be uncomfortable, and he would not be able to sit for long periods of time. This, he reasoned, was for the better. If he were to disappear from view for any great length of time, someone would be sent to see to him. It was better to go for short periods of time and then to resume his sitting and pacing until he could stand it no longer.

July 20. As we move more steadily forward, reluctance grows within me. The prospect of California, which once seemed as heaven to the righteous, now holds the terrors of hell to a sinner. Everything I had conceived of California was wrought in terms of my life there with Michael. In not having Michael, all has changed, and California seems a cruel and barren place, and I wish nothing to do with it. Father, whose sorrow and disappointment are not as great as mine, but are, nonetheless, real and not to be discounted, presses on, sure that even without Michael, we will find ourselves a new and better existence. I would sooner do my own self harm than to dishonor my father by rejecting what he holds so dear. I would believe him and accept his vision of a new life in California as my own, but I cannot. These plains that we cross seem endless and empty, and so, too, does my life and California.

July 22. I have asked father to tell Mr. Estes that I would listen to his proposals after all. Father, of course, refuses to hear of it. But I see now that I must stop my journey to California, for that place is buried with Michael. To look upon it is to look upon the end of all hope, of all joy, if there is any left. I cannot conceive what evil I have done to deserve such a life, but neither can I conceive of a God so willing to strew torments in the path of the righteous who follow Him.

July 29. Mr. Estes has claim to land in the southern section of the Arizona Territory, near to the Mexican border. It is a claim of nearly 800 acres of land, which he finds advantageous to the raising of cattle and horses. There is, as he describes it, water from two rivers and a variety of streams, as well as an abundance of water under the ground which can be reached with a minimum of digging. It is an agreeable bit of land, which could be made to prosper with some effort. To begin such effort, Mr. Estes assures me and Father, will require considerable sacrifice. But so, too, will the sacrifice promise great reward. Of a sudden I find the promise of success where I had thought none possible.

July 31. He is an agreeable man, Mr. Estes. He is softly spoken and polite. Like myself, he finds himself surprised by grief and unsure how to husband it. I have no great affection for him, nor do I fear him. I imagine that I could live a life with him, more agreeable than with many of the other men I witness daily. To go with him to Arizona would be to free my parents from the restraints of the plans made with Michael.

No, he thought. She cannot go with Mr. Estes. Though he seemed agreeable and polite, surely he would misuse her or simply fail to appreciate her. Mr. Estes would neither understand nor value her in the way that Ned did. He thought it was all wrong and wondered if there was a way to prevent her from taking this foolish, drastic step. He felt an unaccustomed panic in his breast, an unaccountable fear, as though she were slipping away from him.

But of course, she had taken that foolish step. It was in the southernmost part of the Arizona Territory that they had found the diary. She had been there. She had decided. His own wishes in the matter counted for nothing.

There is further the matter that California will, in my mind, forever be inhabited by Michael and the designs we had drawn for a life together. How much more attractive at this point is the opportunity to settle in a new place, remote from both memory and prospect. I have never feared either work or its attendant discomforts. In the brief moments when my poor brain is not struggling against the currents of grief and disappointments, I am reminded that having learned to love one man, I might learn to love another. I am sensing hope where there was none. Through the darkest of nights, I sense more than I see the approach of new light in the east.

He remembered to come out of the bushes and sit, book concealed, so that his long sojourns out of sight would not attract suspicion. The diary had become essential to him and gave his life shape. How well he felt he knew Mary! She knew what he knew and felt what he felt as though she were some other part of him. But she could put that terrible knowledge into words, and that was something he could never do. The voice he heard in his head was her voice, but it was his as well. Such a strange situation, to find yourself reading the thoughts of another and taking them to yourself so that they became your thoughts and the person thinking them became you!

He had concocted a plan to turn the diary over to the captain, saying he found it out by the latrine, where its presence could cast suspicion on everyone and, therefore, no one. But it became more and more dear to him, and he thought now that it would be terribly difficult to part with it. Mary, like himself, understood the great unfairness of life and the world. To lose what you cherished most in the world was to hear, in the distance, the world laughing at your plight. In that world, there was no one now more important or valuable to him than Mary.

"I still can't talk to you," Birdwood said as he set down the morning rations of bread and coffee. "So don't ask me nothing."

Ned put his hand over his mouth, partly to indicate his silence and partly to stop the smell of Birdwood's licorice, and shook his head no.

"That's probably a good idea. I don't think you're here much longer. I heard them talking a bit ago, and the captain's still plenty hot about you beating Bliss the way you done, but he's better. Him and Bliss both. And they're sending Brickner up to Bowie pretty soon, and I think you're going with him. But don't ask me nothing about it because I ain't allowed to talk to you."

Still with his hand over his mouth, Ned nodded vigorously.

"That's good. Because before, I didn't think you was understanding me very good. You're pretty smart, after all, for a book reader and all."

He drank his coffee and ate his bread. He was anxious to get back to the diary but restrained himself, not wanting to attract attention his way. He watched the troop assemble for morning roll, feeling awkward and embarrassed at his remove from the rest of the men. He saw Bliss, who fell in with the rest but looked bruised and swollen, and slow in his movements. He would need to apologize to Bliss, but he was not able to in his confinement and felt some relief at that.

While the troop marched in morning formation, he marched in a tighter and tighter circle around the tree, doing his best to move smartly within the confines of the shackles. When his tether allowed him to go no farther, he reversed direction and continued the morning march. Every part of his body hurt from the confinement, but most of all his back and legs. The movement seemed to do him good, and he promised himself he would keep at it.

August 16. Two days married and one day separated from my family and the rest of the train that proceeds to the coast of California and north from that. Though my wedding was less than what had been planned with Michael, it was a celebration well attended. An Independence Day wedding seemed so right, though both mother and father seemed as stricken as if it were a very different, more somber kind of occasion. But there was music and dancing and the eating of delicacies that had been long stowed in various wagons. And we have had surfeit of those other, more somber occasions. It is time that we put that behind us and march bravely forward.

We move steadily south. The sky remains nearly limitless in front of us. I find myself now and again confused. The sky is an infinite dome, traversed by the sun at such an angle and ferocity that it must not be seen. I mistake south for west and believe that we are still moving toward California and that other existence. Then I catch and correct myself. We are in the Territory of New Mexico, headed for Arizona. California has ceased to exist. Perhaps it never did exist. We move across a sea of grass, studded with rock and the occasional stunted, gnarled tree. Moving from tree to tree has become the object of all motion and desire.

August 19. He is a patient man, Mr. Estes. We ride together for long hours. I struggle for things to say to him, though we are man and wife, possessed of histories that must be taught and learned. Still, I find myself with little to say, and he is much the same. So often am I caught up in the battle with the past that I cannot form the least image of present or future, and he, seeming to regard that, keeps his silence as well. When a topic does present itself, I am nearly heartbroken by the alacrity with which he rises to the topic, glad to be speaking, freed from his own thoughts, which must be as forbidding and forlorn as mine own. Still, as the conversation fades, as it necessarily does, he retreats into solitude without becoming quarrelsome or petulant. We have little to connect us but death and the future.

August 22. We move farther south and farther down toward the center of earth, which is surely hell. I have learned to fear thirst. The days grow longer and more hot. We travel in the early morning and make camp in the afternoon when the sun is at its most ferocious. Each day the landscape is more stunted and burnt. We have two barrels of fifty gallons each attached to the sides of the wagon, but each day there is less. Mr. Estes counsels me not to worry, that we will have the opportunity to refill them before they are exhausted, but at the same time, he reminds me that a little thirst now can save a bigger thirst later, so thirst becomes my constant companion. I think of bathing as a luxury out of another life than the one that is mine. As I look at the rock and grass and the twisted shrubs that make up this desert, I cannot even imagine where water might be, or that it has ever been here before.

August 27. I find the responsibilities of a wife wearing but satisfying. I take some turns at the reins so that Mr. Estes may get out of the sun, and I do all the cooking as well as help to tend the oxen and Beulah, the sorrel mare, who, tied to the back of the wagon, follows us faithfully. I find some relief in sewing garments that received hard wear, but these are few. Mrs. Estes was faithful to her duties. I would wash clothes if there were water to spare for that. Those other responsibilities of the wife that are spoken of in hushed tones are not yet mine.

August 28. We came today to a stream with actual flowing water. From several miles away we observed the distant tree line that announced it, and the animals, the oxen — Faith, Endurance, Hope, and Prosperity (for so I have named them, having asked Mr. Estes their names only to be answered with a shrug and "Ox and Ox, Ox, and Ox.") — and Beulah the gentle stepped up their pace. It is a small stream that comes out of the mountains just to the west and can be easily forded. But it gives us enough water that we can refill the water barrels and know that we have enough to last us to our destination, and I washed our clothing and later myself. (Kneeling, very nearly naked in the river, I thought that Mr. Estes might be spying on me and my skin immediately contracted so that I felt I could burst out of it, but I was too embarrassed to turn to see whether it might be true. I felt like Susanna among the Elders. Mr. Estes is an elder, truly, but he is more so a gentleman.)

He had to put the book down. He saw her there, by the small stream, much like the small stream that ran past the camp. "Very nearly naked." The words were galvanic and the image of her there, kneeling by the stream, "very nearly naked," seemed seared into his brain. He had not ever seen a woman or a girl, near grown, naked. He trembled at the thought. She seemed near now, but still so very far away. He thought to see her and meet her and say her name. And she would say his as she thanked him for rescuing her, and thanked him again with a kiss, much like the one he had received from Miss Edith Woodruff, though more urgent and demanding.

September 12. I have not written in such a long time that I fear I have lost the skill. We have a house that is made of mud. Mr. Estes and the hired man Augustine, whom we encountered in the pestilent village of Lordsburg, New Mexico, dug earth, packed it to bricks, dried it, and built us a house of it. It stays tolerably cool during the day's heat. Various creatures move in and out of our house because it is no different than the very earth they have dug through to get here. Such creatures they are! Pack rats and odd desert squirrels, mice, and even rattlesnakes and scorpions, centipedes, and gila monsters regularly take their leisure in our yard and house. I have learned to step nowhere, reach nowhere, until I first look to see if the spot is currently inhabited. Of the stinging and biting creatures, though, none is so feared as the skunk, of which there are legions. They are called in these parts, by the few who live within a day's ride, "Hydrophobia Cats," for almost all carry the rabies. I keep the shotgun ready, and I do not hesitate to fire at the first moving spot of black and white I see. For the more-gruesome-looking but ultimately less-dangerous rattlesnake, I have learned to favor a shovel.

September 28. It is a miracle. Mr. Estes and Augustine have completed the most urgent tasks of living here — providing shelter for ourselves and the animals and putting in a winter garden — and have grown weary of toting water by the barrelful from the stream some 800 yards away. (I had suggested that we build at the edge of the stream so that we would ever have a constant supply of water. But Mr. Estes, who seems quite familiar with this place, though he is as new to it as I, insisted that a house next to a stream is in grave danger of being washed away during the floods that occur in the summer months. We have passed through the summer months now, and I have seen nothing of the sort.) Augustine began only several days ago digging a well some hundred yards from the house. Yesterday, they struck such an abundance of water that it came to the top of the well and continued to flow, spilling out onto the ground. The men, with some assistance from me, are busy constructing bulwarks so that the water will stay away from the house and the stables.

Mr. Estes calls this well "artesian" and says that it is infrequent, but not unheard of in this part of the country. In the evenings, we retire weary but feeling buoyed by the good fortune we have received. Indeed, it seems as if we are considerably blessed in our new location.

He felt unaccountable loss. She had abandoned the memory of Michael and taken up with Estes. He could curse her for her stupidity and willfulness. He wished he had the chance to reason with her, to let her see that to take up with Estes was to simply give up on those who, like him, would care for her and treasure her.

But, of course, Estes was dead. He had been one of the men found at the ranch and buried. And the other would have been Augustine. But she was alive. There was still the chance to reclaim her from her mistakes, and in doing that, to do likewise for himself.

He had learned to get comfortable with his confinement. He wanted to be up and about, but to sit and to read was its own small comfort.

October 2. I fear that loneliness has overtaken me and know that I am a fool to be surprised by its ferocity. It was always there, in front of me, and I chose blindness to it. Almost nothing of my old life remains to me. I have my grandmother's china, some books, my clothes, and little else. Gone is my home, my furniture, my friends, my very mother and father, and, of course, my dear Michael. What I am left with is an endless expanse of grass, spotted with rough, low trees. One can see from one jagged horizon to the next without the interruption of a single building or tree of any sufficient size. I feel that I am surrounded, as I am, by nothing. But this nothing is foreign and hostile and intends to do me grievous hurt. Each day it crowds itself closer to me as if it were intent on taking my very soul.

In the middle of the expanse are only our crude buildings of mud. To call them houses would seem to deny the existence of houses. And perhaps houses have ceased to exist. Massachusetts seems a faraway dream, as foolish as a child's dream. My attempts to make a home of our pile of mud are met with contempt from the world and the mud. How is it possible to keep a place clean when it, all of it — floor, walls, ceiling — is made from dirt? And what is worse, I have taken to eating it, as if to devour it and remove it from the earth or, even worse, to take it into my self and thus become it.

Though the practice disgusts me, I find myself scratching the very mud from the walls and quickly, before anyone can see, stuffing my fingers into my mouth and sucking down the flat, dull earth, enjoying the feel of the grit between my teeth until I realize what it is and then am caught up in revulsion. Each day, each hour, I promise myself that I will put an end to the practice but find that I cannot.

October 6. He is a good man. I repeat that and repeat that to myself, like a prayer or psalm, though the recognition of the truth of it provides little balm. He would no sooner beat me than he would one of the oxen in the corral. He is a gentle man with a grace of spirit that no one might deny. I see him fling rocks at the coyotes and javelina that are our constant visitors, but never would he pick up the shotgun and simply dispatch the creatures. He believes that we are on their land, and they have more right to it than we, though he feels no need to offer up our chickens or shoats as tribute to these mean landlords.

Still, I see him as a man driven by some dark malice that I cannot quite apprehend, but whose effects I feel daily, though he is loath to utter even one cross word to me, despite my inexperience with the duties I suddenly find mine. It is unfair and it is shameful to feel this way. But I am becoming, each day, more unfair and shameful, despite my best efforts to do otherwise.

This I blame on the country itself, its harshness and lack of grace imposing itself on all who venture to survive here. Perhaps once the skunk and the rattlesnake were creatures of delicacy and kindness, but have over long years been driven to the viciousness and depravity of their current state. Perhaps the scorpion, with its sting like fire itself, was once as harmless as the crayfish it so resembles, but has been transformed by the dry and unrelenting heat of this place.

And then so must I be transformed. I see myself in my old life in Massachusetts as a vain and frail thing, a concoction of egg white and sugar, as insubstantial as a meringue. What I was and who I thought I was were as illusory as the dreams that occupy the mind during the performance of trivial tasks. They have no substance save escape and denial of the obvious. What I am becoming, or who I truly am, frightens me more than the herds of javelina, those packs of wild pigs who consume everything in their path with their terrible sharp teeth. Perhaps I, too, will become what they are — rough versions of what was known in the worlds of civilization — all bristling hair, fearsome teeth, and a constant grunting and squealing as they quarrel with everything around them, even one another.

October 13. We were visited today by Indians. What fear their approach set up in my heart as well as those of Mr. Estes and Augustine, I cannot even begin to tell. It was as though I saw our death approaching, slowly, relentlessly, astride a string of ponies. But they meant us no harm, and indicated by means of signs and a few words of English, which soon gave way to Spanish when they discovered Augustine, for they seem quite fluent in that language.

They had brought us firewood. Just bundles of sticks, really, but hardwood — juniper — which burns hot and long and gives off a sharp but agreeable smell. In return, they asked to water their ponies at our well, a favor which was granted at no cost to us. To show them that we meant only good, or perhaps to show them and myself that I could overcome the fear that nearly paralyzed me, I offered them eight eggs I had just collected, as well as a loaf of bread I had just taken from the oven. This seemed to please them a great deal, and their stony, solemn faces were transformed by smiles and even laughter at our unexpected gifts to them.

They are not like Indians depicted in the books given to schoolchildren in America. They wear neither feathers nor beads, nor do they paint their faces. They are small men. Each of them who came today was shorter than either Mr. Estes or Augustine, but they are very pleasantly proportioned. They wear no trousers, but rather long loin clothes that reach nearly to their knees. Most of their legs are covered with long leather moccasins which feature quaint tabs at the toes. Their hair is worn long, like a woman's, but held in place by pieces of cloth, wound and tied around their foreheads. Some of them wore shirts or jackets, but most, even though temperatures are beginning to drop, rode with their muscular chests bare.

They dismounted and took their ponies to drink at the well, and I was surprised at the laughter that came from the group as they took their ease. Perhaps I should have been aware that laughter sometimes conceals or even reveals evil intent, but I was not. Rather I was cheered by the sound as if I were again hearing the laughter of boys in the schoolyards, playing games.

November 3. I do not know how long I can continue to live on a floor of dirt. There is dirt everywhere. I long to hear a footstep on a proper, civilized wooden floor. Mr. Estes has promised me that once we have sufficient monies, he will build a new house, and it shall have wooden walls and a wooden floor. But our crops are meager, barely sufficient for our own needs, and I do not think that a proper house will be built anytime soon.

November 16. One of the Apaches who brings us wood in exchange for eggs is a spritely little man known as Dezeekinee. I have no notion of how that may be spelled or if the translation of that to speech comes even close to the sound of his name. For the Apache tongue does not fit a New England mouth, and when I attempt the name, he bursts into merry laughter, so I have taken to calling him Zee, to which he responds happily.

November 20. I have insisted that we observe Thanksgiving, that we may be grateful for what we have. I have found myself lacking in that regard of late and must push myself to give thanks for what I have. I went to Tucson, though the trip took me four days. It is a full day's ride to the stage line, and there is no guarantee that the stage will stop when you arrive there, for if it is full, it continues its journey, but to ride so far as Willcox will make the trip even longer. It was my good fortune that we waited a short time, not two hours, and the coach did stop and take me aboard. It is then another ten hours to Tucson, but that was time easily spent, for in the coach was another woman, a Mrs. Starr who resides in St. Louis and was traveling to Tucson to visit her sister.

What a joy to have another of your own sex to converse with, even if much (not just much but too much) was of her family and their doings and accomplishments. But I have been too long in the sole company of men who seem to wake each morning with a renewed desire to conquer the landscape around them. No matter that they are kind and good men, each is a little Napoleon, attempting to dominate a little world, exultant with each small victory, destroyed and whining like little boys at each setback. And it is my role, no, my duty to support and comfort them, for Augustine is nearly so bad as Mr. Estes in this regard.

Mrs. Starr was, I suppose, exulting in her own victory, raising a daughter soon to be married to a man of prospects (how that did send shivers through me). But we met as comrades, and there was much in her talk of the world I have left behind and longed for, and even as she wrote out for me a recipe for "a most glorious apple pie," I was delighted to have it and to have this small reminder of a world where simple pleasures take precedence over the continual labor to exert one's influence on a broad and hostile world. I did not even bother to tell her that there was nowhere in that world I might find something so exotic as an apple.

In Tucson, which prides itself in its attempt to convince the world that it is a town and not a random scattering of mud hovels, I was able to acquire, along with the staples — flour, sugar, salt, baking soda, and very much tobacco — untold luxuries such as potatoes, carrots, a small, precious box of cinnamon, walnuts, raisins, and quite unbelievably for me, apples, small and hard and worm-pocked, but apples. And I bought a good-sized pullet that we will eat for Thanksgiving and spare our good laying hens.

I stayed the night in The Congress Hotel, by which I spent far more of our meager supply of money than I should have, but where I passed the night in a comfortable bed. I should report that the noise coming from the saloon on the first floor of the hotel, which was directly below my room, gave me considerable time to enjoy the luxury of the bed before I was taken by sleep.

When I returned, Mr. Estes was waiting for me in the wagon, and I found myself, if not glad to see him, at least reminded that this was a man who took my interests to heart and a man who had spent a good deal of his working day in the journey and who waited for the stagecoach for the sole purpose that I not be deposited alone in the middle of the desert for any length of time.

November 30. It was a fine Thanksgiving, and give thanks I did. Not for the pullet, which cooked up nicely, and the potatoes, carrots, and pie (which was indeed "glorious"), though I did give thanks for those, as did both Augustine and Mr. Estes, with perhaps more enthusiasm than I. But I gave thanks as well that I am here and well, and that the intensity with which I grieve the loss of my home and parents, friends and good company, and still, to this day, with an intensity that seems stitched into the fabric of my being, Michael, too often prevents me from seeing that I have life and purpose, and though this is a hard land, it has, too, its charms. There is a small plant that grows here called fillaree. One must look carefully for it, for it is tiny and grows flat to the ground. But the tiny flowers of the fillaree are delicate and beautiful with their five small, purple petals as fine as any of the large and showy blooms that offer themselves in other parts of the world. And the ocotillo, which for most of the year is a sharply spined bundle of sticks, well suited for the making of corrals and pens, puts out small green leaves, and then, of a sudden, sends out from its ends brilliant crimson flowers that can be seen from a great distance. And even the stalks of that plant that Augustine cut for fencing the chicken yard refused to acknowledge their own death and put forth flowers.

I do spend great hours counting my regrets. But I am resolved that I should leave regrets behind and give myself over to the small pleasures of this life. I would learn to be the fillaree if that I could.

December 9. There was snow last night. It was a light snow, barely more than frozen air, but it hung on the plants, especially the thorned plants, in a delicate and graceful way. It did, I admit, add to my homesickness for Massachusetts, but it also showed me something quite wonderful in this world I had not seen nor could have suspected. I hold out hopes that it should snow again at Christmas.

"Come on, Marybelle, we got to get gone directly. It's your savior, redeemer, good shepherd, and best friend, Obediah. What you doing back there in the bushes all the time, Marybelle? You got the squirts?"

The voice was expected, though not welcome. He tucked the diary into his blouse and exited the little alcove of bushes pretending to button his fly.

"I have the key to your heart here, Marybelle." Brickner held up a key suspended from a steel ring. "You've been reassigned. This is your lucky day. Luck and prosperity have made you theirs." Brickner knelt and undid the hobbles, then put the key into the shackles that held Ned's wrists. "You ain't going to jump me, injure me, and do me great harm once you're free, are you, like the dangerous convict you are?"

He felt the shackles fall open and his arm come free. It was the first time in a day he had been able to move the arm more than a few inches and the first time he had been able to move it without dragging the other with it. "I'm not going to do a damned thing."

"Well, that's where you're wrong. You and me is off to Bowie again. And you're going to be the posted guard while I handle the team. Your talent with the carbine has won your freedom in no time at all. Here's a lesson for you, boy. They don't confine those who are of value to them for long enough to create an inconvenience. That's some powerful knowledge if you choose to put it to use, which I doubt you will, you being a good Sunday school boy and all."

"But I'm the aide-de-camp."

"So it would appear, my boy. So it would appear. You seem to have caught the fancy of the quality up on the ridge, there, Marybelle. You're to guard the wagon. Your ability with the carbine has bought you out of your shackles. And the captain wants you to deliver something to the colonel. I hope it's not an order to hang you, though I suppose not. The captain has a fondness for you, Marybelle, despite your willingness to beat holy tar out of your comrades. The captain seems to find that a lacking in you, though I always thought Bliss would be of better use as a corpse. So, you've made a great success of it. You've got yourself the best job any young man could hope for in this man's Army, riding guard with me, and you've got half the camp thinking you're a raving lunatic they better not cross. I got to hand it to you, it's a better deal than I ever figured you might negotiate. And I apologize for having my doubts about you. First you take me on, which didn't succeed so very well for you, and then you damn near kill Bliss. You're a fice, Marybelle, savage as a meat ax. I would salute you, Marybelle, but it pains me to give my hand to anyone."

"So, I'm riding with you?"

"Yessir. We're off to the civilized parts to do the business of the Army. I think this will be an enterprise of some fortune for you. I have a mind to solve some problems for you, Marybelle. What was you doing back in them bushes, loping your pony?"

"No."

"It's all right if you was. Nothing wrong in that. But if you got the squirts you better let me know. I purely can't stand being hitched with someone in that particular condition."

"How long do we have in Bowie?"

"We have to pick up the mail, the supplies, and that message the captain is all in a pucker about. But I have a mind to engage in some commerce that might ease up on some of our miseries. Would you be of a mind to get back some of those instruments, Marybelle, and reduce your indenture to the Army?"

"You know I would."

"I guess I do know that, don't I? Well, I think I got a line on where they went to. They wasn't much more than curiosities, anyway. I'm figuring now we can buy them back for no more than half of what we got for them."

"I didn't get anything for them."

"That's a matter of how you eye it, Marybelle. I seem to remember you being pretty pleased with your breakfast, and more than that, you got a fast friend out of Obediah Brickner. Your main weakness, the way I see it, is that you just don't know very much, Marybelle. And I know more about the ways of the Army than any ten men. We're a powerful combination here. You're going to see to that."

"You know, Marybelle, with that chunk out of your head, you really do look like a shave-tail."

Ned reached up and touched the bare, sore spot on his scalp.

"That's right. Remember, you're a shavetail, and you got to be teamed with me if you're going to survive without making a fist of everything. You just do what I do, and you'll be all right. You do what you think you should, and you're heading for disaster."

They were just beginning the climb up the low hills that separated their camp from Camp Bowie. Brickner was urging the mules on with a series of taps at the reins and a series of grunts that sounded almost as if he were having a conversation with them. Ned sat with a .52 rimfire Sharp's on his lap, looking hard at the land in front and to either side of them, keeping an eye out for any sign of the Apaches, looking hard so that he did not have to think about how his lot had changed.

"Don't chew up your eyeballs looking for the Indians. If you can see them, they ain't intending no harm. The ones going to give you trouble you ain't never going to see unless you back trace the arrow sticking in you. Besides, them Indians, the ones everyone is so afraid of, they ain't around here no more. The captain is barking at a knot, trying to run down that bunch. All that little excursion we made the other day did was to push them a bit further south. And you keep going south, it's going to Mexico. The

Indians that is here is the one's we always got, and they been watching us for a good while. You and that rifle is nothing more than a show of respect for them."

They rode in silence then, Brickner's head nodding as he slept. Ned understood then Brickner's fondness for the job. Once underway, he needed merely to point the mules in the direction he wanted, and they, knowing the way, would follow it. And Ned was, he supposed, another of the mules, following the rest because any other way he was lost.

The approach to Bowie from the southwest was gradual and open, unlike the approach from the north they had used the last time. It was good defensive placement, he could see, with excellent lines of sight. Bowie itself seemed more grand than it had the first time he saw it, and he assumed that the change was because he had become used to so much less than this. Brickner slowed the mules, who, recognizing a place of rest with food and water, were beginning to pick up their pace, anxious to get the tedious trip over and done with.

"We're going to be here for a little bit, but we got other things to do as well. You might want to use your time here wisely. There's whores over in Sudsville. You can get your uniform clean and your prick dirty all at the same time. I recommend the approach. There's other amusements, too, if you want."

"What other amusements?"

"Whatever you want. Whisky, other rotgut, opium, and a plentitude of warm places to put your prick. Of course, you have to have people who know where to find these things. Lucky for you, you got me."

"I don't have money."

"Well, see. There you are. We're back to that again. It ain't money that's the root of all evil, it's the lack of it, and you got plenty of that. You might want to think about getting some before you lose your immortal soul to poorness. I can be prevailed upon for a loan pending completion of future business arrangements. I believe you have prospects that would augur well for a significant loan."

"Whatever it is, I'm not going to do it, and I'm not going to borrow money. Besides, I have to go see the company commander."

"My, you do have expensive tastes. Ask around and find me if you need me." Brickner fished in his pocket and extracted a small stack of coins. "Here, take this."

"I don't want that."

"Take it. Consider it ballast to keep the first good breeze from blowing you straight to hell. And find a more likely whore than an officer."

The commanding officer's quarters was a large two-story building with porches, railings, and scalloped shingles on the roof, set back away from the parade ground that anchored the camp. The parade ground, he guessed, would be visible from the upper windows of the building. It would be a handsome building, though neither imposing nor impressive, back in Hartford, but here, in the middle of the desert, it was a miracle — a wooden building, lording over the rest of the mud adobe buildings that were most of the fort. He wondered, vaguely, where they had got the lumber. There were plenty of trees in the mountains to the north and south, but that was a long way to tote lumber, and the frame of the building seemed planed and the columns that held the roof over the porches were nicely tapered. He supposed the wood had been hauled in from Tucson, or even farther. The Army, he understood, had a great deal of money and a willingness to spend it on projects that made sense only to the Army.

Inside, the building was cool and the

varnished floors were dotted with rugs, and there was paper on the walls, which were lined with the banners of several posted companies. He made his way down a dark hallway to the commander's office at the back of the building.

A soldier at a heavy cherry desk blocked his entrance to the colonel's office. He was taken aback to see that the man was a lieutenant.

"Private Ned Thorne, D Company, Camp Ramsey, here to see the colonel on orders of Captain Franklin, D Company."

"Have you an appointment? I don't see any indication that you do."

"No. No appointment. The captain told me to come here and see the colonel. I'm his aide-de-camp."

The lieutenant regarded him coldly. "Life in the field is difficult, no doubt. Do you not have a clean uniform?"

He was aware now of what he had previously only sensed with a vague dread — that this was a real Army post, and he was a poor and unkempt excuse for a real soldier, and that the lieutenant before him was a true aide-de-camp, a role at which he played only a rough approximation. "This is my clean uniform."

"You would need an appointment to see

the colonel."

"Then please make an appointment for me."

"All right, then. How would tomorrow a week be? It would give you time to get your uniform cleaned."

Both stunned and stung, he nodded and turned to go, then turned once again to face the lieutenant. "We have ridden a full day to get here. I have a letter from Captain Franklin that is urgent. This cannot wait a week. I must deliver this letter, personally, to the colonel immediately, under orders of Captain Franklin."

"There's a problem, then. For I am under orders to let no one see the colonel without an appointment. And a colonel outranks a captain, and so your orders mean nothing to me. You can deliver your letter to me to give to the colonel or take it back to your captain."

"But it's a matter most urgent."

"Then deliver it to me that I may forward it on to the colonel."

"But I'm under strict orders to deliver it personally."

"Then you do, indeed, have a problem. Take a seat and let me know when you have worked it through." He indicated one of four chairs lined up against the wall facing the lieutenant's desk.

Ned stood for a while, thinking what to do. In truth, he would have preferred to simply cry, for the problem seemed to have no solution. He thought vainly that he might just stand, letter in hand, until the colonel came out of his office, or until the lieutenant gave in and admitted him. "It's a matter of life and death," he said finally.

"Then perhaps you should work it through a little more quickly. Please, take a seat." He motioned again to the row of chairs. When Ned remained standing, the lieutenant tapped the bar on his shoulder and said, "You misinterpret. That wasn't a polite suggestion. Take a seat." And Ned sat.

So he cooled his heels. And he thought what an odd expression that was. He supposed that it had something to do with putting his feet up, though there was nowhere for him to put his feet here. But the expression made him more conscious of his hot feet in the woolen stockings he was issued in Jefferson, and he could not find any way to sit that gave any relief. He sat and shifted his position from time to time. There was some comfort, though, in sitting in a chair. He had not been in one since he left Tucson, some weeks ago. He sat mostly on the ground or on his cot, on tree stumps or rocks, and sometimes on the bench seat of the wagon or in the saddle, but he had not sat in a chair for a long time. What an odd thing that was.

Soldiers came in and out of the office, greeted the lieutenant, gave him papers or received papers from him. Things were done, he saw, with a quick efficiency, and the lieutenant was a crucial link in the chain of operations at the camp. Only occasionally did the lieutenant waste a glance toward him somewhere between mild disapproval and indifference. He, however, could not stop looking at the lieutenant, whose bearing and appearance gave credence to the idea that an aide-de-camp was, indeed, more than a charwoman, or manservant, but someone of responsibility and respectability. He felt himself elevated in the presence of the dapper lieutenant whose clean uniform, bright eyes, and well-waxed mustaches were striking. The man's hands were clean and able, moving pieces of paper from one side of his desk to the other, quickly scratching at them with a pen he dipped into a polished brass inkwell. When he rose to go into the colonel's office, which he did twice, his movements were brisk and sharp, as if he had made the artificial moves of a soldier as natural as standing or walking.

When the lieutenant rose a third time, Ned rose as well. "Excuse me, sir. If you are going to the colonel's office, perhaps you might deliver this letter from Captain Franklin. I will wait for a response."

The lieutenant stepped forward, took the letter, and turned, knocking once on the door of the colonel's office and then disappearing inside. He was inside for several minutes, and when he came out, Ned was still standing where he had been when he handed over the letter. "You will favor us," the lieutenant said, "with more sitting. Please." And so he sat and waited as more soldiers came and went from the office, as the lieutenant handled more papers and went into the colonel's twice more.

Ned wondered what Brickner was up to, then thought that it was best not to know. He was hungry and thirsty and bored, and he could not stop thinking of the discomfort of his feet. But he felt, at the same time, strangely exhilarated, as though, with a little effort, he could become what this lieutenant was, a man with purpose and with use. Since he had nowhere to look, he looked at the lieutenant and tried to memorize his movements and features so that he might emulate them later.

When a small bell to the right of the

colonel's door rang, the lieutenant put down his pen, rose, and went immediately into the office without knocking. When he emerged, he motioned to Ned to come forward. As they stepped into the office, Ned was overwhelmed with the splendor. There was a large carpet of intricate designs he thought to be Chinese or Persian. There were books along all of one wall in glassed bookcases. It could well have been the Reverend Spiller's home on Farmington in Hartford. A map nearly six feet long occupied the opposite wall, and in front of him, flanked by the United States flag and regimental banners, behind an intricately carved desk, sat the colonel, whose long hair was red though his mustaches were gray.

"Colonel," the lieutenant said. "This is Private . . ."

"Ned Thorne," he said, coming to attention and saluting.

"Thorne. Aide-de-camp of Captain Franklin, at Camp Ramsey. He has brought the letter you have before you."

The colonel raised one finger of his right hand to near his eyebrow as a means of returning a salute. He motioned to Ned to come forward as he handed the letter to the lieutenant.

"I have read the captain's letter," he said.

"You can assure him of that. And you can assure him that you delivered it to my hand, as the lieutenant's hand is mine as well. The lieutenant is preparing a response, which I shall sign, and you may return to your captain and thus carry your mission to completion."

"Thank you, sir." Ned eyed the chair beside him, thinking it probably even more comfortable than the one he had just left. The colonel did not indicate that he should sit.

"While Lieutenant Brook is preparing my reply to the captain, I need you to understand something, that you may convey it back to your captain. Listen carefully."

"Yes, sir."

"There is no reply to the captain's letter from General Crook. Do you understand? There is no reply."

"Yes, sir."

"And he must understand that that is the general's reply. The general's reply is no reply. Do you understand what I am telling you? I am conveying that message to Captain Franklin, but I want him to understand that there is no oversight or accident involved in the lack of reply. The lack of reply is his reply."

"Yes, sir."

"Now, in the matter of the ranch that was purported attacked. Do you know the location of that ranch?"

"No, sir. Only that it is east of our camp. It was discovered before I arrived, sir."

"Did Captain Franklin order you not to identify its location?"

"No, sir. I am ignorant of it, sir."

The lieutenant returned with a paper, which he placed on the colonel's desk. The colonel looked it over, signed it, and handed it back. "You will pick up my reply to Captain Franklin on your way out."

"Yes, sir." He stood, now confused as to whether he was dismissed or the target of more of the colonel's scorn.

"The door is behind you. Avail yourself of it."

He turned toward the door, then turned back and saluted. The colonel idly raised his right hand again near to his right brow.

"Sir?"

The colonel looked up, peevish now. "What is it?"

"My weather instruments, sir. When I was last here, a trunk of weather instruments was missing from our wagon — a thermometer, barometer, anemometer, hygrometer — a number of quite good instruments."

"And?"

"I thought you might know of them, sir."

"Are you suggesting that I have your weather instruments?"

"No, sir. Of course not, sir. It's just that they were missing the morning we left here, and I thought they might have turned up."

The colonel scowled. "Tell Lieutenant Brook to look into it."

"Yes, sir." He saluted again.

"The door. With more success than in your last attempt."

Back in the antechamber, the lieutenant stood by his desk, holding a letter addressed to Captain Franklin. "Give this to your captain as soon as you return."

"Yes, sir." He took the letter. "Sir, I have lost a trunk full of weather instruments — a thermometer, barometer, hygrometer, anemometer — the colonel suggested you might help me find them."

"Where would I find such things?"

"I don't know, sir. They were lost here. They were missing from our wagon. I thought that maybe they could be located. It is my mission, sir, to record the weather. They are very valuable."

"If they are valuable, you should not have let them out of your sight, should you?"

"I was sleeping, sir. I had not slept for

some time. They were packed in our wagon, and when the dawn came, I found that they were no longer there. So they must be here somewhere. I thought, perhaps, sir, you might make inquiries."

"No," the lieutenant said. "I don't make inquiries in such matters. But I can give you the name of someone who might have knowledge of your things." The lieutenant picked up his pen and scratched a name on a piece of paper. He waved it to dry the ink before handing it over to Ned.

"This says Mr. Brickner, sir."

"So it does. So it does."

"So, you spent your time with the officers, and I spent mine with the whores. We spent our time much the same, only I would think I had the more enjoyable time of it." The way back to camp seemed to him interminably long.

He took his encounter with the colonel as a personal defeat, though he realized that the defeat was not his but the captain's. That did not matter. The captain had not suffered the looks or the scorn of the colonel or his lieutenant. He supposed that the letter he had buttoned inside his blouse would displease the captain, but he believed that grown men did not suffer humiliations the way boys did, and he could not imagine that the contents of the letter, which he knew to be unfavorable to the captain, would cause not just anger, but pain and embarrassment well beyond the limits of his own.

"Marybelle," Brickner told him. "Whatever it is that got you so chawed up likely isn't worth the powder you're spending on it. One thing I know about officers is that they like to convince the world that their problems is worth a share to us all. And that ain't the likely case. Officers' problems is officers' problems. Don't go toting them. Anything you get from an officer is something he don't want for himself. And in case you haven't figured this out yet, you handle an officer by saying, 'Yes, sir. Yes, sir.' And then whatever he hands you, you drop, because it ain't yours to worry on. That's twenty-three years of life in the United States Army speaking, and I offer it to you, free of all charge. How much worrying do you think you can get for thirteen dollars a month? I never figured out why officers always think that thirteen dollars is going to buy them relief from all their cares.

"There's good times ahead of you, and I suggest to peer towards them. When we get back to camp it's going to be payday. And right after payday comes Mr. Donovan with his wagons, because pay is worthless unless you got something to spend it on."

"Who's Mr. Donovan?"

"Why, Mr. Donovan is the saint of the frontier, that being Saint Nicholas and Saint Valentine all rolled into one. Mr. Donovan is the wonders and pleasures of the known world right in camp. What he is is everything you ever wanted or needed just spread out before you, because you have just been paid by the United States of America for all the misery you've endured in the last sixty days. Mr. Donovan is the cure for whatever it is that ails you."

"My feet are what ails me."

"Oh, you're still wearing Army issue, ain't you? Woolen stockings in the middle of the desert. You go see Mr. Donovan. He'll fix you right up. Stockings made of cotton, stockings made of silk. Stockings wove from the hair of angels. Your poor feet are going to be thanking you. In the meantime, you and me are going to make a little detour here. I need you to do a favor for me. And Obediah Brickner never forgets a fellow who's done him a kindness."

He did not respond. They rode in silence for a good while, the rocking of the wagon making his eyes heavy and his mind light.

"I think, sometimes, that the life of a

cowboy is the best."

He jumped at the sound of Brickner's voice. He had come full awake, seemingly without transition from one state to another. Brickner stared straight ahead, holding the reins as though he, too, had not been sound asleep only seconds before. "It would be a better thing to associate with animals rather than human beings. Think about it. No more orders from officers. The harshest sound you'd ever hear would come from the backside of a cow. Just you and your horse. You'd probably never have to fire a gun the rest of your life. It sounds like heaven to me. Here, hold these." He handed Ned the reins, climbed over the seat, and relieved himself off the back of the swaying wagon. "How about you. You ever think about being a cowboy?"

"At home. I thought about it when I was a little boy at home."

Brickner snorted. "But not now? Now, when you're in the proper place to become one. It don't make any sense, does it?"

"What?"

"When you was a little boy, way back East, you wanted to be a cowboy. Now, when you're grown, out in the West, you ain't thinking about being a cowboy anymore. That just seems contrary, doesn't it?"

"I'm a soldier. And I'm going to be one for a long time yet."

"You ain't thinking right, Marybelle. You're a soldier because you told a lie to become one. Everyone understands that. Everyone. You could stop soldiering at any moment you choose. All you got to do is to tell the truth. You say just one true word, and you're out of the Army. Then you could be out on the range with the cattle, just like you dreamed when you was little. I ain't never had a horse, cow, or mule tell me one damned thing I didn't want to hear. You wouldn't have to get up before sunrise just to take a cow its morning coffee, and you wouldn't have to wash its pantaloons, either."

"But, then, I don't have to shovel the captain's shit, either."

Brickner snorted. "Are you thick? That's exactly what you're doing every damned day of your life, and what you're going to continue doing every damned day of your life. And I do it, too. Everything that comes out the back end of one of these mules comes out on the express orders of the captain. It would be a good life, I say, to be out here, on your own, watching over a beef or two. It would be a life for a real man."

"I guess it would."

"Hell yes, it would. It would be a real life. Free as a damned bird. The way a man was supposed to live his life, not as a slave to the damn Army, which is a slave to the politicians, who are slaves to the rich men, but sleeping under the stars, eating what he wants to eat, when he wants to eat it, taking a drink whenever he's in need of it, and never polishing another pair of boots because some officer is so proud of his own face that he has to see it in another man's shoes. A cowboy knows he's a man and a mule is a mule. A soldier ain't ever sure."

"Well, I guess that's right."

"You're damned right, I'm right. And I'm betting you'll make one hell of a cowboy. I think a young buck like you could damned well write his own ticket in a place like this."

"Do you think so? Do you really think I could get out of the Army and become a cowboy?"

"Marybelle, you stay close in with me, and that deal is done. In fact, you're going to do some cowboying today. Just so's you can see what the deal is. A *vaquero,* which is what they call them in Mexico. And Mexico is where you need to be. It's where we all need to be. All this here used to be Mexico. Everything you can see. It was great land back then. But now it's the United States of

America. And like everything else the United States of America touches, it's damned near ruined. And it ain't coming back."

"How can it be ruined? Just because the United States bought it?"

"Bought it? Took it. Ain't spit's worth of difference. If the United States can't kill someone with a twelve-pound howitzer, they'll throw money at him until he's dead. It's the way the government does business, and all that the government does is business. Look around at what's here. What ain't spoiled is what the government hasn't had the time to spoil. And you know what we are? We're the spoilers, Marybelle. You and me and the Captain and all the others. We're the spoilers, and we cost the government thirteen dollars a month to do their dirty work. They get to keep their hands clean of dirt and blood, all for thirteen dollars a month.

"No, boy. Look yonder. Way down to those last mountains there. You know what that is? That's Mexico. And Mexico is where men like you and me want to be."

He wanted to say that he was not a man like Brickner, despite the uniforms they both wore. But he thought better of it and stayed quiet.

"Marybelle, I'm going to do you a kind-ness. You, being a young man of education, would question why I would ever do you a kindness. And that's some consideration. I can't exactly say. I might have some use for your talents, though I suspect the talents that I need are not so highly developed in you. No, it's more like a man who has stepped in a hole and forgoes the amuse-ment of watching others fall into the same hole and warns them instead.

"You need to get out of this Army and this company. But the captain's got you buf-faloed into this idea of honor and what you owe the Army. God knows what the lieuten-ant has got hold of. So you ain't going to do it. You're just going to sit where you are, and you're going to let them kill you. And they will kill you. Don't doubt that. You just stick your hand up to your head and you feel that scab there, and every time you pick at it, you just think, 'This was just a warning.'

"The captain is going after those Apaches again. And he's going to take you and me with him. And he don't care if he gets his-self killed. And he damned don't care if he gets us killed, too. He's looking for some-thing he lost, and a man looking for some-thing he lost is a man who can't think straight. You ever lose something? Maybe you lost your dog once. And you go damned near nutty trying to find it? Even though it's more than likely something you don't need or you could get yourself a new one. They's God's own abundance of dogs. But, no. You go on looking for what you lost because it's yours and you think that's important. And that's what the captain's doing. He's looking for what he thinks is his and he don't give a damn for the cost of looking for it."

"What's he looking for?"

"The soldier he thinks he was. Not the soldier he was. Truth is he wasn't that good to begin with. But he thinks he was, and he thinks he got a raw shake back a few years ago. The truth is, he didn't get a raw shake. He's alive, and alive is a hell of a lot better than the shake the men who rode with him got. They ain't but a few of us alive to tell the story, and most of us tell the story different, but the story works out about the same in every telling, and that's a whole bunch of dead. You don't want to be joining them, Franklin's Ghost Riders. You get yourself enlisted into that outfit, you ain't never getting out. And you're headed straight for it."

He didn't trust Brickner. He had learned

that much, that Brickner was a liar and a cheat, a man who possessed no morals he could identify. But still, he felt something in the way Brickner spoke, a certainty he had, combined with the anger that propelled it, that made him give some credence to what Brickner might have to say. He felt, no, he knew, that it was important to hear him out.

"What are you talking about?"

"What am I talking about? What am I talking about? I'm talking about what happened up on the Pit River a few years ago. I'm talking about how our captain and our lieutenant got a lot of men killed. That's what I'm talking about. You know about Crook and the Pi-Utes? You ever hear of Infernal Caverns?"

Of course, he had not.

"This was three, almost four, years ago, up on the Pit River, not far from the Boise. It was part of General Crook's tour, only then he was Colonel Crook, the captain, he was a first lieutenant and the lieutenant, he was, well, he was a second lieutenant. Some men find their ultimate destination early. I was a sergeant major.

"That's right, a sergeant major. It was Crook who figured out that mules was better than horses for the kind of work we do, and I was a *muletero,* probably the best damned one in the Army, and suddenly along comes George Crook and my future is made. I mean, I was sitting on top of the heap. Indian fighting is not so hard as a lot of people make it out to be. We got the weapons and the numbers. They know the land, but it don't take that long to learn it. If you're not a damned fool, you can be an Indian fighter. You're holding all the damned cards.

"But Crook, he's something special. It's sort of like you. Lots of men can shoot a rifle. It's not a mysterious science. But you got a calling for it. God knows why, but you do, and Crook, he's got a calling for fighting Indians. Mules, Indian scouts, that's all Crook's doing. He done figured all that out. So we was all in the catbird seat serving under the best damned Indian fighter there ever was. We had our careers made for us. And then Franklin has to go and show he's better than everyone else. Or maybe it was the lieutenant; it's a hard thing to say. Sometimes you'll be talking to a man and understand that you're talking to his missus. It's his mouth, but the words coming out of it are hers. Sometimes it's like that with Franklin and Austin.

"There had been a big fight in September of '67. Some Pi-Utes had been picking off scouting patrols the colonel had been sending out. But he knew that they were camped in a mass of rocks between a couple of bluffs, not far from the Snake River. He thought to go in and wipe them out before we lost more men.

"It was by the Pit River, near to where California becomes Oregon. We'd been following these Pi-Utes for a while and caught up to them up there where they was meeting up with some Malheurs and the local Pit River Indians, maybe some Modocs. I never was clear on it, only that there was a bunch of them. More of them than of us, I know that for sure.

"They kept moving away from us and we kept moving forward until we backed them into the lava beds up there. It was all huge chunks of rock that looked like they had been thrown there somehow. And it made for big open areas, like caves, in between the rocks. And when we got there in the early afternoon, them lava beds was just infested with Indians."

Brickner stopped, took his clay pipe and tobacco from a bag at his feet. While he packed the pipe, then fired it, his eyes stayed focused on the horizon, looking at something Ned did not see. His round face was sweated, great rivulets of it dripping from under his cap down into his beard. He puffed hard on the pipe and his breath was a little ragged and fast.

"Crook sent in a couple of parties to flush them out of there, but they was in there real tight and soon as the soldiers made their way up to where they could get shots off, it came just a rain of bullets and arrows. And it was all rock, so every bullet that missed came off a piece of rock and got a couple of extra runs at people. And the Indians were well hidden down in there, but we were up top with the sun behind us so we stood out like ducks at a shooting gallery. A couple got killed and some more wounded, and we didn't do a great deal of harm to the Indians.

"We broke off the fight in the late afternoon and spread out a camp around the rocks so that the Indians couldn't sneak off at night. Crook's good at that, knowing what the Indians are going to do before they do it. And that night it was a hell of a storm, all lightning and thunder and rain. I was one of the ones went into the rocks to pull out the bodies of the ones killed and wounded. It was all slick treachery trying to climb over those wet rocks in the darkness.

"Come morning, Crook sent a party in to scuttle up those rocks and down into where the Indians was hid. It took them most of the morning to go forty or fifty feet through the rocks and boulders, shooting and dodging bullets as they went. But they made it and just poured in right on top of the Indians so they ended up using their carbines as clubs because they were too close to shoot, and the Indians fought them off as long as they could, and then they lit out of that place and we took it over.

"We spent the day burying the dead and tending to the wounded. There was still some Indians holed up down there and you couldn't just stick your head up and look around or some Indian or the other would favor you with an arrow or a bullet in your head. It was an ugly place, all rock covered with blood and gore. You wouldn't have wanted to look on it.

"And we got up the next morning and went out to clean up the rest of the Indians out of their little crevasses and hidey-holes and damned if the Indians we drove out yesterday hadn't come back in the night and set up shop just where they'd been the day before. It was like it had never happened except to those who got shot up. And we spent that day the same way we done the day before, scrambling over rocks and dodging an abundance of bullets and arrows, and when the day was complete, we weren't any better off than we was the night before. We had lost a couple more, and there was several of us trying to plug up bullet holes and whatnot.

"During the night, Crook spread us out all the way around the area so we had it circled. In the morning we was going to go in to where we had those Indians trapped and we was going to wipe them out. Only the next morning when we charged in there what we found was just what they left behind, a couple of women and babies and a bunch of them dead. There was some cave in there that they had just crawled out of in the middle of the night, because they knew the landscape and we didn't. They was clean gone, and Crook was jumping back and forth between being happy they was gone and mad that they got away.

"So he got up a patrol and ordered them to hunt them down and bring them to ground if they was able and to send back for reinforcements if they wasn't able to gain the upper hand. And I don't think I got to tell you who was in command of that patrol, your commander and marse and his schoolmarm.

"They had some Indian scouts, because that was Crook's signature, to make sure that when Indians was pulling foot, it was Indians leading the chase. We rode hard, pushing after those running Indians, who, like almost all Indians, can outrun an Army horse on foot. And we was getting deeper and deeper into territory that we didn't have any notion on.

"But Austin, he was in signal corps, so the deeper we went into their territory, Austin would keep posting signalers with flags at the highest point, so we had contact all the way back to Crook's camp in no time at all. Austin swore it was the best and latest thing, and Franklin, he just adored the way that boy thought on things. So we just pushed on.

"But you got to understand that Indians may be as ignorant as the dirt about the strategies and tactics of the Army, but they ain't stupid. They ain't animals. They can think. And all they done is send some Indians back and killed 'em a couple of those flaggers, and the whole plan come to nothing in a hurry. Only we don't know that at the time and we keep pushing on.

"And then, we come up on a thicket of trees and the air just comes alive with bullets and arrows, and we're stuck out there in the open, and the Indians are in the cover, and we got two dead before we can even get dismounted, and Austin has one of his flag men just beating the air something fierce to get us reinforcements, which we don't know ain't coming.

"And we waited all day, and, of course, no one's coming. And then out of his great brain, Austin extracts the grand idea a eight-year-old could have seen in about two minutes. The signal line is broken, and Crook don't know we're pinned down. And there's some rocks maybe three hundred yards to the east and Franklin orders us to make a run for it. About a third didn't make it, because those Indians had all the best real estate.

"Things got quiet at sundown. Franklin says we're going to have to do things the old-fashioned way. Someone is going to have to make a run for it back to Crook and the reinforcements. That man, of course, is Obediah Brickner, who always gets his pick of the choicest chores. Why it doesn't occur to him to send one of the Indian scouts, I haven't a notion, except he claims he didn't trust them like he trusts me. When it gets dark, and it gets real dark because there is another storm coming, I take off and head back the way I think we came.

"I rode all night, and I never found the camp. The next morning a couple of

Crook's scouts find me and lead me back to Crook, who is moving up towards Franklin's position. I had missed the camp by about ten miles to the east.

"So we make it back to where Franklin is pinned down, and Crook sends a couple of columns into the copse from different directions and after about an hour or so, most of the Indians is dead, and so are a lot of us. And when we're sorting out who's dead and who is just wounded, Crook begins to sort us out.

"Franklin is a fool for putting his trust in Austin and Austin is a fool because he reads too many books. They've got fourteen men killed and another dozen wounded in what is supposed to be a quick tidy-up from the major battle. And I'm thinking that this ain't right because Franklin and Austin made a mistake, but they're not idjits, they just made mistakes, and Crook turns on his heel and points to me and says, 'And the man you sent for help was deserting.'

"That damn near froze me. I lost my way in the dark and the coming storm, and now Crook is measuring me for a rope. Franklin is sticking up for me, but you can see that he's selling no stock to Crook, who sees this whole flapdoodle as a stain on his career. I'm looking at Franklin and Austin, and I'm thinking I never signed up to get hanged with these two.

"Later, Crook calms down and remembers that Franklin's father is some mucky-muck in Washington and that his career is headed straight for the trench if he hangs him. So he turns to me. And I'll give Franklin this. He stood up for me. He said I wasn't running, I was just lost, and you can't hang a man for getting lost. And finally Crook give in.

"The upshot is what you see. Franklin is a captain now and Austin has crawled up to first lieutenant, but they're sent so far away that Crook ain't never going to lay eyes on them again and has plenty of time to plug his ears if someone takes a notion to say their names. I'm a corporal now instead of a sergeant major, and I ain't going to ever get any higher than that no matter what I do. And the worst of it is that I'm forever hitched to the shucks what got me busted back down here. I ain't a grand fan of your captain and lieutenant, in case you missed the point of that little tale, and I would caution you to learn from my mistakes.

"You will remember that I need a favor of you. You should be agreeable now that you had your time to sleep on it."

Around them was a broad sweep of prairie,

deep in grama grass. It was an unlikely place to find a favor that needed doing. "What kind of favor?"

"A favor. Really it's a favor for a friend of mine, but you don't know him, so for you it's a favor to me, which will be repaid. Agreeably."

Under the low umbrella of a mesquite tree, two horses had been left, saddled and hobbled. "You have a preference?" Brickner asked as he pulled the mules up.

"In what?"

"In horses. We'll be needing to use these horses. They've been left for us by my friend. I prefer the roan here, but you can take him if he suits you," he said as he took the hobbles off the roan.

"What are we going to do with these horses?"

"Well, here's where the story gets good. We're going to do some cowboying. You'll get to see how you like the life. To my way of thinking, it's perfect for you. But you'll need to find that out for yourself. My friend, he's lost some beeves around here. And it being a busy time on the ranch and all, he needs some help getting them rounded up and penned where he can get at them. And since we have nothing better to do, I said that we would give him a hand.

And you could be giving me a hand getting these animals tied to the wagon here."

"We're supposed to be getting back to camp."

"We won't be going much out of our way. That's why I said I would do it. And if we are late, we wouldn't have been if this damned wagon hadn't busted down. General issue ain't worth spit these days. It's going to take us some time to get back up and running."

"There's nothing wrong with the wagon."

"It's busted, Marybelle. It's busted because I said it is. Who knows more about wagons, me or you?"

"You."

"That's right. Now you get out and come get your horse. We got two dozen beeves we have to round up. Now let's get moving while we still have time with us." With the two horses tied to the back of the wagon, they started back down the road that led to camp.

When they had gone another half hour's worth, Brickner pulled up the wagon. "Out there's the beeves. We just got to go out there and move them a bit. Then we can leave the horses here and make it on back to camp. It ain't going to be a big imposition on your time, duties, or mood as far as

I can see." Brickner handed Ned the field glass.

With the glass, he could see distant clumps of cattle grazing in the grass. Their task was to ride out to the cattle, then to herd them back past the wagon to the entrance to a box canyon not far from where they had left the wagon. When they had herded the cattle, they would close up the entrance to the canyon and head back to the camp.

"Now, you've no doubt read about cowboys swooping down on beeves, whooping and hollering and driving the beef toward the corral," Brickner said as they rode out toward the farthest of the cattle. "That ain't how it's done. This, like most other chores, takes a steady hand and some easy calm. We ain't going to drive the beef anywhere. We're going to walk it. Attend to that word. Walk it, to the entrance to the canyon. Take a big loop of that rope and just lay it across the animal's back if it starts to lag or head off the right way, just as you appreciate a gentle reminder when you stray from the path. Don't hit it, don't whoop, don't holler. Don't try to throw a lasso. That's a fool's chore. Keep your horse behind and to the side of the cattle. Keep a steady pace. It's hot out here for you, me, the horses, and the cattle. We're going to keep this as peaceful and easy as can be."

"Just who is this friend of yours?"

"You don't know him. Name's Tim Milligan, if you've a mind to look him up in the social directory. He's got a little ranch a few miles beyond those hills. We're saving him a little time and effort by rounding up these cows so he can bring them back in to the ranch. It's a small thing, but it means a good deal to him. He's a nice fellow who deserves a small break once in every great while."

"We're rustling these cows, aren't we?"

"Marybelle. Those books you read are turning your brains into mush. Too many people just waste their time on paper when they could be learning how to think and act in the real world. Of course we're not stealing these cattle. We're moving them. You'll see. From over there to right over there. Not much different. If we was rustling, I'd move them way the hell gone from here."

He did not necessarily believe Brickner and his Tim Milligan story, but it felt good to be on horseback, moving through the grass toward the cattle. He thought that maybe he looked like a cowboy, even in his Army suit. He could see his shadow perched on top of a shadow horse, and in his mind his shadow was not wearing a uniform but chaps and a sombrero that made his shadow a cowboy's shadow. He wished he could see himself the way the shadow looked, like a drawing in a book. He would need a better hat. That was important.

When they reached the farthest cattle that eyed them and moved only a little ways, suspicious of their intent but more interested in their grazing, they had counted twenty-two beeves. "Well, that ain't all, but it's a good bunch of them." Brickner scanned the area with his field glass. "I think we ought to move these into the canyon. Probably the others is close by somewheres and will follow this bunch. They ain't a bright crowd. If they see the others going someway, they'll likely join in and follow. They're like people in that way. If worse comes to worst, twenty-two out of twenty-four ain't bad."

The cattle were docile, having been moved from one place to the next most of their lives. When he and Brickner had brought themselves behind the small herd, it was largely a matter of moving forward, one on either side, gently nudging the herd forward. Brickner kept up a steady stream of chatter that may have been directed at the cows or at Ned. He couldn't be sure. But it kept the cows moving, probably out of annoyance.

They brought the cattle up the long slope of the plain and up to the entrance to the canyon, which was open to them through a gap in the trees. As he got closer, Ned could see that someone had lashed tree branches from tree to tree to form a crude fence. Some of the makeshift rails had been taken down to open up the canyon so that the cows might be brought in.

It all seemed easy enough, and that bothered him. If it was so easy to do, why did Mr. Tim Milligan need help in doing it? But as the lead steer came up the entrance of the canyon, he balked, and it became much less easy than it had seemed. The steer did not like the narrow entrance, preferring the open space and thick grass of the plain they were just leaving. The steer stopped, and the rest of the herd did, too.

"Go on. Get in there," Brickner shouted as he rode up and cracked the steer across its flank with his lariat. But the steer refused to move forward and, instead, turned and wheeled to its right.

"He's yours, boy. Get him. Don't let him turn the herd on us."

He spurred his horse and brought it toward the lead steer at something more than a canter but less than a gallop. He took a swipe at the head with his lariat, but it was in his left hand, and the motion was little more than an awkward swipe through the air that did nothing to turn the steer. He wheeled his horse hard right and took off now at a gallop. The steer, sensing the urgency of the horse, responded, picking up speed. He was surprised that an animal that size could run as fast as it did.

His horse seemed to understand what was needed here and moved outside, to the left of the steer. With his right hand he was able to lash at the steer with his lariat. The horse kept gaining on the steer so that as he lashed at it, he was turning the steer in a wide turn to the right. As they came nearly full circle, the horse, unprompted, moved to the steer's left and drove it back to the rest of the herd, where it joined up and resumed its plodding.

"Just keep them going. Head for the entrance to that canyon back there. I'm going to come up with the wagon so that we don't have to walk all the way back over here to fetch it."

His horse had settled down, understanding that the steer had also calmed and joined the herd, so they plodded, steadily, toward the box canyon.

"You looked like a real cowboy out there. You must have the call," Brickner said, bringing the wagon up on the other side of the herd.

"That was great," Ned said. "Did you see the horse? That was all the horse. He just knew what to do."

"She. That's a mare, not a gelding. I know you're not entirely clear on such matters. Now, I'm going to pull the wagon up to the entrance to the canyon. You just keep going the way you are, only move up to the front of the herd just a bit and crowd the lead beeves toward the wagon. That way, there ain't no way to go except forward and in. You got that?"

He did.

The herd moved his way a bit as Brickner pulled the wagon alongside them. But his horse refused to give ground, and the cattle settled and continued to move forward. When he had secured the wagon beside the canyon entrance, Brickner unhooked the roan from the wagon, remounted, and rode behind the cattle to keep them moving forward. The lead steer balked at the entrance to the canyon, but Ned moved forward on his mare, pushing the other cattle inward until the steer had no option except to enter. The rest followed easily.

"You done good, Marybelle. Damn good. Now over yonder you should find some fence rails. All we got to do is leave the horses inside, put up the rails to secure everything, and we're all set and on our way home. Barely a couple of minutes of time out of our way here. Everything slick as bacon grease on a knife handle."

The rails were still green, recently cut and trimmed to fit the posts he now saw had been driven into the ground at intervals across the canyon entrance. The mare watched with a kind of detached interest as they built the fence up, then went to grazing inside the canyon.

"Now we need to cover this fence with some brush and trash so it doesn't stand out like a Hebrew at a convention. Then we're done and back on our way."

He carried arms full of small branches he guessed had been stripped from the fence rails. "I guess Tim Milligan is going to be happy to see this," he said.

"Who?"

"Tim Milligan. Your friend."

"Right. Milligan. I guess he's going to be right pleased. You should be pleased, too, having done a kindness to a good man."

"Having rustled a herd of cows."

"That's an ugly word, Marybelle. Don't use it in polite company, and don't use it around me, either. We're just helping out."

301

"By rustling."

"To rustle, you got to take cows that belong to someone. These don't. These are cows that have disappeared in the middle of a business transaction. It's as if I was handing you a dollar and it slipped out of my hands and rolled down a gopher hole. The dollar's gone, but it ain't my fault and it ain't your fault, either. And it sure as hell ain't the gopher's fault. How anyone could call that gopher a thief is beyond me. Gophers is innocent creatures just the same as you or me."

"Gophers don't get hanged."

"Hanged? You worried about being hanged, Marybelle? You needn't. I wouldn't let them hang you. If I was to see that you was about to be hanged, I'd just shoot you. It's the least I could do after all the services you done me."

"Whose cows are these?"

"I guess you'd have to say that they belong to the gopher. They's gopher cows."

"There's no Tim Milligan."

"Now, that's a lie. There is certainly a Tim Milligan, and these was once his cows. He's a good, Christian fellow, and a friend of mine, though I can't rightly say he and I ever met. He's got a ranch over yonder, and he raised up these cows, but he sold them to the Army last week."

"But we stole them before he could deliver them."

"No. No, that ain't right at all. The Army is supposed to come out here and round them up and head them back to Bowie this week. Tim Milligan has already got his money, so he's done with it. But when the Army comes out here, they ain't going to find any of the cows they left out here after the sale, except maybe the two we couldn't find. So the Army's going to be out some twenty head of cattle that they already paid for. What are they going to do?

"I'll tell you what they're going to do. They're going to have to buy some more cattle. And that's where another friend of mine comes in. He's going to arrive at the camp with some twenty beeves he's looking to sell."

"You're selling the Army its own cows."

"We, Marybelle. We. You're a part of this, too. Matter of fact, it seems to me that you're the one who kept insisting that we were stealing these cows."

"I am not a cattle rustler." He turned to Brickner, who held a Sharp's rifle in the crook of his arm, pointed at him.

"Then don't keep insisting that that's what we just done. There's a cure for

303

rustlers, and it's what I got in my hand here."

"You're not going to shoot me?"

"Only if I have to. And not because I want to. Like I explained, only as a kindness. You have to listen to reason, here. The rancher that raised these beeves has been paid by the United States of America for his efforts. But the Army, being the Army, has neglected to bring them on in. Someone is going to find them and take them in to Bowie and sell them to the Army, which will pay for them, because they've lost the ones they bought. Everyone gets paid. Including you."

"I'm not taking any money."

"Yes. You are taking money." Brickner pulled a few bills, two tens and a five, from his pocket and stuffed them into the pocket of Ned's blouse. "There. You are paid for services rendered. That's twenty-five dollars. That's nearly two months' pay, which is owed you by the United States Army, which believes it can buy your life from you at the rate of thirteen dollars a month. Even you, Marybelle, are worth more than that."

"I'm not keeping this money. You lied to me. I didn't intend to steal any cows."

"Marybelle, think on this. I can, if I must, put another beating on you. Think how much pleasure you took from the last one.

304

Then think what's going to happen when we arrive back in camp, and it's plain to a blind man that you've been fighting again. How's the captain going to react to that? You don't even have to think on it, do you? Because you know he's going to drum you right out.

"You're here because of what you done back east. And you're here because you got to stay here. Boys like you don't join the Army because they want to sight wonders and take marvelous adventures. No. They join the Army because they ain't got nowhere else. You ready to face that? You ready for nowhere? It's where you're going if you cross me. It's the way of the world, Marybelle. You do something you oughtn't, and you start coming beholden of people. Now you're beholden to me. And you don't want that, but you should have thought of it before you did whatever it was you did."

"I'm not keeping the money." He took the bills from his blouse pocket and offered them back to Brickner.

"No. That's your pay for what you done. I ain't taking it back."

"Then I'm just going to throw it away."

"That's what soldiers do with money. It's your right. Do with it what you will. It makes no difference to me. I paid you for the services you rendered unto me. I got no control over what you do with it."

Ned let the bills flutter from his hand. The small swirling wind picked them up and carried them into the grass some ten yards away, then picked them up again and spun them farther away.

"Feel better, Marybelle? Come on. Get in the wagon. We got to make up some time back to the camp. You know, lots of people is born poor and stupid. And then there's others that just work their way to it. Guess which one is you."

He watched the bills flutter through the grass, and he thought of how his feet were cramped and sweating and how the sun had burned his face and neck. He sorely wanted to go get that money, tainted as it might be. And he was just about to get off his horse when Brickner dismounted and crashed through the brush, plucking bills from the ground.

"There you go, Marybelle," Brickner said, folding the bills and tucking them into his own pocket. "Now you're a cowboy. And a fool, but you was that before. Wasn't you?"

Lieutenant
Anthony Austin

He did not have to ask about the reply from George Crook. He saw it in the set of Bobby's jaw, in the way that he pulled his head back, the way a turtle does when it's threatened, pulling into itself and away from the world outside. He did not speak, except to conduct the most mundane business. How Bobby thought that Crook would react differently he could not understand, except that somehow, somewhere, Bobby believed in a destiny that defied the known and obvious.

They were here, in this last outpost of the world, because that's where George wanted them, out of his way. It was clear to him, as once it had been clear to Bobby, that given their chance and having failed it, there would not be other chances. But in time, that realization had faded from Bobby's consciousness, though he must somewhere in his mind understand it, and he had allowed himself to hope, once again, that there were other chances.

Hope was a cruel thing. Those who spoke of it so fondly and nourished it blindly as a quality of fortune, or a measure of God's love and kindness, did not see hope as it was: a failure to accept the obvious. How fortunate were the lesser beings of the world, who having no ability to grasp the obvious, lived and died oblivious, and, he supposed, happy, or at least not despondent. What had happened on the Pit was his fault, his own miscalculation, and he had looked long for a way to rectify his error, but he had found none and, finding none, had understood that rectification was an illusion.

And it was despondence that gave heft to the weight he carried. He understood, as he had been told by surgeons and physicians, that he suffered from melancholia, a condition that was neither uncommon nor untreatable among men, though it was more the province of women. And whisky, especially the finer whiskies of Kentucky and Tennessee, had a palliative effect, though only temporarily. Once that effect wore off, the darkness again abided.

He uncorked a bottle of Kentucky bourbon whisky, one of only three remaining, and set a glass on his makeshift desk, thought better of it, and drank a long pull straight from the bottle. He calculated. If he marshaled his store well, and did not go to excess (but how does one not go to excess when excess is precisely what one requires?), there was enough whisky to share with Bobby and to perhaps drag them both from their funks before Mr. Donovan's arrival in two days. If he did not share, there was ample sufficiency, but what good did it do to elevate his own mood if Bobby's remained stove in? To see one you love suffer is to suffer yourself. Suffering in moderation was its own palliative, and he resolved after one more long pull to take greater care with the whisky, so that they both could ease their days.

He walked the grounds of the encampment, headed, ultimately, to Bobby's tent, which was a mere ten yards from his own. But he thought to take the long way, circumscribing the perimeter of the camp, to let the whisky take its full effect and to make a showing of himself, knowing that he had not been much in evidence the last several days, especially since the fiasco of the bakery.

The bakery, which was now being roofed

with long slabs of split pine, filled him with what he knew to be a needless anxiety. It was his building. He had designed it from the pacing off of the dimensions, through the felling of the trees, to the actual construction. But it was tainted, as was most of the world. It was tainted by the death of Borchert and the fight that put the boy back into jeopardy of being drummed from the service, though he suspected that Bobby felt as deeply responsible for the welfare of the boy as he did and had no desire to cast the boy out and forever lose sight of him.

He gave wide berth to the corrals and mules. Though he thought to stop by and see Wanderer, for whom he had great affection, he did not out of distaste for the possibility of encountering Brickner. He assumed the world would be better without Obediah Brickner, and he knew he most certainly would. But Bobby insisted that they keep him close. He was very good with the mules, and George Crook saw the mule as essential to all of the missions in this harsh country. But the main reason, he knew, was that you never took your eye off of a rattlesnake once you had it spotted. Brickner was the sort who would use whatever he had against you, and he had a good deal on them that he could use. He was of greater utility tethered than free.

Up the rise from the corrals and bakery, men were digging in the rocky ground to lay a foundation for the officers' quarters. He looked forward a good deal to escaping his tent and having an actual room where he might set up a desk and shelves to display his specimens. He was an officer in the United States Army and, all in all, would prefer to live like one.

They had not, perhaps, done such a bad job here. The camp was becoming established, with the bakery nearly done and officers' quarters, stables, and enlisted men's barracks to follow. They had mapped a good deal of the territory around them. Well, perhaps not a "good deal." Bobby had done some of it, before he was distracted by the business of the ranch and the woman. It was too bad about the weather equipment, but the weather showed little change anyway. Cool mornings were quickly followed by hot late mornings, followed by hotter afternoons, which were, in turn, followed by cooler evenings. He was confident he could guess the temperature at any hour within a few degrees with some certainty.

And the business with the woman? It was neither their mission nor their responsibility to go in pursuit of the woman, if she even existed. The dead men at the ranch could well have been Nancys. It was not out of the question, though Bobby would certainly bristle at the suggestion, owing to his loathing for the type. But if she did exist, did not they owe her some degree of concern for her protection and safety? While it was true that the protection of the citizenry was not explicit in their orders, wasn't it implicit in the orders of every soldier who served? So while they were at some variance with their orders, they were not exactly remiss, either.

Sorting through these details, he came up short as he walked through the trees and directly into Bobby, who did what he always did in times of discomfort — he paced. "I gather the news from Bowie is not good?" he asked in a tone as neutral and emotionless as he could manage, knowing that Bobby did not receive sympathy well.

"There is no news, except a curt note from Colonel Golden requesting that we desist from inquiring in the matter and that we instead turn it over to him."

"Did the colonel forbid you to pursue the Apaches?"

"Not expressly, but his position is clear, and that is that we should concentrate our energies on maps and bakeries and the other minutia of Army life."

"That's important, too," he ventured. He wished to remind Bobby again that there might not even be such a woman, but he refrained. Bobby believed in the woman because he needed to believe in the woman, like a reformed sinner needs to believe in God.

"What isn't important?" Bobby pulled up short and took a letter from inside his blouse. "You had a letter. In the mail."

Tony took the letter, trying to ignore the context in which it was delivered. The small reminders of Bobby's light regard for his pursuits stung like bees. But like bee stings, they did not kill.

"And the boy?"

"What of the boy? He performed a simple task, and performed it simply. He did not remain chained to the tree, but neither will he walk in the sunshine of our grace. I am sorry for the boy's troubles, but they are not mine, nor, may I remind you, yours."

"Oh, I understand, Bobby. You know. I understand full well." He turned quickly and walked away, offering Bobby a prolonged look at his back. He walked with no particular direction, save away from Bobby. When he had walked far enough to be out of sight, he stopped and took the letter from inside his blouse.

The letter was from Dr. Stanhope at the Philadelphia Museum of Natural History, his dear friend and mentor, whom he had never met.

My dear Lt. Austin,

Received last week your wonderful specimen collected in the Arizona Territory. I am pleased to report that you have correctly identified it as a member of the family Calypte, a family that is known to inhabit the deserts of California, but not, until your fine specimen, the Territory of Arizona.

I am further and more greatly pleased to tell you that a preliminary examination of the specimen indicates that this is, indeed, a species not yet identified. Though this species cannot, at this time, be said to exist, I have undertaken steps to rectify that. I am today packing and shipping the specimen to the museum of Comparative Zoology at Harvard University in Boston.

There it shall be further examined, and if another example of the same species is not already found, a short article describing the species and its capture will be published. If there is no objection, the species shall, indeed, be named *Ca-*

lypte austinus, or Austin's hummingbird.

Though one must always guard against putting the cart before the horse, I am fairly confident that the studies at Harvard shall produce no identical creature. So, I would recommend that you begin the writing of the article, not to exceed 1,000 words, describing the specimen at its capture, along with any details you observed that will aid in the placement of this most marvelous discovery. You may send same to me, and I will forward it for you.

Again, I must caution both of us against getting ahead of ourselves, but it is my opinion that you have, indeed, discovered a new species, and that you are most certainly about to join the ranks of those rare individual naturalists who have discovered new species, and who will have that species carry their name through eternity. You will be granted immortality, my dear Lt., by a tiny and beautiful creature. I remain

Your friend and servant,
Orville Stanhope, PhD

He had, then, done it. He had realized his fondest dream. *Calypte austinus.* Saying the name to himself produced a current not unlike electricity through his body. He had difficulty regulating his breathing.

He would tell Bobby, but he feared that Bobby, so caught up in his own problems, would fail to understand what this meant. And to Bobby, it meant nothing. Or worse, it meant that Bobby was the failure, while he had managed to wrest success from the grasp of fate. It was not supposed to be his part in the play of their lives to be the success. That part, they had both imagined, went to Bobby, while his part was to play the role of the helpful and devoted friend and confidant. To take on that role would likely kill Bobby. He had, as he had never fully realized before now, a strength that Bobby did not. He had been able to put his past behind himself and find success in another direction, while Bobby would be forever fated to keep attempting a new version of the old failure.

So he would not tell Bobby. And he would not tell the boy, Thorne, though he thought that the boy just might understand the import of what had just happened and though the boy was the only other one here who had sufficient intelligence to appreciate what he had done.

PRIVATE NED THORNE

Rumors swirled. At breakfast they were heading out at company strength, and by evening mess they were staying put while troops from Bowie took over the mission. Still other rumors, scattered like dust in the feeble breezes, had patrols setting out on missions to the south to cut off the Indians' angle of retreat. In the meantime, they continued to fell trees and to dig the trenches and gather the stones that would form the foundation of the new officers' quarters. They ate fresh bread and complained of the heat, which kept building day upon day and threatened never to break.

He was assigned light duty, performing small tasks for the officers, preparing and serving coffee and breakfast, and straightening their quarters, which needed little straightening, though the lieutenant was more careless in his habits than the captain. And he took his turn as vedette, riding around the camp at a leisurely gait. Two things caught his attention on his rounds. Each day clouds began to appear over the ridge to the southeast, and each day the columns of the clouds rose higher than the day before. The river, too, was showing signs of change. Though there was still only the slightest stream of water to mark the river, the small pools they counted on were growing bigger. In the pool where he had fashioned his instruments, the level of the water had risen nearly an inch, and the bottle, taken back to the stick, would reach the end of its tether in only six seconds.

No rain had fallen since he had been in camp, but he reasoned that rain must be falling somewhere to the southeast, and that it must be moving toward them.

"Let it come," Birdwood said. "Old Scratch himself couldn't take this much heat without some water on the side. It spit some back in February. Don't get your hopes up. We'll be paid by the end of the week, I would guess. Take that good news, and don't go begging for more."

After evening mess, the talk turned to the coming of the paymaster, and with him, the coming of Donovan. The men sat in a circle and passed razor, scissors, and water from man to man. The soldiers paired off, having arrived at a system where each cut the other's hair, assuring an equitable cut as the man having his hair shorn would soon have the scissors in his hand.

"You figure Donovan will have his whores?"

"How could Donovan not have his whores? It would be akin to the paymaster not having Donovan. Without Donovan, what good is money? Without whores, what good is Donovan?"

"I believe I would prefer to take my pay and spend it on a liberty."

"I sure hope Donovan still has that old wall-eyed Betty."

"Just where the hell would you go for liberty in these parts?"

"If Betty ain't dead, she's still with Donovan. Can't imagine who else would actually want her."

"I'm fond of that old gal."

"Then you, my friend, are a soldier, because none but a soldier would have anything to do with that old, beat-up, splayed whore."

"Well, Tucson and Lordsburg ain't that far."

"Maybe Mayapple is afraid President Grant called Betty up to be his own personal whore."

"Why, it's over a day's ride to either place. You'd no sooner get there than you'd have to turn around and come back. And both of them's snake pits to boot."

"Or that the Lord has called her up to be one of his sweet wall-eyed angels."

"Hold on there, what you're saying. Some things ain't to be tolerated."

"Tucson is as fine a town as ever there was. Why, it's possible to be throwed out of six different saloons in one night in Tucson. And I know that's the truth because I done it. More than once."

"Well, I wouldn't send a dying cat to Lordsburg. I got my harmonica stole there once."

"If the Lord is merciful just as it's said He is, why wouldn't He want Betty for an angel? She's been a great comfort to many a soldier."

"Stole it right out of my pocket, they done."

"They ain't no scrofulous, poxed angels. I can tell you that for sure."

"Well, why the hell not?"

"Angels is perfect, far beyond the knowing of mortals like us."

"Are you saying that God wouldn't have an angel with the pox?"

"I am, indeed."

"What kind of man would steal another man's harmonica?"

"So, some little virgin girl, who ain't never done nothing wrong in her life, catches the pox, she can't be an angel?"

"And in Tucson, when they throw you out, they throw you out real gentle like, so you'll want to come back later."

"If she's a little virgin girl, how'd she get the pox?"

"She just did."

"Ain't no just did. You get the pox the way you get the pox and that ain't by being a little virgin girl. The pox is its own sign of damnation. You show up at the gates with the pox, you're turned right away at the door and sent straight to hell."

"Damn, that sounds like Tucson."

"I been to Tucson, and if heaven is anything like Tucson, I ain't going."

"You wouldn't want heaven to be like Lordsburg, would you? If it was, the heavenly host would rob you blind before you even got in the gates."

"Maybe it's just that they don't appreciate harmonica playing there. I really ain't all that fond of it myself."

"You ain't going to heaven anyways. Don't fret yourself on it."

"You be careful now, speaking for our

Lord and Savior. There are things that can't be tolerated."

"It's the trouble," Fenner said. He joined the group and sat heavily on the ground, lifted his leg, and began picking at his boot. "Churchers can't tolerate this, and then they can't tolerate that. It's an intolerable bunch if you was to ask my opinion, which, I understand, you ain't done. But it just seems to me that churching and soldiering ain't a good mix. Of course, I ain't saying I'm up on everything." He removed his boot and began unwinding a strip of linen he had wound around his foot in place of a stocking. It was a slow process, the mixture of sweat, dirt, blood, and open sores making the linen and the raw skin a single compound.

"I've never held much with the churchers," he said, pulling the last of the wrap from his toes, then carefully laying it out on a rock to dry. "Their believings don't seem so much to a soldier."

"You be careful, now. I'm a Christian man myself. I don't appreciate hearing such talk."

"Well, you see, there it is. Churching renders a man too delicate about the ears for my taste. Every little thing causes him discomfort, and so on he goes, wailing like a babe with a diaper full. Not that I don't believe a Christian man can't fight. He can kill and maim as well as the next man and has been doing such for centuries now. It's just that their believings don't offer much comfort for a soldier. All that floating around clouds and playing on harmonicas don't offer a bit of comfort."

"Lay off the harmonicas. We done solved that one. Harmonicas are out."

Fenner stopped, picked at his toe, and went on. "It seems to me that the old ones had a better way of thinking for a soldier's lot. And it's thinking we need to adopt. Wortham, for example. We say he's in Fiddler's Green with all the others that have ever died in battle. But what he's doing there, we haven't a clear idea. But the old ones, they had a good notion of things.

"They believed, the old ones, in something like heaven but better. None of this flitting around with wings and such. What soldier would ever find flitting around with wings and harmonicas a reward for what this life puts you through?"

"Stop with the damned harmonicas."

Fenner regarded his bent and blackened toes, which even in the clear air of evening raised a stench that made others move away from him.

"No, the old ones believed in the Fields of Alyssum. Fields where a warrior could go and take his ease, naked in his glory and clean as the day his mother bore him."

"Don't you be going on about naked, now. Your feet alone are more than a man can bear."

"In the Fields of Alyssum," he continued unperturbed, "a man, a warrior, mind you, has nothing to do but ease about and eat manna and drink nectar, which is like whisky but without the headaches and stomach troubles."

"What's manna?"

"If it's for soldiers, you can wager it's beans."

"It's the most wonderful thing a man ever ate. It's something so good that if a living man was to eat it, he would die at once."

"Spoiled beans."

"And you don't have to get up from where you're sitting to get the nectar and manna, either. No, sir. It's brought to you. And it's brought to you by lovely maidens, naked as God made them. And they are perfect in their skin, lovely as dawn, and no shame or foolishness about them, either."

"And do you get to poke 'em?"

"If that's what you've a mind to. Beautiful young girls. Not a mark on them. Bosoms as white as snow, small enough to fit in the palm of a man's hand, whole. And little pink teats, hard as pebbles. And between their legs, a tiny little tuft, soft as the down of a chick. That's a warrior's reward in the Fields of Alyssum."

"Just tiny little ones you say?"

"Aye. Bosoms not much more than a slight swell from their chests."

"I don't believe I'd be much in favor of that," Putnam said. "I believe I'd prefer a full-growed woman. One who's got something. Give me a construction of flesh I can grab a hold on and bury my face in. That's what I want."

Fenner looked over at Putnam. He fished out his pipe, packed and lit it. "You, sir, are a profane and disgusting man."

LIEUTENANT
ANTHONY AUSTIN

He woke from penitential dreams. All night
he risked injury and death, throwing his
sleeping self from cliffs, falling from trees
and roofs. His body took bullets and arrows
that brought agony without death. A child
in the uniform of a U.S. Army officer, he
was subjected to an unseen hand that took
him by the hair and pushed his face toward
the mess he had made of his life and career.

Fretting through these dreams, he had
broken free into wakefulness in the middle
of the night. He had been too liberal in dos-
ing himself with whisky. His happiness and
excitement over the news of his hummingbird had required modulation. Happiness was a structure made of cards. The
higher the structure, the more prone to col-
lapse. The descent from elation to despair
was precipitous and terrifying, and he would
avoid it at all costs.

Awake to no light and only the small

sounds of the wind in the trees and the slight scrape of hoof on stone as the vedette circled the camp's perimeter, he weighed his choices. To get up meant freedom from the torment dreams brought. But to remain awake, he knew, meant carrying the burden of fatigue through a long day, made longer by the presence of the paymaster and then inevitable arrival of Donovan and all that entailed.

His mind could not choose between poor alternatives, so he left it to his body. He lay on his back, in the dark, his eyes open to the blackness, listening to what might have been distant thunder. There came a time when he could not tell whether his eyes were open or closed. He felt the tiny hands of demons reaching up from within to pull him back into the cannon fire and destruction of his dreams.

Captain Robert Franklin

The morning was clear and bright, but held the promise of greater heat than yesterday. Lately, the temperatures had been on a steady rise, though they had no thermometer to record it. He stopped that thought before it took him further than he wished to go. He took coffee and bread with jam from Thorne and reminded himself to be thankful that the boy could brew coffee and carry out the several tasks he had been assigned, and to forget the boy's shortcomings and the loss of the weather implements.

It might be worth the ride, he thought, to go to Bowie and demand that the colonel investigate the theft of the instruments. If he was not going to be pursuing the woman and the Apaches who took her, he would do what it was that he was able, which was to explore this part of the Territory, and he would let the colonel know that though he was outranked, he was not outsoldiered by a brigade commander in an outpost nearly as remote as his own.

Just after 9 a.m., the paymaster and his escorts arrived in camp and immediately set up the table and books. He was pleased to see that Tony was awake and about and in his dress blues, though their maintenance was less than it should have been. The men worked at their routine duties, but just barely. Like children awaiting Saint Nicholas, they were too distracted to be of great use.

In their dress blues, he and Tony received their pay first — $300 to him, $250 to Tony. They took their money, saluted, and stepped back to let the rest of the company receive their pay, in their undress blues but with the white gloves of their dress uniforms. They reported by rank, and Sergeants Triggs and Stonehouse led them, setting the example for the rest. Triggs first approached the table the paymaster had brought in on mule back. He saluted, then bent to sign his name on the payroll. After signing, he removed his right glove and took his pay — two months' worth, forty-four dollars. After receiving his money in his bare right hand, the sergeant saluted with his left, faced left, and returned to the ranks.

For a crew that distinguished itself mainly through their inability to perform the smallest of missions with any ease, they threw themselves into payday like the finest soldiers in the army. Going up to the table, they squared off the corners of their approach, facing quickly and straight. They gave crisp salutes, declined, to the man, the Army's offer to withhold some pay for savings, payable at discharge, and marched smartly back to rank.

He felt his lips tighten and twitch toward a smile as he watched them. One could easily imagine this a real company of the Army, and oneself an officer with prospects for advancement.

He left Tony in charge of the payroll and went back to inspect the camp. The men would be given full duty today, though he knew, as the men knew, that as soon as Donovan had set up his camp they would be dismissed to begin the thirty-six-hour liberty that would culminate payday. He listened to the sawing, digging, and log splitting, the beginnings of the new officers' quarters. And like all the others, he listened behind the sawing and splitting for the sound of Donovan's wagons. What work would get done today would be inferior — shoddy and likely to need redoing.

He was moving back toward his quarters when he saw Tony coming across the just-cleared bare ground at a jog.

"There's a problem with the pay."

"What problem?"

"The boy. The new man. Thorne. He's not on the payroll."

"These things take time. It's the Army way. Nothing gets done when you expect it to. And we shouldn't expect differently."

"But he isn't getting paid."

"He will in two months' time. They'll have caught up with him, and he'll get his pay, plus back pay for this period. Fifty-two dollars. A handsome sum for a boy."

"But everyone's paid but him. He feels like an outsider and a misfit as it is. I think we should advance him some money until the next pay period."

"No. Your compassion is admirable. It always is. But the boy stays a boy unless we help him become a man. He has to withstand disappointment. It's what a man does."

"At what price? For God's sake, Bobby. It's twenty-six dollars. Or thirteen. We can just give him one month's pay."

"He hasn't even been here a month."

"But he's been in the Army for more than a month."

"Then it's the Army's problem. Don't give him money. He doesn't need it, and I don't think he's very good with it. He has attraction to the drink without the capability of managing it. We'll be doing him a favor by letting him go for a while without money to worry about. He gets his meals. He has a place to live. He doesn't need money."

"Damn it all, Bobby! Everyone needs money. You need it, I need it. And, by God, the boy needs it, too. Why are you doing this to me?"

"To you, Tony? Why am I doing what to you?"

"You know what. You're pulling rank, and you're pulling rank only because you can. Because you have appropriated the boy as aide-de-camp you think you can claim possession of him. I only want to do him a small kindness. And this a boy who needs a kindness the way a man lost in the desert — and he is such a man — needs water. Why won't you allow me that?"

"Our aide-de-camp, Tony. Our aide-de-camp. Not mine. *Ours.* And the boy is a soldier, or trying to be one. And I aim to make him one, not a lapdog, not a favorite nephew, or whatever else you have in mind, but a soldier. So shall he be."

"This is not over, Bobby. This is not over

at all." And with that, Tony turned on his heels and marched back to quarters. No, he supposed, it was not over. Tony would retreat into drink, and when he had drunk sufficiently, it would come up again, thrown in his face as proof of his inadequacies as friend, companion, and human being.

He rode across the south fork of the river, splashing up the water that had pooled there over the last few days, up a long rise to the plateau where Donovan's wagons, four of them — ancient, patched Conestogas, left over from the great exodus from the East during the first half of the century — were circled up in a small camp.

Donovan's whores were at work setting up the camp. They had tethered and tended the oxen and cleared the area encircled by the wagons of brush and weeds. Some gathered wood for the fire that would burn all night as the center of activity and as a beacon to any stray soldiers who had neglected to fall out directly to their camp. Two others, big women, stripped to the waist, their breasts bouncing and glistening with sweat, the sinews of their arms and backs popping up from beneath their skin, drove stakes for the tethering of the wagons. He thought that if pitted against his own men doing similar work, the whores would win easily. Others of the whores tended to the interiors of the wagons, preparing them for what he did not wish to speculate upon.

He moved closer to the camp, picking his way over loose stones and through the soft silt that the river had deposited some time before. Donovan worked with his whores, shirtless, an obscene and disgusting spectacle. Sweat splashed from the folds of a body that had grown now to over three hundred pounds. He moved boxes and set up stores, pausing only to wipe sweat from his spectacles on a filthy rag that hung from the waistband of his trousers, soaking up the sweat that darkened the fabric of his trousers from waist to midthigh. He saw the captain and stacked a couple of cases of canned peaches, nodded in his direction, ducked into the wagon, and came back out with a bottle. "A fine day for both business and pleasure," he said, proffering the bottle.

"I intend to buy," the captain said, nodding at the bottle Donovan held.

"Of course. No question. It's a sample that shows the quality of the goods and closes the sale. And good it is."

He reached and took the bottle, uncorked it, and smelled it. The fumes shut his eyes and choked his throat. He turned his face from it.

"Go on. Try it. It tastes better than it smells. It's the best Mexico has to offer. They are getting the hang of whisky, I think."

"I'm on duty."

"As am I. We do our jobs as best we can. Go ahead. Give that one a try."

He took a sip only, held it in his mouth, moved it from side to side across his palate, and swallowed. It was, in a word, vile. "And we should hang whoever made this. American. Please."

Donovan nodded. "There's a problem there. I don't have as much as I would like. I have only a case, and that's promised to a colonel at McDowell. He's paying bottle price for it, too."

"That's near to a hundred and twenty dollars. Almost a month's pay."

"A little more, actually. There are taxes on distilled spirits."

"Which we both know you do not pay."

"But still they exist and must be observed. Now your Mexican whisky is plentiful and quite reasonable in price. And your Mexican is not big on the taxation."

"This is outrageous."

"True enough. I expect to hear the same

from the colonel as he unties his purse. It is a hell of a thing. A man works his whole life for his country and what does it get him? He has to work an extra month just to buy himself a small sip in the evening. I sometimes think that governments are instituted among men for the pure purpose of provoking them."

"What for the Mexican?"

"It will become more agreeable in time. That is the way with spirits. Liquoring is a disagreeable practice at the outset that one convinces oneself to enjoy. The distilling of whisky does not come natural to your Mexican, but I think you'll find they are discovering the secrets. Your Kentuckian does it best, but I think we're finding your Mexican a quick study."

"The cost."

"Twenty a case. I will throw in some Mescal. Between you and me, it works wonders on the fungus of the feet. Frankly, it's fit for nothing else, save an enlisted man."

"Both. The American and the Mexican. One hundred and twenty-five for both."

Donovan gave a wan smile and shook his head. "My dear captain. I'm afraid not. One-forty for the both."

"The men could be contained to quarters tonight."

Donovan shook his head. "It would be more trouble than it is worth. To both of us. I have whisky and the lieutenant has a great need of it, and we both know he is a man of discerning tastes in all things. You must have it, and I must sell it. And the dear colonel is not here to fight for his interests, so let us make an arrangement. One-thirty for the both. A pleasant compromise, I think."

Only then did he dismount, untie the strings of his purse, and pay Donovan. "Send this over this afternoon. And if you should happen, quite unexpectedly of course, to find another case of the whisky, keep the colonel in mind. He vastly outranks a lieutenant."

Donovan took the money without counting it and nodded. "Don't fear. As it appears, it shall be. Now, what else might I interest the captain in?"

"What have you?"

"I know your interests, and I think you will like this." From the waistband of his trousers he extracted a small pistol and handed it, butt first, to the captain. "A forty-one-caliber Deringer. A real Deringer. Many are called derringers, but this is an actual Deringer, as you can see for yourself."

It was a cap-lock, the checked grip hand carved walnut, the lock engraved "Deringer/

Philadelph." It was not five inches long. It was tiny and intricate, and he liked it very much.

"It is genuine. You see that."

"Yes. Of course. How much?"

"Two hundred."

"That is outrageous."

"Yes. Of course it is. But it is rare. And I like it very much. I assign it a very dear value. If someone else assigns it greater value, it shall be his. It will not go down in price. I am very fond of it, indeed. A man might buy that at two hundred right now and then sell it sometime later for considerable profit. There are many imitations, as you know, but you are not a man who has interest in imitations, I know that."

"I am not a man who pays two hundred dollars for a gun. No matter the rarity."

"I would throw in some time with the whores if that might influence your decision."

"I am an officer of the United States Army. Have you anything else?"

Donovan shook his head. "And I am a civilian businessman. But, I'm afraid I have nothing more you would find of interest. I have a variety of weapons, ranging from the cheap to the dear, from those suitable for shooting targets to those suitable only for shooting oneself. But none are unusual. I will keep you in mind though." He took the Deringer and stuck it back in his waistband.

"Do that." The captain felt a deep disappointment in not getting the gun, but he neither needed to nor approved of spending money for the temporary pleasure spending brought. "All right, then."

"Come back anytime," Donovan said. "I will be here until tomorrow. The Deringer will not be here when I return at the next payday."

Private Ned Thorne

He stood last in line, and when the next to last in line had gone up, signed his name, took his pay, and saluted, he stood and waited for his name to be called. He stood. The paymaster shut his book and looked toward him as though he were an oddity on display at a medicine show.

And he felt like an oddity. The whole thing seemed just curious, as though he had stumbled into the wrong place, but there was no other place. "Thorne, sir," he said finally. "Thorne, Edward, Private." The paymaster continued to stare at him, but the curiosity had changed to annoyance.

"I don't have you," he said.

"No, sir," Ned replied, unsure of what else he might reply.

"You're not in the book."

"No, sir?"

"No. Goddamn it. No. Who are you?"

"Thorne, sir. Edward. Private. I came here

some days ago."

"This is simply not acceptable. Where did you come from?"

"Jefferson Barracks, sir. Missouri."

"Your papers haven't come through."

He had no response to that. He wanted to say something to the paymaster, to tell him that it was not his fault that the papers were not there, or that he was still standing here at attention after the paymaster had closed his book. "I suppose not, sir."

"How in God's name am I supposed to pay someone when the papers are somewhere between here and Missouri, certainly not here? How am I supposed to do my job under these conditions?"

"I am not getting paid, then, sir?"

"Of course you're not getting paid. I can't pay anyone without papers. You're out of the equation. It's as if they believe this is an easy job, working under these conditions, setting up in the most remote corners of the earth to make a proper ceremony of paying the troops. It's outrageous that I should have to put up with such nonsense." And with that, he took his book in one hand, his folding table in the other, and turned and stalked back to where his horse and wagon stood.

Ned stood. Again he fought the impulse to cry.

LIEUTENANT
ANTHONY AUSTIN

He had left Bobby angry yet again. It seemed that he could not have a civil conversation these days without it disintegrating into anger and recrimination. He did not know what he was going to do, except that he was not sure he could continue forward doing what they were doing. It was perhaps time to think about requesting a reposting to someplace far away where he could teach and work with the specimens he had collected. But these were the thoughts of anger, and he knew it a mistake to act on anger. Anger, however, seemed to be the only emotion he had in ample sufficiency.

He heard the thudding coming from behind him and was first startled, and then curious. He could not see the source of the noise, but it was not far from him. He walked back past the bakery and into the stand of pine the troop had been felling.

There the boy, Thorne, stood pounding on a tree with a sledgehammer, tears streaming down his face. He looked to see if the boy was pounding a wedge into the tree, but no, he was simply pounding the tree.

"I fear it will take a long time to drop the tree that way, Private." The boy stopped, startled, and brought the hammer down slowly to the ground. He continued to cry, and his face was a set mask of rage. "I hope that tree is not substituting for one of your officers."

The boy shook his head. "No. No, sir."

"But it is substituting for someone who has angered you mightily. The Army perhaps."

The boy nodded. "I guess," he said. "The Army, me, everyone, God maybe."

"Then one would say that you're not angry at anyone. You're just angry. I commend you on your choice of outlets, though. Better to pound on a tree than on one of your fellow soldiers. It is a good choice, though the lumber may be somewhat worse for the experience."

"I'm sorry, sir. My anger gets the best of me. I did not get paid today."

"So I am to understand. And your anger is justified, though you seem angry a good deal of the time, too much of the time for such a young man. Have you always been burdened with anger, or is this newly risen in you?"

"I don't know. I had some fights."

"Are you a fighter? Is that why you are here? Have you joined us because your love of fighting needs greater opportunity?"

"No, sir. I mean, I don't know, sir."

"You don't know?"

"No, sir. I do not."

"How can you not? Do you fight frequently?"

"No, sir. No, I don't."

"But in the ten or so days you have been here you have been in fights with Brickner and with Bliss. Granted that those two are obliging when fighting is proposed, but you are setting a rather remarkable precedent here."

"I don't like to fight, sir. Only . . ."

" 'Only,' what?"

"It's my temper, sir. It controls me more than I control it. I do things, sir. I do things I shouldn't do. I do things I don't want to do."

"Like beating Bliss."

The boy hung his head. "Yes. Like that."

"Tell me, please. What did Corporal Bliss do to deserve such a beating?"

"He didn't deserve it, sir. I just gave it."

345

"But what did he do? Did he become familiar?"

The boy shrugged. "No."

"No? He didn't want you to do things?"

"I don't know, sir. He didn't say."

"So why did you beat him?"

"He called me a killer, sir."

He rocked back on his heels, then sat on the ground with the boy, his left leg splayed out in front of him, his right tucked under his buttocks. "It is a very hard thing, killing. We join the Army knowing that that might become our lot. Some of us fear it. Some of us, I'm afraid, are eager for it. But when it happens, we are not prepared for it, for the enormity of it, the taking of a life that we are not sure we have the right to."

"Yes, sir."

He reached out and touched the boy's shoulder. "It was a good thing you did. It was not an easy thing, but it was good. It was your duty. You will come to understand the honor of it as you understand, even more, the enormity of it. If it were easy, it would not be honorable at all. It is the understanding of the great significance of what we do that makes soldiering an honorable profession. We kill, but we are not killers. We are soldiers, who make diverse sacrifices for honor and country. Others do not understand that, and we buy our own understanding of it at great cost. Can you begin comprehending that?"

"I suppose, sir. But . . ."

"But what?"

"It wasn't the first, sir."

"What, killing?"

"Yes, sir. I've done it before."

"What? Where? Is that why you are here?"

"Yes, sir. Back home. I killed someone back home. In Connecticut."

"Who? Tell me. What is this weight you carry all the time?"

The boy opened his mouth twice only to let nothing out. His expression did not change, though the blood visibly drained from his face. He did not look at the lieutenant but at nothing, or at something in the farthest distance. "My brother," he said. "I killed my brother."

"Your brother?"

He nodded. "Sir." Then he looked the lieutenant in the eye. "Thad, sir. My younger brother. I killed him. And Bliss called him a 'bloodsucking louse.' "

"Your brother? How? It was an accident. Surely."

"I don't know, sir."

"You killed your brother and you don't know if it was an accident?"

"Maybe it was. I can't say. I don't think I ever meant to hurt him. But, maybe, just for the briefest time, maybe I did. Maybe I wanted to kill him. I can't decide."

"Do you want to tell me?"

He sighed, and as he did, tears welled into his eyes and began the long, slow slide down the side of his nose. He shook his head.

"I think you do," he said. "I think you want to tell me. I think you need to tell me. I think you've been needing to tell someone for a long while."

The tears rolled steadily, but there was no sobbing, no ragged breathing. His breathing slowed, and he reached up and wiped at the tears with his sleeves, first one side, then the other. "He was nearly twelve," he said. "It was just over a year ago. My brother, Thad — he was almost twelve, but I just said that — asked me to help him build a tree house in the chestnut tree behind our house. He had some boards, but they weren't very good, so I asked our father if I could have some that the workmen had left when they repaired the store."

"Your father has a store."

He nodded. "Hardware and groceries. And everything. 'Edward Thorne, Dealer in Dry Goods, Groceries, Hats, Caps, Boots, Shoes, Provisions, Hardware, Crockery,

Drugs, Medicines, Paints, Oils, Perfumery, and &c.' And I worked there. After school and on weekends and summers."

"And he gave you boards."

"He gave them to me but said that I would have to earn them, working extra hours at the store, for Father believes that what is free is not valued. I agreed, though I was already working most of my free time at the store. He never suggested that Thad might work also. It was always me. Thad never had to do anything because he was the baby and was 'delicate.'

"So I took the boards, each one of them an extra hour of work that I would have to put in that month, because delay led only to neglect, said my father. And Thad and I set to work to build the tree house. I began by sawing some boards so that the house would have a firm place to sit. Thad wanted to saw the boards. And I let him, but he was so slow and so awkward that he kept cutting them crooked. And when they were too short, they would not work. And each cost me an hour of work.

"And when I went to hammer the boards to the trunk and branches of the chestnut, Thad wanted to do that, too. He wanted to do whatever it was that I did. And I know that that was because he was a little brother, but it was also because he did not want me to enjoy something that I was doing when he could be getting the enjoyment of it in my place.

"And so I let him hammer. And he was no good at that, either. He just made a fist of the whole thing, bending the nails and splitting the boards. And every board an hour, and I was wrathy that he was wasting my hours like that."

He was beginning to talk faster now, as though the story were a stone rolling downhill, gathering momentum, becoming unstoppable.

"Before we had gone into the tree, our mother had made me promise that I would watch Thad and be sure that he did not fall and hurt himself. But I could not watch him and work at the same time. Maybe she thought that I should let him do the work while I watched him, but he was just no good at it. But every time I took over the job he wanted to do, he would cry and stamp his feet until I let him do it for himself. So I had to take the hammer away from him and do the work myself. I set him to straightening the nails he had already bent. But because I couldn't nail and watch him, I tied a rope around his waist, and the other end to the big branch that ran just over our heads. That way, if he fell, the rope would keep him from falling to the ground.

"We were doing well, making good progress, with the uprights going in to support the floor. I cut three boards to make floorboards so we would have a place to stand, and I was hammering those in when I heard him banging on the other end. Before I could even look up, the board I was working on split right in two. It was another hour of sweeping for me. I knew enough to blunt the end of a nail to keep it from splitting the wood, but he did not. He had run a sharp, bent nail into the other end of the board and caused it to split right down the middle.

"I told him to stop, to not nail any more boards, but he went right on banging at them like he was trying to whack them to death. I could see he was going to split more of them. I reached over to take the hammer from him, and he pulled it back. Maybe to hit me, maybe to keep it from me. But it made me mad. I gave him a shove. Hard. To the chest. He took one step back and over the edge. The rope I had put on him he had slipped off partway, so that it was now under one arm and over the other shoulder. When he fell, it came taut around his neck and arm. I saw him fall and he did a little bounce at the end of the rope, his feet still two or three feet from the ground."

He stopped then and took several long breaths, trying to slow and regulate his breathing. His hands had begun to tremble slightly, as though he were taking a sudden chill.

"And I didn't know what to do," he began again. "At first I started to pull the rope up, but that only made things worse. It just tightened the rope, and he hung there, right arm up, the rope tight around his neck, his tongue stuck out. I climbed down the tree as fast as I could, and I grabbed ahold of his legs and I lifted him up to take some of the strain off the rope. I told him to pull the rope from his neck with his free hand, but he did not move. I yelled at him, but he did nothing. His body bent at the waist a little and kept more pressure on the rope. I yelled for our mother, but she did not come. She had gone to the neighbor's two houses down and could not hear me. So I held him as best I could, hanging onto his legs, holding him up, but he just kept bending back over. I yelled and I screamed, and I walked in tiny circles trying to make his body come upright so that we would put some slack in the rope, but it did not work. If I let go of his legs to try and get the rope off, he came further down and harder on the rope. Whatever I did only made it worse."

His face had gone blank and colorless. His eyes took on a faraway look, seeing what no one else could see, what he did not want to see.

"I do not know how long it was when finally my mother came screaming into the yard and then went screaming away again, and then the men came and they took his body and lifted it, and one of them loosened the rope from his neck, and they pulled him down and tried to make him breathe. But he did not, for I had killed him."

The boy looked at him then, his eyes meeting his own, but somehow not attaching and holding. A tear or two made its way down either cheek, but he did not cry, though the lieutenant wished he would. It was more horrible to see the blank, detached look on the boy's face than it would have been to see him overcome with weeping. "It was an accident. How horrible! But it was an accident."

"That's what they said. Accident. I had to talk to the sheriff and I had to talk to the reverend. And they all said that it was an accident. And I tried to believe that. They were all nice about it. But I could see in my father's eyes. He knew it was no accident.

He knew I did it, even though he kept telling me it wasn't my fault. But I knew. I knew."

He had told the story fast, nearly breathless, but, aside from the few tears that rolled down his nose and cheeks and the snuffing back of the tears, he told it calmly, as if it were the story of something that had happened to someone else who just happened to be him.

"They kept on looking at me. My mother and father. Even people on the street. I was the boy who killed his brother. And my father never raised his voice or hand against me, but in his looks, it was anger. And my mother. So sad. So sad. And it was me who made her that way. Maybe I should have gone to jail."

He reached out and touched the boy lightly on the shoulder. "You did. You've put yourself in jail and you've forged bars and locks out of your own mind, and those are the hardest to break. If you did wrong, and I'm not sure you did, you will have to learn forgiveness. It's not an easy lesson, but you must learn it. What you have done is to make a mistake. It was an error in judgment. Nothing more. We are imperfect creatures, and it is our lot to err. Usually the wages of error are slight and soon forgotten, though they seem great at the time. But we all make great errors, as well. And those are not forgotten. Those are the ones we must learn to forgive, because it is only we who can or will."

"That's not all. I stole. When I couldn't stand the way they looked at me anymore, I went into Father's store in the middle of the night, and I stole almost two hundred dollars. And I got the train and I went south. In Baltimore, I met the Army recruiter. I owe everyone money, and I don't make any money. I was going to pay my father back the two hundred dollars, only I lost most of it gambling, and then when I came here I lost the weather instruments and now I owe the Army four hundred dollars. I owe six hundred dollars and I can't pay it back."

"Your presence here repays the Army. The captain needs to tell you that, but he won't. I won't go into the reasons for that; he just won't. I would be surprised as well if a father who has now lost two sons grieves the loss of two hundred dollars at all, or if he even considers it. Does he know where you are?"

The boy stared straight ahead. The tears had stopped rolling now, and his blank-mask face, long gone into the distance, began to slowly flicker recognition.

"Write a letter. To your father. Your mother. Tell them you are safe." He felt himself starting to constrict in the throat. "Try to forgive yourself. If there is a God, He did it long ago. Now you must forgive yourself."

The boy nodded once, and as though they had breached a dam, the tears began, and then the shaking that precedes the sobbing. The lieutenant reached out and put a folded bill into the boy's pocket, then took him by the shoulders and pulled the boy to him and held him and repeated at just above a whisper, "Forgive yourself. Forgive yourself. Forgive yourself," as he had repeated and repeated so often before, alone in the various darknesses.

Private Ned
Thorne

"Here," Birdwood said. He held out ten dollars to Ned.

"I can't take your money, Jarbal."

"Why not? It's good money."

"It's yours, not mine. I have some."

"Not if I give it to you, it's not. Take it. Save your money. If you don't take it, Brickner's going to take it from me in dominos. He always does. I don't have much use for money. I'm going to Mr. Donovan's and get myself some licorice. That's all I need is licorice. I got sixteen dollars. I can't eat sixteen dollars of licorice in two months. I doubt that Mr. Donovan even has sixteen dollars of licorice. I buy three dollars worth every time, then I lose the rest to Brickner at dominos."

"All right. I'll take five. I'll owe it you. Next payday, I'll give you the five back. Next month, you'll have thirty-one dollars instead of twenty-six."

"Just give it to Brickner. He's going to get it anyway. He's a whiz at dominos. Hell and villainy, I don't even like to play dominos."

"Then why do you?"

"It's payday. The dominos come out on payday."

At the command of "dismissed," the company broke ranks and scattered in various directions. They had been expecting roll call all morning, and when the call came, they were barely able to stand in rank. Dismissed, they fought to be first out of camp and across the river to where Donovan had set up his wagons.

A number of the men headed for the corral to pick up mounts. He followed them until he was caught from behind.

"Forget that. Come on," Birdwood said.

"It'll be faster."

"No, it won't. Besides, you want to be too drunk and tired to ride tonight, anyway. Just quick-step it."

Ned and Birdwood took off in a headlong scramble across the lower end of the camp. At the south fork of the little river, they leapt off the five-foot embankment and hit the bed, slipping and sliding over stones and small puddles, and scrambled up the other side, kicking dirt and rock back into the mostly dry riverbed. On level ground they kept running, dodging trees and brush, through the thick grass down the slope toward the desert floor. They passed other, older soldiers walking, running, or limping, broken and winded. At the bottom of the hill, mounted troopers began to pass them, riding at full gallop as though being pursued by all of the misery of the last months, threatening to haul them back into themselves.

On the desert floor, the run became more challenging. The temperature rose as the land dropped away and vegetation turned from tree and grass to chaparral and yucca. They ran together, keeping each other on a pace, neither trying to get the edge on the other, though they both knew that later this would turn to all-out competition. But right now they ran for the joy of the run, just barely in control of their movements, gravity and inertia exerting the greatest force. The sound of their boots pounding the hard ground, their breath coming hard and fast, their sweat flowing free now and their eyes sweeping the terrain ahead, watching for the rocks and cactus that would have to be jumped, they ran and they laughed.

Footing was treacherous. Going upslope, their boots pulled sand and gravel loose and

sent them windmilling for balance. Down-
slope, the pull of gravity taking them faster
than the pace of their own running, they
had to make quick, hard turns to avoid the
obstacles that sprang up in front of them.
Ahead of them, a rider tried to take a jump
at full gallop. His mule lost its footing, going down hard and rolling over the rider.
Other riders came by, and when they made
the jump, the fallen mule got up and followed, leaving the rider behind. More riders
passed him by and did not stop.

They came to the plateau winded and in
full sweat, Ned running the last two hundred yards full out, but two steps behind
Birdwood. Four wagons had been pulled
into a semicircle. Behind the wagons, small
tents big enough for no more than two
people had been erected. In the center of
the semicircle, a pile of board and brush
rose nearly as tall as a man. Around the pile
milled the whores — tall and short, fat and
bony, most ugly, all dirty, but women, real
and miraculous.
    Over everything creaked the sound of a
concertina playing a bright and lively tune
he could not recognize, pumped by a fat,
redheaded whore. The soldiers who had
reached the plateau before them were

mostly lined up at the first wagon, where the stream of silver going in was broken only by the bottles of whisky that came out. Though one of the men was dancing a spastic jig to the music of the concertina, and another had managed to loose the breasts of a large whore and burrow his face into them, most of the men stood around like boys at their first church social. The spoke to each other only and passed the new bottles back and forth, casting only sidelong glances at the whores as if they were afraid that at any moment the whores were going to put them on report for lechery.

"Whores and liquor," Fenner sang. "Whores and liquor, whores and liquor. It's a soldier's life for me." He, too, danced a little jig, but he did not approach any closer to the whores.

As it darkened, the pile of brush was lit and became the focal point of all action of the encampment, which became more and more like a church social than anything else, save that the couples that wandered off were engaged in quick commerce. Most of the soldiers took seats around the fire and drank and sang as the whores circulated among them. Others feasted in the failing light. A large piece of beef roasted on a spit at one end of the fire and the whore in charge sold thick slices of it for fifty cents each. He wondered, briefly, if it was part of the cattle he had helped Brickner to rustle. A case of canned peaches had been purchased and eaten in the first hours of the festival, and sticks of hard peppermint candy were nearly as common as cigars, jutting from the jaws of the soldiers.

He had eaten one of the sticks of candy and a couple of peaches that came by in an open can, and he had drunk quite a bit of whisky, despite his promise to forgo or moderate its use, without spending a single penny from his own pocket. He watched the whores come and go, their laughter a constant counterpoint to the singing and caterwauling of the soldiers. He left the circle for a piss and wandered back to the lead wagon where the stream of commerce that had been eight soldiers deep had lately tapered off.

"What's your pleasure?" He was suddenly confronted by a large man, a double-barreled shotgun cradled in his arms and silver dollars for eyes.

"Nothing. I don't know."

"You don't know?" The man bent forward, put the barrels of the shotgun behind Ned's neck, and pulled Ned toward him. He saw then that the man's eyes were not silver dollars at all, but the lenses of spectacles reflecting oil light in the near darkness. "You don't know your pleasures? A man who doesn't know his own pleasures is no more than a dog with a can tied to his tail, being run all over kingdom come, all in a panic over what he doesn't know. That's no way to live. If you don't know your pleasures, you best be studying on them."

"I don't know. I'm sorry. It's the shotgun."

The man leveled the shotgun at him. "This? A fine weapon. It gets the attention of all who behold it from the wrong end. Perhaps you would like to purchase it?"

"It's for sale?"

"Everything is for sale. What do you need? You have found the whores and the whisky. I know that. So you must be looking for something else. You are, perhaps, a man more wise than your years, a man who looks for comfort that has some duration to it." The man pulled him closer with the shotgun until he was resting against the man's girth, surrounded by his odor.

The odor was not mere dirt, nor sweat, the smells he had lived with the past weeks. Not spoiled, exactly, but something like it — a smell from his life before the Army, a smell from Connecticut and the store. Rancid. It was the smell of rancid butter.

"Do you know what I have in that wagon?" The man pointed with the shotgun. He put his mouth to Ned's ear and spoke just above a whisper. "Stockings."

The word hit him like a shock of static. "Stockings?" He was again acutely aware of the burning of his feet, the chafing and the suppurating blisters.

"Two pair for a dollar. Fine cotton stockings from the mills of Georgia. Stockings that will make you believe your feet are wrapped in clouds, as perhaps they are. Isaac Donovan understands the life and needs of the soldier. He provides for them. Did he not, he wouldn't be here today. Hoist yourself into yonder wagon." The stock of the twelve-gauge came around and gently but firmly pushed him toward the back of the lead wagon.

"I recommend without hesitation the pleasures of the ladies outside, skilled in arts learned in the Orient and the palaces of Europe, and of the whisky that flows from springs in the green hills of Kentuck that is responsible for the well-known bravery of the men, the beauty of the women, and the speed of the horses that are there raised. But I understand, as well, there are men whose tastes are so discerning that the merely extraordinary holds little charm for them. For such men, I open this wagon. It is not for every man. Be certain. But for the rare man who seeks it out, it holds pleasures and wonders that few can understand, much less enjoy."

The inside of the wagon was a construction of pine shelves built with lips and rails to hold the contents steady against lurching and rolling. Everywhere there were boxes and jars and cans of every description and size, piles of blankets and clothing, racks of rifles and crates of ammunition. In front of him appeared two pair of men's cotton stockings, white. He parted with two dollars and bought four pair.

"I could use a hat, as well."

"Some protection from the sun that will, at the same time, mark you as a man of distinction, I should think. This, I think, is what you seek." He produced from behind him a straw hat with an extraordinarily wide brim. "Your Mexican is a man who has lived his life under the fiercest of suns. This sombrero represents the wisdom of ages in this land. You may have it for five dollars. It is worth your very life."

"I can spend only three dollars."

Donovan took the hat from his head, spun

around with surprising speed for a man of his girth, and replaced it with another, seemingly the same. "Three dollars it is, then. And, furthermore, you look like a man who has some experience with a rifle." And as suddenly as the hat had appeared on his head, a Springfield rifle appeared in his hands. It had a curious sight attached to the stock, just behind the hammer. "United States Army surplus, much like the one you have, though thoroughly reconditioned by yours truly and outfitted with a sight of my own design. It can throw a fifty-caliber slug some seven hundred yards with remarkable accuracy in the right hands, which, I think, may be yours."

Ned shouldered the rifle to get the heft, then examined the sight, which had a thumb screw to hold the almost solid slide against the concussion of firing. "Seven hundred yards?"

"In the right hands. And provided those hands have fifty dollars. It is a remarkable weapon. I have tried to interest the United States Government in the sight, which, as I believe I mentioned, is of my own design. They have shown little interest, though some of the indigenous people have understood the wisdom of it."

"You sell these to Indians?"

"Only those who can afford it. Here you are, soldier. Four pair of cotton stockings that will wear like iron while they feel like feathers. You won't be disappointed in the quality. And one sombrero of distinction, proof against sun, rain, wind, and the ill wishes of the jealous. I regret the necessity of taking from you your precious dollars, but I deal strictly in cash, for the habit of extending credit is a destroyer of friendship and ruination of the souls of those who accept it. I come every two months to validate the efforts of the paymaster, because money is good only to buy things with, and the paymaster has nothing save the tender."

Ned took the socks. He could not resist holding them to his cheek. They were as soft as newly hatched chicks. Behind Donovan's head hung a string of hair and feathers. He strained for a closer look.

"Apache scalps. Still a cash commodity in some parts of Mexico that I frequent. A deplorable and disgusting custom, and I keep them as more curiosity than as an item of commerce, though everything here is for sale if there is interest. And if you have scalps, I will pay top dollar for them."

"Aren't you afraid that the Apaches will see those, since you trade with them?"

"I have others. Including, and I mean no

offense to you, some taken from white people, who it would seem were enlisted in the service of their country. Some of them quite fair, not unlike your own hair, there." He took the Springfield from Ned's hands, caressed it, and added, "I would hate to think that some Indian might wish to trade me your hair one of these fine days." He held up the Springfield. "Fifty dollars. And I will take your Army issue weapon in trade for twenty-five of it, if it has been well maintained."

He scanned the wagon, half afraid, half excited about what new fascinating and exotic horror he might find. It was in a corner, lashed to a shelf. "That," he said, pointing to it.

"A curious device," Donovan said. "A rare commodity. A predictor of the future, if you will, fashioned by master craftsmen in Europe. It is too rare even to set a price on. Sixty dollars, however, could make it yours."

"It is a mercury barometer. It is my mercury barometer."

"It is, perhaps, the first, but most certainly not the second. I bought it at a bazaar at the far reaches of my trading route."

"You got it at Camp Bowie, where it was stolen from me in my sleep. I want it back."

"Well, then. Excellent. I would be happy

to get it back to you. I believe everything longs to find its rightful place, a place where it is esteemed, treasured, loved even. I am in the business of helping things find their rightful place. Have you sixty dollars?

He shook his head. "I have fifteen."

"An unfortunately insufficient amount."

"It is what I have."

"In currency. What have you that might better belong somewhere else?"

"It is mine."

"Not yet. What have you?"

"It is mine. I will have the captain come here and vouch for me."

"The captain has been here and left. What have you that might occupy the space vacated by this wonderful device?"

"A forty-five Colt, center-fire, revolving pistol." He had the disquieting thought that he was home, doing what he did best, bargaining for goods. He was, perhaps, a born and bred shopkeeper.

"You do not. You lie."

"I do."

"I could be interested, then."

"There was a thermometer that matched this piece."

"That would require considerable interest. I do not think I am capable of mustering so much. I think I would want cash in addition to the firearm."

"I have ten dollars left."

"That is not enough."

"I will sell it to someone else, then."

"All right, then. But I want to see the Colt. And I want to see it soon."

"I have no ammunition for it."

"That shall reduce the price I am able to pay for it a good deal, I'm afraid. A gun without cartridges is not of great use."

"The thermometer and barometer for the gun. There is no other bargain."

"And ten dollars."

"Five dollars."

"Eight dollars."

"Six."

"Run. Fetch it."

The sun was down as he started to camp, though there was still enough light for him to see. The trip that had been short as he and Birdwood made their way over had stretched to its own dismal length again. He had had some of the vile whisky that had passed through the ranks, hand to hand, and a dull weariness began to set in despite the excitement of finding the instruments. If it were not for the freedom from indebtedness and embarrassment, he would let Donovan keep the instruments rather than hike back to camp and then back once more to Donovan's.

More than halfway back to the camp, he broke into a slow trot to kill the monotony of the trek. This time, dodging rocks and cactus presented little challenge except that it was now dark save for the light of the three-quarters moon. In the distance the last visible mountains would barely illuminate in infrequent lightning, so far distant that the rumbles of thunder came long after the pulse of light and were barely audible over the sound of his own breathing, which had just begun to deepen as he jogged. He made his way down the embankment of the dry riverbed and back into camp, dodging puddles of water that had pooled there.

He was stopped twice at the borders of the camp; first, by the vedette who had had the misfortune to draw guard duty on payday and who cursed his luck and everyone who did not share it. He demanded details of the goings-on back at Donovan's and groaned as each one was listed.

Shortly after he had passed the vedette, he came upon Lieutenant Austin, who asked if he had seen the captain. When he replied that he hadn't, the lieutenant said only "Hell and damnation" and spurred his horse across the riverbed.

Back in his tent, Ned uncovered and unwrapped the Colt pistol hidden in his belongings. Tucking it into the waistband of his trousers, he started the trek back to Donovan's camp. As he crossed the south fork of the river, he stopped at the pool where he had left his stick-and-bottle current indicator. When he reeled in the bottle and let it go, it reached the end of the rope before he counted two. He thought to calculate that, but instead he jumped the pool and made his way back toward Donovan's and his instruments. Before he reached Donovan's camp, the rain had started. It fell light and slow, then picked up force and volume. By the time he had reached Donovan's it was a steady rain, falling cold and determined. There were bright flashes of lightning, and thunder followed almost immediately.

LIEUTENANT
ANTHONY AUSTIN

He was of two minds. He thought he should apologize, because that was what he did. He was the peacemaker, the one who backed down first, knowing Bobby had no skill in that craft. But he was still angry Bobby would even suggest that he showed the boy favoritism, because Thorne was a young boy and needed some favoritism. He was also angry that Bobby understood more of what he felt for the boy than he wished him to.

While heavy clouds built to the south, the sky became overcast, cutting the sunlight considerably. A scattered sprinkle started to fall. All in all a most pleasant afternoon. A good rain, he thought, would brighten things considerably, and both the flora and fauna would change to the trained eye. There were, perhaps, whole species whose presence was not felt until the rain began to fall in earnest. So did the creatures of the earth adapt to the conditions in which they lived.

He heard Donovan's encampment before he saw it. And he spurred his horse forward toward the music and the cacophony of laughter and raised voices drifting out past the chaparral. It reminded him of fairs when he was a child in Illinois. And he felt the same little trip-hammer of excitement that caused his back to stiffen as he leaned forward, spurring the horse to a trot.

Barely dark, there was a good-sized fire going at Donovan's and music, laughing, and screaming. He could see the whores dancing around the fire, and troopers with them in various stages of dress. The light had failed sufficiently that he could not make out the faces of any of the company, nor did he care to. So long as there were no deaths and no serious injuries, he preferred to ignore what the men did, and he took a course away from the fire and around the wagons to where he knew he would find Donovan.

"There is only one case left of the Kentuck," Donovan said. "And that is promised to a colonel at McDowell, who is fully prepared to pay bottle price for it, which would be a quite exorbitant one hundred and thirty-five for the case. It grieves me even to tell you that, but it is the last case and colonels must be accommodated."

"That is outrageous."

"Truly. But I am helpless against the fluctuation of prices in an unstable economy such as we find ourselves burdened with. I travel to Kentucky to buy this whisky especial, and each time the trip is more difficult, burdensome, and expensive. And I arrive there only to find that the prices have again risen."

"You do not go to Kentucky. You travel no farther than Lordsburg."

"But the whisky does. And the costs rise, whether I pay them directly or indirectly. One twenty-five is the best I can do."

"I'll not pay it."

"All right. I have some very nice Mexican whisky here that has shown great charm for the enlisted men. Thirty a case."

"And I cannot abide Mexican whisky. It is vile. It is so little aged one would think it bottled tomorrow."

Donovan shook his head sadly. "It is improved over the last batch. Not a single fatality so far."

"I must have my whisky. It is the only palliative available for my condition. It is a matter of my health, of my very life."

"A case of the Kentuck and a case of the Mexican for one forty-five. Otherwise the voice of the colonel grows loud in my ear. One suspects he suffers as well."

"No. It is an outrage. I shall take two cases of the Mexican, for its medicinal value is my primary aim. What else do you have?"

"Curious. Interest is an odd commodity in that it can be determined only from the view of the beholder, and even then is quite temporary. Everything is of interest to someone; nothing is of interest to everyone. And what interests one man today may not tomorrow. What interests the men in your command is of no interest to you and vice versa. Men are curious creatures, beset by interests as flexible as weather. It is difficult for me to say what I have that might be of interest to you at the moment. Why don't you tell me again what it is you desire, and I will show what I have that might satisfy such."

"Specimens. Of the natural world. Oddities and indigenous creatures. What have you?" He took another sip of the Mexican whisky. It was vile. Medicine that tasted like medicine.

Donovan held up one finger and went to the wagon. He was a disgusting and reprehensible man, a fat, grotesque whoremonger who fed off the honest labor of others. But he was also a remarkable person, an oddity in his own right. He had adapted spectacularly to his territory as if he had been produced by it. In his few wagons, he could satisfy an enormous variety of the wants and needs of soldiers across hundreds of miles, thousands. It was not so much that he carried everything with him. It was more that he could anticipate the needs of his clientele with great accuracy.

"These may not be quite appropriate," Donovan said, backing out of the wagon, naked to the waist. "Still they may provide an amusement." His deeply furred girth seemed to have grown further furred, and then animated. Patches of reddish-brown hair crept across his bare chest and arms. "Quite fearsome appearing, are they not?"

The "they" he referred to were large, hairy spiders, the circumference of a man's hand. Donovan took one from his breast, placed it on the back of his hand, and held it out to the lieutenant. "They are dears, actually. Gentle as lambs, though they look as though they could each of them devour a lamb or two. Go ahead, stroke its fur. It provides a pure pleasure in the touching."

"Tarantulas. They are common."

"And how true that is! Think how often

the most fearsome exterior hides the gentle soul, and vice versa. Too often the meek exterior conceals the most ferocious of hearts. A puzzlement, isn't it? But you are right. Common. I buy them from children in Mexico at a penny each. Many of the soldiers keep them as pets. They are gentle, and their fur is soft and luxurious, and they are not so much bother as a dog, though they must be provided with food. They are often favorite implements with your jesters. Of course they would not interest you. The only other thing I have is similar. You know these, of course?"

From out of his trouser pocket he held out a horned toad — a flat, squat lizard, with a rough skin and a corolla of thorny scales around the back of its head.

"Those, too, are common."

"Also gentle and an amusement to bored and lonely soldiers. They bleed from the eyes when threatened. A most saintly lizard."

"Yes, I know."

"That is what I have. I don't generally deal in livestock. Soldiers have little interest in living creatures unless they can be fondled or killed for sport. If there is something you would specifically desire, I would be glad to have my sources hunt it down for you."

"No," he said. "There is nothing in specific. I had hoped only that you might have something I hadn't seen before."

"Oh, that I do. But it is not a creature of the desert. I have any number of things that you have not seen before. I gather that you have an interest in the unique oddities of the natural world." He took a small, leathery object from a pouch tied at his belt and held it out to Austin.

"It's an ear," Austin said.

"It is not just an ear. It is the ear of our dear President Lincoln. It was taken from his body during the postmortem examination. It is a rare and valuable specimen. If such a thing were possible in this world, it would be called 'priceless.' There is not another like it, because only one was taken."

"It is, most likely, the ear of a Mexican or an Indian."

"It would be likely, yes. A high degree of probability. Most certainly. But it is not. It is his, and it is precious and extremely dear."

"If one wanted such a grotesque and gruesome specimen, how much would you charge for it?"

"How much are you willing to pay for it?"

"Nothing. I would not be willing to pay a cent for it."

"Then there is nothing to discuss, my dear lieutenant. I don't set prices on objects that are not likely to be sold. To do so would waste the time of all involved and would create an illusion that objects have value unto themselves. This, for example." He held the ear up so the lantern light shone on it, turning it translucent brown. "This has no value to you. It might be the ear of an Indian or a poor Mexican or our beloved president. But, whatever it is, it has no value. Except that another man might find it has a value that is not clear to you. But there could be no such discussion with you." The ear disappeared. "It is valueless, and it is gone.

"Now this would seem to belong in a similar category." He extracted the walnut-handled Deringer from his waistband. "Most likely, it holds no interest for you and would seem to have no value at all. But it has great interest to others, and for you would make a most impressive gift, a token of affection and regard of great value, indeed. A value nearly inestimable."

"How much?"

Donovan smiled. "Aah, and so is value conferred. Two hundred."

"That is outrageous."

"And the esteem and regard of our friends is also outrageous?"

"You shall not use my affections to line

380

your pockets."

"My pockets are already lined. Purchases out of affection are quite in order today. This would not be the first by any means. That whisky in your hand there might not require the exertion you are planning on to bring it to taste."

"Bobby?"

Donovan smiled. "I would never spoil a surprise."

"But two hundred for the little gun is truly an outrage, and I won't let my affections be used as a lever toward its purchase."

"There is something else. Brand new, just acquired. It is the newest thing. A rare item, in that its rarity relies on its newness rather than age. Behold the weapon of the future." He unwrapped a piece of flannel and held the gun out for Austin's inspection.

"What is it?"

"A forty-five, center-fire, Colt revolving pistol. This is the first I have seen, though I have heard rumors of its existence for some months. For the serious connoisseur of firearms, this is truly an exceptional piece."

He took the gun in his hand. It was smaller and more compact than the .44 Remingtons that were standard issue. Where those were long and heavy, this was short and light, a better combination for a side-arm. Though he hadn't Bobby's love for firearms, he saw the charm of the graceful pistol.

"And how much for this?"

"One hundred dollars."

"I don't know. That is dear, as well."

"As are friendships. I'll throw in two boxes of ammunition. Three. I have cases of the cartridges that I haven't been able to use. I bought them cheap, but too soon. No extra charge. That pistol will fire six continuous rounds and be reloaded in only seconds to fire six more. It is a remarkable weapon. Truly revolutionary."

He held the gun and took another sip from the whisky. The sharpness of it drove his eyes closed in a tight squint. "And I have no need to purchase a case of the Kentucky?"

"There is always a need to purchase Kentucky whisky. There is nothing finer on the earth. And to buy it would be to deny a colonel. That, in itself, recommends the purchase. But, no. There is no immediate need. It could wait until my next visit."

"Done."

"Is there a more melodious word in the English language? I think not."

PRIVATE NED
THORNE

Around the campfire, which had become somewhat subdued by a slow, steady rain, soldiers danced, some in uniform, some in union suits, and two bare as babes, with naked whores on their arms. The party had gathered momentum in his absence. The concertina had been joined by Pack's scratchy fiddle, and the voices of a dozen or so soldiers pointed in the same approximate direction.

The two most popular commodities — the whisky and the canned peaches — had become one as soldiers poured whisky into the peach syrup of their nearly empty cans while others poured the syrup from the cans into the whisky bottles. The result was a varied mixture of syrup and whisky that was thick and sweet enough to gag a man, but an improvement over the original whisky. From every direction, bottles or cans of the stuff circulated as private ownership faded and a kind of joyful communalism of alcohol, sex, music, and rain took over the evening.

He sat by the fire, which various soldiers kept feeding against the rain that would neither turn to a real downpour nor completely quit. He held the thermometer and barometer, for which he had traded most of his money and the Colt, against him with his right hand. They rested in the box Donovan had kindly thrown in. Burned into the top was the legend "U.S. Army." He took drinks from the bottles of whisky and syrup as they came by. He had a powerful longing to have a go at one of the whores, old and beaten as they seemed. Yet he stayed where he was. He had little money to spare and no desire to increase his debt to Birdwood or anyone else. And under no condition was he going to let go of the weather instruments, the loss of which had already cost him so much.

The officers were here somewhere, and he had some concern for that. But none of the rest did. Liberty, it seemed, belonged to one's self to do with as he pleased. So, he sat, drank small amounts, listened to the music, and watched the cavorting of the other soldiers. It was not unpleasant to do so. The music was passable, if the standard for passability had been sharply lowered, and it was counterpointed now by the music of frogs or toads who had materialized as if by magic with the rain.

Taken all together, he was a happy man, free of the shame of having lost the instruments, though the captain did not yet know he had them back. Cool and clean in the small rain, his senses were delightfully blurred by the thick liquor and a whore, naked as the day she was born, not four feet from him, bobbing in time to the music, her breasts performing a kind of magical dance that surpassed any wonder he had seen thus far in his life.

And when she stood in front of him, in her nakedness, and extended her hand to him, he was both flabbergasted and embarrassed. "Come, pretty," she said. "Let's dance together, an old and wonderful dance. One I bet you're very good at." She took his hand and pulled him up.

"I don't think so. I mean, I don't know."

"Then I shall show you." She guided his hand to her breast, which was slick with sweat and grease, but the most wonderful thing he had ever touched in his life. He was amazed by the way its weight shifted in his hand. "And there you have it, love," she said.

"I don't know."

Around him the men had begun to clap in unison. "Have at her, boy. Jump on and ride."

He was embarrassed and light-headed with drink, and he wanted to run and hide, but he wanted to keep his hand on her amazing breast as well, with the nipple that seemed to grow larger and harder in his hand. "I have no money," he said.

"None," she said, guiding his hand from her breast down her belly to the thatch of hair and the hidden wetness.

"No, none."

She pulled his hand away and pushed him back, and then something hard struck him in the back and another on the head. There were small flashes around him in the fire-light. He understood that the soldiers around him were throwing coins at him and the whore while they laughed at his embarrassment.

She pulled him back in to her and her hand was suddenly inside his blouse, pinching at his nipples just as he was pinching at hers. She continued to laugh and to dance, and he tried his best to dance with her, in time with the clapping of the troopers, while she unbuttoned his blouse and then went after his belt. The coins kept bouncing off his head and back, but he barely felt them. "My love," she said. "You are so pretty. Come to me. You're a god in a shower of silver. Honor me."

"Come on, soldier. For the glory of D Company. Show her what you're made of."

He was laughing now, caught up in the liquor and clapping and the mirth of the naked whore, who was dancing and turning in the firelight, presenting herself to him from every angle, letting his hands go to whatever part of her body he wished to explore. The coins kept coming, bouncing off his back, shoulders, and head. Other whores appeared to scoop them from the ground.

And then he was standing, not dancing, in the firelight, unable to move because his trousers were around his boots, and all the soldiers and all the whores were cheering now as he stood naked and erect before them. And she reached out her hand and took him in it, pulling him to her until he felt himself pulled into the warm wet of her and his knees buckled, and he thought that maybe he had lost consciousness and was falling to the ground. But instead, he was standing upright with his pants below his knees, feeling dizzy and embarrassed as the whore danced around the assembled, cheering, applauding soldiers, displaying her slick, glistening body in the firelight.

It was still dark when he awoke. The fire was out but the smell of smoke drifted over everything. He sat up and strained to see. Around the wagons there was a good deal of activity as Donovan and his whores packed up to move on to the paymaster's next stop. He could hear the sounds of horses and of tack, the thud of wooden crates on the floors of wagons. Behind all other sounds, the call of the toads was relentless.

Next to him was the crate with his weather instruments. He touched it just to reassure himself that he really had it, that its return was not just some dream. It was cold, and he opened the crate and struck a match. Fifty-four degrees, the thermometer read. But his eye was caught by the barometer, which had plunged during the night.

He shook Birdwood and woke him. "We need to get back," he said. It's going to be dawn and there's rain coming."

"It ain't raining. That was last night."

"It's raining somewhere. Pressure's way down. It's going to rain some here, too."

"Who you think you are? God?"

"No. A man with a barometer. You have a

good time last night?"

Birdwood struggled to his knees and then vomited.

"Me, too. Can't wait for the next payday."

They made their way back slowly, trudging over the brushy, rocky ground. Ned struggled, carrying the box of instruments, and Birdwood stopped three times to vomit. It was a source of pride that Ned had been able to moderate his drinking to the extent that he had only an aching head to show for his efforts. He had made progress. He heard the crack of the whips and then the groaning of wood and leather as Donovan got his wagons moving. He looked for the whore who had danced naked with him, but she was nowhere he could see. When he heard the horses coming, he knew it was the officers heading back. He told Birdwood that they needed to hurry, to get back before the captain and lieutenant did. They took the lower route back to the camp, mindful of the narrowing of the river. After what he had seen in the afternoon, he was afraid that there would be water, and they would need a tight, shallow crossing.

They both heard it, though neither could see it. They were standing in the bed of the river. There were small streams of water winding through the bed, but otherwise it seemed as dry as usual. It rumbled to their right like a locomotive, or two locomotives, loud, powerful, and fast. They could feel the trembling in the sand under their feet. They stopped and looked at each other, reading their own fear in each other's face. Then, they ran the few yards to the opposite bank and began clawing their way up, suddenly understanding the reason for the deep banks and wide bed of a river they knew only as dry. Birdwood made good progress up the bank, but Ned struggled, using only his right hand, his left occupied by hanging on to the box of weather instruments. He slipped back, all the way to the bottom of the riverbed, which continued to throb with the vibration of a tremendous force. When he looked to his right, he still saw nothing, but panic began to build in him. He threw the box of weather instruments to the top of the embankment and began scrambling up on all fours.

He made it to the top of the bank and rolled across the flat of the land, trying to get as far from the sound as he could. The sound was growing incrementally, as though the sky were a vessel for it to fill. Other soldiers, whom they had passed, gathered at the banks to look, though there was nothing to see. Ned closed his eyes and gritted his teeth against the sound that seemed to fill his skull and threatened to break it open.

"Jesus, the Lord."

Whether it was the cry or the noise or the sight, none of them could say. But they all jumped back as a front of water twenty yards wide and five feet deep tore away part of the embankment just above them and threw it at them. The front of water threatened to come straight at them, then negotiated the slight curve just ahead and came past. In the blinking of an eye, the dry riverbed was transformed into a swirling, wildly running river, spraying water over all who stood within ten feet of the bed. The box of weather instruments rocked for a moment at the edge of the riverbed. He made a grab for it, only to be held back by Birdwood. The box spun once around and was gone.

The light was just beginning to break in the east and they stood by the river, marveling at the sight in front of them. The water was ragged and brown, seething with whitecaps that foamed like lace. Bits of tree and brush ran along through roil of water, as well as, he could swear, rock, the bones of the long dead, and the bodies of newly dead animals that the water had picked up along the way. A large Palo Verde tree, bright green, became a huge broom, riding the water around the curves of the river, sweeping things in its way, its wide root structure as large and exposed as its branchy top. And then he saw the horse coming sideways, hooves first, and the blue-clad rider hanging on, and just behind that a mule, all wide nostrils and terrified white-rimmed eyes, and behind it, another blue body spinning down the river like a piece of flotsam, powerless in the sweep and rush of tons of water.

He was running, headlong and flat-footed, along the bank of the river with the rest of them when he had the revelation, perhaps because his mind had just sorted out what his eyes had recorded or because of the cries of the other soldiers running with him down the bank of the river, that what he had just seen go down the river were their officers. They ran as fast as they could, but the river outpaced them all.

By noon the water had subsided. The river flowed past the camp nearly bank to bank, but steady and controlled. The soldiers, suffering from lack of sleep, the effects of bad whisky, and the disorientation of those who have seen the world turn itself inside out, wandered the camp in a rough approximation of clean-up duty, though the actual work done was minimal.

Where they went, whatever small tasks they found to occupy themselves, they avoided the tents of the officers, the one inside his tent nearly dead of drowning and the other on the plank outside his tent, where he had been since he was retrieved from the tree that had wedged into the bank of the river and caught him as he swirled and tumbled past, simply dead. In the early light, with the quick rise of temperature as the sun finally came from the ridge of granite to the east, the body had steamed and oozed thick brown water. Now, naked and blue, the body seemed to be settling into a solidity that had more to do with the river and the trees than with the mute, hungover soldiers who moved in any direction save this one.

Stonehouse, who had assumed command, kept them moving. He did not expect them to accomplish real work, though there was real work to be done. The wall of water that had moved through in the early morning had carved a new bed for the river, and in so doing had taken with it two posts, a good section of the corral, and three mules. Mostly, the soldiers wandered, picked up sticks and brush, threw them into the river, and went back for more.

The troopers assigned to rebuild the corral did more measuring, usually by pacing off the distance and staring at the river that had appeared more suddenly than such things are supposed to, than they did repairing. It did not matter much. The river had created its own natural boundary for the southwest corner of the corral. No horse or mule was going to try that. But the mules, like the men, came every now and again to look at the river, though the horses mostly stayed at the far end of the corral in fear of what they had witnessed earlier. Perhaps, he thought, they also grieved for their corral mates, especially the horse that, following the orders of officers, had done exactly what its instincts had directed it not to do and who was now forever lost.

So man, horse, and mule continued to pace off the boundaries of the world suddenly transformed. It smelled different. Overall was the smell of water and the dirt picked up by the river and deposited in soft wet rills everywhere. And the smell of juniper, wrenched from the mountains and scattered at every turn of the river, and the sweet, sharp odor of creosote.

And the sounds were new. The small

trickle of the river that could be heard only if you were on the banks of the north fork had been replaced by the rush of water that came at the camp in two directions and cut it off from everything else. There was a constant chorus of toads that, having slept for months or years or centuries, were suddenly awake and desperate to mate in a world temporarily wet enough to support the lives of tadpoles that would be aquatic for the first weeks of their lives in the desert.

Ned's duty was to stay where he was and watch the lieutenant sleep. He wondered if this was the same sleep he knew or some other, darker sleep that he also knew, though not in the same clear and obvious way. His main job was to note any signs of consciousness in the lieutenant, and if he saw any, to call Sergeant Stonehouse or Triggs immediately.

But there were no signs save an occasional cough followed by the sleepy seep of water from mouth and nose that he had come to see as the natural order of things and no cause for either hope or alarm. Instead he refined his duty as keeping away the flies that circled and tried to land on the sleeping man in anticipation of a new breeding ground. He waved away flies with a pine bough, and he read.

January 4. Christmas came and went, and then the year turned. There was little to acknowledge either. I did my best to keep the days festive, cooking a fine venison brought to us by Zee and his comrades. But for Mr. Estes and Augustine, those were yet further work days, marked by the need to provide shelter for the animals. Both of them thanked me for the shirts I had sewn for them for the Christmas celebration, and then went back to work. There has been no further snow, but the air continues to cool and there is often frost in the mornings. The days, mostly, are quite pleasant.

January 18. I pull myself from my funk and think how much richer is my life now than it once was. I can do all of those things that are expected of a woman and a wife, and I learn I am capable of so much more. I tend to the chickens and the milk cow with no help from the men. I have learned the art of stringing barbed wire, and I stretch it and hammer it to mesquite posts with large, sharp staples, if not as quickly as a man, with as much skill, and my fences shall last as long as theirs. I cannot imagine the reaction of my friends and family from the old life should they see me in canvas trousers, wrapping a strand of wire on a post with one hand as I nail it with the other. Or, as I did yesterday, taking charge of a recalcitrant shoat, grabbing hold of it by the ear and rear leg and lifting it from its trotters while it shrieked the most awful sound at the indignity. When I threw it down where it belonged, it looked at me with a mixture of anger and regard that told me it wanted no more of me if it could help it.

I have become an able dispatcher of rattlesnakes. I know the sound of their rattles immediately and can locate them without thinking, should I hear it. I rarely go near shade without a hoe or shovel, which are fearsome weapons to a snake. Where once they near froze me with terror, now I slice them up as unconcerned as if they were rocks or weeds.

He would stop in his reading and attend to the lieutenant, who continued his sound sleep. With the pine branch, he would fan him for a while, brushing away the flies that had come in abundance with the flood, laying their eggs in the dead that the flood had left behind. He would let the needles brush against the lieutenant's face in the hope that the soft tickle or the sharp scent of the pine would wake him. Occasionally, the lieutenant's eyes would flutter a bit, or he would grimace, even grunt now and again. But he did not wake.

He came to the reading of the diary with anticipation and left with regret. He was somewhat disturbed to read of Mary's transformation into a ranch wife, even a cowboy, for he saw her always in dresses and crinolines, her hair tucked into a fashionable bonnet from the East, her features delicate and kind. That she would kill a rattlesnake by herself, though, pleased him, in part due to the contrast with the delicacy of her aspect. What an appearance it would be to see the well-groomed, pretty Eastern girl hacking a large rattlesnake into pieces. But he should have to alter his picture of her, he supposed.

They were, he thought, similar spirits, transplanted from New England into the Arizona desert under the harshest, most forbidding of circumstances. He thought, perhaps, he should write his story of coming into the West. But he was a fratricide, a thief, a rustler, and an Indian killer, and not worthy of being the hero of his own tale.

And that was the worst of this duty — the time given him to think. He had left Hartford looking for a way to never think again. He had thought that the Army would be perfect for that. In the Army, he imagined, it was all "take orders and obey without thinking." He had thought that he would be so engaged in fighting that there would be no time to ponder anything, that his only thought would be to keep himself alive.

And that had happened to him once. The rest of the time his thoughts were free to torment him as they wished. And they did. And this duty, sitting here beside the lieutenant, taking no action other than brushing a pine bough over him every few minutes to startle the determined flies, gave him the most time of all.

He thumbed ahead in the diary.

July 9. There is nothing so inconstant here as the rain. In the winter we have days of small, sleety rains that threaten never to end. A couple of showers grace the spring and give the seeds their start into the year. Now each afternoon, we can watch the clouds move in from the south and travel over us until they are stopped by the mountains to the north.

Then the next quantity bumps into those and the rain starts and comes down hard, harder than I have ever seen rain, with great booms of thunder and lightning that trace intricate paths through the sky. There is little warning, but beware the man or creature who is caught out in the downpour. The earth, being dry for so long, sheds water into the many washes that lace the lowlands, and what seem, for most of the year, to be stretches of sand become great torrents of water that cannot be crossed by any means save a bridge (and who in this country knows what a bridge might be?). By the next morning, the washes have become gentle brooks or stretches of wet sand. But likely, in the afternoon, the clouds will again push up from the south and the cycle will begin anew.

"What are you reading?"

He jumped at the sound of the voice, which was, in fact, a voice from the dead. The lieutenant lay, eyes opened but squinting, as if just awakened from a nap.

"Sir?"

"I asked what you are reading. You appear engrossed."

"It's just a book, sir."

"Let me see it." The lieutenant reached for the book, gasping in pain as he tried to rise from the cot. Ned hesitated but handed the book to him.

"I can't see it. Hand me my spectacles."

"Your spectacles are lost, sir."

LIEUTENANT
ANTHONY AUSTIN

He had no time to respond, to ask how his spectacles might have been lost, before the boy left the tent on a dead run. He did not know why he was waking into the full light of day. Had he overindulged the night before? He could not remember. There was very little whisky left, he knew, and the paymaster and Donovan, close behind, were due today, or was it tomorrow? He needed to speak to Bobby, but he could raise neither his head nor his voice. He shut his eyes and slipped back into the swiftly moving currents of sleep.

"Sir. Sir."

He broke free into waking again.

"It's Sergeant Triggs, Lieutenant."

Of course. Of course it was Triggs. He had to get up and put an end to this strangeness and foolishness. He had drunk too much the night before. He was sure of it. But what had he done? Had he made some embarrassing scene? "Sergeant," he said. He rose and came into the grip of a profound weariness. He lay himself back down.

"Be easy, Lieutenant. You've had a bad time of it. Don't be pushing yourself, sir. Just rest."

"What?" he asked, knowing it was an inappropriate question. He was starting to anger. No matter what he had done the evening before, he was not to be treated as an invalid. He needed to get up, to prove himself, to show that he was stronger than the drink that occasionally bested him.

"The flood, sir. Do you remember the flood?"

In the Bible? Of course he remembered the flood. Noah and Ararat. First the raven, then the dove. But what had that to do with anything of the present?

"You were caught in the flood. You were crossing the river when it came. You had no chance, sir. It was all of a sudden. It was like nothing anyone had seen before. It had you trapped between its banks, sir. We got you some miles down."

He had tatters of remembrance, but he did not remember any specific thing or event. What he remembered was a series of shocks. Galvanic pulses through his body. The sudden awareness, the impact and spin, the struggle against the water. Yes, water. He remembered a bit more. Water. A great deal of water. The world suddenly gone to water. He had struggled against it. And there was more. "Wanderer? Wanderer. How is Wanderer?"

"Your horse, sir?" Triggs shook his head. "It was no good. He was gone."

He felt himself pressed into the horse's neck. His hand grasping at its mane, trying to make himself and the horse one, counting on the horse to save both of their lives. He shook his head, though that hurt him enormously. "Damn fine horse."

"Yes, sir."

"And how long have I slept? What is the time?"

"It is near to eleven, sir. But you have slept for two days. We have been greatly concerned for you, sir."

"I'll be getting up, then. Tell the captain that I am all right, bruised and tired, but all right." He read the rest of the story in the look that passed between Triggs and Thorne. "No." He could think of nothing more. "No."

"He was coming behind you, sir. He tried to pull you out and it took him as well."

"You're sure?"

"Of what, sir? We have him. We found him

404

before we found you. It was a miracle that we found you alive. We had already found Captain Franklin, caught up in the branches of a Palo Verde tree, sir." Triggs stopped then, struggling to say no more, to hold back the story that wanted to come rushing out, to wear itself out and become powerless in the telling.

"Bobby," he said. "Bobby." He whispered the name.

"Sir," Thorne said. "He was a hero, sir. It was a great thing he did. He sacrificed himself to save you. He was an example to us all."

He waved the boy off. There was nothing more he wanted or needed to hear. He just wanted them away from him. He felt shock and grief, but more, he felt a deep and abiding weariness. He heard, in the distance, someone wailing, a low, long moan, and then knew it was himself.

He called for Thorne when he had composed himself. "My uniform," he said.

"It is there, sir." The private pointed to the stack of blue on top of the crates that served as his desk. "Do you need help, sir?"

"No. Leave me. I will be there directly."

"There is no need, sir. The sergeants have the camp in order. There are repairs being made. There is nothing that needs your immediate attention. Not for a day or so."

"Bobby."

"He is being prepared, sir. For . . ." The boy paused as if he could not remember the term for the practice, or did not wish to. "For Camp Bowie, sir."

"No," he said. "Not yet."

"Sir. There is not much time left. He needs burial soon, sir. I beg your pardon, sir. It is just that . . ."

"Leave me. I will see to it."

When the boy was gone, he began an inspection of his own body. There seemed to be nothing broken, but he had taken a bad beating. There were bruises and cuts everywhere. His right hip was purple and yellow and streaked nearly to the knee. He had to sit on his cot and gently work his trousers over his foot and up the leg by inches. Putting on his blouse, he found he could not fully extend either arm. Pushing his left arm into the sleeve brought tears to his eyes. Both legs were so badly bruised and aching that he could not put on his boots. He went out dressed and barefoot, walking like an old man who had fallen into the firewalker's pit.

The company greeted him with surprise and concern. He could feel the attention more than he could either see or hear it. He returned salutes with his hand raised no higher than his chest. The journey was no longer than one hundred yards, but it took him a long time. He moved with small steps on his painful white feet. He kept his eyes on a spot on the ground some ten yards in front of him to save the exertion of raising his head. His arms rode slightly behind him and barely bent at the elbow. From any distance, he would have been taken for an old man, badly gone to the rheumatism.

The bier had been made of planks and was on two sawhorses set up between pine trees, in sight of both the officers' quarters and the parade ground. A rope had been stretched between the trees and just above the planks. A blanket was draped across the rope as a tented shroud. A soldier, Bird-wood, he thought, stood at one end of the bier, holding a pine bough. The distance between himself and the bier seemed barely to diminish as he made his slow progress toward it.

A human body is a fragile thing. This thought had come to him more times than he could or cared to remember. He had seen death many times before. He had been responsible for it, had tried to prevent it, had inflicted it. He had never regarded it lightly. As a man of science, he held death not in awe but in respect. Yet as he reached his hand to the blanket that covered the body, it trembled as though this were a completely new experience for him. The rough wool of the blanket may as well have been a sheet of lead. He grasped a small edge of the blanket between his thumb and forefinger, yet he did not have the strength to lift it. He made the easier, more natural motion of pulling it toward him.

The sight of the body knocked him to his knees, and as he went down, he nearly took the makeshift bier with him. Two soldiers, Birdwood and some other, rushed toward him and held him before he could fall forward, onto the bier. He struggled to his feet with help from the soldiers, then pushed and waved them away with small, painful motions.

Bobby's eyes were swollen shut, yet there was about the face an expression of alert attention — a set of the jaw, also swollen, possibly broken on the right side, a pull to the upper lip, an unusual lift to the brows. His mustaches, unwaxed now, hung below the corners of his mouth. The body was white, in the early stages of bloat. *Pupal.* He could not ignore the term that pushed its way into his consciousness. Large patches of purple had turned him piebald where he had smashed against rocks and trees on his way downriver. The left arm, crossed over the right at the puffed belly, was broken. A two-inch splinter of bone jutted through the skin.

The right leg, too, seemed broken, lumped at an odd position, turning the foot toward the other. His dress uniform lay neatly folded and stacked between his feet. The dark hair, which had lost all luster, was a tangled mess, full of sand and leaf. The chest now seemed small and fragile, somehow caved in. The hands — right open, left clenched — were battered and blue at the tips. The penis had shrunk to a mere cap to the testicles, laying heavy against the battered legs.

At the juncture of the neck and shoulder, a piece of branch had been driven through the skin and deep into the body. If Bobby had not drowned, then certainly this was the hurt that killed him. He reached out and touched it, tentatively at first, then grasped it in his hand. He was afraid to pull, sure he would cause Bobby more pain. As ridiculous as the thought was, he had to fight against his own instinct to apply any force to the branch. Suddenly, it moved a fraction of an inch, then stopped.

"Sir." Triggs was behind him.

"Clean him up. I will come back and dress him."

"Yes, sir."

"And get that stick out of his neck."

"Sir. Beg your pardon, sir. It has penetrated deep into the body."

"Then saw it off." His own body shook with an unaccustomed fury at the sergeant who stood before him, thick as a pine log, looking at once confused, guilty, and pitying.

"We shall bury him this afternoon."

"Sir. We thought to prepare the body for transport to Bowie."

"No. Here."

"But, sir. His family. The senator. They will want his body back East for a more fitting burial."

"Then they can come here and dig him up and kiss my ass while they are about it. Dig a grave over there next to Borchert and Wortham. He would want that, to be buried next to his men. Right now, I care a great deal more about what he would want than what the senator wants."

"Lieutenant. We're cut off here. I have a detail working on a raft, a kind of ferry to get the wagon with his body across the river. We've lost about a quarter of the camp, and we're cut off from the outside until the water abates."

"Pull the detail off the raft and onto digging a grave. The river can't stay like this for long. Bury him before the sun goes down."

"Yes, sir."

When Triggs had gone, he continued to stare at the body. As battered as it was, it was incomprehensible that Bobby would not heal, wake, and return to his duties, return to him. As often as he had seen death and acknowledged it, he could not comprehend this one. It seemed that as long as he had been alive, so had Bobby, and since he was still alive, then so must Bobby be. But the body did nothing, and when he bent to it and kissed the cold, dry lips, the recognition that Bobby was gone, completely gone, came out in a strangled cry of horror, grief, and sickness that took him from his feet and onto the makeshift bier, sending them both to the ground.

The thunder, lightning, and rain came and went while he stayed to his cot, neither awake nor asleep, but stuck in some between state where the dream world caught up with the waking world and altered it, though not sufficiently. Bobby moved in and out of his tent, stopped twice, and talked with him, though now, fully awake, he remembered nothing of their conversation. What he did remember was that Bobby was dead and buried in a place he had come to hate, in a terribly short time. He could not wake out of that.

He roused himself from his cot and began putting on the clean uniform folded on the chair next to the cot. He could not find his spectacles and remembered then that they were lost. And then he remembered that he had worn this uniform at Bobby's funeral, standing straight and silent to hold the uniform in place, but in fact far distant from the crude ceremony. He had dressed the body with painful slowness, pulling the fabric over limbs that no longer articulated correctly. He had combed Bobby's hair and pulled leaves and sand from his beard. It had been the most difficult task of his entire life. He took his own uniform off and began dressing in a set of fatigues that were long past clean.

Up and dressed, he sat back down. He should go forward and assume command of the post. Since Bobby's death, the post had gone on under the command of someone

— Stonehouse or Triggs — and it remained on the face of the earth, just as it had. He had heard the bugles and commands, and even now he heard the voices of the men and someone barking orders in the distance. It was his job to get up and take command, at least until the word of Bobby's death had reached Bowie, where the decision would surely be made to send a new commander. It was his job to take command whether he felt like it or no, but the Army was built for contingencies, and the post was going on without him, most probably better than it would go on with him.

In the drawer of his campaign chest, he used his hands to sort through the effluvia of his career because his eyes, in the failing light, were of little use. Finally, he touched on the wrapped leather pouch and pulled it out of the contents. Inside was a pair of spectacles, old ones, scratched and crooked, not as strong as the ones he had lost, but serviceable when there was nothing else.

Coming across the parade ground, he accepted and returned the salutes of soldiers who stopped in their tracks and brought their hands up as if caught completely off guard by his presence. They were, he supposed, surprised, even frightened to see him, but acting out of pure duty and routine. He presented a strange picture, bedraggled and slow, moving in a stiff gait and soiled uniform.

He refused offers of eggs and bacon, fearing he could not keep them down, but he took coffee that had boiled too long and a loaf of bread and a plate of butter. He took sips of the bitter coffee and then obliterated the taste with hunks of bread he dragged over the butter. He dismissed Thorne, who had come to the bakery on a dead run, having failed to anticipate the lieutenant's return to the world of the living. When Sergeant Stonehouse approached and saluted, he merely motioned to the bench across the table from him. The bread and butter was having the opposite effect from what he expected. With each bite, he became more ravenous than he had been before.

Stonehouse reported what had happened in the days of his confinement. He thought it odd that the sergeant would use a word normally reserved for ladies giving birth. Could there be a situation less similar? He listened to a litany of the mundane. Sections of corral were washed away, stock was missing. Crews had been formed to berm the banks of the river where it was weakest and the camp most vulnerable. The Apache scouts, who had their loyalty first to Captain Franklin and only second to the Army, had left the day before. They were now, officially, deserters.

He continued to poke buttered bread into his mouth. He shook his head vigorously, and at the term "deserters," he waved it away with his hand. The Apaches had little to do with them or they with the Apaches. They were better let go. There was no sense in provoking trouble over a term of which the Apaches certainly could have no conception.

"And what are your orders, sir?" Stonehouse asked.

He started to reply, then pushed in more bread and chewed. He had no orders. He swallowed, drank some coffee, and swallowed again. "Carry on, Sergeant."

Stonehouse hesitated. "Very good, sir." He started to say something else.

"Bread?" Tony held up part of the ragged remains of the loaf.

"No, sir. Thank you, sir."

"Carry on, then."

There was no getting around it. He would have to go through Bobby's things, and though it hurt like the Devil itself, he thought it better to do it now than later. He had a sense that his memory of Bobby was already wearing away at the edges as though it had been handled a little too often, and yet he also feared that if the memory were not exercised, it would fade to oblivion.

He found himself dismayed at the bulk of what must now be touched, thought about, handled, and decided upon. It was a ten-by-twelve officer's tent, one cot, one desk, one chair, and two trunks. Compared to his own, it was the very definition of emptiness and sterility. Anyone else could come in and dispose of the contents and strike, fold, and pack the tent in less than two hours' time and still take tea.

But what appeared to the eye was only warp and woof. Each item, carefully put away and arranged, carried with it a jumble of associations that, assembled, constructed the history of the man who had owned them. The possessions of the dead occupy a distinctive position in the world. They remain, for the meantime, part of the narrative of the life they ornamented. But their connection to that life becomes steadily more tenuous. They slip slowly back into the world of pure things. He found the sense of history, Franklin's and his own, overwhelming. The possessions revealed the real man, not the idealized memory he would become in time. The sight of a book Bobby had borrowed and failed to return buckled Tony's knees and pushed the air out of him. To go through these things was to go through Bobby's life and day. That most of those days were also his was nearly unbearable.

He had, then, the desire to take something of Bobby's and wear it as his own as though it were a disguise. A blouse or pair of stockings would be sufficient. But in the handling and movement of the years, their clothes had been a tangle. They had borrowed each other's clothing that they could wear. As Bobby had aged, he had grown heavier and his older blouses and trousers became Tony's. He took one of Bobby's blouses and found it too big. His trousers were worse, and he could wear nothing with an insignia sewed on. The wide straw sombrero that Bobby had worn on patrols he took for his own. It was a little large but the band could be stuffed with batting to make it fit, and there seemed nothing more intimate than a hat.

He sorted the things, stacking them in three piles. What he might use — kerchiefs, stockings, coats, older blouses — he put in the first. That which he had no use for — trousers and boots, mostly — he put into a pile to distribute among those who might be able to use them. A last pile was to be returned to general stores, being more of the Army than of Bobby. These included blankets, arms, livery, and issued equipment.

It left a pile of personal effects. These loomed, in his mind, large as a mountain. There was a Bible. Bobby had, in New York, a family. And they would want this. Though it had been less read than pounded upon and slammed to the desk to enforce a point, it would become a thing mystical. It would be, forever now, Bobby's Bible, as though it contained his soul rather than his sweat and the oil of his fingers. With it he would be remembered not as he was, but as they wanted him to be. He pushed the things aside and began removing insignia from the uniforms to enclose with the Bible, for these were the sorts of things that families wanted of their dead, no matter that there were many things far more intimate to the man that the family would have nothing to do with.

How odd, he thought, that we remake in death those who we cannot make or remake when they remain stubbornly alive, bent on fashioning their own lives. After a death, those who were near set about the business of refashioning the departed like a troop of industrious insects, not satisfied until they had reduced the dead to what they needed. "Honor thy family, boy." And the dead, less human now than a small terrier, did just as they were asked, walking on their hind legs and barking on command. With that thought, he felt the presence of Bobby wrench away from him just a hand's length further.

He looked for what else the family might want. He took a pair of binoculars, Bobby's dress gloves and helmet and saber, and added them to the pile. They would create a fitting monument for the family and would compose a portrait of which the family would approve, especially since there was nothing of Austin himself in it. Here were remnants, the physical evidence of an officer and a gentleman, one whose fine hands were fit for both the silk glove and the steel saber but who never, trembling with desire, touched the body of a fellow officer.

For himself, he took a meerschaum pipe that smelled as Bobby did and that brought his memory back with alarming speed. Bobby's razor, ivory handled, was the thing that had been closest to his skin, that glided gently over it, taking the thinnest layer with it as it went. His flask, a pint, done in silver, was monogrammed *RGF.* He uncapped it and smelled. It was the bourbon he himself had. And he realized that among the enormous losses he had suffered, he had lost his whisky and with it a good deal of his ability to cope with the great sadness he was just entering into. He dipped the flask back and took a swallow. The flask was nearly full, so he took another. Of the things that Bobby did well, and there was a great number of them, drinking was not one of them.

Later, a good way to drunk, he went through the papers Bobby had left. His journal was one of duty. He had lived his life in the motion of it, not in contemplation, meditation, or examination. Despite his adoration of Marcus Aurelius, Bobby had fallen quite short of that man. The entries were short, a few sentences, hardly sentences even, that delineated what he had considered progress, or what he knew the Army had considered progress. "Reveille at five-thirty. Two reported for sick call. The rest assigned to maintenance. Taps at ten."

He went through the journal haphazardly, looking at entries in a random fashion, stopping at one page or another, pulling it close to his face and peering, squinting at the handwriting, looking for something, though he did not know what it was. He could not believe that Bobby had reduced their careers in the Army, from West Point to California to here to hell, to nothing more than short notations on the small labors that separated the beginnings of days from the beginnings of sleep.

Even the incidents of 1867, which had altered their careers and lives so utterly, were noted in the briefest fashion. "In pursuit of Indians fleeing the battle at the lava beds, we were attacked from behind. Lost six men." And later, "Investigation inconclusive. Gen. G.C. to reassign to southwestern divisions." "O. Brickner demoted to corporal, G.C. having honored my request that he not be cashiered." And that was it. A brief notation of facts, without emotion or reflection.

He woke in the dark. Fumbling at the ammunition crate beside his cot, he found matches, rose, and lit his lamp, stumbling and clattering over something as he stepped toward the lamp. When the light had taken the lamp and spread, he saw it was his supper that he had stepped on, supper that someone, Thorne probably, had brought and left, unable or unwilling to wake him. There were beans and something that might be canned tomatoes visible under the overturned plate. Next to it there was a hunk of bread. He stooped, picked it up, and ate it, without bothering to brush it off. At the flap of the tent he tried to judge the hours. There were lamps in the distance and he heard the voices of soldiers attacking their boredom. He had not heard Taps, so he knew it was not yet 9:30. He was weary to the bone but fought against going back to sleep. Both his and Bobby's watches had been ruined in the flood. But then, time seemed simple and inconsequential.

Bobby's flask was empty. He pushed the papers back into the pouch, slung it across his shoulder, blew out the lamp, and made his way to his own tent. The sound of toads was that of one huge, breathing creature. Even in the faint light of the moon, the motion of the toads was evident, a constant movement at foot level that could not be identified as such, but more as an excitation of the earth itself, as though it had suddenly become very anxious and agitated about something.

"The end is not likely."

The words stopped him. He stood still where he was and tried to identify the source of the sound. He neither heard nor saw anyone who might have said it. Around him the wind was swirling easily, dropping the temperature quickly. He wanted to know who had said it and what it might mean.

"In the fatal rain," another voice said.

"Good evening," he called. "Who is there?"

There was no answer beyond the wind brushing the leaves and small branches around him. They were discussing the events of the last days, obviously — the "fatal rain," the rain that had taken Bobby and had nearly taken him. Or had the speaker meant "rein"? Had someone else died? Had there been a riding accident? Or "reign"? Was someone comparing their command to a monarchy? Was he being blamed for the deaths of Wortham and Bobby? Or was this in the future tense? Were they predicting death and destruction at his hand?

"Who is there?" he demanded.

"Lieutenant?" A voice echoed from a good distance. He heard boots coming at a jog or double-time step. "You're up, sir. Are you all right? Can I get you something?"

"Thorne?"

"Yes, sir?"

"You were speaking of me?"

"When, sir?"

"Just now."

"No, sir. I was playing cards with Private

Park, sir. We were just chatting, sir. The way you do in a game of cards. Idle conversation."

"About the weather?"

"Not that, sir. Just things. Trivial. I can't remember them all, except Park has an amusing story about Indianapolis."

"Are you afraid of me, Thorne?"

"Afraid of you, sir? No, sir. I mean, you are our commander. But, sir, begging your pardon, I'm more afraid *for* you. You've had a terrible hard time of it, sir."

"A hard time of it. Yes. Yes, quite a hard time. And terrible."

"Sir?" Thorne stood expectantly.

"Yes?"

"The men, sir. They found the captain's saddle and some of his belongings, sir. Would you like me to bring them?"

No. He would not like them brought, but he could not say that, and Thorne turned and took off at a run to retrieve the belongings.

They were not Bobby's belongings. They were his own. The saddle was ruined, having soaked in river water for a good time. One stirrup was nearly severed. It could, perhaps, be mended and oiled but he did not think so. It was a good saddle, but it

424

was a saddle and the Army had plenty more.

He was more interested in the wooden crate that, when opened, revealed six bottles of the Mexican whisky still unbroken amid the litter of the other six bottles. The irony was not lost that this vile concoction should survive while the fine Kentucky whisky was forever lost in the river. Still, despite the allure of the maker's art, whisky was more about effect than the delicacy of its blending. Six bottles were not much, but they were better than none.

And finally, he unwrapped the oilcloth from around the center-fire Colt and the boxes of ammunition that seemed to have survived quite well, though the boxes for the cartridges were water damaged. He looked at the cartridges and found them in good shape. This was the last present he had bought for Bobby, and now he presented it to himself in lieu of Bobby.

The bundle of letters was in the pouch with the rest of the paperwork. He recognized the hand of Thorne and knew these were recent letters, not yet sent off. On the flap of the envelope, Thorne, in a small, tight hand, had written the contents of the letters as was customary. "In the matter of the white woman. The Bakery. Mapping."

He considered whether or not to open the letters. They were meant for Bowie, that was evident. And there was, perhaps, Bobby's final decision on the matter of the white woman. He wished he knew what that was, but they had not discussed it. He thought to open it and read it but did not. He could have Thorne simply write out another envelope for the letter and send it on. But he did not open it.

He was coming to understand grief as a vast ocean circling the world. When you were in its presence, it came at you in waves, some of them larger than others. Some were barely more than a ripple, and others picked you up and sent you to kingdom come with the vengeance of a power you did not know, except that it existed.

And that's what the next wave did. At the first thought of "dead," the wave crashed over him, balling him up and throwing him down. Full of whisky, he had no choice but to go with it. He was spun in the churning power and felt himself no more than a stick, certainly nothing of consciousness, will, and power on his own.

He did not remember leaving his feet, but he came to consciousness — though, by conventional thinking, he had never left it — on the ground floor of his tent, looking up at the jars of specimens from which the rattlesnakes — western diamondback, timber, Mojave, sidewinder, and speckled; lizards — gecko, various whiptails, horned, and skinks; and scorpions; tarantulas; centipedes; and lubber grasshoppers stared in the unchanging distance of death.

It must be boring, death. And now he felt regret that he had condemned the one person he cared for most in the world to the constancy of that boredom. The pain that had hit him and taken him down had let him back up now, and he felt the relief of the sick man who one day realizes that he is no longer ill, but well. Still, he was not well. He understood that behind the clean, sharp pain of grief lay the other. And he understood that it had always been there, waiting for him. Now it was rising up, and he was already feeling himself pulled back down.

This despair of the unrelenting had taken him before. Twice before, once at the Point and later after the war, almost killing him. Despair had not only shown him strength, but also that it grew within him, like tar, thick and heavy, and when it rose up and caught you, there was no escaping. It left you stained and let you know you would never be free. And he knew that the next time, he would not be strong enough to fight it back down.

He went to his makeshift desk, took the oilcloth bundle, and unwrapped the Colt he had bought from Donovan. He hadn't the love of weaponry Bobby had, but this was a beautiful gun, small and compact and delicately curved. He flipped open the chamber and filled it with all six bullets, though that was five more than he needed.

He sat on the edge of the cot and held the gun in his lap. There was, truly, nothing more left for him. What he had become was what he was going to become. There was nothing beyond that. He squinted at the future and found nothing of interest in it. He put the Colt to his temple and cocked the hammer. It required only the small pressure of his finger on the trigger to bring the whole affair, the foolishness — for he now considered his life just that, foolishness — to a conclusion. He stared forward, keeping his eyes open, for he wanted to enter death that way, to see what it was, how it was formed, for nothing was more speculated on and less scientifically examined. He held the gun there, then lowered it, unable, finally, to muster the small strength required to end this.

He was not afraid. At least, he did not

think he was afraid of death, nor did he long for it. Heaven and hell were chimeras of the human imagination placed there by those who could not stand the thought of nothing. He looked up at the animals swimming in their small dark seas of alcohol, and for no reason he could explain to himself or anyone else, he knew the certainty that the next move was to mount up a patrol and go after the woman.

Triggs registered dismay with only his eyebrows. He nodded his comprehension of the statement and, seemingly, his agreement. He spoke the words "very good, sir," with only the slightest movement of his lips. When this agreement had been acknowledged, he began the slow process of tearing it down. "The lieutenant is feeling better, then?"

"Quite."

"Very good, sir. You look some improved."

He smiled with the barest corner of the right side of his mouth. "Some," he said.

"You gave us a considerable fright."

"Can you have the men ready to ride tomorrow?"

"I can, sir. But, sir. If we take as many men as you have proposed, we leave this camp with less-than-adequate defenses."

"Against what?"

"Why, the Apaches, sir. That mountain is their home. There are hundreds of them up there. More of them than of us."

"Right now, at this very moment, are there not more of them than of us?"

"Of course. Four or five times as many."

"Then it is small matter if there are four or five times as many or eight or ten times, is it not?"

"I should not think so. Then there is the matter of the scouts. They know this camp. They have reported back to the Apaches everything they know."

"What the scouts know, they knew before. There are no secrets here. The Chiricahua have always known how many of us there are, how many horses we have, the extent of our armory. They have known this from the first days of our arrival. The scouts can tell them who has a fondness for sweets, which of us snores, and who has the best voice for singing. It is not such valuable information. We live here at their pleasure. That has not changed."

"But we are talking about mounting an attack upon a band of Apaches. Our scouts, Apaches, have left us rather than to participate in an attack against them. If we go and leave this camp inadequately defended, the

Apaches will attack it."

"I think not. Our scouts do not want a part of an attack on another band, that is clear enough. It does not make particular difference to them if we go after this band or not, so long as they are not endangered. We see them all as Apache. They see themselves as Chiricahua and Arivaipa. The Chiricahua will see it as business between us and the Arivaipa and nothing to do with themselves.

"Think of it in terms of the United States. Were Pennsylvania to attack Missouri, Kansas would certainly not wade in on the side of Missouri, for whom they have no particular fondness. Rather, they will see it as none of their business. It is why the Apaches have so much difficulty understanding why soldiers come after them for attacking farmers. What business is it of the soldiers? Farmers are not soldiers, and Arivaipa are not Chiricahua. They see things separately. We see them together."

"Still. I do not like it."

"That is abundantly clear. And it shall be as it may. We shall begin preparations to ride. Reveille will be sounded at five on Wednesday, with 'Boots and Saddles' at seven."

Triggs stood as if fishing for some answer

to this. But there was no answer to an order except to salute and say, "Yes, sir."

He peered at the maps in the light of the oil lamps. Without his proper spectacles, he had to lean close to whatever he attempted to read, as he saw the near better than the far. It was a struggle to achieve comprehension, but he assumed that he would soon grow used to the world in its new unfocused form. On top of the map, he had Bobby's journal. He read from the journal and tried to fit that scanty information on the map that Bobby had been filling in piecemeal. What he knew of this place, he knew well. But what he knew was a small area, studied intently, as was his way. Bobby had known a much larger area, but looking at the journal and maps, it was as if he had not known it at all.

The sense he was able to make of it was that the Apaches had decamped for the time being in the mountains that began some forty miles to the southeast. It was a small range that ran some twenty or twenty-five miles south by southeast. It was most probably where they were headed and now encamped. It had been over two weeks since the attack on the hacienda, but having gained the Peloncillos Mountains, the

Apaches would remain there. Those mountains crossed, at about two-thirds of their length, the border between the United States and Mexico. As long as the Apaches stayed in the northern half to two-thirds of the range, they could be pursued. Beyond that, he had no authority. Of course, he thought, sitting back, he had no authority beyond his own on any account.

Later, and a couple of small drinks more, he undressed listening to the sounds of the guard as they rode patrol in the reduced area of the camp. The toads were getting steadily louder as the waters receded, making their short mating period perilously close to over. One could hear the desperation in their rhythmic croaking, like a long, labored inhalation and exhalation in unison. He put out his dress uniform, and he cleaned and oiled the Colt revolver, which he had not yet fired. He opened the cylinder and slid the cartridges out. It was this that amazed him most, the ease with which the weapon could be loaded and unloaded. He slipped the cartridges back in again. Loaded, unloaded, loaded again.

He blew out the lamp and stripped off the rest of his clothes and sat on the cot, naked. In the dark, the frantic singing of the toads became the rhythm of his own breathing.

Taken by a sudden thought, he rose in the dark and made his way to the pile of Bobby's belongings he had brought back to his tent in preparation of sending them to Bobby's people. He took the saber and moved it from Bobby's pile onto his own clothing for tomorrow. Tomorrow he would become not a staff officer, but a line officer, responsible for the success of his mission. That done, he went back to his cot. He lay back and listened, waiting for sleep to take him. When it did not, he slid his hand down his chest and belly to his phallus and tried to coax it into response, but there was none. He continued to lay on his back, hands crossed on his chest, aware that he must appear, must even want to appear, dead.

PRIVATE NED THORNE

They were given the rest of the afternoon after the burial of the captain. There was little in the way of duty for them anyway. He kept attentive to the needs of the lieutenant, but it became abundantly clear that the lieutenant's greatest needs did not involve him. The river found its banks and slowed, but each afternoon more rain in the mountains rolled off the saturated ground and into the river and its branches. They had erected a temporary corral north of the old one, a quarter of which had floated downstream some days ago. They went through the routines of cleaning and keeping order, but it was difficult, if not impossible, in a camp that changed daily as the river rose, fell, and changed course.

Everything was now mud. Mornings broke clear and hot, and the ground steamed, then firmed briefly. But after noon it clouded from the southeast. And, he learned, clouds from the southeast brought rain, and lots of it. Often by two or three in the afternoon, the skies opened and the rain poured down faster and harder than the ground, their tents, and their clothes could absorb it.

Now that he finally had new stockings that did not sweat his feet, he was reduced to walking in wet boots, wet stockings. His feet were no longer hot, but no less miserable.

The calling of the toads was constant. It was a new sound in the mix of sounds he had learned. The toads themselves were everywhere. It was as though they had fallen from the sky with the rain. The color and size of the rock that littered the ground, the toads suddenly set the ground in motion. With nearly every step he took toward his tent and bunk, a toad, disturbed, leaped to a new position and took up its calling once again. They were frantic in the short season of rain. While the water stayed above ground, the toads had to find mates, breed, lay eggs, and get them hatched and into adulthood before the water disappeared. In their small lives, the desert was a wet place. The ones who saw the desert as it was most of the year did not survive it.

He moved across the parade ground, letting the toads watch for themselves. Legions sprang from in front of him as he walked.

They avoided him, but others who had not been so fast lay flattened in the mud, often in the middle of a hoofprint or boot print. He was beginning to feel revulsion toward them. Their plenitude, their packed bodies spilling gut at mouth and cloaca, their desperation to mate and die began to disgust him. Only his desire to see no more of their guts prevented him from stomping them flat as others did.

His boots stuck and sucked in the mud. Clouds had piled in over the mountains again, and he could hear the distant roll of the thunder. It would be here in a few hours, perhaps only minutes, and it would be pure fury — the rain coming hard and cold as ice, the lightning long and jagged, moving across the horizon in broad forks, the thunder sustaining itself for several seconds like the sound of heaven being ripped apart.

"Have you heard?" Jarbal stood at the fly of the tent.

"Heard what?"

"What they are saying."

"What are they saying?"

"We're leaving. We're packing up and heading out."

"Says who?"

"Says everyone. It's a well-known fact. Everyone knows it. Everyone is talking about it."

"I believe everyone is drunk."

"And why is everyone drunk?"

"Because you've been into the whisky."

Birdwood considered this, snickered, snorted, and gave himself over to giggles. "We've been into the whisky," he agreed.

"We buried the captain not three hours ago."

Jarbal pulled himself upright. "Right. And that's why we're leaving. The captain. We're leaving here because the captain is dead."

"Leaving for where?"

"Bowie to start. We're going back to Bowie where we belong. Where there is food and beds and whores and beer. We're going to live like real soldiers back in Bowie."

"I'm not sure."

"Yes. Yes. Yes. The lieutenant. The lieutenant is taking us back to Bowie where we belong. He's giving this up."

"But it's not his to give up. They might send us another captain, but they're not going to just shut this camp down because the captain drowned."

"Yes. No one in Bowie wants to come out here. Everyone says so. There ain't good beds or food, and there's only whores every couple of months, and no captain wants to live like that. So we're all going back to Bowie."

"Captains don't decide where they want to go. Colonels decide where captains go. And there's a colonel at Bowie. I met him. Captains are going to go where he tells them to go, beds and whores or not."

This stopped Birdwood, and he began to pull hard on the shock of hair that fell onto his forehead, something he did when he got agitated. "No," he said. "Park said, and Pack and Hermann and Foster. They all said. We're going back to the world."

The world. It was a thrilling word, *world.* He thought momentarily of trees, his house, a bed, warm food, his parents, Hartford, and Edith Woodruff. And, ultimately and inevitably, Thad and his absence. It brought him up short. He'd left the world of his own choice, running from his mistakes. No matter the allure of the world, it was better to be in the Army, where mistakes were frequent and expected, and all you really needed to do was follow orders. And beyond that, no one really cared what you did, and most mistakes were someone else's.

"You're drunk," he said. "Get on your cot and sleep some."

"Sleep, hell. I'm going back to the world."

"Not very likely. You been listening to the idle and feeble. Go to sleep."

Birdwood threw himself down on his cot.

"Wait. Sleep outside if you're going to be sick. Don't go stinking up the tent."

"Hell and villainy." Birdwood rose up from the cot and, unsteadily, to his feet. "I ain't going to be sick, but I could use a nap. Make up your mind."

Ned watched him wobble to the tent fly and outside. He could tell Birdwood was far gone to the whisky, and his boots had gone round and threatened to pitch him to the ground. If the lieutenant or one of the sergeants came by, Birdwood would be toting the post for a good while. Disgusted, Ned threw himself off his cot and went to get him.

Jarbal sat at the base of a pine tree, already asleep, though he could not have been down for more than a few seconds. Ned bent down and shook him until his eyelids struggled open. "Get up. You're going to get caught out here. Get up and back to the tent." Birdwood began to shake his head in the negative, but that dissolved into a mere wagging of his head as he floated back into sleep. Ned took him by the shoulders and shook him hard.

"Wake up."

The eyelids fluttered open again. Bird-wood's pupils drifted in their sockets, struggling to latch on to some image, but never quite catching. Ned kept shaking him as if to find a field of focus by accident. Bird-wood's eyes rolled and the lids came down again. Ned picked Birdwood up by the arms and hoisted him to his feet, pulling Bird-wood to him, ready to carry him the rest of the way to the tent.

Carrying was not entirely needed. Bird-wood got his feet moving in an awkward shuffle so that Ned was barely pulling him to get him moving. He maneuvered them through the tent fly and over to Birdwood's cot. He had him aligned toward it, ready to let him fall backward into it, when Bird-wood's eyes opened once again. They focused on Ned's eyes and Birdwood opened his mouth to speak. But as soon as he did, a torrent of thin, whisky-fouled, licorice vomit hit Ned squarely in the chest. Birdwood looked apologetic for just an instant, but he smiled as Ned jumped back. Birdwood sat heavily on his cot, rolled to prone, his legs still dangling off the edge of the cot, and slept.

At the north fork, there was a group of boulders that formed something of a natural ring. By adding large rocks around the boulders, they had built a pool of calm water, above waist deep, clear and clean, the water being flushed out every few minutes. By kneeling at the bank and leaning over, Ned was able to wash out his blouse and trousers with a bar of pine soap. The smell of old whisky was still strong enough to nearly gag him. He stripped off his union suit and held it into the water, then stepped into the water himself, able finally to wash both his clothes and himself at the same time.

He sat naked under a pine tree, his uniform and union suit spread on sprawling juniper branches to dry. The sun warmed the sky at the same time that a small breeze came up and kept the heat from becoming oppressive. Above him, jays scuttled through the branches of a pine, quarreling with each other, with other birds, maybe with the world itself. With the rough bark of the tree at his back and the ground thickly carpeted with pine needles, he felt relaxed and whole as he had not felt in a long, long time.

He wished he had the diary the lieutenant had taken, even though its contents had lately vexed him. Events no longer marched forward as they should, but dissolved into tears and complaining. With no events to keep him going, he was lured by the voice of her in his own head, a voice that he recognized as clearly as the voice of anyone he had ever known. He wished to hear that voice again, just as he wanted to hear the voices of Thad and his mother and his father and Miss Edith Woodruff. He wanted to hear their voices speak of the events of the day.

Life was about events, was it not? This he knew from school and church. Each life led toward conclusions that became evident as events unfolded. It was not possible that George Washington could have become anything other than president of the United States. Everything in his life pointed that way. But perhaps that was only great lives. Perhaps lesser lives, like his, did not have such patterns and eventualities. Had the events of his own life led to Thad's death? Surely they had. In the small decisions of his life — whether to sweep out the store or hook it to play with his friends, to read history or to read about the lives of the heroes who fought the wild Indians or of outlaws who boldly robbed banks and stagecoaches — he had been steadily moving on a path laid out by the Devil, steadily away from the Heavenly Father until he was so lost he became part of the Tribe of Cain.

He was lost. That was certain. But did not Reverend Spiller say that no life was ever lost? That however one strayed, whatever horror one had found, God would take you back? He wanted God to love him, and he wanted to love God, though he knew God was, at best, disappointed in him and found him an unfit vessel, weak and lacking in all good traits. He would give himself over to God to do whatever was His will. But was the voice of God so easy to discern? It seemed to him that God's voice was not so far from the voice of Satan. Neither of them had the clarity of the woman's voice. How did one know for sure whose voice spoke to you?

He wished he could speak with Reverend Spiller. Or Lieutenant Austin. But the reverend was a thousand miles away, and Lieutenant Austin was farther away than he knew. The lieutenant lived now in the land of Grief, and Ned knew from experience that that was a terrible place.

His only hope was to do something great enough to overcome the wrong he had done. If he could rescue the woman, he could, perhaps, tip the balance. It seemed that they were getting ready to go, though the colonel had forbidden it. It would be done without his knowledge and without the orders of General Crook. But so much depended on her rescue. It was imperative that they retrieve her.

He reached up and touched the wound on his head. It no longer hurt, and what remained was the bunching of the skin where the lips of the cut had knit themselves back together. The hair around the wound was growing back already, stiff and prickly. He kept running his fingers over it, enjoying the slight tickle as his fingers brushed the tips of the hairs. He touched the scar on his cheek, which did not hurt but still had a bit of swelling.

Within an arm's reach to his right, a small pool remained from the cresting of the river. It was laced at the edges with webs of sticky toad eggs and flecked with black at the bottom. He lowered himself to the ground so that his head was directly over the pool. When he extended a finger to the surface of the water, it broke into a frenzy. Hundreds of tiny black tadpoles, nothing more at this point than heads and tails, thrashed through the water in primitive terror of his finger. In just seconds, the swirling settled, only to be begun again as his finger again broke the surface of the water. Strange creatures. Teeming toward a life they could have no conception of, startled into frenzy by the mere flick of a finger.

He lay out prone on the pine needles, naked, head cradled in his arms, and watched the tadpoles. The wind came across his back, cool on his skin. And, watching the blind hurtling of the tadpoles, he was momentarily aware of his body as something other than a means of dragging himself from one place to another at the pleasure of the United States Army, which could never see his body as anything other than an object to be moved.

He pushed himself upright, feeling a great relief as though it had come in on the wind and freed him from his brooding. Like the tadpoles, he was alive in this instant, and maybe he did not need to know any more than that. He thought of Mary, who told in her own words of being naked, as he was now, in the river on the way west, letting the water cleanse and cool her. He thought how she must look, kneeling at the river, loosening her garments, bringing the water up to her bosom to bathe it. The word *bosom* had thrilled him, though he had heard and read it many times before. Still, to read of it from the secret writings of a woman was dark and mysterious, and it made the hair on his arms rise. It was as if the world were suddenly, briefly, stripped bare for him, its mysteries and secrets revealed. He was aware, too, that he understood nothing of women and their ways. He had, months ago now, behind the meeting house at a church social, received a kiss from Miss Edith Woodruff, and the kiss had followed on a delicious squeeze of his hand. The force of the two actions, taken together, had propelled him to a near ecstasy that quickly gave over to confusion. What had that meant, and what was his response to be? He felt sure he should know but surer that he did not, and that, in turn, confused him more. Should he not know? Wasn't that the sort of knowledge that came with manhood, and did that mean that he was still far from that state, maybe never to attain it? Miss Woodruff certainly knew her role, and his lack of knowledge revealed the vast gulf between them.

As surely as if he had come out of the brush and caught her, he saw Mary in the river before him, naked as the day she was born, letting the cold, clear water slide over her. Her body, naked, was the body of the whore and could be his for the touch. Her nipples, like the whore's, were hard and warm as her breasts shifted under his hands. The very thought of it made his phallus stir as if he were, in truth, watching her at this river just in front of him.

And now the Army was going toward her. In another day, maybe two, even three, they would find her and rescue her from her captors. And he would be a special hero. As he had killed the old Indian at the *cienega,* so would he vanquish her tormentors. And she would love him, as one can love only the one who has given you back your own life. She would reach out, ignoring her dishabille, for the Indians had used her badly, and she would tremblingly touch him, asking him to move closer, to hold her and protect her. And she would want, he knew, for him to kiss her and then to enter into her.

The touch of his hand caused him to catch his breath so hard he nearly choked. In the river, she stood, standing straight up, fingers to her mouth, her eyes on his, unblinking in fear or urgency. Holding himself, he scrambled across the dirt and pine needles and into the pool of water.

Though the shock of the water cooled him and his imagination, he was soon adjusted to the cold and again had her image before him. She was crouched now on the opposite bank, dipping her hands into the water and bringing it up to her neck and chest. It ran there in rivulets, coursing its way over her breasts, stiffening her nipples. He thought of the feel of breasts, their wonderful shifting weight and the warm moistness between her legs.

He pushed himself up from the pool to the bank of the river and leaned back on his left arm, so that only his lower legs were still submerged, leaving his right hand free to transubstantiate itself into her and him, and Miss Edith Woodruff and every man and every woman in the world.

It did not take long. Strings of semen curled across the surface of the water, clumped, clotted, and then slid past the rocks and away down stream. Clots of it caught in the sticky mess that held the toad eggs and formed a new gelatinous mass. He pushed farther back, resting his shoulders on the ground at the edge of the pool, letting his head loll back, and he recaught control of his breathing. Above him, the sky was deep and blue, but already it was edged with clouds. He stretched out his arms and let gravity pull him tight to the earth, his legs still bent, his feet dangling in the water. His eyes closed against the blue, and he felt himself begin to drift.

"That's it?"

He scrambled awake and up, rolling over

to his stomach, then crabbing backwards to the pool. Brickner stood there, shirtless and sweated, an empty bucket in his hand. He smiled. "Looks like you beat the hell out of it, there, Marybelle."

"Get out of here. Leave me alone."

Brickner smiled a wide smile and lurched toward him until he was standing over him, legs spread, the left hand still holding the empty bucket. "You don't want company? Because it looked like you was craving it."

"No."

"Could have sworn you did. It did appear for a bit as though you were deep in need of company."

"What do you want?"

Brickner looked down, frowned, then cocked his head as if considering the question. "To be of service to my fellow man. That's all I ever wanted." He squatted down closer until the smell of him caught in the back of Ned's throat and stung his eyes. It was a potent mixture of dried sweat, ammonia, mule, and things he could not identify. He had a quick memory of a dog he once had that would roll in anything dead or disgusting and wear the scent like a new suit.

"Leave me alone."

Brickner regarded him with a slight smile.

"I got work for you. We're going to have to pack some *aparejos* for the mules, because we're moving out in the morning. You're assigned to me the rest of the day."

"To Bowie, then?"

Brickner snorted. "Your world must be a pleasant place, Marybelle. A pleasant place."

LIEUTENANT
ANTHONY AUSTIN

He sat in his tent, sipping coffee Thorne had brought earlier. Outside, in the deep dark of early morning, he could hear the sounds of movement. Stonehouse had the men up and moving. By lamplight he studied the maps Bobby had drawn. They were, of course, not to scale. There were notations referring to scale and distance that Bobby had written, but they made no sense to Tony.

The lack of scale did not bother him. The directions were clear, and they would ride in those directions, noting the landmarks Bobby had indicated. It would be difficult to predict riding time, but they would find the canyon where they had encountered the Indians easily enough. It would have been easier with the Apache scouts, but he had Triggs to guide them along a trail he had already followed.

And now he had the diary Thorne had

turned over. He opened its pages at random and dipped into them here and there, looking for nothing in particular, except the life of someone not himself.

September 7. I am coming to find the company of men nearly unbearable. It is as if they are another species, inhabiting a world not quite mine. Their placid maleness, hardly beyond the existence of cattle slowly grazing and chewing cud, drives me near madness. I would dearly love to sit and talk with one of my own sex, but the nearest is many hours' ride from here, and I dare not leave the men to their own devices any more than I would let the stock wander where they may. The lives of men exist on two principles — construction and destruction, and the first is only handmaiden to the second. Having succeeded in building shelter, they would knock it down in their blind ambling toward food or sleep. Both Mr. Estes and Augustine are superior examples of their kind, as the great bull who dominates the pasture is a superior example of his. I shudder to think what I would become if I had teamed with worse. I do not, on purpose, think what life might have been with Michael. I cannot bear it.

September 28. The desert broom is putting out its small, yellow flowers, tiny blooms against the flat brown of the countryside. But that is not the great gift. The plants are covered with a multitude of butterflies, some sort of small monarch butterfly, though I think not so brightly colored. But they are wondrous, teeming on the plants, scattering in swirling clouds when one walks through, wheeling from one plant to another, settling and resettling, painting the sky a lovely orange. The rain, long past, has made the world a vibrant place in its absence.

October 3. I wait for the Apaches to come and bring us firewood. I set aside things I think they may like in addition to the flour and beans that we trade them — bits of cloth and ribbon, all bright, for they are almost childlike in their fondness for bright color. The last time Zee was here, I gave him purple ribbon, not a lot, perhaps two feet of it. I wait to see if he has given it to someone in his own camp, sister, mother, sweetheart, wife, or if he wears it himself.

Foolishly, I anticipate the latter.

November 16. When do the dead leave us entirely? I go for hours but never days, certainly not weeks, without thoughts of Michael. Should his memory leave me forever, I do not know whether I would be free or dead. Is there a difference?

January 3. Aunt Gertrude's clock has run down. I have neglected it, and now we have no way to tell time. The sun rises and sets. In between, the day is marked in chores — starting the fire, fetching water, feeding the chickens, making lunch, making dinner. When next Mr. Estes goes to Tucson, he can take the clock and wind and set it. Until then, my days are formless, except as a series of chores to be performed. Time has become endless, or it does not exist.

January 17. The Apaches came down from the mountains today, hauling three great travois full of wood for us — the rough-skinned juniper and the nearly white sycamore. For though it is not as cold as a Massachusetts winter, it is cold nonetheless. You never see the Apaches coming, though they were mounted and dragging the great loads of wood. Suddenly they are here, and as suddenly, my heart is racing. They dismount and lead their ponies to water and they are all smiles and laughter. At first I thought that Zee was not among them, and then of a sudden from behind another I saw him smiling his great white smile, a piece of purple ribbon trailing from his hair. I thought my heart would leap from my bosom.

January 29. I believe madness continues its conquest of me. I am devouring our house, unbeknownst to Mr. Estes. I search for new secluded places where I can scratch the mud from our walls and suck it into my mouth. I reach behind the furniture, I scratch into the wall behind the fireplace. I would eat our house whole if I could, then the tack room, the barn, the smokehouse. I think that I am trying to eat the world around me, to devour it as it devours me. This land is so vast and empty, so lacking in comfort, that I take my comfort from swallowing it down.

I cannot stop myself from thinking of Zee, the Apache, the savage. As Mr. Estes performs his weekly labors, my injured mind transforms him into Zee, and I want to reach up and touch the hardness of his arms and back, but I do not, knowing I would touch only Mr. Estes. I know that this is the reason for my failure to conceive, but I hide that from Mr. Estes, as well. Hiding has become my avocation, and my need to hide what I think and do grows daily and will soon overwhelm us.

February 12. I wait for the Apaches to bring us wood, though our supply continues to grow faster than we can use it. In the smell of the juniper smoke in the smokehouse, I can dimly make out the outline of Zee. I see him clearly in my mind, but I know that the picture I see is neither true nor accurate, and each time he comes into view, he alters the workings of my mind. When I bathe, it is not my hand that cleanses me, but Zee's, moving over me, washing this life from me.

It was of little use, except to confirm that there was a woman, and that Bobby's suppositions were credible. And it hurt his eyes to read with the old spectacles, so he read only occasional bits, but those bits gave him the picture. Clearly, she was a madwoman. Had she gone with the Apaches willingly? The diary seemed to show that she appreciated the Apaches more than her own kind. Or had they merely become careless, letting a band of Apaches ride up on them because they thought all Apaches friendly? It told nothing, though he was angry at Thorne for not turning it over to Bobby. It was the loyalty of a boy. It was easy enough to trace the diary back through Thorne to Birdwood, who had been on the patrol at the ranch, but the boy would never admit that. Bobby probably would have beaten the story out of him, but he was content to let boys be boys.

It was his job now to do what Bobby had been unable to accomplish. There was a woman, and she would be rescued. And to rescue her would be to redeem the reputation of Bobby from his own blunders in Idaho. It would be simple enough to bring back the woman and then report that she had been saved by the captain. He did not need accolades, but Bobby always had. And, besides, he had his little bird, making its way to Harvard, bearing his name into the future. The rescue of a white woman from her own foolishness would be an act of heroism that could be attached to Bobby as easily as a service ribbon is attached to a uniform.

"Sir."

He picked Triggs's voice out of the darkness. He returned the salute he could not see, and, realizing that Triggs could see him no better, he added, "As you were."

"Brickner is preparing the mounts. The supplies are packed."

"Good," he said, not even in Triggs's direction. "Good. All the preparations are done, then?"

"Almost, sir."

"Very well. 'Boots and Saddles' in an hour?"

"If that is the lieutenant's order."

"That is the lieutenant's order."

He listened to Triggs's bootsteps retreat back toward the camp, and he tried to read in them what he could not read in Triggs's voice. Acceptance? Scorn? Apprehension? Acquiescence? But not respect, never respect.

PRIVATE NED THORNE

"I guess you better go to mess, then."

"I guess I better." Jarbal Birdwood sat on the edge of his cot watching Ned pack his few personal items. "You ate?"

"I had some biscuits. I got to see to the mules."

"I wish we wasn't going."

"No you don't. You're afraid you will get killed. You probably shouldn't do that. If you're worried about being killed, you get yourself killed."

"Is that true?"

He didn't know. He was afraid it was, though he hoped it wasn't. He was terribly afraid of being killed. He was glad that, in the darkness, Birdwood couldn't see his trembling.

"Well, maybe I would. I have a bad feeling about this. I can tell you that. I wish we wasn't going. That's what I wish. Really. I wish we could stay here and shovel mule shit. That's a better thing than getting yourself killed."

"Is it?"

"I guess it is. I never been killed, but I shoveled a lot of shit and that's an all right job."

"But we're going to save that woman. The one from the ranch."

"Well, I guess that is doing some good."

"I believe so."

"Then, me, too."

"Well, I got to see to the mules. I guess this is it, then."

"Nah. This ain't it. We ain't going nowhere except to get that woman. Do you think she's pretty?"

"I think she is. I'm pretty sure."

"Well, we're going to come back heroes."

"Yeah. Well. I got to see to those mules." He stuck out his hand, and Birdwood took it.

"Don't get killed."

He shook his head. He wouldn't get killed. "You don't get killed, either."

"I guess I can't. Still a lot of shit to be shoveled."

"Kid. Come here." Exeter, a fat lifelong corporal, held up a bridle. "Look at this. It's torn. Right here at the D ring. Run and

461

fetch me another."

He shook his head. "I got to see to the rest of these mules. There's more tack in the shop."

"No. It was your job, and you didn't do it. Besides, you're the lowest dog in this pack. Now you go get me a new bridle and be careful with your lip." Exeter lurched forward and into Ned's arms, knocking them both to the ground. He set up a howl like a shot dog. Ned looked up and saw Brickner, standing where he had just kicked Exeter in the britches.

"Go get the thing yourself," Brickner said. He straddled the two of them about knee level.

"You didn't need to kick me, Brickner. I think you broke something. It was his job. He should have done it."

"He does what I tell him to do. And I say for him to see to the mules. And I say for you to either get yourself a new bridle or ride with the one you got. You got those two choices. If you don't like either one of them, I'm going to kick you again."

Exeter rolled off Ned and struggled to right himself, his face contorted with pain. "Damn you, Brickner. Something in me is broke. You hurt me bad."

"I didn't kill you. You're lucky. I'm not.

462

Get on with those *aparejos,* Marybelle."

"Yeah. You go on, Marybelle. Goddamn, Brickner. Why you kick me again? I didn't do nothin'. I'm getting all broke up inside."

"Don't you ever call him that," Brickner said, aiming another kick to Exeter's ribs. "I'll break all your insides up."

The *aparejos* were large leather sacks, shaped like butterflies. His job had been to stuff them with grass as padding and was now to put them on to the backs of the mules, including the shavetail in front of him. It took the weight of the *aparejo* calmly. He took his time, gentling as he went, and when he reached under to cinch the *aparejo,* the shavetail took the gesture with equanimity.

Once the *aparejo* was secured to the mule, the job was turned over to Brickner. The construction of a pack was a feat of engineering and intricate knotting. The mules were capable of hauling unthinkable loads, but even the best mule could not carry an unbalanced load. Brickner would survey the pile of material to be loaded, point at something, and Ned would hand it to him. He held it while Brickner snaked out coils of rope, wrapped the item with the rope, and then tied it down. Then they moved to the other side, Brickner always calculating,

463

constructing, and balancing. There was a grim purposefulness to Brickner now. Every movement, every detail, was filled with both promise and risk.

LIEUTENANT
ANTHONY AUSTIN

He took them out by fours, under full colors
— the U.S. flag and the banner of the
Eleventh Cavalry. There were only seventeen
troopers (Exeter had reported for sick call,
badly bruised, or worse, from a mule kick),
plus Triggs, himself, and Brickner, and
Thorne bringing up the pack mules. The
numbers called for riding in twos, and so he
would regroup them in twos later. But for
now, they looked smart, coming out four
abreast, splashing through the fork of the
river, the colors unfurled above them. He
thought it good for the men, and for himself
as well, to be putting on a show. They
needed a sense of pride and presence now.
He himself had taken Bobby's saber and attached it to his belt. He was, under his own
appointment, an officer in the U.S. Army
Cavalry.

He had set the line of march with Triggs,
and though he rode at the head of the

column now, he would move back and let Triggs, who knew the country, take the lead.

He took them out in a line of march roughly south by southwest, heading first toward the depredated ranch, then on toward the base of the Peloncillos mountains. The Peloncillos were something of a corridor to Mexico, rugged and difficult in terrain. The Apaches had always inhabited them. Now that the boundaries of the Territory had been drawn through them, the Apache range extended to two countries.

He knew the Chiricahua Apaches watched them as they came up the draw in the south side of the Chiricahua mountains, rode the crest, and came down the backside into the valley. They did no more than watch. They let themselves be seen, so the soldiers would know they were watched, and then they disappeared.

He had been confident that the Chiricahua would regard them with dispassion. He was not an authority on the aboriginals, but he had made them an object of some study. Still, he was gratified to have his opinion borne out, especially as it affected his men. He knew of the aboriginals' extraordinary ability to hide themselves, but he found it disquieting in practice to actually be observed by watchers who blended into the landscape as completely as the fallen leaf or pine cone.

Coming into the valley, Bobby's reports unfolded in front of him. The long plain of stirrup-high grama grass stretched before them. Then, as if reinforcing the strange variety in the landscape, within a few miles came thick forest at the top of the mountain, then scrubbed plain, lea, and desert. For Bobby, this had suggested a prospect of prosperity and a difficulty of defense. To him, the variations in the earth's surface, the presence of a mountain in the path of prevailing winds, demonstrated the variety and adaptability of creation, as Darwin had shown, years before.

More as scientist than as soldier, he had determined that the logical place to start their pursuit of the Apaches, without benefit of Apache scouts, was at the beginning. Their first sight of the ranch, from a long distance, came at mid-morning. It was a disappointment that grew as they came nearer.

From the significance it had assumed in his life, he expected something more grand, perhaps something more sinister. Instead, it was a pile of mud, much like so many others that erupted in this land, a minor disordering of the flat earth that surrounded it. There were three small buildings visible from the distance and some corrals, nothing more.

When they came upon it, the force of the plain became more evident. Though he could read from the height of the grass what had once been cleared and cultivated, the grass had spread all the way to the door of the house and even through it. It had been short weeks since the Indian attack had left the place deserted, but it could well have been years. The door to the house had been left open, or had blown open, and the plains and its inhabitants had made inroads into it.

He walked around the building, taking reports from the troopers who had been with Bobby when he first came onto the scene, shortly after the attack. He put together, from the accounts, a suitable understanding of what had happened here, and it seemed to clarify his thinking. In truth, the scene of the devastation gave him not the slightest clue as to where to go next, except toward the canyon where Bobby had encountered the Apaches and where Wortham had been killed. He had known all along that was the place to start, not at the beginning, which told him almost nothing.

As they neared the Peloncillos, which they saw on the second day, he became more sure that the Apaches and the woman were there. There was considerable territory to cover, but they had sufficient supplies for a two-week expedition and the ability to replenish those supplies through forage. He felt that he had the advantage. What this expedition needed now, more than the eye of the strategist, was the eye of the naturalist. He wished his worked better. Everything was smudged and indistinct, lacking the outlines that made for clarity.

All living things are the product of their habitat. They adapt to that habitat and, if successful, thrive. Taken out of what had engendered and nourished them, they weaken. They gravitate, therefore, to the habitats that spawned them and that now give them strength. These Apaches, who had been attacked, decimated, and pursued, would return to the landscape they knew and understood.

As he had studied and learned the habits of the grouse, the western diamondback, and the kangaroo rat, so he had learned, indirectly, the habitats of the aboriginal. As he had learned to find the specimens that he collected for his study, he had learned enough about the Apaches to know where to look for them. Where Bobby had looked from the view of a military commander, he would look as a disinterested scholar looked at a library. And he understood that as you learned the language of the land, it could be made to give up its secrets.

They came to the foothills of the Peloncillos in the early hours of the third day and began a steady and strenuous ascent. In the early afternoon, he halted them in the same *cienega* that Bobby had stopped his patrol and gone on foot to the canyon where he had made contact with the aboriginals and where Wortham had met his end. Austin gave the order to graze the horses on the rich grass of the meadow.

He, Triggs, and Shattuck moved slowly up to the edge of the canyon. It was small and was fed by a thin brook. Though there was no evidence of habitation, the canyon was perfectly suited to the needs of a small band of Apaches, offering shelter, water, game, and a vantage point from which to survey the narrow ways that led to it. He considered the possibility that, this being such an advantageous refuge, the Apaches might have come back to reinhabit it. He rejected that, understanding that if the Apaches were still here, the soldiers would have heard from them long before this moment.

Triggs pointed out the site of the battle. The copper casings of shells fired that day were beginning to crust over with a green patina. As he looked across the canyon, he saw what a perfect place this was for an ambush, and it became clear that a couple of old men could, indeed, hold off a patrol for enough time to let the rest of the band escape. It was clear, as well, how easily a soldier, even one as experienced as Bobby, could be drawn into such an ambush. That this site was not so much different than the one in Idaho was not lost on him, and it could not have been lost on Bobby, either. Bobby had come into this canyon well aware of what might, what probably, lay ahead. A quick chill of fear came through the lieutenant as he imagined himself in the sight of an Apache carbine, and then it left as quickly, being just the stuff of imagination.

Around him, jays scrabbled in the leaves, and the wind made a soft percussion in the upper branches of the pine and sycamore of the mountain. The men made their way down into the canyon, moving sideways to keep traction against the descent in the loose soil and pine needle. He sent Shat-

471

tuck in search of rock to build a cairn while he tore a page out of his notebook and wrote in pencil:

On this 8th day of June in the year 1871, in this spot in the mountain range called Peloncillo, in the southeastern section of the Territory of Arizona, I hereby have the honor of naming this location Franklin Canyon in perpetual memory of Captain Robert Franklin, commanding officer, D Company, 11th Cavalry. May it be so known to all who pass this way for now and all time.

> Anthony Austin, 2nd Lieutenant,
> D Company
> U.S. Army, 11th Cavalry

As they gathered wood for fires — small fires, just enough to heat beans and coffee — Washington returned from his scout. "About three miles north and west of here," he said, "is a small Apache *rancheria*. They've left it now, but not so long ago."

He went with Washington, Shattuck, and Richmond, pushing their tired mounts a bit longer than they needed to be pushed. The territory was hard and they rode a bear trail, splashed every few hundred yards with the scat of bear, loose and runny, peppered with seeds.

The *rancheria* was in another, smaller *cienega* farther up the side of the same mountain. Three *wikiups* still stood, small, domed creations of sticks bound by woven grass, which were easily erected and easily abandoned. The site was extraordinarily well chosen. The canyon where the attack took place was more easily detected and less defensible than the site where they had actually camped, which commanded a long view of the countryside.

"They're on the run," Washington reported. "Take a look over here."

Under a small pin oak they found the bodies of five dogs, side by side, abandoned, their throats slashed. They were in the early stages of bloat, not long dead, and at the soldiers' approach, swarms of flies lifted from the bodies and hummed through the air around them.

"They're in full retreat. When they need to move, fast and quiet, they kill the dogs."

He shook his head. "It's a sad, sad sight."

"The Indians weren't happy about it either, you can wager. They like dogs, and they always seem to find them."

"And the dogs are what to them?"

"Sir? They are pets, sir. Same as us."

473

"We'll go, back and bivouac for the night where we left the rest. We'll resume the track in the morning."

It was almost always the birds that woke him. They felt the approach of the sun and got to their business. When sober, he would get up with them. Triggs was already awake, gathering small sticks for a fire. How Triggs woke, he did not know. The vedette, he supposed, though he sensed sometimes that Triggs did not sleep at all. He felt good, better than he had in a while, despite the conditions. He had taken a small bit of the whisky while the rest of the troop made their beds for the night, and he had slept well.

"Let's get the fire going that we can be back on the trail at first light," he said, his voice at a normal volume to begin the process of waking the rest of the patrol.

Triggs bent forward, blew on the little stack of sticks and let it flare up. "It will be ready."

They spotted the Indian a few hours later, on top of an outcropping some four hundred yards to their front left. He stood still as the rocks themselves, and it was mostly the white of his loincloth that caught their attention. Even then, it was not clear that he was actually there, an Apache, watching them.

By the time they had the sighting confirmed, stopped the march, and shouldered arms, the Indian was gone.

PRIVATE NED THORNE

Dearest Thad,

We are pinned down now by the Indians. I supposed it is just this we have been waiting for. We are in some low mountains, and though it is not nearly so hot as it was a couple of days ago, I am pressed up against a stone that burns my face. But I dare not move for fear of an Apache arrow or bullet.

In a little while, you and the world will know what to make of us. Heroic soldiers or the forgotten dead in a land far away. But right now, I wish this rock were just cooler and softer. I know, though, I must get used to the hard and the hot. There is little else where I am headed. I envy you paradise, but I do not deserve it. You do, having been killed by . . .

Your brother

LIEUTENANT
ANTHONY AUSTIN

The cramping began early on. He could move his right leg a little, but it was insufficient to quiet the pain. He was belly down in the dirt and litter of twig and leaf, his right leg pushed up, awkwardly, by some large stones. He had his carbine at the ready and his cartridge case off his belt and open before him. He wanted to stand and put pressure on his leg to relieve the cramps, but he could not. Bobby's saber was further torment, allowing him only a few degrees of torque before the hilt pressed on his kidney.

It took the patrol an hour and a quarter to complete the scout. He held the rest of the troop where they crouched, sat, or lay under what cover they found. When he received the report from the patrol, it confirmed what he already knew. It had been a lone Apache, sent back to scout their position. They had never been in danger. And he knew that, though he had to assume that all contact was hostile and that every rise in the landscape contained an ambush.

He let them move about before remounting. They were still and edgy from the wait, achy and complaining, but also reinvigorated by the sudden break in the march, the promise of some action, even though none had come about. While it was important to get back into the saddle and resume pursuit, he also knew that they were not as close to the Indians as they might believe. The Indian they had seen was a scout, and he most certainly had put great distance between himself and the rest of the band before he put himself into a position where he might be discovered.

They resumed the march following as best they could the trail of the Indian they had seen. The Indian would, of course, alter his direction a number of times to throw them off, but they had no other direction to choose from. The Apaches could make their way through the countryside as quietly and efficiently as any of the animals that lived there. It was one thing to understand the ease of the Apache within his own landscape, but it was not until you, yourself, traversed that landscape that you fully understood how adept he was at moving through hostile country.

Apaches rarely traveled on horseback when they needed a tactical advantage, relying most on their own facility for movement. When they did use mounts, it was in large part because the mounts provided a ready source of food when they slowed down. They were remarkable people. Truly remarkable.

By the fifth day, they had moved over one hundred miles but only twenty-five of them in one direction. The Apaches, on foot, were tacking a tortuous route, moving first one way, then another, trying to shake the Army or to at least put some distance between themselves and the soldiers. The Apaches could go where horses could not, so the patrol had to find ways to circumscribe the Apaches' trail, which often went up nearly vertical rock faces.

But he was determined that they should not relent in their pursuit. They were not gaining appreciable ground, but perhaps they were not losing any, either. They had occasional contact — a sighting of smoke, a bit of cloth. Twice they had found the Indians' abandoned encampment, and one more time they had seen a scout, though from a long distance.

They camped for the night, grazing and

watering the horses, the men in small groups, stretching and shaking off the day's ride, which had been hard, with much difficult climbing through small draws that had little solid ground. They were in decent spirits, but the march was wearing on them. He let them have a small fire — an Apache fire for all practical purposes — which was sufficient for only coffee and beans. They were all tired of hardtack and cold beans, and as they rose up through the mountains, the nights grew colder. Yet to stay with the Indians, to overtake them, they had to travel as the Indians traveled. And though the Indians knew where they were at least as well as they knew where the Indians were, they needed to protect their position as best they could. Should the Indians lose track of them, if there were any chance of that at all, their chances of catching the Apaches would improve dramatically.

Triggs brought him coffee, which he accepted though he had just finished a cup, his ration for the evening. He thought to decline Triggs's offer, but he understood that the coffee represented something more important to the sergeant. They squatted together on a ridge of rock above the main encampment and looked over the small patrol, taking their ease.

"It is going well?" Austin asked. He knew the answer.

"As well as can be expected. The men are doing well. The horses and mules are holding up. Things are going as well as can be expected."

He nodded. The sun was down and it was getting harder to see in the gathering gloom. "Very well. Very well." He waited for the sergeant to speak, knowing that something was worrying him about the edges. He thought it best, though, to let the sergeant bring it up of his own accord, without prompting from him.

"Sir," Triggs said, finally.

"Yes. Go on, Sergeant."

"Sir, do you know where we are?"

"Pretty much. It's not mapped territory, but we know that we are deep in the Peloncillos, moving along a ridge that is near to the top."

"Mexico, sir. I have been trying to keep track. It is very difficult. We have been changing directions a couple of times a day, backtracking, side tracking. So, while I cannot say with certainty . . ."

"You think it likely we are in Mexico."

"I can't be certain."

"Nor I. But I suspect you're right, Sergeant. If we are not in Mexico, we are very

481

close to it."

Triggs looked puzzled, as though he had worked out an entire argument and now found himself in an entirely new location within that argument and had no idea how to proceed.

"Are the men speaking of this, Sergeant?"

"Not directly. No one has said anything to me."

"Good. If there is grumbling, I want to know about it."

"Of course, sir. But, sir."

"Sergeant?"

"We have no business in Mexico."

"Not officially, no."

"We are going to continue, then?"

"Of course. Of course we are, Sergeant. There is the matter of the woman. We are in pursuit of this band in order to recover the woman. Until we have done that, we will not give off the chase. Wherever that chase leads us."

"Very good, sir."

"I think so, Sergeant. I think it is very good. But we shall see. We shall see."

Private Ned
Thorne

At the very least it was not hot. He repeated that to himself and repeated it again. There was no comfort. It was not hot, but he had grown sore and miserable. His legs and back ached, and the seams of his trousers raised welts from the rubbing of the saddle against his thighs. He had never ridden so far at a stretch. Even in his new cotton stockings, his feet burned inside the leather of his boots.

During mounted intervals, he thought only of the dismount. After a mile or two of dismount, his feet ached badly and he wanted to remount. In the end, he guessed, it did not matter. It was misery, and the mounting and dismounting was only trading one misery for another. Differences in misery seem slight.

He spoke to Birdwood, who rode to his right. "Where do you think we are?"

Birdwood did not acknowledge that he

had heard at all. But that was Birdwood's way. He took all communication from another human being as significant, and he did not answer without giving the question due attention. "Mountains," he said, at last.

"You think we are in Mexico?" The orders of march specified silence. Though, in a march, there was not silence but, rather, a constant clatter of shod hoof on ground and stone, counterpointed with the continual creak of leather from saddle and stirrup, and the clank of metal bits and rings. So, they talked, and so long as they talked quietly, and not too often, they were not reprimanded.

"No," Birdwood said, looking around as if he knew the landscape well and was cataloging the familiar details. He shook his head. "Not Mexico."

"I don't know. We're a long way south. I think we might be."

"Hell, yes, we're in Mexico," Mayapple said from in front of them. "Been here more than a day."

Neither responded. Ned worried what this might mean, them in Mexico.

"I guess not," Birdwood said. "I'm an American soldier, and you are, too. American soldiers are in America. If we was in Mexico, I'd be a Mexican soldier. I ain't no

Mexican. I can't even talk their talk."

They had a twenty-minute dismount in a small canyon, where a braid of water not a foot wide spilled over a granite ledge and fell ten feet to a small, clear pool. They watered the horses and filled canteens and the large pouches carried by the mules. Though there were orders against swimming and bathing, they made their way bootless around the slick rocks of the pool and took turns holding their heads under the cascading water, which splashed and wet their blouses and trousers and cooled them down.

As Ned came back around the edge of the pool, balancing himself by walking sideways, his new cotton stockings freshly washed and wet, he was caught by Triggs. "Get your boots back on and report to Brickner."

He wrung his stockings. "Are we headed out, then?"

"Soon. Soon. We have a difficult march ahead of us for the rest of the afternoon, and Brickner is going to need help with the mules. He will tell you what he needs."

"This here canyon," Brickner said when Ned came to him, "is the entryway to a larger canyon. And there ain't no easy way around it they've found. We're going up over a ridge, yonder." He pointed upward, vaguely east, but all Ned could see was the buff rock of the canyon walls, studded with cactus and scrub. "It's going to be a difficult climb, even for the mules, and we're going to have to take them single file."

Brickner had unpacked the *aparejos* of Grace, the lead mule, and of the shavetail. "They got to be repacked," he said. "Grace can take whatever gets thrown at her, but this shavetail has to be balanced just so. It ain't got the good sense to keep itself balanced." He had two of the water pouches, one under each arm. Ned had some trouble moving one full pouch on his own. Brickner threw them on Grace's back and tied them off.

"You're going to bring up the rear. You're going to watch what I do, and you're going to do the same. Just as I do. You keep your ears open, and when you hear me say something, I don't want you taking time to think about it. I want you to do it almost before I say it. You got that?"

He nodded.

"There are times for thinking, but this ain't one. You start to think, you're going to kill us all. You got that, too? All right. Most of all, you got to keep your eye on those mules. They are going to follow one another hoofprint by hoofprint. If any one of them" — he hit the shavetail, hard with his fist, on the shoulder — "and I'm especially meaning this one, gets out of line, you are going to have to get it back in before it can cause us any trouble."

"How bad is it?"

Brickner shook his head. "I don't know, but Triggs says it's bad. He's worried, and Triggs has seen a goodly amount in his life. If Triggs is worried, I'm worried, too. Prepare for the worst, so you don't get surprised by it. Life is full of surprises, and if you expect the worst, all the surprises you get are good ones."

They backtracked out of the canyon with the pool, swung to the north, and started up the hillside that skirted the canyon. To their left, the mountain rose steeply and the climb was difficult. He could see, though, that the other side of the canyon was rockier, with ledges that rose nearly sheer and at other points seemed to drop nearly away. The trail they were on was steep and rugged, but it was a trail. There was bear crap everywhere, and he thought it might just be another bear trail, though Indians or hunters or traders could have made it as well. But it was thin and did not get much traffic.

As they wound through the trees, he

caught glimpses of the canyon they had just been in. The sound of the waterfall followed their progress up the mountain. The mules struggled with the climb, burdened with the weight of the *aparejos.* The loads shifted back and forth, the leather creaking against the ropes to the rhythm of the mules' gait, but they pulled the loads and maintained their balance, following one another up the side of the mountain.

The small river that had carved the canyon below kept falling away from them. As they came up, the difficulty they faced began to present itself. The canyon where they had stopped was a small adjunct to a larger canyon, which grew deeper and wider as they pressed on. The little river had at some time carved its way deeply into the mountain, and what it had left for them to traverse was slight. He saw that the trail ahead of them continued to narrow and that their march was bringing them steadily closer to the edge of the large canyon.

He tried to keep his eyes on the progress of the mules in front of him, but to his right, the landscape continued to open as they passed out of the realm of the trees. The canyon was enormous. As far as he could see to the right were rugged passages of the river, studded with rills of rock that often rose a hundred feet or more but were still below the level of the point they now traveled, which was the highest point around. He had the feeling that he had found the top of the earth, and that if his eyes were good enough, he could see whatever he wanted, even the world.

They moved steadily up the side of the mountain. The distance between the upslope of the mountain and the drop into the canyon diminished. They stopped twice to regroup, and they were moving up in single file now, four horse lengths between each. Though it had not been stated, the spacing ensured that slips would be isolated.

A length of rope ran from Brickner's saddle horn, along the canyon side of the mules, to Ned's saddle, where it was tied onto his saddle horn. It provided a tactile guide to move the mules back if they strayed too far to the right and the edge of the trail. He gave the shavetail two lengths, keeping the rope slack but off the ground so that it made constant contact with the mule's legs.

Brickner was just out of sight, around an outcropping, when Ned heard first the screams — of horse and man — then the shouts. Later he would remember it the other way around, but it must have been the screams and then the shouts. The rope went slack on the ground, and this terrified him until he realized that the danger would come when the rope came suddenly taut. He stopped his horse, stood in the stirrups, and tried to see what was going on. There was commotion, but he made no sense of it, though he understood it was bad, very bad.

"Lost one," Brickner said when Ned walked up to him. "Royal Kent, I think. Man and horse right off the trail to the bottom."

"We have to get them."

Brickner spit and nodded toward the canyon. "Look at that. What's the reasoning on going down there? Ain't no one alive down there. Besides, we're in a bad place here, and we got to get out of it before the Indians find out just how bad it is. Now, I want you to listen to me. I don't want you looking into the canyon or thinking about what happened or praying or anything else. You listen to me.

"It's a bad spot up here, a washout. It's passable, but it's a rough go, as you just found out." He pulled off his hat and whacked it against his thigh. "We're going over it, but we're going to switch positions. You're going to lead us over, and you're going to pull Grace behind you. She'll come as you pull her, and she'll pull the rest.

"And what it is, is I'm going to take the rear, and we're going to pull that rope taut. The rope runs from me to you, and it's like a rail to keep the mules from drifting out and taking us over the side. Grace won't be a problem, but we can't let that shavetail move an inch. I'm going to hold the rope hard, but you are going to have to pull hard, and you can't hesitate. Once that rope comes loose, there's a good shot we're going down into that canyon, too. You understand that? Those mules go, we all go. We're putting our lives in your hands. Grace will help you out. Yours ain't the hardest job, but I won't lie to you; it's going to be some tough work. But I know you can do it. Once you start, don't you dare to stop."

He nodded and swallowed, his mouth gone dry.

"You want to go up and look at what we got to go over?"

He wasn't sure he wanted to see it. Maybe it would just be better to charge the area and take it as it came. He was pretty sure that knowing would only scare him more. Still, he nodded yes.

Water from the rains had cut rills into the soil on its way down into the canyon. It was dry now, but in several places, it had cut away all the soil until it exposed bare rock. The trail didn't exist here at all. Most of the washouts were fairly small, a yard or two, no more. Here, he and Brickner kicked at loose rock and dirt that might throw the horses or mules. "It will still be like this. These riders got to go over first, and they'll kick up more loose rock." He nodded at the handful of mounted troops still on their side of the washout, looking down into the canyon where Kent had disappeared.

"We could wait for them to cross, then come back and clear out the rocks again."

"No. We got to get to moving. We can't be isolated back here away from the troops. We got to go across with them. Come up to here, see the rest of it."

The rest of it was a washout four or five feet across. The dirt and rock that had washed away revealed the rounded edge of a granite boulder, sloping toward the canyon. Brickner walked across it, and Ned followed. It was not as bad as he thought, though he placed his feet carefully as he came. "It's not so bad."

"You want to try it while wearing iron shoes then, carrying two-thirds your weight on your back as you go. It's bad enough."

"What are we going to do?"

"We're going across, and we're going across fast. I want you to put spurs to your horse as you go. The least time we're on that rock, the least chance one of the mules is going to slide into the canyon. You do your job, and we'll be all right. You don't do your job, I'm going to be in hell, waiting for you. And hell is going to be a much worse place once I get there."

They retied the rope to Ned's saddle horn and tested it. They moved up to the washout once more, then came back and retested the rope.

"Right there." Brickner pointed to a stunted tree that grew from a fissure in the otherwise solid wall of rock, a dwarf tree no more than three feet tall. "Right here you lay spur to that horse and you don't stop. When you feel that rope go short, you got to keep going. When you hit the washout, you got to be moving like the Devil hisself is right behind you. That rope goes slack, and one of those mules runs wide, and you're going to see the Devil sooner than you expected. It ain't good enough just to get yourself across. You got to get us all across. Otherways, we die. You got it?"

He did have it. He did not wish to understand it or even to think about it, but he had it, and his stomach was churning, and he was afraid he was going to be sick or was going to embarrass himself.

They took the mules back and rechecked the ropes one more time while the rest of the patrol went across. As they passed them, no one looked him in the eye, not even Jarbal, who looked at him for confirmation of the smallest things. Now Birdwood was hunched forward, jaw set, eyes straight ahead and unblinking, as he spurred his horse and leapt forward toward the washout.

Across the washout, the rest of the patrol had dismounted and formed a semicircle to give them cover. "Go on," Brickner said. "Take your run. Don't think."

He resat himself and leaned forward and gave his mount a kick.

"Go," Brickner yelled. "Go now. Go hard."

When the horse felt the spurs, he hurled himself forward. In front of him was the semicircle of troopers with rifles at the ready. It was easy to believe that the fear he felt was fear of the rifles, not the canyon. When he came to the tree, he spurred again. Behind him, he knew the mules were running, but now he was moving faster than they were, and when the rope suddenly came taut, he heard it whine and felt the sting as it snapped against his leg. He thought for a second that they were going over backward, but instead they continued to pull, and the weight of Brickner and his mount slowed them enough to keep a good pace for the mules. His horse continued to pull, trying to get away from the pain of the spur.

He saw the washout from far away. It seemed that it got no closer, and then, suddenly, he could not see it at all. Instead, he heard the quick clank of the horse's shoes on the rock. The danger was in two parts. If his horse slipped, he would take them all over, but even if his horse made it, a slip from one of the mules would pull them down as well.

He heard himself scream before he understood he was flying free of the saddle, and then he was seated again and they were all at a flat run across the ground of the trail. Brickner had let the rope go, and around him, troopers were whooping and hollering. He pulled his horse up and turned to see the mules come pounding up behind him and behind them, Brickner, standing in his stirrups, waving his hat in the air.

When they got under cover of a stand of pine, they dismounted. He tied the mules and saw that his hands were trembling.

"You should have been a jockey," Mayapple told him. "That was some riding. Real cowboying."

"I would bet money on him in a race," Randolph said. "But only if he was dragging a piano behind him."

He sat with them, smoking a cigar offered by Mayapple, feeling a part of them for the first time.

They moved up for the rest of the morning and into the afternoon, though the ascent was not so steep now, and they had passed the canyon and the steep drop-off to the side. He was next to the last in line, leading the mules and following Brickner. Birdwood now rode behind him as rear guard.

It was Birdwood who saw it and stopped, then called for Ned to stop as well. It was well off the trail and would have blended into the ground if it had not been for a small flash of pale blue. Birdwood dismounted, and Ned, getting the mules under control, watched Birdwood, and then knew what it was that Birdwood had found, and he dismounted, too, and came up behind Birdwood.

It could not be her. It was not. She was too old, too dead. It was not her. He thought he would vomit, and then he did. It could not be her, but it could not not be her, either.

She lay some twenty yards off the trail, on her back, legs straight, arms folded over her breast, as though someone had taken the trouble to lay her out as if she were sleeping. She wore a dress that was gray, though perhaps it had once had a color. The collar, turned up, was blue, and it was this that Birdwood had seen. Her feet were shod in men's shoes, ankle high and worn through at the soles. He could see her suppurating feet through the remains of the leather.

She was old, not as he had imagined her, years past what he had seen in his mind. She was not so old as his mother, perhaps, but old nonetheless. It was difficult to tell, because he did not fully understand such things. There were girls his own age and younger and then there were women who were older.

Her eyes were open. If someone had taken the trouble to lay her out as if she were sleeping, he had not taken the trouble to close her eyes. Though, he remembered that dead people's eyes came open, which was why coins were put on the lids. Her eyes were a dull gray, perhaps blue once, but clouded and unseeing. The stare of the dead unnerved him, and he looked away.

But he had to look back. Was it her? She was white, and it wouldn't be common for a white woman to be here, just abandoned. He looked at her hands. They were dry and hard, and the nails were worn down as if she had clawed at something. He tried to look away again, but he could not keep his eyes from her.

The ants were starting at her, and there were flies all about, and he guessed that they were at her, too, and those thoughts sickened him. If you knelt too near her, the smell was awful, sweet and sickening, and it called the insects to her. Birdwood, who stood at his side, stared at her and, Ned guessed, at the ants and flies. Birdwood just repeated the word "damn."

But what he could not stop staring at was the rope. It was around her neck and under her arm. He vomited once more.

He saw Birdwood looking up into the sky, and when Ned looked up, he saw what Jarbal saw. Turkey vultures were gathering above them, wheeling in great, graceful arcs, their wings tipped up. From a distance they were beautiful birds that could be mistaken for eagles, but up close they were uglier than death itself. He did not even have to think. He reached down, took the Springfield beside him, aimed at one of the birds, and shot at it. Ned heard the quiet snap as the bullet went through the bird's feathers. It faltered, then continued its slow circling. He was opening the breach to extract the shell when Birdwood crashed into him, sending them both sprawling to the ground.

"Hell and villainy," Birdwood said. "Don't do that. We're under orders of silence. The lieutenant will have you hanged."

Ned struggled to get up, to get another shot at the vultures, but Birdwood hung on until they heard the boots coming up behind them.

"I'll be damned." It was Brickner, who had stopped when they did, and came up now behind them. "He found her. I would have bet a year's pay that he had no chance of ever finding her. You're getting awfully delicate about the deceased there, Marybelle, for someone in our line of work. Give me that carbine. Birdwood, you run up and get the lieutenant. Tell him he is a success at last."

Lieutenant
Anthony Austin

He gave orders to keep the rest of them back. Thorne had been sick and had stood by, pale and confused. He and Triggs knelt above the body. The sweet odor of decay cloyed at the back of his throat. "What do you think?"

"A couple of days, I guess. I don't think much more than that. Maybe less. You can't really tell about these things. It's pretty dry around here. That slows the rot some. Not really bloated, though that may have come and gone."

"No. Is it her? Is it the one we came looking for?"

Triggs shrugged. "It's a woman, white, dead for a short time. Out here in the middle of nowhere, on the line we know the Indians took. Who else could it be?"

"Did they kill her?" He kept staring at the length of rope around her neck.

Triggs moved his hands over the woman's

small body, describing an outline of her head and torso. "Can't find wounds. No blood. Neck don't look broke. That rope was for leading her. I think when she fell, they just let it go. You want to take her clothes off?"

"No. I don't think that's necessary, do you?"

"She's dead, naked or clothed. It don't make much difference to us, none to her. I think she wore out. We've been putting pretty good pressure on them, I think. Likely, she couldn't stand the pace. Her shoes are pretty much gone. I think the trip killed her. She wasn't real young."

"Then we killed her."

"You could look at it that way," Triggs said. "It wouldn't be my way, but you could. We didn't kidnap her. We didn't kill her husband and the other one. We weren't going to sell her in Mexico. We did what we could to save her. That's how I see it."

"But in chasing the Indians, we caused her death. She wouldn't have died if we hadn't gone in pursuit."

"Maybe. Maybe not. They were headed this way. All we did was follow. It's a long, hard haul, whether someone's chasing you or not. It's going to take a toll. And what if we didn't come after her? Most likely this is a kindness, if you consider the other possibilities. You did your duty. We all did our duty."

"And our duty killed her."

"Look at it how you will. You're the officer. I'm just an enlisted man, and I don't know about such as that."

Austin looked at the woman's burned and drying face, the mouth open to reveal a swollen tongue, the insects already at her. The Army had done its duty. To her. To God and to Country. "Get up a burial detail."

While the burial detail scratched away at the hard clay of the canyon, he sent scouts off in the four directions at a distance of five hundred yards. It was a bad place, low ground from all directions. Thorne's rifle shot had surely put the Apaches on notice that they were here. He looked again at the spot. He wouldn't want to defend it. But all indicators pointed to the continued flight of the Apaches. It was a small band. Of that, he was positive. And they had been routed by surprise at Fort Grant, so they were likely not well armed. Caught and cornered, they would fight. But he thought that they would not attack. They would not choose to stand and fight with the Army, even a patrol as small as this.

The discovery of the woman had brought an end to the stated purpose of the patrol. Still, it was more certain that they must push on now, even though his reason told him not to. While Bobby had argued for the pursuit, he had argued against it and had stalled them. As a result of his conservatism, his fear that something would go wrong, he had cost the woman her life. Had Bobby gone when he wanted, kept in pursuit with the Apache guides, she would be alive now. And so, ironically, would Bobby be alive. He had cost both Bobby and the woman their lives, and this patrol would neither bring them back to life nor settle scores. He knew that. And he knew that now, more than ever, he had to run the Indians down and take them.

He owed it to Bobby, and he thought maybe he owed it to the boy, too. The boy had come deflated, finding now no reason to go or to do anything else for that matter. He had an image of the boy, on tiptoes, dancing small circles, trying to hold up the body of his little brother, trying vainly to keep the younger boy's weight off the rope while the body, unconscious, kept bending and twisting into the rope no matter what the boy did to prevent it. The ability of the world to configure ever new horrors to inflict went beyond the power of any man and suggested that there was some higher force, brutal and malevolent and mocking. He would go on. They would go in pursuit of the Apaches and avenge the woman and Bobby, who died not at the hands of Indians but by the same hand that was propelling them forward.

They had not seen the Apaches in two days, but this camp was only a day old, perhaps two. The Apaches were a little farther ahead of them than they had been, but they were still close. The Apaches had the advantage of the local knowledge, and they knew where they were going and how to get there. Apaches traveled lighter and, on the whole, faster than the patrol could. He had the advantage in numbers and supply, though. The mules, while weary, were still sound, and a steady pace, not too hard, would keep them moving for some time yet. The Apaches were on foot. They had been running for over a month now.

He had cut rations three days ago. There was grumbling and discontent, but the men could travel for a week on such rations, though they would not be happy doing it. Whatever they ate, mostly hardtack and canned vegetables, it was more and better than the Indians were getting, and so long as they maintained pressure, the Indians would get no more food, neither by hunting nor raiding. If he could keep moving them, he would keep them from replenishing their stores. Patience is what the job wanted, and he was determined to stay patient, moving always forward.

The men were taking their ease while Thorne and Birdwood buried the woman. It was an odd country here, beyond high desert, with rock and buckthorn, sotol and cholla. The brush attacked the country with a persistence he admired. The plants drilled their roots through fissures a hair could not pass through, and then split the fissures wide and made their way into the earth below. In one such fissure, amid a scatter of rock and plant matter, a lizard, a chuckwalla, he thought, watched them warily. The birds were the standards for that part of the world — flicker and Phainopepla, an assortment of wrens, finches, and hawks. And the turkey vultures, which still circled above where the woman had fallen.

Mayapple brought the word. The northernmost vedette had begun circling his mount at a trot, indicating the presence of the enemy at not too great a distance. He dispatched Park back into the canyon for

Thorne and Birdwood and sent Mayapple up to get the vedette's report. He ordered Triggs to prepare the patrol for mounting.

The northern vedette had seen someone, an Apache, certainly. Probably a boy. He could not be sure because the sighting was at considerable distance. The Apache was staying close to the ground, moving slowly, trying to get a read on their position. There could also be no doubt that the Apache was a scout, and that the main band was some distance beyond. But the patrol was close enough again to make contact, and that meant they were closing the distance between themselves and the Indians once more.

He tightened the column, pulling in both the advance and rear guards. He detached Shattuck, the best horseman, to be lookout. He moved them out single file and kept them close to the hills and outcroppings, where they would be exposed on only one side. He tried to keep them to the rock rather than the dirt. Though it was noisier and harder on the animals, rock did not raise dust that could be seen at a far distance. He kept them tracking east by southeast.

The greatest concern now was water. In the last two days, they had found no more

506

than a few trickles, and their own stocks were getting thin.

The appearance and disappearance of the Indians at almost regular intervals suggested that the Indians were allowing themselves to be spotted, that they were leading them. It was not for ambush. He was certain of that. Even from the best of ambushes, and the Apaches were good at ambushes, the small band would be no match for the Army. No, he decided, they were not leading him toward anything. They were leading him away from water, trying to wear the soldiers down with thirst, just as he was trying to wear the Indians down with hunger. He sent Park to scout the hills to the west for water.

At sundown, they bivouacked, as the Indians were likely doing as well. The Apaches did not fight at night, and neither did they like to move much in the nighttime, when the owl spirits were in charge of things. This could be used to tactical advantage, a chance to gain on them while they rested. But the Army did not know this territory, and to travel at night was to leave themselves vulnerable to unknown dangers. He supposed that the best advantage at the moment was to rest both the men and the animals. Water had been located some miles northwest, and they had passed within a few hundred yards of it earlier in the day. Triggs had dispatched four men to fill bags and canteens, and in the morning they would move out refreshed and with a four-day supply of water, enough to last them until the capture of the Apaches.

Private Ned
Thorne

In his dreams, bodies continued to fall apart, hers and others he both knew and did not. Ants unlaced the bindings that held bone to bone. Maggots mined deep in the recesses of the corpses. The most private of parts floated free, bubbled to the surface, rose and floated on the effluvium of decay until trapped in the cage of bone.

He had seen more of the human body than he had ever wished to. He shut his dreaming eyes and, blind, tried to hold her body together. But his lids had become glass, windows through which he saw coyotes and turkey vultures, crazed, clumsy surgeons, reduce her to her components. The thing that had been her was as precious as a child he would protect, even to the end of his own life.

He took the sweet, rotting thing to himself to hold it together until he could wrap her in the earth and store her away. Everywhere, eyes were on him, ready to take another bit of her away from him and into themselves. He gripped her more tightly, even as he felt her pulling herself apart, rushing toward her own disintegration.

He woke, sweating and shaking in the dark. Beyond him were the slow sounds of men sleeping, snoring, muttering in their dreams. He had not screamed in his sleep, though he continued to feel the ache in his jaw from trying to scream or vomit without result.

Dear Thad,

I think I begin to know what death feels like, as you are drawn to that place you always knew you were going, though you do not want to go. We are in pursuit of a band of desperate Apaches who have killed white people, including a very agreeable woman, who I had to bury. I surrender her to your protection. I am anxious to catch up with them, that we can stop the killing, though I know once we catch them, there will be still more killing.

Some are saying we are in Mexico, but I do not know that to be true. We are on half rations and may drink only small amounts, for there is little water to be found. I am as hungry and thirsty as I have ever been in my life, and I hope to never be so again.

If I am killed, I would hope that people would say that I was a brave soldier and not afraid of what lay before. That would be a damned lie, but it might give comfort to our mother and father.

He felt a growing numbness. It was as if he had traveled back in time several months. It was the same feeling he had had just after Thad died. The rope at her neck, the rope he had loosened and carefully slid from around her neck, had cancelled out the last months, his small attempts at restitution for his crimes. Death was back in front of him, mocking him, bullying him, letting him know just how unworthy he was.

There was no redemption now. Rescuing the woman had been his only hope of restoring his life, and now that was gone. He saw that his hope of saving her and bringing her back, unharmed and grateful for his heroism, was the stuff of boy dreams. And he was a boy, not a man. He was impotent in the world of men, where his best intentions neither fit nor signified.

As he waited for the Apache arrow or bullet that would surely take his life, he grew more hopeful that the Indian who would send it on its way would hurry and get this miserable life over with.

They had watered the mules, though not much, had drunk a little themselves, and had eaten hardtack and canned tomatoes, which was a better combination than he had expected. Small fires built to heat the coffee and tomatoes were extinguished as soon as those tasks were done.

He smoked one of the cigars he had been given when he was the hero of the canyon crossing. That seemed like a long time ago and like some person other than him. The duty of burying the woman had weighted him heavily. They had scraped through hardpan and rock with shovels that weren't suited for the hard ground and rock of the mountain. He had fought in his own mind to decide whether or not it was her. She looked much older than he had believed her to be.

He had grown weary of death. He had known of this woman, cared for her, perhaps loved her, and then buried her. He had been nothing to her. She had not known he had been born or had ever lived. Yet he knew her from her diary, and he had put her in the hole he had dug. He had touched her and loved her.

But her grave was not even a hole. It was a shallow depression, hurriedly dug. They had piled rocks around her body, gradually letting them rest on and finally cover her body. Ned had yelled at Birdwood when he went too fast and let stones as big as a loaf of bread drop on her. He felt the embarrassment she surely would have felt at the odor that was expelled from her body when the stones fell. Hurt, Birdwood had slowed and placed the stones. That only made his anger grow.

"I want to kill the Indians," he said. "Bastards."

Birdwood said nothing, only went on placing stones.

"If you lined them up. Right over there. I would put a bullet into the brainpan of every single one of them, and I would be happy to be doing it, too."

Birdwood considered this. "All right, then."

They mounted and rode, picking their way through narrow canyon trails — bear trails, most likely, or Indian trails. If this was Indian fighting, it was damned poor work. They were five days in the saddle now, and they didn't even bother to talk anymore as they rode. There was nothing to say. The man in front felt as tired and miserable as the man behind, and so on. Ned wanted the Indians to start shooting. He thought that even if he died, it would be preferable to this steady climbing through the mountains, looking at the back of Park's head. At dismounts, they milled around and muttered their discontent, though that was not news to anyone.

They huddled around their small fire, heating their equally small rations. It was already near to completely dark. They had unsaddled the mounts, fed and watered them, and they had now just a few minutes before it was time to put themselves down for sleep.

"This is incursion. That's what this is," Foster said.

"It ain't incursion. We ain't incursing," Park responded.

"I tell you it is. We are in Mexico. There can't be any doubt about it now. We been here a couple days now. There's no arguing that."

"And what if we are? What's it going to matter? We ain't doing no harm to any Mexicans. We're just hunting Indians."

"It'll cause a war. That's what it will do. It will start another damned war."

"A war my behind. Mexico don't want no war with us."

"Otis Park, you are a damned fool. If we're in Mexico, Mexico got no choice except to go to war."

"Well, then. That's Mexico's problem. We ain't doing them no harm. If they start a war on us, they got what's coming to them. That's what I say. What do you think, Thorne?"

"I don't know if we're in Mexico. Maybe. And maybe we shouldn't be."

"Aw, he ain't no good in a argument. Ask Birdwood there. That boy's a caution. Ask him."

Birdwood shook his head fiercely.

"Come on, Jarbal. We're asking you. You got to answer."

Again, Birdwood just shook his head.

"Don't be shaking your head, son. You got to answer. You got to be giving your opinion. It's a rule of the civilized world."

"I ain't got no opinion," Birdwood said. "I ain't of no civilized world. I'm an American, and in America, poor people like me ain't got no opinions. You want to get yourself an opinion, you got to be able to afford it. I ain't got the cash."

"See, what did I tell you," Park said. "The boy's a caution."

■ ■ ■ ■

He had drawn duty as third vedette, so he had a few hours to sleep. It was better to draw first duty and do your shift and then sleep straight through until the morning. He hadn't drawn first shift for the whole patrol, though. He knew Triggs did not like him, and as long as Triggs was doling the shifts, he wouldn't get any of the good ones. He wished he could start over out here and tell everyone he wasn't what he pretended to be and become just one of the boys again. His exploits at the canyon had given him a moment of fellowship with the men, but now that had faded from memory. He was back to being the outsider, and he knew that when they looked at him, they saw only someone who was using up part of their rations.

They hated him. At least, all but Birdwood did. They hated him because they hated Brickner, and he had no way to tell them that he hated Brickner more than they did. Brickner's attack on Exeter back at the camp was proof in their eyes that he was Brickner's boy and was, therefore, aligned against them. So he stayed to himself as much as he could, away from the rest of them and as far from Brickner as he could manage. There was nothing he could do now to salvage his reputation and to become one of them. Nothing.

He was awakened by a boot in the back. It was not a kick but a push, designed to waken him and get his attention, not to punish him. Still, he longed to be back in a world where you were not wakened with kicks. It was Shattuck, who had taken second shift. He roused himself in the dark, pulled on his boots and hat, and took up his rifle and cartridge belt. He reported to Mayapple and was, in return, sent to the west where he would relieve Richmond, who would then walk back to camp and kick someone else in the back until all the vedettes had been changed.

He walked away from the sleeping troopers and took a position on top of an escarpment under a ragged tree not more than eight feet tall. He was well concealed and had a view of considerable distance to the front and sides of him, less to the rear. There was good light, and in that moonlight, the scraggly canyon growth had turned white and skeletal. He made out distinct shapes in front of him, though he did not always know to what they corresponded. He kept his carbine at the ready, across his chest and cradled in his left arm. Every several minutes he would break open the breach and reach in and finger the cartridge just to reassure himself it was there. It always was, though in his imagination, he continued to find himself facing an on-slaught of Apaches with an empty carbine. After touching the cartridge in the breach, he worked his fingers under the flap of his cartridge case and felt the rounds there, then brought his rifle back up to his chest until the next time.

An outrider made a circle of the perimeter some yards behind them. He heard the hoofbeats long before the rider reached him and, in fact, heard them before the soft exchange between the outrider and the ve-dette stationed to his right. When the hoofbeats approached, then stopped, he shouldered his carbine and challenged the rider to stop and identify himself.

"Foster," the voice came back. "What of your post?"

"All quiet," he replied. The hoofbeats resumed and gradually faded.

Though he did not much care for the company of his fellow soldiers, he did not relish the loneliness of vedette duty. The feeling of vulnerability was difficult to overcome. His lookout was a good one, and secure. But he was overwhelmed by the notion that he could not entirely protect himself. No matter how secure the post, there was a way for the enemy to penetrate it. That this enemy did not fight at night did little to alleviate the perceived threat. Had he had his back against a wall of solid rock, he would have felt that someone, somehow, could appear between his back and the rock. Apaches were capable of things that others were not. He half expected that the blade of an Apache knife was already at his throat, and he had failed to notice it.

He passed the four hours of his watch moving from states of terror to torpor. He watched the landscape ahead of him wide-eyed, with a concentration that made everything in his range of vision vibrate and jump. In the middle distance were paired trees, each fifteen or twenty feet tall — either pine or juniper. He could not tell at this distance. They would make perfect hiding places among the sparse, low vegetation that made up most of the landscape. Twice he saw the northernmost tree move slightly as though it hid someone who watched him. He neither shot nor called out, but watched harder, convincing himself that it was not moving, even as it moved once more. He wanted to call out, but he knew it would be a false report. It was his imagination, nothing more. Still, if it was not, the entire patrol was at risk. He left his watch weary from the effort of looking, his eyes sore and burning.

He was the last relieved and had an hour or so more of dark in which he would not be able to sleep. When asked what he had seen, he looked back to the trees that stood stock-still in the early morning dark. "Nothing."

He walked the several hundred yards back to camp quickly, moving as fast as he could, keeping an eye on the ground in front of him. Though he was behind his own lines, he felt the muscles in between his shoulder blades tense in expectation of the bullet or arrow that was surely aimed at him. He wanted desperately to smoke. He had no cigars left, and the flare of a match against the dark would earn him lashes if not an Apache bullet, anyway. Perhaps in the morning he might be able to buy or beg one from someone who had had the foresight to bring enough.

"Watch where in hell you are going." He was grabbed and pulled roughly off his feet and brought hard to the ground. "You damned near ran into me," Brickner said.

"What are you doing out here?"

"Sometimes the company of my own species is nearly revolting to me. I stay out with the mules. They smell better and have better sense. They watch where they're stepping, too."

He thought that the stock was still a few hundred yards to his right. He must have wandered a bit on his way back. He looked around, disoriented. "Where am I?"

"Where this is, is the doorstep of dead. That's where you're at."

"Are the Indians here?"

Brickner made no answer for a few seconds, then pushed a bottle toward him. "Here. You'll feel better for it."

He took the offered bottle and drank, though it was still so early the sun was not up. He enjoyed the burn of it in his throat and waited for it to settle and calm him.

"It's the blind leading the blind. Or the ignorant following the blind. I don't know, but it's the damnedest thing I have ever been involved in, and I have involved myself in all sorts of foolishness. But this fool is leading us to a massacre. We're going to be the first detachment of the U.S. Army to lose a battle with the Indians, and he don't give a damn if we live or die, because he don't give a damn if he lives or dies."

"The lieutenant."

"The same. Hell, he's a damned lieutenant in the Signal Corps. He has no business leading troops into a fight. He's no soldier. He's a schoolmarm squinting through spectacles, taking the children out to chase butterflies and ants. He would have us all in short pants or dresses if he could. We need to turn around and go back the way we came while we still can."

"We can't."

"The hell we can't. He has no authority to take us out on this patrol. We found the damned woman. That's what we was supposed to be after. What the hell are we doing now?"

"Chasing the Indians."

"No. Following the Indians. The same Indians that outsmarted the captain. The same Indians that killed Wortham. And the captain knew what he was about. He was a cavalry officer, a line officer, not a damned staff officer. He knew enough not to get us killed. A lesser man would have ridden right into that ambush, and we would both be dead. And now that lesser man is leading this patrol. And we're dead. We just ain't fallen yet."

"We can't just stop."

"No. We can't. They'd hang us. They'd strip him of his commission, but they'd hang us. One way or another, Marybelle, you are as old as you are going to get."

"We can beat that scrap of Indians."

"They are leading us. They could have lost us a few days ago, but we're still right behind them. I don't like that much. We ain't got no Indian scouts. We're right behind them because right behind them is where they want us."

"They're leading us into a trap?"

"They did before."

He could still smell and taste the cold, dusty rock where he had pressed himself down, trying to become too small for a bullet to find. He could hear the angry buzz of the bullets that had passed over him. He saw Wortham, dead, his face drained of blood and his blouse all gore.

"I never signed on to follow the schoolmarm at all," Brickner said. "And I certainly didn't sign on to follow Austin to the grave. I don't believe I have a mind to do it."

"You'll be hanged."

Brickner let out a low chuckle. "If I refused to go on and just turned back and went to camp, yes, I believe I would be hanged. It would be a damned stupid thing for me to do."

"We'll come out of this all right. I know we will."

"I'll come out of it all right. I'm already out of it. You're stuck belt deep in it."

"But, you said . . ."

"I said I wouldn't refuse to go on. That's not what I'm fixing to do. To hang us, they would have to have us. You can't hang what you don't have. And they ain't going to have us, or, at least, they ain't going to have me.

"This here is Mexico. We been here for a couple of days. Just before we hit the mountains, we come into Mexico. A body doesn't even need to run away. 'Away' is where we already are. You take a side step and you're a free man, well beyond the reach of the Army, because the Army ain't got nothing to do with Mexico. And the best of it is that it was the Army that brought us to Mexico. The Army ain't got no business here, and I'm guessing the lieutenant can't ever admit where he was or where he lost us. Son. We have invaded a foreign country."

"But it is Mexico. They don't even speak English here."

"*Sí, muchacho. Hablamos solo Español aquí.*"

"Why are you telling me this?"

"Because it's your last opportunity. I have invested my time and my effort into you. I have made offers an intelligent man would jump after, and you have ignored me like I was the very mule shit you wipe off your boots. This here is the last chance I am going to give you. Throw in with me, and you'll end up a rich man with everything you could ever want. Stay here, and you don't have to make no more decisions, right or wrong. Go with me, and get a life of wealth and pleasure. Stay here and die. It's your choice. Make your decision. You choose wrong and it's your last one."

"I don't believe you."

"About what? Mexico? You better believe you're in Mexico. The lieutenant? Up on the Pit River, it was me that saved them. It wasn't neither Franklin or Austin. It was me, though Franklin got the brevet. If I hadn't stumbled onto Crook and the rest, they'd both be dead now along with a bunch of others, and the Army might be better off for it. And for my trouble I got busted back to corporal. Sixteen dollars a month for the last four years. No opportunity for further advancement, as they say. So, I have helped myself to the Army's things. I won't deny that. But they helped themselves to my things first. They were the ones that started the stealing. I didn't do more than what was done to me first.

"Franklin was a fool, and Austin's the greater. Up on the Pit, Austin thought that a string of flags kept us safe. I was the one that broke through and got word back to the major that we needed help. By the time we got back, half was dead and the other half was lined up to follow. And I was the coward who had run away. Not the hero that saved them, the coward. And all this is because Franklin trusted Austin. The fool loves another fool. I wouldn't follow Austin into a cathouse if some miracle gave him the inclination to go to one."

"I am not a deserter."

"Neither am I. Yet. And you ain't dead. Yet. Let me put it to you plain. The lieutenant has loaded his gun, cocked it, and put it to your head. Right about here." He stuck a finger into Ned's temple. "And now he's saying that he's not going to hurt you, but he needs to pull that trigger just a little bit tighter right now. And he's doing that because he's too much the coward to put it to his own head, and you're too much a fool to duck. You have no prospects, Marybelle, save what I offer."

"I don't want prospects. I'm done with them."

"You'll change your tune once we're out of here and on our way deep into Mexico.

You'll be needing to consider your future then, Marybelle."

"And why is that?"

"Your story is told now, Marybelle. There isn't a man in camp who don't know what you done."

"I don't know what you mean." His stomach tightened, and he felt his flesh grow cold.

"Yes. Yes, you do. You killed your brother. That's what you done, and everybody knows it. Ain't one man back at the camp going to hear your name, his throat won't want to tighten against puking."

"How do you know?"

"How do I know? How do I know anything? It's a small camp, Marybelle. Anything worth knowing, I know it."

"The lieutenant promised."

"What? He promised what? That he wouldn't tell? Hell. He didn't need to tell nobody. You want something secret, you don't ever let it find its way to your mouth. Something like that finds air, it's gone. It belongs to everybody, then. Why do you think the lieutenant give you to me? You think he didn't like the way you tote his coffee in the morning or the way you wash his inexpressibles? You been cast to the outer darkness, Marybelle. Your lot's thrown in with me, now."

And he thought that he would vomit. Only his parents had suspected that the death of his brother might not have been an accident, and he hadn't been able to stand that they suspected, or even that he himself suspected. Now he was in Mexico in a troop of men that believed that he had slain his brother in cold blood. And as bad as the situation was, it was about to get worse.

"A deserter is the lowest thing in the world, and I'm done with running."

Brickner snorted. "Deserters are alive, and the living make their way in the world walking over the dead. No living man is lower than a man of honor dead and buried, or, even worse, one who has turned himself into vulture shit. And that's what is about to happen to you. I don't know what it is those Indians are up to, but they are up to something, and it ain't something in our favor, and we are doing exactly what they want us to do."

"You should tell that to the lieutenant."

"He's not my lieutenant. It's him that got Franklin killed, and now he's working on the rest of us. That man is death's aide-decamp. The first time I seen him, up on the Pit, his mopey queerness just about made me throw up. I saw it was the end of us.

And it was. He just takes his time about things is all. Now, you follow him if you want, but he is going to kill you and everyone else. You follow me, and you'll get to bounce grandbabies on your knee someday."

"What are you going to do in Mexico if you run off?"

"We. And what we are going to do is what I been doing for the last several years. Buying and selling. Working with horses and mules. I'm the best there is with mules. Lots of mules in Mexico, and lots of folks who want them. I know how to get them. Mexico is the land of opportunity. The United States is pretty well played out. I don't see much good coming down the line in the States. But Mexico is a place a man can make a good life for himself. And I can teach you what you need to know. You're bothersome and you whine like a left pup, but you're smart. I can work with you." Brickner moved in close enough for the sweetness of his whisky breath to catch in the back of Ned's throat. He put his hand on Ned's shoulder, then moved it up so he cradled Ned's neck in his hand. "I am going to be a rich man. Those who stay here are going to be dead. I can take care of you. Come with me. You don't want to be dead, even if you think you do. It ain't got nothing to recommend it.

"When I go, I'll come and tell you I'm going. That will be as much as you need to know. All you got to do is jump on a horse and ride. I'll have it ready for you. You'll have to ride hard for a little while, but only a while. They ain't going to go chasing us all over Mexico. There it is. Your very own forty acres and a horse, courtesy of the U.S. Army."

"I don't know."

"You best know. If I come to you and say 'this is the time to go,' and you don't go, I'll have to slit your throat to keep from giving me away. So you tell me now, and you tell me true. I have no wish to hurt you, no matter the pleasure it's given me in the past. I'm your friend. Right here, I am your only friend. But, if I have to kill you, I will. You know I will."

He saw the dilemma clearly. If he told Brickner he wasn't going, he would die right here. "All right. I'm with you."

"You damn right," Brickner said, passing him the bottle. "You with me."

When he was away from Brickner, he tried to see his way through this. He could go to the lieutenant and tell him. He didn't like that. He didn't peach. That might be a child's way, but it seemed to him wrong, and he had difficulties seeing where child stopped and man began. All the lieutenant could do in any means would be to confront Brickner, who would only deny it. Later, Brickner, knowing who had told the lieutenant, would kill him. He knew that was true. Brickner would kill him.

He thought maybe he should go. There was nothing for him now. He was just Ned Thorne of Hartford, Connecticut, just as he had always been. The boy who killed his brother. The boy who swept the store and counted change into the impatient hands of customers who did not want to stay in the presence of the boy who killed his brother. Maybe he should go with Brickner. He was not going to redeem himself, so he might as well go to hell, or, at least, to Mexico.

He thought he was the only one awake except for Brickner. It was cold, and he felt the cold as intensely as he had felt the heat earlier in the day. Around him, men snored, and someone, probably Birdwood, mumbled in his sleep. He thought about running, running away from the Army and Brickner and the lieutenant and Mexico, saving his skin from those all around him who seemed determined to kill him. He was more scared than he had ever been, far more afraid than he had been on the patrol with the captain. Death had become more real now. He had begun to fear his.

Brickner was drunk, and it might have been only the whisky that was talking. Brickner had spent his whole life in the Army and had never left it, at least, according to him. Perhaps it was all just the grousing of a lifetime Army man. Perhaps it meant no more than that he was unhappy with his present situation.

But he was right. They must be in Mexico by now. There had been other talk of it, though that had been quiet. And they had no reason, anymore, to be there. The woman was dead, and there was no genuine reason to go forward, except that it was the lieutenant's command. It was not their job to punish the Apaches, no matter how horrible the thing they had done. It was the Mexicans' problem now. Brickner was right to complain. He knew that. Perhaps it was right for Brickner to desert, though desertion could never be right. Could it? But he knew that Brickner was going. It was not idle complaining. And he had told Brickner that he was going with him.

He moved between rows of sleeping men until he came to two who were sleeping close together, just the width of a man's body separating them, and he lay down between them, so that if Brickner came, he could not wake him without waking the others. He listened to the men breathe. They had been asleep awhile and their breathing had regulated so that they were inhaling and exhaling to the same rhythm. He envied them their sleep. He lay on his back, close enough that some part of him touched each of them and their warm breath touched his face. He closed his eyes and pretended to sleep.

LIEUTENANT
ANTHONY AUSTIN

He was awakened from a thin sleep, that barely held him, by Triggs, who told him. He sat upright and made Triggs repeat it.

"Brickner. He's gone. Sometime last night, perhaps this morning."

"The mules?"

Triggs nodded. "Two of them. He left us one. The shavetail, which was too much a bother for him to take. I can send four men after him. He can't be too far away."

He waved the suggestion off. He was still struggling out of sleep, trying to make sense of what Triggs was telling him. "Keep the men together. How? How did he do it?"

"I don't know exactly. He's smart, Brickner. We found Cranston out cold on the western post this morning. He still doesn't know who he is or what's going on. Certainly, he has no idea what happened to him. Brickner whacked him a good one, that's for certain. And most likely he wrapped the animals' hooves in cloth so they wouldn't be heard. They didn't leave much in the way of prints."

"We don't know which way he's headed?"

Triggs shook his head. "He left headed west. You can bet he's not still going that way, though he would like us to think he is. But I'm placing no wagers. If it was my call, I would send men out in the four directions, riding hard, with orders to shoot to kill. He's a deserter, and he has our supplies."

"And he would assuredly kill the men we sent after him. He's the best man with the animals, and he's our best shot."

"Except Thorne."

"What about Thorne? Is he with him?"

"Thorne's here. He says he knows nothing of it. He came off watch this morning and went to sleep. I woke him when we found Brickner gone. Maybe it's true, maybe not. I can work with him for a while if you like."

"Leave him."

"He may know something. He's the closest thing Brickner has to a friend."

"No. Leave him be. Leave Brickner, too. He's trouble we're best rid of."

"Permission to speak freely, sir."

He looked at Triggs. His face was raw and peeling, blistering at the nose, lips, and hairline. He looked tired and dusty. Austin suspected he himself must look as bad as Triggs, or worse. His own skin burned like lye. "Yes. Go on."

"Two things, sir. Brickner has the bulk of our supplies. And" — he paused — "we're deep in Mexico, sir."

"I know that."

"Well, to get back means foraging our way back. And the more we move around, the more noise we make and the more attention we're likely to draw. It's quite possible we could be discovered. And if we are, it's courts-martial for all of us. Or worse. And if Brickner gets caught, one American soldier, riding with two packed Army mules, they are going to come looking for the rest of us. We desperately need to find Brickner before someone else finds him, or finds us. I don't think we can afford to let him go, sir."

Trouble was akin to gravity. Things go wrong the way hoops roll down hills. They start slowly, but they pick up speed and determination as they go. He could not remember now exactly why it was so important that they follow the Apaches. Certainly that was a mistake, and he had compounded it by continuing the pursuit after finding the woman. They were, he thought, thirty, maybe forty, miles into Mexico. He could feel Bobby's condemnation from somewhere beyond. Oddly, he thought of his little hummingbird, probably at Harvard now, carrying his name into the literature. Why was it a man could have so much difficulty accepting who he was?

"Very well. Take three men and go after Brickner. Be back by dark. If you find him, give him the opportunity to return. If he chooses not to, you'll have to kill him, I suppose. We will remain encamped on this spot."

"Sir. Yes, sir."

Triggs took Foster, Richmond, and Shattuck. They took the freshest horses, leaving the weariest and most wounded to rest with the men. He put Thorne in charge of doing what he could for the mounts that remained — dressing their cuts and scrapes against blowfly, dressing their hooves, keeping them watered and fed.

They needed forage. The shavetail was packing only dry beans and coffee, blankets, supplies for the horses, and some utensils. Brickner had taken most of the food — the hardtack and canned food and nearly all of the water. This became the immediate concern. They were a day's ride, back across the canyon, from the last water they had found, and they needed to water the horses, soak their beans, and cook their coffee. What Brickner had left was barely enough to keep men and horses going, without food.

There were ten of them left. He had to keep four men in position as vedettes. Thorne was tending the horses. That left himself and four others to forage for food and water. Within their perimeter was little — perhaps some nuts and berries, a few rodents and birds. It was unlikely any larger game was going to wander inside that perimeter. There was no water. A dry creek bed lay some three hundred yards to the west. He could send two men to scout up the creek for water, but that left only three of them within the perimeter. They were completely unprotected, and their situation was untenable.

There was an option to send only one man for water, but he would be limited in how much he could bring back. His most resourceful man had deserted, and the second most resourceful was in pursuit of the first, and he had taken numbers three, four, and five with him. The men he had left were best suited for hunkering down, keeping their heads low, and trying not to get themselves shot. The hoop continued to roll.

If everything went well, they could be back

to near full strength by midday. Then they could regroup and backtrack to yesterday's water. From there, they could make a fairly easy ride of it back to the border and across, giving the Apaches the small victory of escape this time.

He didn't, however, like their chances. Brickner, for all his ungainliness afoot, was good in the saddle, even pulling mules behind him. He was smarter than most of them and wiser in the ways of the countryside. Triggs was a good man, but his money would have to go on Brickner. It was Brickner every way he thought it. Brickner had been doing Triggs's job since Triggs had been in short pants.

"They need water, sir." Thorne gestured backhanded at the horses and the mule. "I've done what I could, dressing their wounds and hooves. They're getting rest and some grazing, but mostly they need water."

"Can we get another two or three days' riding from them?"

The boy looked worried, uncertain. He reminded Tony of a schoolboy who had forgotten his lesson. "I don't know, sir. Mr. Brickner would know. I don't."

"But Brickner's not here, is he?"

"No, sir."

"And I need an answer. Can these animals

give us another two or three days' hard ride?"

"I don't think so. Not a hard ride. They're tired."

"I think you're wrong. I think they can."

"Yes, sir." Thorne looked relieved that someone had given an answer and it was no longer being demanded of him.

"Especially if they get some water. Is that right?"

"Yes, sir. Yes, it is. They need water."

And that was it, exactly. He saw now what he had to do and regretted that he had not seen it earlier. While they would conserve their strength by waiting for the pursuit party, the need for water would continue to grow. Their greatest concern now was water. They could not afford an extra day without it, even if that day was one of rest.

"Very well, soldier. I want you to prepare them for march. Take Birdwood and Hermann and get the mounts saddled and ready. We are marching in an hour."

It was simply what had to be done. Without water they were lost. When Triggs's patrol returned and found them gone, there would be only one explanation of where they could have gone, and Triggs would have the explanation immediately. They had gone for water. In this barren place, water was the only thing that made sense, and Triggs would see that, and they would regroup at the water.

Austin took them out, single file, spaced a length apart so that they made as little noise as possible and were less easily seen. He got them up into the tree line quickly, and in the trees they did not stand out. They continued to move through the morning, at a steady pace, making their way back to the stream and pool they had found the day before.

It was slow, moving back up the mountain. He resisted the impulse to push them, instead letting them pace themselves to conserve their small store of food and water and energy. He had miscalculated, then Brickner had compounded the miscalculation, but a careful and deliberate replanning would bring them out all right.

As they rode, the canyon opened up beside them, to their left this time. The crossing at the washout began to concern him. It was made more difficult without Brickner, but they had fewer mules and supplies to bring across this time. Thorne had the experience of having made it once. And, Austin assumed, that would give him confidence to make it back across.

He let Mayapple take the front. He was a

good horseman and a man mature enough to take care with his life and the lives of others. He followed in second position, with the rest behind him, Thorne leading the shavetail and Washington bringing up the rear. It was an easier go, though the ascent was steep. There were fewer of them, and it was earlier in the day, when both the men and the animals were fresher. They had the advantage of cooler weather and more light. The sun was at their backs. The mounts were just enough in need of water to be restive but not balky. Each man allowed himself two lengths ahead and behind.

The looseness of the line gave them two advantages. If they should be attacked at this vulnerable position, they were spread wide enough to allow them time to dismount and find cover. And if a horse should slip, it would take only its rider with it, not the near horses and men.

He did not look down, though he had no particular fear of heights. He knew, though, that to look in the direction of the fallaway increased the chances that he would pressure the tack that way and risk taking his horse to the edge. Instead, he looked ahead to Mayapple's horse, which was delicately picking her way across the rocks. He let his eye go occasionally to the horizon that stretched far beyond, probably back into the United States, in a clear and cloudless sky. He gave the roan little encouragement, but, instead, trusted her to pick her way behind Mayapple's horse to the other side.

Twice the small trail had slid away and the horse had to take it in a small jump. The first was no trouble, but at the second, he felt a thrill of fear as the roan lost purchase and scrambled to regain the trail. He felt her weight go out toward the fallaway and knew that his weight, too, was impelling them toward the edge. He felt her forehooves catch and then a jolt as her rear hooves hit rock and pushed them both forward and onto the solid footing of the other side. He looked back at Brock behind him and saw his horse take the same scree with a delicate jump a child might make at play.

He brought them up short and ordered a dismount. The washout was next, and though he did not wish to magnify its danger and importance, he wanted to make sure that they were all in agreement on the best way to make the crossing. The boy was his worry now. And when he went back to where the boy was, his concern grew.

PRIVATE NED THORNE

Dear Thad,

I believe that perhaps my time has come and I will join you in death. It is my most urgent hope that death has a small foyer, or perhaps a large lobby as in the grand hotels, where we could stop and greet each other for just a bit before we go our separate ways. For I once thought I would redeem myself if sufficient opportunity presented itself. I know now that is not true, and that in death, my residence for eternity will be far from yours, but I hope there is sufficient mercy that I may see you one more time before I am forever cast down.

LIEUTENANT
ANTHONY AUSTIN

Thorne was tightening the rope that secured the mule to his mount. Though Thorne did nothing more than come to attention and salute, Austin could see that the boy was making his way down the dark hallway of fear. "Are you ready, then?"

"I think so, sir. I am securing the lines. She has done it before all right."

It took him a moment to realize that the "she" referred to the shavetail, which was now digging at the ground, nervous and edgy, perhaps feeding on the boy's own nervousness. He considered ordering the boy to tie up to Washington and to rein the mule in as he and Brickner had done on the first crossover. It had been Brickner's idea, and he had let him do it, deferring to Brickner's great experience. But now, without Brickner, he could not countenance it. An error now would take one or more of the few troopers he had to the bottom of the canyon, and he could not accept the risk of it. "Untie the rope from your saddle."

Thorne looked surprised. "Sir?"

"Untie the rope. Lead the mule by hand. And if there is a problem, I want you to let it go. Is that understood?"

"But, sir. This is a shavetail. She needs leading."

"She will follow you, and you will lead her across. And if she falters, she will fall. But if she falls, she will not take you or Washington or any of the rest of us with her. What is she packing?"

"Beans, sir. And cooking utensils, some ammunition, and medical supplies."

"That's it?"

"Yes, sir."

"Unpack the ammunition and medical supplies, then. Distribute them among the rest of the men."

"But that will unbalance the packs, sir. It could throw her off balance."

"Do your best to redistribute the weight. But if she goes, she goes, and we shall minimize our losses. But I am not relieving you of your responsibilities. Is that understood? Your job is to get her across. You shall achieve that."

"Yes, sir."

■ ■ ■ ■

They all waited while Thorne unpacked cases of ammunition and broke them open so that each member of the patrol could take several boxes. Then the medical supplies — bandages, scalpels, forceps, carbolic acid, and various powders — were similarly divided up among the riders. He saw, with concern and regret, the look of doom that crossed the boy's face and knew that his precautions had simply reiterated to Thorne his lack of faith in him. But if the boy went over the side on the crossing, there would be no faith to iterate, he reasoned. When Thorne glumly nodded his readiness, he regrouped the men and gave orders to mount.

He put Mayapple in the lead and Foster behind him. He took a rearward position, behind Birdwood but ahead of Thorne, who was followed by the repacked shavetail mule, then Washington. They went over the washout one at a time, spurring hard for thirty or forty yards, then leaping the washout and landing on the other side. As soon as each man cleared, he dismounted, unsheathed his rifle, and brought it to the ready to provide cover for the next man.

Birdwood gave a sharp grunt, then took the kepi from his head, slapped his horse with it, tucked his head at the horse's neck, and took off at a gallop. He watched Birdwood go, riding low, then rising in a graceful arc as he cleared the washout and came around on the other side. As soon as he saw that Birdwood had cleared out from the landing area, he gave the roan the spurs and tucked down, letting up on the reins and feeling, before seeing, the rise of the roan into the air as she cleared the washout.

He wheeled his horse around and scrambled off, pulling the roan out of the way so that Thorne would have area enough for himself and the shavetail. He pulled his rifle from the scabbard and knelt. He saw Thorne coming, hard and straight, and he looked at the clearing, which now seemed quiet and secure. He pulled back the hammer of his carbine in readiness, though there was no danger that could be shot at.

He heard the shout, or rather the curse, then the scramble and clatter all in one. The scream of the mule came later and hung in the air a long time. He saw, at the same time, Thorne's horse, furiously digging for purchase with its back legs while its forehooves scratched at the rock and dirt, the boy desperately urging it forward, away from the fallaway that was death, and the mule, *aparejo* down, its delicate hooves in the air, doing a futile and dainty dance as it spun and screamed into the canyon below.

He made his way back onto the small trail as Foster rode up, wide-eyed and red in the face. "Goddamn," Foster said. "It was the mule. It went over."

"Thorne," he said. "Thorne. Did he go as well?"

"It went right on over. The damnedest sight I ever saw."

"Thorne, man. Thorne."

"He made it," Foster said, collecting himself. "He let go of the rope just in time. The mule just about took him down, too. But he's there. Right there," he said, pointing in a direction where Thorne wasn't.

"I tried to lead it," Thorne said. He was talking fast, taking gulps of air between rushes of words. "It was no use. I had to let it go where it would. It got scared. I saw it coming, scared. It was just a shavetail. I think the *aparejo* was wrong. Brickner, he knows those. Not me. I couldn't stop it. I don't know. There was nothing I could do. Sir."

"Well," he said, shaking with fear gone to anger. "You have done the rest of Brickner's work for him. That was all the food we had. You've done us in."

"I could go down into the canyon and get it."

"No. You could not. You may not. It's too steep, too far down. There's nothing to be done." He could see that the boy was trembling, coming near to tears. He felt some sympathy, but even more, he felt a rising fury. What the boy had done was a direct result of his, not Thorne's, mistake. He had nearly killed the boy. He had killed a mule and lost the supplies. The hoop was picking up speed. His mistakes compounded themselves, and every agent of that compounding seemed to be mocking him. By losing the mule, the boy had announced to all, finally and irrevocably, that what could have gone wrong had, and it continued to go so. There was no hiding now the fact that they were in serious trouble. "You no longer have an assignment. Fall in with the others. We will resume the march."

"Sir."

"Yes. What?"

"I have some hardtack, sir. I've been saving it out of my rations."

"Oh, very well. You have loaves. That is splendid. Miraculous, even. One assumes you have fishes as well?"

"No, sir. Just hardtack."

He had to believe that Triggs would catch up with and capture Brickner and the rest of the supplies. Though rations were short, almost to nonexistence now that the rest were with the mule at the bottom of the canyon, they had enough to get back to the water and some beyond, and they could probably forage well enough to get back to the camp. Should the worst happen and Brickner elude them, they would have water by nightfall and fresher horses for the trek back. On fed, watered, and rested horses, they could ride for days without food for themselves. It was two, three, no more than four at most, back to the border, where they might forage without fear of discovery.

They continued to make their way back through the rock and brush of the narrow trail, a bear trail most likely, through the late morning and into the early afternoon. After the noon rest, he ordered them to lead their horses and march on foot, conserving the strength of the horses for when they would need it most.

It was still early afternoon when Washington came riding back from his scout, coming hard. "Mexicans. Up ahead. There's a dozen or so near to the pool where we're headed."

"Were you seen?" he demanded.

"Pretty sure. I'm pretty sure I was."

"Who are they? Are they Army? Or farmers? Hunters?"

"Maybe hunters. I don't think they're soldiers. They're not in uniform, but they're armed, and there are a lot of them. I didn't stop to chat."

"Did they follow you?"

"Maybe."

"All right. Take three men. Form a short line up about one hundred yards. If they are in pursuit, challenge, then open fire. Understood?"

Washington flicked a salute, pointed to the first three men he saw and went back the way he had come.

He gave orders to ready arms and establish a perimeter, with the horses in the middle, tended by Thorne. He put at least one man at every direction of the compass, including at the canyon so that they could not be surprised from the rear. There was plenty of tree and rock cover, and all things considered, it was not a terrible place for withstanding a siege. They could hold off a small number for a long time. And if firing began, Triggs and the patrol would no doubt hear it and be able to return and reinforce them.

■ ■ ■ ■

The first shot came at one fifty-seven. He could not say which side fired it, but he was precise about the time. It would be important for the incident report, and that would be pored over at the court-martial. There was more firing, and he reckoned that it was Washington and the forward scout returning the fire. He had to yell at Birdwood to maintain his position as he tried to run up to reinforce Washington.

Whoever they were, they were not looking for a fight, perhaps not prepared for one. They were firing sporadically, halfheartedly, even. He thought to himself that it was the slowest, calmest, most orderly fight he had ever engaged in. Still, it was a fight. Shots rang out, and he could hear the bullets whine overhead. Nearby, handfuls of grass and pine needles jumped into the air, and small branches snapped off trees. The horses, tethered and hobbled, stamped and whinnied, but could not bolt. He felt he must be dreaming, the engagement such an odd one.

He was not surprised when Pack scurried back to tell of the white flag. He moved up behind Pack, two trees farther, until he could see, where Pack pointed, a bit of white rag waving from behind another tree some forty yards up.

The scrap of cloth made its way from behind the tree in a slow, comic dance, appearing first as just cloth, then as a whole scrap of cloth clutched in a hand. The hand grew an arm and the arm a shoulder, until the right half of a man's body appeared, dressed in a dark coat, head still tucked behind the tree, and the cloth still dancing in the air like a puppet. *"Hola,"* a voice called. *"Hola. No tirame."* There was a pause, and then the man's head, hatless and broad, emerged from behind the tree. *"Por favor. No tirame. Por favor."*

He emerged from behind the tree, slowly, tentatively, a good-sized man, dark and unshaven but with a broad and open face, the face of a man of some intelligence and character. He wore a suit of Eastern cut, not particularly unfashionable but old, worn, and soiled, perhaps torn here and there. *"José Epitacio Tafoya. Tafoya. Estoy Capitán. No tirame. I come to you."* He continued to wave the white rag in circles over his head, as though he were about to throw a lasso.

Austin watched the Mexican come out into the open, then proceed toward them in a direct line through an opening in the trees. "Get Thorne up here," he told Pack. "I want someone who can actually hit something to cover me while we talk. I want him on this fellow."

"You're not going out there?"

"I'm not about to let him in here. I die, he dies. Vice versa. Get Thorne up here before he comes much closer.

"Alto," he yelled to the Mexican. *"Me llamo Anthony Frederick Austin."* With that, he had very nearly exhausted his stock of Spanish. He looked around for who else might have facility with the language. Brickner, of course. He rose up from where he knelt and stood erect, his body tingling in anticipation of the bullet.

He told Thorne to kneel behind the large pine and to keep a bead on the Mexican. As he started into the clearing, he took the revolver from its holster and handed it to Thorne.

"Hola, Anthony Frederick Austin," called the Mexican. *"¿Habla usted Español?"*

"Poco. Solo poco."

"All right, then. English. I can speak English. Not so good. But maybe better than you can Spanish. You are soldiers? Of the United States?"

He thought for a moment how he might

deny this. Involuntarily, he looked down at the striped leg of his uniform trousers. *"Militar. Sí."*

"Soldiers. You are soldiers. Us also. But, you will pardon me. This is Mexico. You are *norteamericanos.* You are lieutenant?"

He nodded. Yes.

"And you are authorized to speak? For the commanding officer? There is *capitán?"*

"There is no captain. I am in command of this patrol."

Tafoya nodded gravely. *"Esta bueno.* Good. It is good. I am in charge as well."

Austin snapped off a quick salute. "That is good, then. We can talk together."

Tafoya returned the salute. "Then I must ask this of you. Why are you here for?"

"Indians," he said. "We are in pursuit of the Indians, Apaches. They have kidnapped a woman."

"Yes. *La rubia.* The light-headed woman. We know of her."

"Of the woman?"

"For a long time, we have been looking for these Apaches. We hear from here and there. *Los Apaches,* they have a white woman, *una rubia.* They try to sell her. Very valuable, such a woman. We try to find these Apaches so that we may save her. Always we are pretty close, but we do not find them. It is the same with you?"

"It is. We have been searching a long time. One of our patrols found the ranch where she was taken." He tried to reckon the time. How long ago was that? Days? Weeks? Lifetimes? Centuries? "A long time," he confirmed. "A very long time."

"And to here. You followed them to here?"

He nodded confirmation. "We had contact yesterday. We lost them just by here."

Tafoya nodded and rubbed at the pine needles and dirt with the worn toe of his boot. "*También*. We have followed them to this place *lo mismo*. We see them, we lose them. We see them again. We try to be closer, but we do not reach them." He shook his head. "These last few days we push very hard because we are knowing we are close. They appear to slow down."

Austin nodded. "Yes, they seem to be wearing down. One could almost reach out and touch them."

Tafoya blew out his breath. "*Mierda*. They are very clever, these Apaches. Very smart." He tapped the side of his head with his finger. "It is not by accident then that we have found each other, is it?"

"I would suppose it is not."

"They have led us right to each other. If you are running from a dog, you get that dog to chase a cat instead of you. *Hacen no-sotros los tontos.*"

"Pardon?"

"Fools. They make of us fools. Of you and me."

"I guess that might be the case, mightn't it?" He watched Tafoya's discomfort grow. Within the camaraderie of the duped, the essence of the situation remained and gradually grew more clear. Tafoya's own analogy of dogs and cats had served to foreground what neither wanted to address outright. He thought to suggest that they might join forces and try to push the Indians back into the United States, but it was not his place to be suggesting. The first move must be Tafoya's, and he would let him make it and see if there was room for negotiation later.

"You did not know we are here?" Tafoya asked.

"No. Not until our scout found you at the pool."

"Nor us. We saw you come across *la cañada.* You lost your mule. Mariano, he saw it fall. You lost much of your foods?"

"Most of them. We can forage our way across the border."

"That mule. It is a gift from God for the Indians. They will get to the bottom of the

558

canyon and they will eat your foods. They will eat your mule as well. They will eat anything, these Indians. They eat mules. They eat dogs. They eat rats and lizards. They are more like dogs than men. They disgust me. You are the United States Army. You should kill all of them."

"That's not our intent or our wish. But we have reservations for them. They can learn to grow their own food. These Indians were on a reservation and then some stupid American men attacked them. It is our responsibility to round them up and take them back to where they belong. They won't need to raid into Mexico. It is not my desire to kill them, though I will kill them if I must. We wish to help our neighbor Mexico."

"We will kill them."

"That is your right."

"Yes. Yes. It is our right. You have lost all of your foods? Your ammunitions?"

He assumed that the Mexicans did not know about Triggs and his small patrol, or Brickner and the rest of the supplies. If Tafoya was telling the truth, the Mexicans had just now found them and had not yet found Triggs or Brickner. What you knew was often the greater advantage than the force or armament at your command. "All of it.

We shall forage, hunt, our way back."

Tafoya nodded agreement. "We have some foods. Not too much. How many are you?" It was clear that he did not know and was trying to get a fix on their number.

He himself was trying to count the Mexicans and their horses, but both were well hidden in the trees. He could catch, now and again, some bit of movement from one place to another, but in a pine forest, it was impossible to know what movement represented man or horse or some other creature, or whether there were men moving from tree to tree. Tafoya was keeping his men moving to keep him from knowing just how many there were. He wished he had thought to do the same.

"It is a small patrol," he said finally. "And yours?"

"*Lo mismo.* The same. A small patrol. We have enough to combat with those Indians when we find them. You do, as well?"

"We would not be here if we did not."

"*Verdad.* But this is not good what we find here. Not any good. You should not be here."

"You are right. We should not. We were pursuing our common enemy, though. To get the Apaches back to the reservation would be a benefit to both of our countries.

We are in Mexico only to get the Apaches and take them back where they belong. We are engaged, you and I, in the same pursuit."

"*Verdad.* This is true what you say. And I would be very happy if you had found the Apaches and captured them or killed them to rid me of their pestilence. I would be very grateful to you. But instead we find ourselves here, talking on this mountaintop about things that are bigger than we are. You and I do not decide what is right between countries. But it is you and I who must stand here today and decided together what is to be done about this situation."

"It is difficult," he confirmed.

"Those Apaches." Tafoya spit on the ground. "If we could rid ourselves of them, we would not have these problems. Certainly you would not come to Mexico, but you are chasing those *condenados Indios.* Do you wish to kill me, Anthony Frederick Austin?"

The question startled him as it was supposed to do, and though he made every attempt to hide any emotion, he reacted to it. He gauged his own reaction by the widening of Tafoya's eyes. "No," he said.

"*Está bueno. También,* I do not wish to kill you. This is good. Let us agree that we will discover the solutions to these problems

561

without bringing harm to each other. Can we agree on that?"

"I would hope so. We will not harm you so long as you do not try to harm us."

"*Bueno.* You are looking for the woman? *Verdad?*"

"No. We have found the woman. She is dead."

"They have killed her?"

"That we don't know. She is dead. Only that. We have buried her."

"I don't think they would kill her. A woman such as that would be very valuable. It grieves me to say that there are those in my country who would pay very much money for a *rubia* like that one. The Apaches would try to keep her alive."

"She may have slowed them down too much. That might have given them cause to kill her. Perhaps when we came in pursuit, that became a necessity. Perhaps it is we who have killed her. Still, that is not the issue. She is dead. We do not know how she died. She died."

"Then you need not pursue the Apaches further?"

He looked at Tafoya, trying to judge both what he expected to hear and what he wanted to hear. He did not wish to appear weak, but he also needed to avoid the confrontation if he could.

"They have fled the reservation. We should take them back. But, finally, no, we do not need to pursue them any further. We do not intend to pursue them any further."

"This is good. You want to return to *los Estados Unidos.*"

"Yes. We do. We are on our way."

"You are leaving Mexico?"

"Of course. As quickly as we can." He did not know if this was the right way to go, but it was the way he was going.

"Then you could back up a little. We could back up a little. You could go that way, we could go this way. There is no longer a problem. This is true?"

"Yes. I believe it is. We need water. We have to go that way." He motioned with his hand to where he assumed the water was. "You will need to let us reach the water. We can make it back without food or supplies, but we can't go without water."

"Yes. I understand. You can have water. You need water to continue your journey back to your country. It is hard, being on patrol. It is hard on men, and it is hard on the animals."

"It is."

"I can let you have water. This is not a problem. However, we are in need as well.

It is a most difficult business chasing Indians through the mountains. And when we catch them, their scalps are not worth so much money as once they were. So, much like you, we are in need."

"We have very little. You know that we lost our supplies coming through the canyon. I don't think we have very much."

Tafoya smiled. "How American. You consider yourselves poor when you are rich. You are not so poor. We are poor. You have very fine horses."

"You want our horses?"

"Not all of your horses. Some of your horses. Several of my men are on foot. We can do our job better if we have the horses to do it. You, you will go back to *los Estados Unidos* and you will have more horses given to you by your government. Our government does not give us horses."

"You cannot have our horses."

"*Por favor.* Please. Anthony Austin. Do not be so rapid here. We must work together to solve this problem that now confronts us."

"We will not surrender our mounts or our weapons. That we cannot do. And this is a very dangerous course you are considering. You cannot extort the property of the United States of America."

"Please. Please. Understand. This is a very

difficult situation. You are in Mexico now. You have no business in Mexico. I am trying to resolve the problem that you have yourself created. We will help each other out of this situation. No one will ever know that this situation ever occurred in this place. Do not be quick to accuse me. I wish to go home to my wife and children, and I wish the same for you."

"Do *you* understand? This is a detachment of the United States Army. Do you understand that? This is the United States Army you are dealing with."

"*Claro que sí.* We have this discussion precisely because you are the United States Army. Not the Army. No. A very small part of that Army. And I think no one else in the Army knows you are here. And I also think that no one will be eager to admit that you are here. This is a discussion between us — you and me, not the United States and Mexico. We are here on this mountaintop, a mountain where I have spent much time hunting and riding. This is a place of great beauty, which is put here for the enjoyment of men like ourselves. And men like ourselves must be men of caution. We can walk to the edge of *la cañada,* look over, and then take a step backward so that we do not, like the mule, end up at the bottom. Perhaps now is the time to take that step."

He nodded, unsure what to say. Tafoya had taken control of their situation, and he wasn't sure how he was supposed to react now. Bobby would not stand for this. Certainly. Not at all. But neither would Bobby have allowed himself into such a situation. He assumed that sooner or later, this would come to a fight. He wished only to keep it to later, when he would have the reinforcements to push the balance into his favor. "Do you smoke?" he asked.

"You have tobacco?"

He took his pouch and pipe from his blouse and handed the pouch to Tafoya, who took it, opened it, and smelled it, inhaling deeply. He took a scrap of paper from the pocket of his coat, unfolded it, and smoothed it carefully, rubbing it against his leg. He folded it once more, then tore a small piece of it away, still careful, following the folds. Into the paper, he shook a small mound of tobacco, handed back the pouch, and rolled a thick cigarette. They smoked together.

"There are many deer in these mountains," Tafoya said. "And bears and lions, as well. It is a good place. I first came here with my father when I was a small boy. Always there have been Apaches around, but if you came in numbers, it was not such a great concern."

The terrible silence that had followed the shooting was over. He heard the scrabble of birds and the rustling of the wind in the trees. "It is a beautiful place."

"I have a wife and two children," Tafoya said.

He looked at Tafoya, trying to determine just what he was to make of this information. Nothing. Nothing, he supposed. It was simply the sort of statement one person makes to another while they wait for some small event, like the arrival of a coach or the beginning of an entertainment. Tafoya took another long draw at his cigarette and smiled. "I never married," Austin told Tafoya.

Tafoya seemed to regard this as significant information that required a bit of study before it might be answered. *"Esta bueno. You are married to your Army. Verdad?"*

He nodded affirmation. His career seemed to him a small thing now. It had slipped away from him somehow. He had never had great or even sufficient ambition. He had a curiosity that the Army allowed him to indulge, but he had little else. Except Bobby. And now that Bobby was gone, there seemed nothing that held him. He felt tired.

He had run through the energy of grief that had propelled him here, and now he was simply weary of it all. The mission had come to disaster, and all he had now was the need to take care of his men, whom he had brought into danger out of motives he was no longer certain of. "The Army. Yes, my career. I suppose that would be the case, yes," he said.

Tafoya shrugged. "*La vida no vale nada. ¿Entiendes?* You understand?"

He shook his head.

"Life," Tafoya said. "This is a saying. Of my people. It is worth nothing. Life is worth nothing. Do you understand?"

"Better than you know."

"Perhaps then we are obligated to live up to what has been said before we were born. I hope this is not so true. I hope that we have ways of living our lives that are our own. I remember watching my father die some years ago. His *camisa,* his shirt, it was changed several times a day because there was so much *sangre.* Blood. Everywhere, blood. And this was a good man. He lived a life I would be proud of. And he ended bleeding to death from the inside. I wanted only for it to be over. It was then I understood that death respects no one. How you have lived your life means nothing to death.

Do you understand this, as well?"

"Do not threaten me."

"I do not threaten you. I do not. I want to go home, and I want you to go home as well. I want us both to live awhile longer. Much longer. To die *con nietos y sin balas, verdad?* We should die *viejos.* Old men, surrounded by our grandchildren, not from the bullets of soldiers simply because one of us made a mistake. I did not come into your country with a company of armed soldiers. I was in my own country, doing my job, when you came into my country with your soldiers. I am not threatening anyone. I am trying to help us both out of a situation that you have yourself created. Think, Anthony Austin." He tapped at his forehead. "You come into my country with your many soldiers and guns and long knives. Whom is threatening who, here, Anthony Austin?"

"The Apaches."

"Yes. The Apaches. They have drawn us together in this way. We stand here together, trying to find a way out of this, and the Apaches go farther away."

"We could work together to accomplish what we both set out to do."

"I wish to rid us of these Apaches. And you, as well. Go on."

"Let us get to the water first. Then, I

569

could take my men in pursuit of the Apaches. We will drive them back to you. You have only to wait for them. Then we will be gone. But we need water."

"We will let you have your water. And you go. And what do we get?"

"The Apaches. We will drive them back to you."

"You must forgive me. I mean you no insult. But if a man is caught where he does not belong, he is willing to make deals to get back to where he does belong. If you catch a thief in your house, he will be happy to promise to send you money as soon as he returns to his home, if only you will let him go. But if you do let him go, you are a fool. I don't think you are this kind of fool. Why do you insist on thinking that I am such a fool as this?"

"I give you my word as a gentleman."

"I believe your word as a gentleman. But I think gentlemen give their words to other gentlemen, not to poor farmers who are soldiers without nice uniforms or *sables.* To these, gentlemen may offer their word. But, I think, they do not give it."

"There is nothing to be done, then?"

"Give me six horses. I will go after the Apaches. You can have your water and go back to your country, and all of this will be forgotten. This is what is to be done."

"No. I have told you. I will not give up our mounts."

"Anthony Austin, we have come again to the edge of the cliff. It is time we step away, again. Maybe it is better if we step away separately this time. I am going to walk back to where my men are. I wish to talk with them. When there is not an officer around, men begin to think too much. Thinking is not what they are best at. You go talk to your men. We will talk again." He took out a gold watch. "One hour. We will talk in one hour."

He knelt beneath the ponderosa pine, next to the boy. "Look at me," he commanded. "Listen. Listen as you have never before in your life. I need you now. You must do exactly as I tell you. You cannot hesitate or make a mistake. You cannot ask for clarification. I am going to tell you what to do, then you are going to do exactly what I tell you. Is that clear?"

"Yes, sir."

"No," he said. "Look me in the eye and pledge it to me. Don't just repeat what you have been told. Be a soldier. You haven't had much chance to be one since you have been here. Now you must become one. I need you to do this. The whole patrol needs you to do this. And you will do it. Look around. The lives of everyone you see are in your hands. You must do exactly what I tell you."

"Yes, sir. I will, sir."

He nodded. The boy would do it. He was smart, and Austin was nearly sure that the boy actually wanted to do what was expected of him. "It will not be easy. Everyone depends on you."

The boy nodded. "Yes."

"Good. The Mexican and I will talk again. He wants our horses, and I cannot give them up. He knows that, and I know he is desperate for the horses. I am going to tell him that he can have them. I don't think he will believe me. If he does not, there is nothing more to talk of. You understand?"

The boy shook his head. A negative. "No, sir."

"It does not matter. You will or you won't. But what you must do is keep a bead on the Mexican. When I raise my hand, or if anything should happen to me, you must kill him. Do you understand that?"

"Yes, sir."

"Only not just kill him. You must kill him fast and clean. A head shot. You cannot miss. You must put a bullet into his brain before he has a chance to say anything or do anything. Otherwise, we all die. We are outnumbered. I am sure of that. When you shoot, everyone will charge. But we must have the advantage, and you're the one to give us that. It is crucial that you do this properly."

"Yes, sir."

"It is not an easy job that I'm giving you. You must look him in the eye and kill him. You must blow his brains out. It will be difficult."

This time, the boy simply nodded.

This pleased him. The boy knew exactly what was wanted of him. The enormity of it robbed him of speech. It was as it should be.

"He is not a man. You must convince yourself of that. He is your enemy. He is going to kill you and me and everyone else. Do not hesitate. Do not mistake him for a human being. He is not. He is death, and he is coming for all of us. For you, for me, for everyone. Only you can stop him. If you hesitate, you will die. I will die. We will all die."

"He is my enemy."

"Yes. Your enemy. Death. You must not hesitate. It is better to be too soon than too late."

"All right. All right, sir. I will do it."

"And you will be a soldier."

He moved among the rest of the men, sure that Tafoya was doing much the same among his men. He gave simple orders. At the first shot, they had to mount and advance, hard and fast, taking as much advantage of the trees as they could. But they were cavalry, and cavalry held the advantage only when it was charging. Defense was not the strength of cavalry. To hold back was to wait for slaughter. They had to break the Mexican lines, or the Mexicans would come around them from the flanks and they would be trapped. He had each of them move out and take his horse, one at a time, coming to the ready, ready to melee.

To each he said the same thing. "Charge their position. Sabers at the ready." Carbines were of little use here. Clear shots, if they existed at all, would be rare. They would rely on the ability of a charging horse and a slashing saber to disable a man with a rifle. Faced with the charging horse and the saber, the first instinct of any man would be to turn and run. Simple Mexican irregulars could not stand in against such a charge. They would melee and regroup on the other side of the Mexican line and recharge to take any stragglers missed on the first charge. The sight of them coming out of the trees, mounted, sabers at the ready, would inspire awe. It would engender terror. That would be their advantage — terror. They would terrorize the Mexicans and render them incapable of thinking. What advantage the Mexicans had, fear would take away.

"Give them hell," he told them. "Let them know that the United States Army is coming right over the top of them, bent on nothing but total destruction."

At fifty-five minutes, he took his pipe and filled and fired it. He had to create advantage where none existed. He moved up to Thorne again. "When I raise my hand, that is your signal. Or if anything happens to me. If you are not sure, shoot. Do not, under whatever circumstance, stop to determine if the time is right or not. The time you shoot will be the right time. Better soon than late. Remember. You will remember that, won't you?"

"Yes."

"Very well. I trust you, Thorne. You are a good soldier. As of this moment, you are a good soldier, the best we have, and we are all putting our lives into your hands, because we are confident of you." He reached out and took Thorne's shoulder in his hand and squeezed it. He smiled and released his grip. "Shoot straight."

Thorne nodded. "Yes, sir."

"Very well, then. Again, shoot straight and don't stop to think. The time for thinking has passed now."

He walked into the clearing, smoking his pipe, as if he were simply a man out for a late morning stroll. He felt the sights of rifles on him. That was his imagination, he knew. Yet he also knew that the sights of many rifles *were* on him. To imagine does not make the thing less so. He took the pipe from his mouth, shook some of the bitter liquid from the stem, replaced the pipe, and puffed with his hands clasped behind his back.

Tafoya came forward. He smiled, a small smile, but sincere. He reached forward, and Austin stretched out his own arm and clasped the Mexican by the hand. "My men wish to go home," Tafoya said.

"On our horses."

"It is a long walk, and we are tired," Tafoya conceded.

"I can give you two horses. That is the best I can do."

Tafoya pondered this. "This is good. We begin to talk. We are getting someplace. I feel the edge of the cliff farther and farther from us as we talk. We are talking numbers now, are we not, Anthony Austin?"

"No. Not numbers, horses. I am willing to give you two horses."

Tafoya scowled. "This is not good enough. Let us conclude this discussion and go home. Six horses. You give me six horses, and I let you go to the water and then to home. All unpleasantness ends."

He thought to prolong the discussion. He could not give up the horses or any weapons. It was simply out of the question. The cavalry never gives up its mounts. But they would continue to talk. He would say "three," and later, "four." But when he went to speak, he said, "All right then, six."

Tafoya smiled, held his hands out to his side, and shrugged.

Private Ned Thorne

He saw the Mexican's small gesture, then there was a tremendous thud on the tree just above his left eye, and he was knocked slightly backward. He was out of position to fire at the Mexican. He saw the lieutenant fall and then rise, as time had slowed, and he saw the lieutenant stumble back to where he was, blocking for a second any shot he had, and he saw the lieutenant stutter-step and fall, and he felt the wash of blood come back onto him. He did not hear the shots, but he knew they were being fired. Tafoya spun around and crouched, raising his arm above his head and motioning forward.

The bead fell into the V of the sight like a ball falling into the groove of a child's toy, and when it came to rest, he pulled the trigger.

There was no connection between what he had done and what happened. He squeezed the trigger, a slight pressure, no more. And Tafoya's head came apart in a brilliant spray, sanctifying him in a luminous, temporary halo of his own blood and brain. The motion of his arm coming down pulled Tafoya's nearly headless body to the ground.

He flipped open the trapdoor of the Springfield to eject the spent shell — a seventy-grain infantry shell — but the soft casing had crimped and jammed in the breach. He picked at the shell with his finger, only driving it deeper into the breach. He had to put the carbine down and rummage through his pockets for a knife to pry at the casing. In front of him, the scene swarmed. At Tafoya's command, the Mexicans had come out of the trees and were charging on foot across the space between the lines, dodging from tree to tree.

Behind him was chaos. He could not turn, because prying out the crimped shell casing was now the most important thing he had done in his life. But he could see, in the periphery of his vision, a scramble of men and horses. Certainly he heard more than he saw. Horses screamed and men cursed. The killing of the lieutenant had moved the advantage from the Americans, who had for the most part yet to mount, to the Mexicans, who ran and fired, hitting both horses and men. And now, both horses and men were panicked — the horses wheeling and rearing as the bullets of the Mexicans buzzed and snapped through the air, and the men trying to settle the horses in order to mount and, in the process, making themselves easier targets.

He got the blade of his knife into the breach, under the casing, and twisted. But that just bent the casing the other way. He kept pushing the knifepoint deeper into the breach, twisting the blade and scooping the soft copper, which tore into two ragged pieces. The shooting continued. He could hear bullets all around him now. Behind him, many of the troopers had abandoned their attempt to mount a charge and took defensive positions behind the trees and returned fire. He heard voices, but whose, or what they might be saying, he could not tell.

One trooper at least had mounted. He heard the charge of the horse before he saw it. His attention was pulled away from the casing he was working on as someone he recognized only as a mounted trooper leapt past, waving his saber over his head. Air displaced by the charging horse pushed against his face as he watched the horse do the trick. He had seen other riders put horses through wonderful and intricate stunts many times during shows he had seen in Connecticut, but this trick beat them all. As the horse rose in its jump over a bit of fallen, decaying log, its head was suddenly driven down, and the weight of its huge body followed until it completed a midair somersault, flinging the saber-waving rider forward through the air. The rider hit the ground and rolled once before the body of the horse rolled up and onto him, and then both lay still.

Ned took the front piece of the brass from the breach and began working on the rear piece when he was knocked backward. It was not so much pain as a terrible sense of wrongness. His body was both wrong and wronged. He came slowly to the understanding that the problem was not his entire body, but his knee. He rolled over onto his side and tried to pull his leg up close to his body. The pain came now, and it bloomed over him and surrounded him and became the world he inhabited.

And when the man came toward him, Ned took the carbine by the barrel and pulled it back to swing it like a club, but then he saw that the man approaching him was the risen lieutenant, ashen and stumbling, the front of his blouse dark and shiny with blood. He rose as best he could on his wounded leg and took the lieutenant by the arm to guide him to the safety of the tree when a huge spray of blood and gore hit his face. He momentarily let go of the lieutenant and the lieutenant slipped and crashed into him, dead.

He was in the open, fallen away from the tree, and he had lost his carbine. The bloodied body of the lieutenant lay at his feet. The weight of the pain was more than he was capable of carrying. He found his jammed carbine and used it as a crutch, ramming the barrel into the dirt and then dropping it, for he could not stand the extra burden of the carbine's weight anyway. Around him, bullets were whining and landing in the ground, sending up small explosions of dirt and pine needle. Holding his leg with his right hand, he began to pull himself along the ground with his left arm, working his way back toward the shelter of the tree. The tree was not far. But to put himself behind the tree, he had to crawl in a backward circle, pulling with his free arm, pushing with his hip.

He felt two more bullets thump into his body before he stopped feeling anything.

"Are you dead?"

The voice was distant, yet he felt another thump against his body. Then the voice, closer. "Are you dead?" Another thump that he understood was a boot landing against his ribs, the universal greeting of the United States Army. The voice came again. "Are you dead?"

He did not move. He was alive, and he understood the importance of remaining alive, so he did not respond or move. He listened to the voice, moving farther away now, asking the same simple question, "Are you dead?" punctuated with a kick. He remained still as the voice retreated and came back. Even when he took the shock of recognition, he did not move, except to adjust his head and to barely open one eye.

It was quiet now, much as it had been before. He still could not formulate before what. Just before. He saw a horse on its side and remembered seeing it tumble down as if death had reached up from the ground and yanked it down by the bridle. There might be bodies around, too. He was sure there must be, but he could not lift his head to see. The figure moved into his field of vision from the right and knelt. Then it rose again, swinging a belt and holster over its shoulder, and moved on out of his range of vision.

He knew that the figure had checked all of the bodies and, finding them all dead, was now plundering them. And he knew that the man was coming back, coming back to him, and he tried to think what to do. From somewhere to his right, he could hear a mule snort and stomp. The voice went on. "Are you dead?" Then came the moment of silence that contained the boot to the ribs. No one seemed to answer, and the questioner went on moving from body to body, asking the question, and when it got no answer, taking what it wanted.

He felt more than heard the man stop and kneel over him. "I'm not dead," he said. His voice foreign and scratchy.

"God Almighty. Don't do that. You scare the life out of a man."

"I'm not dead."

"You surely look dead, Marybelle. You surely do."

He tried to raise up on his arm, but he could not. His body was all lead and pain and did not work right anymore. He tried to reach out his arm. "I am alive."

Brickner pushed his arm and let him fall again on his back. "Good God Almighty. How can someone alive look so damned dead, Marybelle? How many times you get shot, Marybelle? You been shot all full of holes, boy."

He raised up a little on his arm and looked down on himself and saw that he was covered with blood. It did not seem possible that he had that much blood in him. Certainly it was not possible that any might remain inside him. He had been shot in the leg and near the left shoulder, and there was pain on his right side. It was hard to tell. Pain had taken over his whole body.

"You been shot in the head?"

"I don't think so."

"You are a goddamned mess." Brickner reached out and touched him above the eye. He drew back a hand covered in blood and gore so that Ned might see. "These your brains?"

He shook his head, remembering the beginning of the fight. "The lieutenant," he said.

"I saw him. He got it pretty bad."

"Dead?"

Brickner laughed. "He better hope so, because if he ain't, he's going to have a hell of a time finding a hat to fit him. Hell, they're all dead, Marybelle. Near as I can see. Of course, I thought you was, too. Might be further mistaken. Who all was with you?"

"I don't know."

"That's all right. Don't tell me. I know there was some chasing after me. But here. Hell, everyone here's dead. Except you and a horse I found a ways back. Don't know how them Mexicans missed that one."

"Jarbal?"

"Dead. And Park. And Brock and Pack and Mayapple and the rest."

"All dead?"

"Yessir. All dead. Even you, though you don't know it yet. I guess you're pretty much dead. Too dumb to know it, I suppose. You kind of leaked out all your blood there, Marybelle. But that's what comes of bad decisions."

"Help me."

"Why, Marybelle, I don't believe I can. You been pretty bad shot. Even if I could help you, it would probably come on me that you wouldn't help me back there, when I was fixing to leave and save your life. No. That would pretty much stop me from helping you, if I could. Which I can't. I bet you wish you had that decision to go back and gnaw on for a while. I knew where the Mexicans was. I wasn't going to get anywhere near them. And I knew the Apaches were taking you right to them. Now, I'm just here to pick up the pieces. Damned lieutenant probably thought I would save him again. Guess he got a surprise, didn't he? Those brains he was so proud of is all over the damned place now. Just another big mess, like his very life. You got anything I can sell, Marybelle?" Brickner patted Ned down, sending waves of pain and nausea through him.

"They will kill you."

"Who? Triggs? No. I guess not. I led Triggs and them in so many circles they damned near drilled a hole in the ground. They might be all the way down in China by now. I don't know. But they're not up to catching me. And when they get back to here, if they ever do, they got to worry about getting back over that border. This scene here is a hard lesson on what happens when you don't leave when the festivities are over. I can't say I cared much for any of these men, but it's a hard thing to see them all here, killed like this. The lieutenant might have done better by them. I will say that."

"I'm hurt."

"Yes, Marybelle. You are bad hurt. They done shot you full of holes. A leaky vessel, boy. A leaky vessel."

"Help me," he insisted.

"I can't do that, Marybelle. This here, what I'm doing, is what they call 'building inventory.' I got to keep moving. Pretty soon, Triggs will be here. He's bound to stumble onto this sooner or later, and I surely wouldn't want to be around if those Mexicans came back. How many of those Mexicans were there, Marybelle? There's about five shot dead over there."

"I don't know. I never saw them all."

"Well, that would be right. You were busy getting yourself shot up. It don't matter. I'll be on my way directly. This was a mighty poor showing, though. I got some sabers and some boots, but not much else worth selling. That and about twenty-six dollars. The rest of it the Mexicans must have took — the carbines and the rest of the valuable stuff. Did you know you all got shot up by old muzzle-loading muskets? That's what those Mexicans had. Hell, I can't even sell them, except maybe as curiosities. But they did the job on you all. It was a mighty poor showing, Marybelle. Mighty poor."

"The horse," he said. "Leave me the horse."

"Can't do that either, Marybelle. I can sell the horse. It's the best thing to come of this little hubbub you all had here. It's the only thing that's done made this little detour worthwhile here. I just couldn't waste it on you. Even if you was going to live, which I think you ain't. Of course, if you have money, or something else of value, we could talk."

He tried to think what he might have of value, only to remember that if he gave it to Brickner, he would only take it. Brickner wouldn't trade. "No," he said.

"Well then, I'll be finishing up my chores here, and I'll be off. When I'm done, I'll stop by and see you off, boy."

He closed his eyes and let his head roll back onto the ground. He was, he guessed, dying. This must be what dying felt like, because it was not like anything else he had ever felt. He was weak and more tired than he had ever been. Still, if he could get onto a horse, he thought he might have a chance to get back to the camp. He thought he deserved a chance. Brickner owed him a chance. He thought that maybe he had never before understood the nature of evil, but he knew it now. He listened as Brickner went on, from body to body, stripping each one of its possessions. Everyone was dead, except him. It seemed an odd thing. Everyone but him. He was having a harder and harder time staying awake.

"All right, then," Brickner said. "I believe I am done here. Are you sure you don't have anything I can sell there, Marybelle?"

"Go to hell."

"Oh. I surely will, Marybelle. I surely will. I been on my way to hell since my very birthing. The funny thing is, Marybelle, you're going to get there before me. Prepare ye the way, boy. Maybe we'll meet in hell as old friends. I guess one just never knows. You wearing them new stockings, boy? They must be worth something." He bent over and pulled off Ned's boots. "The boots is in good shape, too. Some Mexican farmer will be wanting them."

"Brickner."

"I'll tell you what, boy. I always liked you. I was fond of you near the moment I first saw you. I always thought you was going to be my friend. It was a grave disappointment to find out you just couldn't see things clearly. But I did like you, boy. Hell, I could have treated you like a little angel boy. Just disappointment. That's all you are. But, I'll tell you what. I will put a bullet in your brainpan before I go. How's that? It will save you a long and hurting dying. And if the Mexicans come back, they wouldn't be of a mind to treat you well." He reached down and ran his fingers over Ned's face, a gentle caress. "Such a sweet face. Would you like that, boy? Would you like me to put a bullet into your head?"

"Give me the horse."

"You just don't listen, do you? Are you aware of nothing? Here are the choices. You can stay here and bleed to death or get scalped by the Mexicans when they come back, or you can die right here, nice and easy, and save yourself the pain and trouble. It's your choice. It doesn't make no difference to me. You decide."

"Come here," he said. "I need to tell you something."

Brickner moved forward a step and then knelt over him. "You want me to shoot you, Marybelle?"

He shook his head and pulled his arm from behind him. Brickner's look was one of surprise. Whether it was just that Ned had it, or that it was the very same centerfire Colt he had given him, he couldn't know. But the look was surprise, only surprise — not anger, not fear, surprise. And because it was surprise, Brickner smiled at him just as Ned pulled the trigger.

Brickner fell onto him. It was the second time he had been covered in someone else's blood. But now he was also covered by someone else. Brickner was a heavy man, and he was very weak. He worked his good hand under Brickner and tried to push him off. He could raise him only a few inches, and then he came crashing back down on him. He began to worry now that he would suffocate from the weight of Brickner on his chest. He pushed again and could move him no further. Still, blood was coming from the wound in Brickner's face and onto his own face and even into his mouth. Though he was weak and Brickner heavy, he struggled harder now, wiggling his body while he pushed up at Brickner's body, aware that he was now drowning in Brickner's blood.

It was a process of reaching out and pulling himself less than an inch at a time to his right, while pushing Brickner's weight to his left. Slowly he freed his head from the bleeding bulk, and he could stop and, turning his head, vomit and rest and get a clear breath. Then he went back to the pulling and pushing until he was able to free both arms from under Brickner's body and, with a great deal of pain, push Brickner away from him.

When he was free, he began to crawl toward the horse and mules. He could not rise up onto his feet, but he could crawl. The horse was tethered forty or fifty yards from him, and he could crawl only a foot or two before he had to stop and rest. The horse eyed him nervously, and as he got closer, began to skitter against the rope that held him to the tree. He looked at the rope and hoped that Brickner had tied it well. But with animals, Brickner did not make mistakes. He continued to crawl.

The ground was badly cut up from the hooves of horses and the scrambling soldiers and bullets from both sides. There were bodies, soldiers, nearby, but he could not see who they were. Jarbal would be one of them, but he did not wish to know which. The lieutenant, Birdwood, the others. He did not want to know.

He reached the mounts after what seemed to him a very long time, though he supposed in the time of the unhurt, it was not a very long time at all. He took hold of a stirrup and pulled. The horse moved away as far as it could. He pulled again and fell. Whatever amount of strength it took to pull one's own body up a couple of feet, he did not have it. He let go of the stirrup and lay on the ground. Then, realizing the danger he was now in, he rolled back several feet out of the range of the horse's hooves and fell back into unconsciousness.

"Are you alive?"

He opened his eyes and saw Triggs kneeling over him. He tried to nod his head, but he was not sure he actually did.

"Good Lord," Triggs said. "Are you the only one alive?"

This time he felt his head move just slightly.

Triggs held a canteen to Ned's lips and tipped it up so that the cool water flowed into his mouth and down the front of his shirt. "Everyone's dead. The lieutenant, the men, the Mexicans. Brickner. Did you kill Brickner?"

"Yes."

"Do you know where all you're shot? There's blood all over you." He shook his head and lay back as he felt Triggs's hands cover his body, searching for wounds. "One in the leg here. One in the shoulder. Are there others?"

He did not know. He began to cry, though the pain was not as great as he would have thought it might be.

"Come on," Triggs said. "On your horse."

"I can't."

"You can. We have water, thanks to you. Do you understand? We have the water and the food that Brickner took. You got that back for us, and now you're going to get on your horse."

"I don't know," Ned said.

"You will. We'll help you to your horse,

but you will ride. It's going to hurt like hell, but you're going to do it. There's too many dead. You aren't going to be one of them. You're one of us. There's us five, now. Five United States soldiers, and we're heading back to our camp. It's June, 1871, and we were never in Mexico."

AFTERWORD

The characters and events in this book are fictitious. The Camp Grant Massacre in April 1871 was an actual event, well described in Don Shellie's fine account *Vast Domain of Blood* (Western Lore Press, 1992). Likewise, the events of Infernal Caverns, referred to in Brickner's account, are based on the actual incident of 1868, largely drawn from Michael Brodhead's article "This Indian Gibralter," in *The Journal of America's Military History,* Vol. 29, No. 3 (2003, pp. 60–87). I have taken liberties with historical fact, sparingly, I hope, moving up the production date of the Colt .45 revolver, the date of Crook's command in Arizona, and the headquarters at Bowie. I am deeply indebted to Don Rickey Jr.'s *Five Miles a Day on Beans and Hay* (University of Oklahoma Press, 1963) and to Robert M. Utley's *Frontier Regulars: The*

United States Army and the Indian, 1866–1891 (Macmillan Publishing Company, 1973), as well as many other sources too numerous to name, for their accounts of daily life in the United States Army in the nineteenth century.

ACKNOWLEDGMENTS

I would like to express my thanks to the U.S. Army libraries at Fort Huachuca, Arizona, and Carlyle Barracks, Pennsylvania, for the use of their resources. To Donnie Dale, Major General John Salesses, USMC, ret., Brian and Katie Laferte, Rod Siino, Rusty Barnes, Karen Lee Boren, the Flat Sundays group, Glenn Blake, Daniel Asa Rose, and the dozens of graduate students who have read and helped with the book, many thanks. And thanks, too, to Rhode Island College for the grant and sabbatical that allowed me to do much of the initial research. To Colin, thanks for your fine eye, ear, and judgment. And to Amanda Urban, thank you for hanging in when there was no apparent reason to. And thanks to Randy for everything.

ABOUT THE AUTHOR

Thomas Cobb was born in Chicago, Illinois, and grew up in Tucson, Arizona. He is the author of *Crazy Heart,* a novel, and *Acts of Contrition,* a collection of short stories that won the 2002 George Garrett Fiction Prize. He lives in Rhode Island with his wife and teaches at Rhode Island College.

The employees of Thorndike Press hope you have enjoyed this Large Print book. All our Thorndike and Wheeler Large Print titles are designed for easy reading, and all our books are made to last. Other Thorndike Press Large Print books are available at your library, through selected bookstores, or directly from us.

For information about titles, please call:
   (800) 223-1244

or visit our Web site at:
   http://gale.cengage.com/thorndike

To share your comments, please write:
   Publisher
   Thorndike Press
   295 Kennedy Memorial Drive
   Waterville, ME 04901